THREE BEAUTIFUL GIRLS
WHO LIVE ON THE EDGE . . .

ROBIN

She was born to be bad.

This was the second time within a twenty-four-hour period that I had been in a Nashville police car. The fact didn't escape me, nor would it escape Mother darling when she found out.

TEAL

This rich girl breaks all the rules.

I was able to get back into my house and up into my room without being discovered. It reinforced my feeling that I could do anything I wanted if I was just careful and clever enough.

PHOEBE

Wherever she goes, trouble is sure to follow.

He lifted my sweater and I let him take it off. . . . Every few seconds I told myself, we're doing this in school, right in the nurse's office. It made it all seem more exciting—so exciting my heart hammered at my chest and shortened my breath.

V.C. ANDREWS®
BROKEN WINGS

V.C. Andrews® Books

The Dollanganger Family Series
Flowers in the Attic
Petals on the Wind
If There Be Thorns
Seeds of Yesterday
Garden of Shadows

The Casteel Family Series
Heaven
Dark Angel
Fallen Hearts
Gates of Paradise
Web of Dreams

The Cutler Family Series
Dawn
Secrets of the Morning
Twilight's Child
Midnight Whispers
Darkest Hour

The Landry Family Series
Ruby
Pearl in the Mist
All That Glitters
Hidden Jewel
Tarnished Gold

The Logan Family Series
Melody
Heart Song
Unfinished Symphony
Music in the Night
Olivia

My Sweet Audrina
(does not belong to a series)

The Orphans Miniseries
Butterfly
Crystal
Brooke
Raven
Runaways (full-length novel)

The Wildflowers Miniseries
Misty
Star
Jade
Cat
Into the Garden (full-length novel)

The Hudson Family Series
Rain
Lightning Strikes
Eye of the Storm
The End of the Rainbow

The Shooting Stars Series
Cinnamon
Ice
Rose
Honey
Falling Stars

The De Beers Family Series
Willow
Wicked Forest
Twisted Roots
Into the Woods
Hidden Leaves

Broken Wings Series
Broken Wings

Published by POCKET BOOKS

V.C. ANDREWS®

BROKEN WINGS

POCKET **STAR** BOOKS

New York London Toronto Syndey Singapore

Following the death of Virginia Andrews, the Andrews family worked with a carefully selected writer to organize and complete Virginia Andrews' stories and to create additional novels, of which this is one, inspired by her storytelling genius.

This book is a work of fiction. Names, characters, places and incidents are products of the author's imagination or are used fictitiously. Any resemblance to actual events or locales or persons, living or dead, is entirely coincidental.

An *Original* Publication of POCKET BOOKS

A Pocket Star Book published by
POCKET BOOKS, a division of Simon & Schuster, Inc.
1230 Avenue of the Americas, New York, NY 10020

ISBN: 0-671-03997-0

First Pocket Books paperback printing May 2003

10 9 8 7 6 5 4 3 2 1

For information regarding special discounts for bulk purchases, please contact Simon & Schuster Special Sales at 1-800-456-6798 or business@simonandschuster.com

Cover design by Jim Lebbad
Tip-in illustration by Lisa Falkenstern

Printed in the U.S.A.

Contents

BROKEN WINGS

Prologue

Once when we all had a quiet moment, when no one was demanding anything of us and our punitive chores were completed, we sat and watched the sky turn from deep blue to mauve and turquoise.

A sparrow landed on the top rail of the horse corral and tapped about for a moment before settling and staring at the three of us. Teal was the first to notice.

"I wonder," she said, "if birds who live in cages ever wonder why they are in cages."

Robin looked at her as if she were going to say something sarcastic to her and then she looked at the bird and her face softened.

"I suppose we could pretend to be confused about that ourselves," Robin said. "Couldn't we, Phoebe?"

"What do you mean?" I asked. "I'm not confused. I know I don't belong here."

"Phoebe, we're all so good at lying to everyone else,

we're even good at lying to ourselves," Robin replied.

Teal smiled.

"She's right, you know."

"No, I don't know."

"Well, I'm telling you, Phoebe. We don't need to be told or shown why we're like caged birds. We each know why we're here."

"I know why I am. Let me tell you," Robin said.

And then she began . . .

PART ONE

ROBIN

1

Jerked into the Night

"**W**ake up, Robin!" I heard my mother say. I felt myself being rocked hard.

At first I thought the rocking was in my dream, a dream so deep I had to swim up to consciousness like a diver from the ocean floor. Each time my mother shook my shoulder, I drew closer and closer to the surface, moaning.

"Quiet!" she ordered. "You'll wake Grandpa and Grandma and I'll have my hands full of spilt milk. Darn it, Robin. I told you what time we were headin' outta here. You haven't even finished packin'," she said.

My suitcase was open on the floor, some of my clothes still beside it. Mother darling had insisted I not begin until after I supposedly went to bed last night. My mother said I couldn't bring but one suitcase of my things, and it was hard to decide what to take and not to take. She needed everything of hers because she was going to be a country singing star and had to have her outfits and all her boots and every hat as well as half a suitcase of homemade audiotapes she thought would win the admiration of an important record producer in Nashville.

I sat up and pressed my palms over my cheeks, patting them like Grandpa always did when he put on aftershave lotion. The skin on my face was still asleep and felt numb. My mother stood back and looked at me with her small nose scrunched, which was something she always did when she was very annoyed. She also twisted her full lips into her cheek. She had the smallest mouth for someone who could sing as loudly as she could, but most women envied her lips. I know that some of her friends went for collagen shots to get theirs like hers.

Everyone said we looked like sisters because I had the same petite features, the same rust-colored hair, and the same soft blue eyes. Nothing she heard pleased her more. The last thing she wanted to be known as was my mother, or anyone's mother for that matter. She was thirty-two years old this week, and she was convinced she had absolutely her last chance to become a singing star. She said she had to pass me off as her younger sister or she wouldn't be taken seriously. I was sixteen last month, and she wanted everyone, especially people in show business, to believe she was just in her mid-twenties.

Although I was closer to one of her idols, Dolly Parton, than she was when it came to breasts, we did have similar figures, both being a shade more than five feet five. She always looked taller because she hardly ever wore anything but boots. She wore hip-hugging tight jeans most of the time, and when she went out to sing at what she called another honky-tonk, she usually tied the bottom of her blouse so there was a little midriff showing. Grandpa would swell up with anger, his face nearly breaking out in hives, or just blow out his lips and explode with biblical references.

"We taught you the ways of the righteous, brought you up to be a churchgoing girl, and you still dress like a street tramp. Even after . . . after . . . your Fall," he told her, and swung his eyes my way.

That's what I was in his way of thinking: the Fall, the result of "the grand sin of fornication." Mother darling had been sexually active at the age of fifteen and had me when she was only sixteen. Grandpa, despite despising the situation as much as he did, would not permit even talk of an abortion.

"You abide by your actions and pay for your sins. It's the only path toward redemption," he preached then, according to Mother darling, and preached now.

I remember the first time I was arrested for shoplifting. The policewoman knew my grandparents and asked me how I could behave so badly coming from a solid, religious, and loving home. Wasn't I just a self-centered ingrate?

I fixed my eyes on her and said, "My mother didn't want me. My grandparents forced me down her throat, and she never stops throwing that back at them. How would you like living in such a solid, religious, and loving home?"

She blinked as if she had soot in her eyes and then grunted and went off mumbling about teenagers. I was just barely one. It was two days after my thirteenth birthday and the first time I was arrested. I had shoplifted a number of times before, but I was never caught. It amazed me how really easy it was. Half the time, if not more, those machines that are supposed to ring don't; and the employees, especially of the department stores, don't seem to care enough to watch for it. I practically waved whatever it was I was taking in front of their faces. Many times I threw away whatever I took almost immediately afterward. I couldn't chance bringing it home.

Grandpa placed all the blame on Mother darling, telling her she was setting a very bad example for me by dressing the way she dressed and singing in places "the devil himself won't enter." He would rant at her, waving his thick right forefinger in the air like an evangelist in one of those prayer meetings in large tents. He made me attend them with him when I was younger, claiming he had to work extra hard on me since I was spawned from sin. Anyway, he would bellow at Mother darling so loudly, the walls of the old farmhouse shook.

Grandma would try to calm him down, but he would sputter and stammer like one of his old tractors, usually concluding with "Thank goodness she took on your mother's maiden name, Kay Jackson. When she goes singing in those bars, I can pretend I don't know who she is."

"You don't have to pretend. You don't know who I am, Daddy," my mother would fire back at him. "Never did, never will. I'm writin' a song about it."

"Lord, save us," Grandpa would finally say and retreat. He was close to sixty-five but looked more like fifty, with a full head of light brown hair with just a touch of gray here and there, and thick, powerful-looking shoulders and arms. He could easily lift a fully grown Dorset Horn sheep and carry it a mile. Despite his strength and his rage, I never saw him lift his hand to strike my mother or me. I think he was afraid of his own strength.

My grandparents owned a sheep farm about ten miles east of Columbus, just outside the village of Granville. The farm was no longer active, although Grandpa kept a dozen Olde English Babydoll sheep that he raised and sold.

Before she went anywhere, Mother darling would practically bathe herself in cologne, claiming the stench of sheep and pigs permeated the house. "It sinks into your very soul," she claimed, which was another thing that set Grandpa on fire, the farm being his way of life and his living. Mother darling had the ability to ignite him like a stick of dynamite. Sometimes, I thought she was doing it on purpose, just to see how far he would go. The most I saw him do was slam his fist down on the kitchen table and make the dishes jump so high, one fell off and shattered.

"That," he said, pointing to it and then to her, "gets added to your rent."

Ever since Mother darling quit high school and worked in the supermarket and then began to sing nights with one pair of musicians or another, Grandpa insisted she pay rent for her and for me. It wasn't much, but it took most of her supermarket salary, which was another justification she used for her singing, not that she needed any. She was convinced she could be a big star.

I knew she was saving up for something big. Suddenly, she was willing to work overtime at the supermarket and she took any singing gig she and her partners at the time could get, from private parties to singing for an hour or so in the malls in Columbus.

Then one night, she slipped into my room, closing

the door softly behind her. She stood with her back
against the door and looked like she had won the lot-
tery. Her face was that bright, her eyes seemed full of
fireflies.

"We're leavin' this trap tomorrow night," she said in
a voice just above a whisper.

"What? To where?"

"I've got a job in Nashville with a three-piece band
my old boyfriend from high school, Cory Lewis, runs.
He's the drummer and they lost their singer. She ran off
with a car salesman to live in Beverly Hills, which I'm
sure was just an old tire which will go flat before they
get close. Not that I care. It's become an opportunity for
me. We're going to play in places where real record
producers go to listen for new talent."

"Nashville?"

"You don't make it in country music if you don't
make it in Nashville, Robin. Now here's what I want
you to do. Quietly pack one suitcase. It's all I got room
for in the Beetle."

Mother darling had an old yellow Volkswagen
Beetle that looked like someone with a tantrum had
kicked and punched it for hours. The car was rusted out
in places so badly, you could see through to the road
beneath, and it had a cracked window on the passenger's side.

"But isn't Nashville very far away?"

"If you attended class more often, you'd know it's
only a little over four hundred miles from here, Robin.
Four hundred in actual distance, but a million in
dreams," she added.

"That lawn mower you drive won't make it."

"Just shut your sewer mouth and pack," she ordered,
losing her patience. "We're leavin' at two this mornin'.

Very quietly. I don't want him on my tail," she said, nodding toward Grandpa and Grandma's room.

"How long are we gonna be there?" I asked, and she shook her head.

"Girl, don't you get it? We're leavin' here for good. I can't leave you with Grandpa and Grandma, Robin. Believe me, I wish I could, but they're too old to be watchin' after you, bailin' you out of trouble every week. And it's now or never for me. I'm gettin' nowhere singin' in the honky-tonks here. It's nothing for you to leave the school, so don't make like it is," she warned. "You've been suspended a half-dozen times for one thing or another. They won't miss you when the new year begins and you're not there," she reminded me.

"And don't try tellin' me you'll miss your friends, Robin. Those nobodies you hang out with just get you into more trouble. I might be savin' your life the same time I save my own. Be sure you're quiet," she said.

Despite her bravado, Mother darling was still frightened of Grandpa.

"If we're lucky, he won't realize we're gone until it comes time for him to collect his rent. In his mind that was a way of imposin' penance on me for havin' you. Pack," she ordered, then opened the door quietly and slipped out as fast as a shadow caught in the light.

I couldn't help but admit surprise at her courage. For as long as I could remember, she talked about picking up and leaving Granville. But it was certainly one thing to talk about it and another to actually do it. Despite Grandpa's monthly rent and his ranting and raving about saving our souls, we had a home. Grandma cooked our meals, and even though Mother darling and I were supposed to do our share of the household chores, Grandma usually did them for us. She had them to baby-sit for me when I was younger so she could pursue her music career, even though Grandpa thought it was "coddling the devil" to perform "half-naked" in "slime pits." He talked so much about the devil and hell that I used to believe he had been there and back. One of these days, I thought, he will bring out some pictures to show me tortured souls.

When the farm was active, he tried to get Mother darling to work, feeding and caring for the variety of sheep he raised, as well as miniature Hereford cattle. On purpose or not, she was more trouble than value to him, always wasteful when she was shearing. He finally gave up on her, which couldn't have pleased her more. By the time I was old enough to be of any use, he was retreating from the business and there wasn't much to do. He let all his help go.

Anyway, after she had awoken me, I splashed some cold water on my face and finished packing. Of course, she had promised to buy me a whole new wardrobe when we got to Nashville and she had earned big money in the music business. I couldn't deny she had a nice voice and looked pretty up on a stage, but it just seemed so unreal to think of her as actually making records and being on television or singing in front of thousands of people. I didn't tell her that. Nothing would set her off as much as being told she didn't have what it takes. Actually, I envied her for having some sort of dream at least. The only thing I looked forward to when we left was a cup of strong coffee.

She was at the door fifteen minutes later.

"Ready?" she asked.

I had the suitcase packed and closed and I was sitting

on my bed with my eyes closed. I was falling asleep again, hoping it was just a dream.

"I've already got all my things in the car," she whispered. "C'mon, wake up, Robin."

Impatient, she picked up my suitcase. It was obviously heavier than she expected.

"What did you take?"

"Just what I needed," I said.

She grimaced and led the way. Grandpa always kept his hallway lights low to save on electricity. The weak illumination, the heavy thick shadows following along the wall, all made me feel it was still a dream. It was mid-July, but nights and mornings were cold to me. I shuddered, wrapped my arms around myself, and followed Mother darling down the fieldstone walkway to the car. A partially overcast night sky provided minimum starlight. The whole world looked asleep. I felt like I was sneaking into a painting.

The car doors complained when we opened them, metal shrieking. Mother darling started the engine without putting on the lights and drove slowly down the long driveway. I was still in a state of disbelief, groggy, my eyes half closed.

"Good riddance to this," she muttered. "I'm gettin' out. I'm gettin' away, finally."

I turned and cuddled up as best I could with my head against the window and the top of the seat. I couldn't crawl into the rear because she had her guitar there resting on a pillow she wouldn't let me use. Nevertheless, despite the bumps and turns, I fell asleep.

I woke up to the screaming shrill sound of a tractor trailer as it passed us by on the highway. We were already on I-71 South heading toward Louisville. The driver in the tractor trailer sounded his horn again.

"Donkey," Mother darling called him. I groaned and sat up straighter, stretching my arms.

Suddenly, it all came back to me.

"I thought I was dreaming," I told her.

She laughed.

"No more, Robin. Dreams turn into reality now," she vowed.

I saw the road signs.

"I don't see why we have to go to a place where people call people Bubba and Sissy," I complained. Mother darling knew how much I disliked country music. I told her it was soapy and full of tears.

"I told you—it's where you have to go to make it in country music," she said.

"Country music. You've got to chew on straw and be barefoot most of the time to like it."

She practically pulled off the highway, jerking herself around to yell at me.

"You'd better keep that stupid opinion to yourself when we get there, Robin. People in Nashville have been known to hang rock-and-rollers like you by their ears for less."

"Yeah, yeah, right," I said.

"I don't see how you can afford to make fun of anyone anyway, Robin. You're sixteen and you've already got a criminal record. You should be happy I'm takin' you to a place no one knows you. You'll have a chance to start new, make new friends."

"Friends. You never liked any of my friends and probably never will, no matter where we live. In fact, you never liked anything I've done."

"What are you talking about now?"

"When I was in that school play in seventh grade, everybody else's mother or father was there, but not my mother darling. My mother darling was strumming a guitar in some sawdust-floor saloon instead."

"Damn, you never let me forget that, do you? I do the best I can, Robin. It's not easy bein' a single mother, and my parents never helped us all that much. You know Grandpa took my money, even though he condemned me for the way I earned it. You know what he says, 'There's no such thing as dirty money, only dirty people.' He's been punishin' me ever since I got pregnant with you," she reminded me.

"You should have run off and had an abortion. I wish I wasn't born anyway."

"Yeah, right. That's easy for you to say now. Bein' a girl out there alone in the world is no picnic with or without a baby, and it's not been a picnic for me livin' with my parents and hearin' Grandpa complain about you all the time, blamin' me for every stupid thing you do."

"Don't worry, Mother darling. I'm not complaining about your not leaving me back there with them. I'd probably have run off anyway."

"I don't doubt it. I know I'm savin' your life takin' you with me, Robin. The least you could do is be a little grateful and very cooperative. And another thing, I don't want you callin' me Mother darlin' anymore. I know you're just bein' sarcastic 'cause of that book *Mommie Dearest*. Besides," she said, "I told you how I have to present myself as bein' younger. From the day we get to Nashville, until I say otherwise, you're my younger sister. Always call me Kay."

"That won't be hard," I said. "It takes more than just calling someone Mother for her to be a mother."

"Oh, you're so smart." She thought a moment. "Actually, I like that. It's a great first line for a new

song: It takes more than calling someone Mother for
her to be a mother," she sang. She looked at me.
"Thanks."

I shook my head and stared at the floor. She turned
on one of her country music stations and began to sing
along. The happier she was, the angrier and more
depressed I became. This wasn't my dream life; it was
hers. I was like a piece of paper stuck to the bottom of
her boots. She couldn't shake me off, and I couldn't
pull away.

The road streamed ahead. She saw only promise and
glory. I just saw a strip of highway going to nowhere,
which was where I had been.

Why did she ever name me Robin? I thought. She
should have called me Canary.

I'm just like one: trapped in a cage.

All I had to do was tell her and she would turn it into
another song.

2

Getting to Glory

I fell asleep again, despite Mother darling's singing. When I woke this time, I had to go to the bathroom. She moaned about it.

"We're almost to I-65. Can't you put a plug in it?" she whined.

"I have to go now!" I screamed.

Reluctantly, she turned into the first road stop, complaining about the time we were going to lose. I didn't understand why she had to get to Nashville so fast.

"Where are we going to live when we get there anyway?" I wanted to know.

"We're going to live with Cory. He has a two-bedroom apartment, and it's not far from where you go to school," she told me.

Two bedrooms? I thought. She and I weren't going to share one. That was for sure.

"How do you just go and pick up again with some-one you haven't seen in years?" I asked her.

She stared ahead, looking for a place to park. I thought she wasn't going to answer.

Then, when we stopped, she turned to me and with steely eyes said, "You do what you have to do to move ahead in the business, Robin. Cory knows people now and besides, what are you worrying about? I'm the one sleeping with him, not you."

"Who don't you sleep with?" I mumbled. "That's why you never could tell who my father was."

It was the only explanation I knew. From what I could put together, she had been at some wild party and actually had gone to bed with three different boys. She was either so drunk or hopped up on something, she didn't know who was first and who was last. Some wild sperm had seized upon one of her eggs and brought me into this world. Like Grandpa paraphrased, "The sins of the mother rest on the head of the daughter."

"I heard what you mumbled, Robin. Don't be so smart," she said, turning off the engine.

I got out, slammed the door behind me, and went into the restaurant and to the bathroom. I heard her fol-low me into the bathroom. I could never mistake the clip-clop of those boots on tile.

"Thought you could wait until the precious exit," I said to the closed stall on my way out. She didn't reply.

I went to the shop. As I stood there looking at news-papers, magazines, candy, and other things, I remember feeling like I was floating in space. I didn't think I'd miss Grandpa and Grandma, but at least I had a home with them. Where were we really going? Did Mother darling really believe I would be better off in Nashville, or was I just like some old suit of clothes, stuffed in a bag and dragged along? She had made it crystal clear to me that she didn't want me to call her Mother. How much easier would it be if she could just drop me off on her way to a new life.

Back in the car, after we drove off and were on the highway again, I pulled the entertainment magazine out from between the sections of newspaper. She watched me do it and nearly turned off the highway again, jerking the car and hitting the brakes.

"Did you steal that? Did you? Did you put that magazine in the newspaper first and then just pay for the newspaper? I know your tricks."

"No," I said, but she fixed her eyes on me like two small spotlights and scrunched her nose.

"You're lyin', Robin. I can always tell when you do. Are you ever goin' to stop stealin'? Don't you know you could have gotten me in trouble, too, back there? And me on the way to Nashville. How do you think I would be able to explain that? Sorry, I couldn't make the audition because my daughter shoplifted a magazine and we were arrested on the way."

She continued to drive.

"Why do you do these things?" she asked, but mostly of herself. "Maybe my father is right. Maybe people do inherit evil."

"Who did you inherit it from then?" I fired at her.

She glared at me for a moment.

"I don't think of what I did as so evil, at least not as evil as my father does. I was young and into stupid things like drugs and alcohol and I was very frustrated livin' in that house and bein' told that everythin' I liked and everythin' I wanted to do was bein' inspired by Satan."

She turned back to me, glancing at the magazine again.

"I'm warnin' you, Robin. If you get into trouble in Nashville the way you did back home, I'm not goin' to come your rescue. I won't want anyone, especially people in the business, to know I gave birth to a petty thief. Do you understand me?"

"You already told me you're going to pretend you're my older sister, didn't you? No one will blame you for giving birth to anything."

"Don't be so smart. Oh damn," she said, grimacing. "I was hopin' we would have a nice trip and you would be as excited about all this as I am. We're startin' a new life!"

"You're starting a new life," I corrected.

She sighed and shook her head again.

After a moment I took out a pack of cigarettes and lit one. She spun around even faster than before.

"Where did you get those?"

I shrugged.

"You stole them, too, probably. My God, the trouble we just missed. Didn't I tell you I don't want you smokin' around me? Didn't I tell you how bad it was for my throat, my voice? I can't chance strainin' it, not now. Stop makin' me shout!"

"I'm not making you," I said.

"Throw that cigarette out the window!"

I took one more defiant puff, rolled down the window, and flipped the cigarette out.

"Throw out the whole pack," she ordered.

"The whole pack? But—"

"Throw it out, Robin. Now," she said, and I did.

Then I sat back with my arms folded and pouted, until we both heard the police siren and she looked in the rearview mirror and exclaimed, "Oh no!"

As she slowed down to pull over, my heart began to pound. Had I been seen back at the store?

"Now you've gone and done it," she wailed. "I'm ruined before I even begin."

The state trooper got out of his vehicle and sauntered over to my side, moving his hand in a circle to indicate I should roll the window all the way down.

"Let me see your license and registration," he ordered Mother darling. He looked ten feet tall to me and broader than Grandpa.

Mother darling hurried to dig it all out of the glove compartment and her purse. It took a while, and all that time, he stood there glaring at me. I'm caught again, I thought sadly.

He took the license and the registration.

"Where are you going?" he asked as he read it.

"To Nashville, Officer. I'm a singer and I have an opportunity to improve my career. My daughter and I are goin' to start a whole new life," she continued. I thought she was pathetic, trying to sound so sweet and innocent.

He didn't smile.

"Do you realize," he began, looking more at me, "that you could start a serious fire tossing lit cigarettes out of the window and into the dry grass back there?"

"Oh," Mother darling said, obviously relieved I wasn't being arrested for shoplifting. "Yes. I mean, no. I didn't realize she had thrown a lit cigarette out the window. I thought she had snuffed it out. Didn't I tell you to do that first, Robin?" she demanded with a face full of steam.

I looked at her without answering. He would have to be a very stupid policeman to buy that, I thought.

"We've had some serious fires here recently, and with the drought and all . . ."

"Oh yes, Officer. You're absolutely right. We weren't

thinkin'. You know how two young women can git sometimes. We were listenin' to music and talkin' because we're so excited about startin' a new life."

"Umm," he said. "I really should cite you for this."

"We don't have much money," she wailed. "Just enough to get ourselves goin'. I swear we won't do anythin' like that again. Will we, Robin?"

"No," I said dryly. "Never again."

He nodded.

"All right. You watch it, and watch your speed. I notice your right rear tire is too worn. You had better get that changed soon."

"Oh. It's so like me to neglect my car. But," she said, flicking her eyelids, "I never neglect my men."

He finally laughed.

"I'll bet," he said. "Have a good trip."

"Thank you kindly, Officer," she told him.

I could have puked, but I swallowed hard, closed my eyes, and pressed my lips shut.

"Okay. Good luck in your career. What's your name in case I hear about you later?"

"Kay Jackson," she said. "And you will hear about me."

He broke a smile, tipped his hat, and returned to his car.

Mother darling released a hot, trapped breath.

"There," she said, satisfied with herself. Let that be a lesson to you. If you're nice to people, they'll be nice to you. Especially men," she added, and started away.

"If you're so nice to them, how come you never had one ask you to marry him?" I asked.

In my heart of hearts, I thought the reason was really me. Most men didn't want to marry a woman who had a child to raise, and as I grew older, that became more and more a problem. I used to have nightmares in which Mother darling did decide to marry someone, but only if I remained with Grandpa and Grandma. She would come to me in the dark dream and say, "You can't expect another man to take on the responsibilities of raisin' someone else's child, now can you, Robin? I'm sure you understand." I'd wake up as she was leaving the house, and for a long moment, I would wonder if it hadn't happened. The dream was usually that vivid.

"What makes you think no man has asked?"

"You never talked about any," I said.

"Plenty have, but I can't pursue a singin' career and keep house, can I? And what if he wanted more children, huh? What would I do, hold a baby in my arms and record songs? I don't need a marriage. I need a break in the business," she declared.

She looked at me.

"I'm not sayin' marriage is bad or nothin', Robin. It's right for almost all other women. Someday, I hope you find a good man. It's just not for me," she said. "Remember that song I wrote: 'I'm not the marryin' kind, so don't go bendin' your knee for me,' " she sang.

"I remember. I'm just trying to forget it," I muttered.

"You're goin' to be sorry you said all those mean things to me, Robin. Someday, you're goin' to be lookin' at me up on the stage of the Grand Ole Opry and be sorry you ever made fun of me and country music. At least it's honest; at least it's from the heart and not like that rap talk or bangin' and screamin' you think's music."

I closed my eyes and tried to sleep again. She was quiet and then, as we drew closer to Nashville, she began to get very excited. She found some new radio stations and sang along whenever she could.

I opened my eyes and looked at the beautiful day, one of those days when there are just a few scattered soft puffs of cloud against the aqua blue sky. An air force jet began to trail a line from one horizon toward the other. I imagined I was in it, just sailing toward something blue.

"Oh, I can feel it," Mother darling cried. "I can feel the changes comin', Robin. Can't you?"

"No," I said, but I said it sadly. I really wished I could feel what she felt. She was glowing with expectation. Would I ever be that radiant with happiness?

She ignored me because she was concentrating hard now on the directions Cory Lewis had given her to a section called Madison. Either he had left out something or she was confused and I wasn't much help. Finally, she pulled into a gas station and got better directions. About a half hour or so later, we made a turn down a residential street and came upon Garden Apartments.

"We're here!" she declared, pulling into the parking area. Cars were parked under carports. She found Cory Lewis's apartment number and pulled in behind what I imagined was his red pickup truck. For a moment she just sat there, smiling. "We made it," she said. She took a deep breath and added, "The rest will be easy."

I raised my eyebrows. Maybe it wasn't so good to have high hopes and dreams, I thought. Without them, there's no disappointment, and if there was one thing that described my life, it was disappointment with a capital D.

We got out of the Beetle. She said we should find Cory first and then bring along our things.

"He'll help," she told me.

The apartments looked seedy to me. The stucco was

stained and discolored after years of rain. On some of
the balconies, I saw old furniture, rusted exercise equipment, and sick-looking plants. The walkway through
the complex was cracked and chipped and, at one point,
gouged, with a chunk of the cement gone. There was a
swimming pool, but it was empty and there wasn't anyone around it. As we passed it, I looked down and saw
all sorts of garbage at the bottom, including what
looked like a little child's tricycle.

Cory Lewis's apartment was on the second floor,
number 202. Mother darling, still smiling from ear to
ear with excitement and expectation, pushed the buzzer.
I didn't hear anything. She pushed it again.

"Maybe it doesn't work," I suggested.

"Oh." She knocked, but there was still no sound
from within. I knocked harder, practically pounding the
door.

"Robin!"

"Well, maybe he has the radio on. Doesn't everyone
in Nashville have the radio on?"

She scrunched her nose and then the door finally
opened and we looked in at a tall, lean man with a thin
nose and thin lips. He had what looked like a two- or
three-day beard, stiff enough to sand off paint. His light
brown hair hung listlessly down the sides of his head to
his shoulders, where the split ends curled. Dressed in a
black T-shirt with the faded words Bulls Are Always
Horny and a pair of jeans, he stood barefoot and looked
like he had just woken up. His blue eyes were glassy. I
saw he had a small scar just under his right eye. It had
tiny spots in it like it had been created with a dinner
fork.

"Cory, it's us!" Mother darling was forced to declare
because his face hadn't recorded any recognition yet.

"Whaa . . ." He ran his hands over his eyes and blinked. Then he smiled. "I'll be damned. So it is. Kay Jackson herself," he cried. "Never thought you'd do it, Kay. We was just thinkin' about lookin' for another singer."

"You'd better not," Mother darling said. "I told you I'd be here, and I'm here."

"Yeah, but you been tellin' me that for some time now." He turned to me. "And this is . . ."

"Robin Lyn."

"I like to be called just Robin," I said quickly.

"Whatever you like, sweet thing. Well, I'm sorry to say the place ain't exactly in prime condition, Kay. I had the boys here last night playin' cards until three in the mornin'. I didn't get a chance to clean up or fix up the other bedroom yet."

He stepped back and we gazed in at the small living room. The coffee table was covered with empty beer cans and a pizza box in which two dried pieces remained. There was a bowl with cigarette butts in it and various articles of clothing scattered over the sofa and the two easy chairs, each with thick arms and what looked like holes burned into them by dropped ashes. Pieces of newspaper were scattered about, and I saw what looked like a racetrack form under the table.

"What the place needs badly is a woman's touch," he said. Before Mother darling could say it, he flipped his forefinger at her like a pistol and added, "Make a good song."

She laughed.

"Still the same old Cory. Well," she said philosophically. "We didn't expect it would be a picnic right from the start, now did we, Robin?"

"Never that," I said dryly.

"Why don't you go back to the car and start getting our things," she told me. "I'll help Cory get organized and then maybe he can come out and get the heavier pieces."

"That's a good suggestion," he said. "It's been a while since I was organized."

I started away.

"Oh," he said, looking out the door after me. "I forgot. Welcome to Nashville."

"Thanks," I said, and walked on.

I wished I could just keep going and never stop.

3

Settling into Nowhere

If ever I felt lost or out of place at Grandpa and Grandma's in Granville, it was nothing compared to how I felt at Cory Lewis's apartment. At least at my grandparents' home, I could find space for myself, escape to my own music, into my own little world. Living in this apartment, I knew what bees must feel like in a hive, I thought. Nothing was mine. Nothing was truly private, and everyone's conversation was buzzing in everyone's ears whether he or she wanted it or not.

Besides the fact that my room was about one-third as big as the room I had at the farm, the real problem was, there was only one bathroom and because it wasn't very big either, I had to keep most of my things in my room. I could see that the only time I would have any real privacy was when Mother darling and Cory had to go to the garage owned by Del Thomas, one of the other musicians, to practice and prepare their music. At least for a good part of those days, I would have the apartment to myself, not that there was much to do in it. There was only one television set and Cory wouldn't pay for any cable or satellite reception, so the set was able to show only local stations pulled out of the air by a rabbit-ear antenna. Some improvement to the life we had, I thought. At least Grandpa had cable and I had my own television set there.

Mother darling saw it in my eyes.

"This is just a temporary residence for us, Robin. As soon as I start makin' big money, we're gonna have a place of our own."

"By then I'll be on social security," I said, and she came as close to slapping me as ever.

"It would help," she said, standing in front of me with her hands on her hips, "if you would be a little more encouragin'. I'm doin' this for both of us."

"Right," I said.

Cory watched our little arguments with a wide, stupid grin on his face. Most of the time he wouldn't say much. He would just shake his head and go, "Robin Lyn."

"I'm Robin," I shouted at him. "Not Robin Lyn."

"Heck, girl, most of the girls I know here got two first names."

"I'm not from here."

"Right. You're from a bigger, more sophisticated town," he said, and laughed. Mother darling laughed too. It wasn't long before I felt like it was me against them. She sided with almost anything he said or did.

For my part, I couldn't see where he was so connected and important in the music business. If he knew so many influential people, why was he living like this and why didn't he have another singer, one with more experience or fame than Mother darling? I couldn't believe how much hope and faith my mother was putting in him. From what I could see, he didn't even seem as successful as the musicians Mother darling played with back in Granville. It was as if she was blind or just didn't want to see. I actually felt sorry for her, but it wouldn't be long before I would feel sorrier for myself.

In fact, I felt sorry for her the very first night there. Cory called his two other band members and told them to come over, supposedly to talk about their music and hear Mother darling sing and play her guitar. She got as nervous as a hen. It was as if she was already auditioning to play the Grand Ole Opry.

"What songs should I choose? Which ones do I do best?" she asked, more of herself than to me as she flitted about the small apartment, going from the room she was sharing with Cory to the bathroom and back, barely concerned at all about my room and how I was adjusting to this.

She paused once to say, "Oh, you have a view of the street from here. That's more interestin'. We're lookin' out on the courtyard."

"Right. I'll spend my time watching cars go by," I said.

"There's nothin' to stop you from fixin' this room up any way you want," she said. "Cory said that would be just fine. He was only usin' it to store things and occasionally let someone sleep over when he had too much to drink or somethin'. I'm not sure what shirt to wear. I've got that one that sparkles like the Electric Horseman. Bet that would be good, huh?"

I didn't answer. I just continued to take my things

out of my suitcase and put them in the drawers of the rickety, old, chipped, and faded dresser. After I cleaned out the spilled tobacco and gum and other junk, that is. The closet was crowded with Cory's clothing, cartons of sheet music, six pairs of old boots, and a guitar with broken strings.

"Where am I supposed to hang things?" I asked.

"Oh, hell," Cory said, overhearing me. He rushed in, scooped up clothes, lifted them off the rack, and threw them in the far left corner of the room. "Don't matter if this stuff's hangin' or not. The closet is yours completely, Robin Lyn," he said with an exaggerated stage bow.

"Robin," I said sharply, and he laughed. He had already opened a bottle of beer. It seemed he didn't move without one in his hand. I noticed a tattoo on his right forearm. It was a picture of a heart split in two with tears dripping from it and the words My Heart Cries for You underneath. He saw me staring at it.

"You can read it better like this," he said, turning his arm so I'd have a better view.

"Why would you put that on your arm?" I asked, grimacing.

"Oh, didn't your mother . . ."

"Sister," Mother darling corrected from the bathroom where she was fixing her hair. He laughed.

"Sister, I mean, tell you I once had a song on the charts called 'Broken Heart'?"

"No, she left out that little detail," I said.

"Kay Jackson. You never told her the important guy you're working with?"

"Oh yes, she told me that," I said. He sucked on his beer bottle and then smiled.

"You want to see the rest of the song?"

I didn't, but I could see it was important to him.
"Sure."

He opened his shirt and there were two lines tattooed on his chest with that broken heart between them.

Each time it beats a beat,
My heart will cry for you.

He took his shirt off completely and showed me his back, where there were two more lines tattooed.

Each time I see your face,
My heart will cry for you.

He turned back to me, undid his jeans, and lowered them and his briefs almost to his private place. Another two lines were on his abdomen.

When I see your hand in someone else's hand,
My heart will cry for you.

Then he turned around and dropped his pants and briefs to his knees. There across his buttocks was tattooed:

Until the very end of time,
My heart will cry for you.

He pulled up his clothes and turned around to sing some more of his song.

"So take me back and hold me tight and never let
* me go.*

*Please mend a heart that's torn in two,
A heart that loves you so."*

He laughed.

"I couldn't get the whole first verse on me. Well, what'cha think?"

For a moment I had to convince myself I had seen what I had seen.

"What I was thinkin'," he continued, gulping some more of his beer and not waiting for me to respond, "is I might have the woman I love tattooed with the rest of it. Then, whenever we stood naked together, we would have the whole song between us. Huh?"

He looked at Mother darling and then at me and burst into laughter.

"Look at her face, Kay."

Mother darling did, and then she laughed, too.

"Let's call the boys and tell them to come over earlier. We want to get this thing goin'."

He looked at me again and sang, "My heart will cry for you."

Then he put his arm around Mother darling and went out to the living room to call his fellow musicians.

If anyone's heart's crying, I thought, it's mine.

Before the musicians arrived, I left the apartment to explore what looked like it would be my new neighborhood for some time to come. Down on the lower level, in front of the apartment closest to the street, I saw a girl who looked about my age, with licorice black hair tied in a ponytail. She was sitting on a lawn chair and seemed to be singing to whatever was coming through her earphones. She wore a T-shirt with the sleeves torn off to her shoulders and jeans. I thought the T-shirt was splattered with red paint, until I drew closer and saw the red dots were all connected to form a pair of lips. Underneath it read, Don't Give Me Any Lip.

When we made eye contact, she took off her earphones.

"Quién está usted?"

"Excuse me?"

"I asked you who you were in Spanish. That's what I'm doing with these earphones, learning Spanish."

"Oh."

"So?"

"What?"

"So who are you, or is that a secret?"

"My name's Robin Taylor," I said, making sure to leave out the Lyn. "My mo . . . sister and I are staying with a friend for a while."

"Quién?"

"What?"

"I thought you might have figured it out by now. Who? Quién? Get it?"

"I don't speak Spanish," I said sharply. I was just going to keep going, but she leaped out of her chair.

"Neither do I. That's why I'm studying it."

"Why?"

"I'm going to run off to Mexico and live on a beach and drink tequila and not care what time it is, ever," she vowed. I guess I looked pretty skeptical. "I am!" she insisted. She looked back at the front door of her apartment. "I'm tired of my stepmother telling me what to do, what to wear, what to eat. My father never says anything. She's got him wrapped around her you-know-what."

This time I smiled.

"Quién está usted?" I asked, and she broke into a wide smile.

She had a round face that made her dark brown eyes look too small. Heavy boned, she looked a good twenty pounds overweight. It gave her a more matronly look, especially with her big bosom and wide hips. I imagined that when she said her stepmother was telling her what to eat, she was trying to get her to lose weight.

"Mi nombre es Kathy Ann Potter. And I'm warning you now, don't call me Pothead," she said with a face bracing for a fight. Then she smiled again. "So, who is your friend?"

"Friend?"

"Who are you and your sister living with?"

"Oh. Cory Lewis."

"The vampire? That's what my stepmother calls him because he's out all night and sleeps all day."

"Musicians usually do," I said, "and so do singers. My sister is a singer in his band, or will be."

"Peachy keen," she quipped. "Where are you going?"

"I don't know. Just for a walk."

"Forget it. There's no place to go around here. You've got to get into the city. You wanna go to Stumpin' Jumpin' with me and my friend Charlotte Lily tonight?"

"What's that?"

"A dance club. You got to be twenty-one, but we can get in. Lots of college boys go there."

"Twenty-one? How are we going to pass for that?"

"Charlotte Lily's sister's boyfriend is one of the security guards. Lots of kids under twenty-one get in." She glanced at her watch.

"Can you meet me here in about an hour? We'll take the bus and meet my best friend, Charlotte Lily, downtown by the Tennessee Fox Trot."

I smiled in amazement. Talk about someone making friends fast, I thought. For all she could know, I was a serial killer.

"Well?"

"An hour?"

"You need more time to dress?" she asked. "You're not going out in just a pair of jeans and a shirt like that with sneakers, are you?"

"Oh, no. What do you wear to this, what did you call it, Somethin' Jumpin'?"

"*Stumpin'* Jumpin'." She smiled. "Something sexier," she replied. "It's very hot."

"What's the other place? What did you call it, Tennessee Fox Trot?"

"Oh, the carousel at Riverfront Park." She tilted her head with suspicion. "For people coming here to be in music, you sound like you don't know anything about Nashville."

"I don't," I said. "Except it's the home of the Grand Ole Opry, where my sister intends to sing."

"Oh, sure, her and about two million others," Kathy Ann said.

"She might make it," I muttered. Funnily enough, I could be critical and skeptical about Mother darling's chances of becoming successful, but I didn't like anyone else being that way.

"I hope she does," she said without much emotion. "Well, you going or not? I have to call Charlotte Lily and let her know, make sure it's all right with her, too."

"What kind of a place is this?"

"Fun with a capital F," she replied. "Are you afraid of fun?"

"Terrified," I said dryly. "Okay, I'll see you in an hour."

I went back up to the apartment. Mother darling was dressed in one of her outfits and was picking on her guitar. The bathroom door was closed with Cory obviously in there.

"I'm going out with a friend," I told her.

"What? You have a friend already? How could you do that? You just walked in and out of the apartment."

"She lives here, too. She was just downstairs."

"Great. Where are you goin'?"

"Riverfront Park. They have a carousel."

"That's it?"

"I'll just learn about the city and then I'll know where to go myself," I told her, and went to pick out something to wear from my meager wardrobe. In the end I decided to borrow one of her western blouses and do what she did, tie it at the bottom and show some midriff. Cory was still in the bathroom.

"I want to fix my hair and put on some makeup, but I don't have a mirror. What's he doing in there?" I asked loud enough for him to hear. Just then there was a knock on the door and Mother darling let in Del Thomas and the third musician, a man named Ernie Farwell, who was way over six feet tall, with long arms and a long neck. He had dirty blond hair as messy as Cory's and dull brown eyes with lids that looked poised to shut. Del was the neatest of the three, with well-trimmed dark brown hair and a trim beard. I thought he had an intelligent look, and I would soon see that he was the most serious of the three when it came to their music.

Mother darling introduced herself and then me. Cory finally emerged from the bathroom. While they talked, I fixed my hair and put on some makeup.

"Where's she goin'?" Cory asked Mother darling.

She told him. "Who'd you meet?" he demanded as if he had become my legal guardian.

"Her name's Kathy Ann Potter."

"That fat girl? Didn't know she did anything but listen on her earphones and eat and smoke dope, I bet. Mother's a looker," he told Del.

"Thanks for the rundown on the neighborhood. Let's get busy. We've got a lot to do," Del said dryly.

"Sure." Cory turned to Mother darling. "You gonna let her go out lookin' like that?"

She looked at me hard, turning her eyes into two steel balls of cold threat.

"Don't you get into any trouble here, Robin. We don't know a soul, except Cory."

"Who says he has a soul?" I quipped, and the three men laughed. "I need some money," I added.

She got up, went to her purse, and gave me a twenty-dollar bill.

"We have to watch our budget, you know," she said. "Be home by eleven, and I better not hear about you smokin' no dope, Robin."

"Right," I said.

"Robin Lyn," she called after me. She always added my middle name when she wanted to emphasize something.

"Robin Lyn," Cory chorused. "Don't you sin."

I shut the door on the laughter behind me and hurried down to Kathy Ann's apartment. She was already out and waiting.

"Don't you look killer," she remarked. She herself wore a silk ruffled sleeveless blouse with a collar deep enough to show the cavernous promise of her cleavage. I thought she had gone hog-wild with makeup, too heavy on the eye shadow and thick on the lipstick. Her skirt was nearly a mini, and she didn't have the legs for it. They were short and stubby, with bony knees. She reminded me of a young girl who had snuck into her mother's bedroom to play grown-up.

"C'mon," she said, grabbing my hand and tugging me toward the street. "I told Charlotte Lily about you, and she's anxious to meet you."

We started toward the bus stop and then broke into a run when a bus pulled up. Kathy Ann didn't seem to notice the way other passengers looked at her.

"Here," she said, handing me a college ID. "Tonight, you're Parker Carson and you're twenty-one."

"Why do we need this? I thought you said we could get in."

"Just in case," she said. "You have to flash something so Charlotte Lily's sister's boyfriend doesn't get into trouble."

I shrugged and put it in my shirt pocket.

"Now tell me all about yourself," she said, sitting back and looking like a five-year-old about to hear a bedtime story, "and don't leave out the sad parts."

I made up a story, claiming Mother darling, who was now known as my older sister, and I had lost our parents in a plane crash. The more elaborate and far-fetched I was, the more Kathy Ann believed and enjoyed the story. I went into how we had to live with our grandparents, who were both old and feeble, with no memories, and how Grandma had set the house on fire accidentally in the kitchen one night. They were both now in homes, and we had left to start a new life in Nashville.

"Wow," she said with envy, "you have had an exciting life already. You're going to love Nashville," she added when I had mentioned my concern about moving here. "You'll see," she promised.

With all the lights, people, and music, downtown was more interesting than I had anticipated. We went directly to the park and to the carousel where Charlotte Lily was waiting for us. She was quite the contrast to Kathy Ann. Tall and stylish in her cowgirl's hat, red fringed-sleeved shirt, and laminated black jeans and black boots, I thought she was pretty enough to be a model. She had long, light brown hair parted in the middle and brushed down, hazel green eyes, and features as petite as mine and Mother darling's, only with a dimple added to her right cheek. She looked me over quickly.

"Hi," she said, and glared angrily at Kathy Ann. "You're nearly twenty minutes late."

"We left when I said we would," Kathy Ann whined. "I can't help it how long the bus takes."

"C'mon," she ordered, and marched ahead of us.

We caught up, and she looked at me again.

"Where are you from?"

"Granville, near Columbus, Ohio."

"Why did you come here?"

"Her sister's in a band and someday will be singing in the Grand Ole Opry," Kathy Ann bellowed.

Charlotte Lily smirked.

"What about your parents?"

"Her parents were killed in a plane crash when she was only five."

"What did you do, Kathy Ann, get her whole life story in ten minutes? Be careful," she warned me. "Her picture's next to the word *gossip* in the dictionary."

"It is not!"

"What's it next to then, Pothead?" Charlotte said, laughed, and impulsively crossed the street.

"I thought you said she was your best friend," I told Kathy Ann as we caught up.

"She is. She's very popular and she can get us into Stumpin' Jumpin'," Kathy Ann reminded me.

"Maybe it's not worth it," I told her.

She looked at me as if I was crazy.

"Give me a cigarette," Charlotte ordered.

"Oh, I left them home," Kathy Ann said. Charlotte stopped walking and glared at her.

"What? I told you not to forget."

"I know," she said mournfully.

"You smoke?" she asked me.

"Yes, but I don't have any cigarettes on me at the moment."

"Terrific."

I looked at the drugstore just down the walk.

"Give me five minutes," I said, and headed for it.

"Five minutes?"

They followed me in. I located the cigarettes quickly, but picked up a box of tampons I actually did need. I checked out the mirrors, watched the clerk behind the counter, and then picked up a pack of my favorite menthol cigarettes, shoving it into my blouse. Then I paid for the tampons and walked out, the two of them standing at the door.

Charlotte watched me take it out of my blouse.

"Here."

"I thought something would ring if you did that," Kathy Ann said.

"Obviously not," I said.

"Why did you steal them? I saw you have enough money to buy them," Charlotte asked.

I shrugged.

"I'll save my money for something I can't steal," I told her, and she smiled.

"C'mon," she said. "I think we're going to have a lot of fun tonight."

Kathy Ann's face brightened.

"She likes you," she said, as if the queen had just granted me permission to live in Nashville.

If it's that easy to win friends here, I thought, maybe I'll have a good time tonight.

Charlotte Lily offered me one of the cigarettes from the pack I stole for her. I took it.

"I want one too," Kathy Ann said.

"You don't get any. Punishment for forgetting," she told her, smiled at me, and continued on. Like a whipped puppy, Kathy Ann remained a few steps behind us all the way to Stumpin' Jumpin'.

I was in Nashville and if Grandpa saw me now, I thought, he'd have me at a prayer meeting in the morning.

Too late for that, I told the voices inside me.

Maybe too late for a lot of things.

4

Getting into a New Groove

~~~

On the exterior Stumpin' Jumpin' looked almost like another one of Mother darling's honky-tonks. There was a blazing red neon sign over the two large black metal doors, at either side of which stood two human bulldogs. Each looked like a football linebacker, with thick necks and shoulders that made Grandpa's look puny. Charlotte Lily exchanged some sort of greeting and message with her sister's boyfriend through their own eye and head signals and then turned to us and said, "It's a little too early. We have to go in when there's a good crowd. We're less conspicuous if we do it that way," she explained. "C'mon, we'll visit Keefer for a while."

"Who's Keefer?" I asked when I saw that Kathy Ann was very pleased by the suggestion.

"An old boyfriend of mine I toy with from time to time. He works in an auto body shop."

"His father threw him out of the house," Kathy Ann said.

"I believe it was by mutual consent," Charlotte Lily told her.

"His father beat him up, didn't he?"

"I swear, Kathy Ann, you still don't know anything about men, do you?"

"Why?" she wailed as we turned a corner into a side street.

"Why? You don't remind a man of a time when he looked a fool or lost a fight. Sometimes I wonder if you learn anything being in my company. She's still a virgin," she told me.

"So am I," I said.

"Sure, right. And there really is a Santa Claus. Oh, good, Keefer's at work," she announced. "The light's on in the shop, and he's the only one who would be working now."

We entered through a side door. A young man was working on a car fender, the sparks flying from his welding torch. There was a radio blasting country rock music. The shop was lit by a half-dozen white neon lights. Next to the car that the young man worked on was a vehicle with its rear end bashed in, a taillight hanging by wires as if the accident had just occurred.

"He hates it when I sneak up on him," Charlotte Lily told me with an impish grin. Then she did just that. She walked up beside him, waited a moment, looked back at us, and with her hands around her mouth, shouted, "Keefer!"

He jumped to the side, the torch nearly turning at Charlotte Lily, who then screamed.

"Damn you, Charlotte Lily," Keefer shouted at her

after lifting his mask off his face. There was a streak of grease down his right cheek. "I told you a hundred times that's dangerous. You nearly got fried."

Charlotte Lily regained her composure.

"Oh, fiddlesticks, Keefer. You've become an old fuddy-duddy at the ripe old age of nineteen."

"Right," he said. He still hadn't noticed either Kathy Ann or me. "What's up?"

"I wanted you to meet our new friend. She just moved here from . . . where you from, Robin?"

"Granville, Ohio," I said.

Keefer turned to me, and for a long moment, we just gazed at each other. He had a strong, square jaw with firm lips, dark eyes, and hair the color of a crow. Although his hair wasn't really long, it looked wild and untrimmed, but somehow, it wasn't unattractive. There was something very natural about it.

"Like what you see?" Charlotte Lily asked, and followed her question with her short, thin laugh.

He tilted his head and looked at her, the side of his mouth lifting just slightly as he squinted.

"What are you up to now, Charlotte Lily?"

"Nothing. We're going to Stumpin' Jumpin' and thought we'd stop by and see how you were doin' first, Keefer," she said with a voice dripping maple syrup.

"Right," he said, and wiped his hands on a rag before walking toward me and Kathy Ann. "You really her new friend?" he asked.

"We just met about twenty minutes ago," I replied. He smiled at my honest and exact reply.

"I'm Keefer Dawson."

"Robin Taylor," I said.

He held out his hand, looked at it, and then pulled it back because it was thick with grime.

"You don't want to shake that if you're going to Stumpin' Jumpin'."

"You wanna go with us?" Charlotte Lily asked him. "We can wait for him to clean up, can't we, girls?"

"Oh yes," Kathy Ann said quickly.

"You'd even take him along dirty," Charlotte Lily told her, and she withered quickly, even stepping back.

"No, thanks. I've got to finish this car tonight. Promised Izzy I'd have it ready for paint in the morning. You here for good or what?" he asked me.

"I think both," I said, and he laughed. "I'm with my sister, who came here to be in a band. She sings."

"Parents let you move off?"

"They were killed in an airplane crash," Kathy Ann volunteered.

"Oh. Sorry."

"It's okay. It was a long time ago. We're all the family we have now."

"I know the feeling," Keefer said. "It's like my parents went down in a plane."

"Keefer lives here," Charlotte Lily said, obviously enjoying our warm conversation.

"Here?"

"In the back," he said. "I have a small apartment Izzy lets me have. It's all one room, nothing special."

"I'm going to the bathroom," Charlotte Lily declared.

"Don't do nothin' bad in there," Keefer warned. He looked serious. I waited until she went in and then asked him what he meant by that.

"She's been known to light up a joint or two or sniff some snow. All I need is Izzy to think I let something like that happen in his place. Ain't that right, Kathy Ann?"

"Yes," she said obediently.

"Where do you live?"

"She lives in my complex, upstairs, in Cory Lewis's apartment," Kathy Ann answered for me.

He shrugged.

"I don't know him. So, are you a singer, too?"

"Hardly," I said.

He laughed.

"You're probably the only one in Nashville who would admit it."

Charlotte Lily emerged from the bathroom, apparently having gone in only to check on her makeup.

"Don't worry," she said when he glared at her. "I didn't do anything that would get you in trouble."

"That's a surprise. Well, I gotta get back to this car," he said, more to me than to Kathy Ann and Charlotte Lily.

"Sad when a young man like that is more interested in working on a car than being with us, isn't it, girls?" Charlotte Lily teased.

He looked back.

"I don't get many arguments from my cars," he told her. "And they appreciate what I do for them."

"Oh, you poor sad boy. Someone done your heart in good. Put that torch to work and mend it," she told him, laughed again, and sauntered back to the door. "Let's go, girls, unless you'd rather stand there and watch Keefer make love to a fender bender."

I glanced back at him. He had his mask on and turned the torch back on. The sparks were flying again.

Not sure myself why I was so reluctant about it, I followed Charlotte Lily and Kathy Ann out of the shop.

"You don't want to get yourself involved with him," Charlotte Lily lectured as we started back toward

Stumpin' Jumpin'. "He's a loser from the get-go. Quit school, has no family anymore, and never does anything with his old friends. That's one boy you look at and know that what you see is what you get. Now," she said, turning toward the dance club, "let's see if we can entice a few of those college boys. They know what fun is. After all, what's the point of being young if you're going to waste it on being responsible, huh?"

She laughed at herself and looked at Kathy Ann, who smiled widely and then glanced at me for approval. I shrugged.

"I don't know if I'll ever be considered responsible," I said, "young or old."

She liked that.

"Yes, we're going to have a good ole time of it tonight. If you listen to us and watch us carefully, Kathy Ann, you might even lose your virginity," she said, and laughed again.

Kathy Ann looked to me, but I walked ahead, still thinking about the way the sparks flew around Keefer Dawson.

There was a long line at the entrance of Stumpin' Jumpin', but Charlotte Lily took us around on the inside of the crowd, and when we approached, her sister's boyfriend glanced at our fake IDs and just stepped out of the way. Kathy Ann looked excited enough to explode.

The moment we entered, the music washed over us like an ocean wave. The dance hall itself was a long, dark room with sofas and tables and drapes, giving the impression you were in someone's house, except that there was a large dance floor and to the right a long bar with a half-dozen bartenders, all with black cowboy hats, black suspenders holding up jeans, and no shirts.

They were all well-built, good-looking men. The bar was already jammed, mostly with what looked to me like college-age women flirting with the bartenders. Small spotlights combed through the dancers as the beat grew quicker and the volume of the music was turned up another notch or two. It was very hard to hear anyone talk, but no one cared, even though people sitting side by side at the bar were literally shouting at each other.

Waitresses in cowgirl outfits and fancy, glittering boots took orders from those seated on the sofas. We were just standing, drinking it all in, when suddenly Charlotte Lily saw someone she recognized.

"C'mon," she screamed, pulling at my arm. "There's Wyatt Baxter. He goes to Tennessee State."

I didn't know how she could see anyone through the thick jungle of swinging bodies. We wove our way through to three young men sitting and drinking at one of the sofa and coffee table setups. One of them recognized Charlotte as we approached and broke into a wide smile.

"Hey, Charlotte Lily, I was hoping you'd be here tonight," he cried, standing.

"I haven't seen you here in a while," she said.

"Busy, busy in summer school session," he said, shaking his head. "Who are your friends?" he asked, focusing mainly on me.

"This is Robin. She's new to Nashville. Surely you remember Kathy Ann?"

"Oh," he said, looking at her. "Yeah, yeah. How ya doin', Kathy Ann?"

"Just fine, thanks," she said.

"I'm Wyatt," he told me, and extended his hand. He was a little less than six feet tall, with an athletic build and dirty-blond hair, the strands of which lay trim over the top of his forehead.

I shook his hand, but he didn't let go of mine. Instead, he pulled me a bit closer because of the loud music and screamed, "This is Axel Farmer." He pointed to the stout boy in the middle with dull brown eyes and a military-style haircut. He looked as big as the security guards at the door. "Axel's a linebacker on the football team. And that there is Birdy Williams," he said, pointing to the third boy, who was lean and had an interesting, sensitive-looking face. "He plays trumpet in the marching band, and he's in a jazz band on the side, thus we call him Birdy, after Bird, the famous jazz musician. Hey, make some room, Birdy," he ordered.

Birdy shifted to the left. Charlotte Lily moved quickly to the open seat.

"You wanna dance?" Wyatt asked me.

The music changed to something more rock than western. I looked at Charlotte Lily, who seemed already interested in Birdy Williams. Grandma would say she had "wandering eyes" and was never satisfied.

"I guess," I said.

"Hey, Axel, order a round of drinks for everyone, will ya," Wyatt ordered. "What do you want?"

I wasn't sure what to order.

Charlotte Lily piped up with, "Get us three Saddle Soaps."

"You heard her, Axel," Wyatt said, and pulled me toward the dance floor. When I looked back, I saw the waitress taking the drink orders and then Axel asking Kathy Ann to dance.

The truth was, I had never been to a dance club before this. I had gone to some of the honky-tonks

Mother darling sang in, and most had a dance floor, but there was nothing that compared to this. The frenzy, the loud music, the exciting lights were all hypnotizing. Wyatt was a good dancer, too. I copied some of his moves and we danced into the next song, which was more country western. I wasn't into the beat as well and unsure of my steps, so he leaned over and shouted, "Let's get a drink."

I found out Saddle Soap was some kind of draft beer. It tasted very good, and after working up a sweat dancing, I found it very enjoyable. I drank it fast. Wyatt saw that and hooked a waitress to bring me another.

"You go to school with Charlotte Lily?" Wyatt asked.

I shook my head.

"No. I just moved here from Ohio. We just met, actually."

"Great. You'll love it," he promised. "We're all having a good time." He howled something which Axel mimicked and then we were all out on the dance floor. Nearly an hour later, and two more rounds of drinks, Charlotte Lily announced she had her house empty. Her parents had gone away for a few days and her sister was at a friend's until very late.

I saw that it was approaching ten and knew that Mother darling would be upset if I didn't get back by eleven, but I wasn't even sure which bus to take. Before I could express any of my concerns, everyone was up and moving toward the entrance. When we burst out on the street, my ears were ringing and my throat felt like I had swallowed sandpaper because of how much shouting I had done to be heard while we were dancing. The beer had just enough alcohol to give me a buzz, and for a moment, I felt a little unsteady.

"Whoa," Wyatt said, taking me around the waist. "You all right?"

"Yes," I said quickly.

"Hurry," Charlotte Lily screamed, "we can catch this bus."

Everyone ran, Wyatt pulling me along. When we got on the bus, I wasn't able to talk to Charlotte Lily because we sat boy-girl. The bus trip only took about five minutes, but as soon as we got off, I pulled Charlotte Lily aside.

"This is my first night here," I told her. "My sister wanted me back by eleven."

"Why? You don't have any school to go to tomorrow. It's summer. We're not college students taking a summer session. We're free, like we're supposed to be."

"I know, but my sister and I just arrived and . . ."

"She'll be happy you made new friends so fast. That way you won't be in her hair," Charlotte Lily assured me. I started to shake my head. "C'mon. My house is just ahead. We've got to do it for Kathy Ann. Axel looks serious."

I gazed back at them. He had his arm around her. Together, I thought, they would sink a rowboat. He looked like he weighed two hundred and fifty pounds. Charlotte Lily giggled and moved back under Birdy's long arm. Wyatt seized my hand and began to ask me questions about where I had lived, what interested me. I was nervous because he was the oldest boy I had ever been with and yet he didn't seem to care about my age. He told me he was going to get a B.A. in public administration, but he might go on to law school. When he asked me what my interests were, I didn't know what to say. I didn't want to sound young and stupid, so I said I was still thinking about it.

"Smart," he told me. "Don't make a decision too

fast. Explore. That's the fun of being young, you know, discovery. If you don't have fun now, when will you, I always say. What do you think?"

I shrugged.

"I guess," I said.

"You guess right," he said.

Charlotte Lily's house was a large, two-story colonial-style home, all gated.

"We can't drink too much of Daddy's booze," she said before opening the door. "He measures the bottles."

"Just put in some water and he'll never know the difference," Wyatt suggested.

Charlotte Lily laughed.

"I've done that already," she said.

The house was as impressive inside as it was outside. She wanted us to stay in the living room–den area and immediately put on some music that came through speakers in every room. Then she and Birdy prepared drinks, measuring the vodka and gin carefully and replacing it with water.

"It's too bright in here," Wyatt told Charlotte Lily. "Can't you do something about that?"

"Sure," she said, and turned the lights down very low.

"Dance?" Wyatt asked me when the music became slower. I looked over at Axel and Kathy Ann. They were already kissing. "C'mon, show me those Ohio moves," Wyatt teased, getting up and pulling on my hand.

"I don't have any moves," I said. He put his arm around my waist and tightened it so that I was practically attached to his hip. Then I felt his lips on my neck. I jerked back, but he held on firmly.

"Easy," he said. "We're just getting to know each other."

"I know enough," I said sharply.

"What you need is a little more to drink. You've got to loosen up," he advised, and handed me the drink that had been prepared for me. He tried to lift my hand to bring the glass to my mouth as if he was feeding a child.

"No," I said. "I don't need it."

"You need it," he retorted sharply.

Axel and Kathy Ann got up and went into the den. Charlotte Lily had already taken Birdy out and up to her bedroom, I imagined. Everything was happening so fast.

"C'mon," Wyatt urged, "get with it."

He put his arm around me and sat me on the sofa, bringing his lips to my neck while he fumbled with the buttons of my blouse so he could slip his hand under it to cup my breast while he pressed his lips to mine and then put his weight against me, driving me back.

"Now, that's better," he whispered, his breath reeking with the odor of his alcohol.

His hands were like spider legs, going everywhere. He had my jeans undone with his right hand while his left went over my hip. In a matter of seconds, he would have me half naked, I realized, and panic set in. I wasn't going to end up like Mother darling.

"No," I insisted, and pushed him so hard, he spun and fell to the floor.

"Whaaa," he cried.

I leaped up, zipped my pants closed, and rushed to the front door.

"Hey!" he called after me. "Where are you going?"

I didn't know where I was going, only out. Once on

the street, I ran for half a block and then walked quickly
to where we had gotten off the bus. Confused and lost, I
realized I was sobbing. I clutched at the money Mother
darling had given me and I hoped to see a taxicab.
Maybe I had enough to get back to Cory's apartment.

The streets here looked empty, however, and I
walked and walked for some time before I recognized
the downtown area where we had been. Then I saw the
side street we had taken to go to see Keefer Dawson. I
strolled down it and saw the lights were still lit in the
shop. Maybe he could give me directions on how to get
back, I thought.

When I entered, I didn't see him or anyone else for a
few moments. Then I heard, "Hey?"

He was sitting back on what was once an easy chair
but now had no legs. Its stuffing leaked out of the torn
arms.

"What are you doing here? Where's Charlotte Lily?"
he asked.

"She's home. I was hoping you could tell me how I
can get back to my apartment."

He sat up quickly.

"You just left her."

"You can say that," I said, and he smiled.

"What happened?"

"One of her college boyfriends thought I was going
to be his good time tonight."

His smile widened.

"C'mon," he said, standing. "I'll take you back in
Izzy's pickup."

"You don't have to do that," I said.

"I'm not doing it because I have to," he replied.

5

Sinking Deeper
into the Dark

I hate being dishonest with someone who bares his soul so willingly and is so trusting with his emotions, but Mother darling's fears and dreams weighed heavily on my mind, and I was afraid she would think I had betrayed her if I told the truth. Keefer just started to talk frankly about himself. It was as if he had not found anyone to talk to before he met me.

"My daddy drinks a lot," he began. "And he gets real mean when he's drunk. I have a scar on my right leg from the time he hit me with the broken end of a beer bottle. He threw it across the room. I was about seven."

"What about your mother?"

"She's what they call a manic depressive. Ever hear of that?"

I shook my head.

"She goes up and down. Sometimes she gets so depressed she won't come out of her bedroom all day, not even to eat. Can't blame her, being married to him."

"Do you have any brothers or sisters?"

"I have a sister, Sally Jean, but she ran off with her boyfriend about two years ago. She had good reason to get away from my father, even better reason than I have," he said, his eyes growing small and dark. "She's out in Texas and once in a while, she sends me a post-card. One of these days, I might join her," he added wistfully. Then he turned to me and said, "I'm one who knows it's not easy to be on your own, so I can appreciate what you and your sister have been going through. I hope she does well here."

"Thank you," I said in a small voice. Guilt made me feel like I was taking a bath in dirty old engine oil.

"But just know that Nashville's so full of people dreaming of stardom, you can smell fantasy in the air," he warned.

We were both quiet until he turned into the apartment complex.

"The apartment seemed farther by bus," I said.

"Yeah, with the stops and all, it would."

"Thank you very much," I told him after opening the door.

"No problem. Next time you're downtown, stop by if you want. I'll show you how to pull a ding out of a car door."

I laughed and got out slowly. He waved and then shifted and backed up. I watched him drive off before heading for the stairs to the upstairs apartments. It was nearly twelve-thirty and I was anticipating Mother darling's rage. Instead, I was surprised to find no one home and even more surprised to find the door unlocked. Was it just that there was nothing here anyone would want to steal?

At least I had the bathroom to myself for a while. Afterward, I got into bed and realized the sheets and the blanket smelled like they'd been made in a cigarette factory. The stench nearly choked me. I decided to put my clothes back on and not use the blanket. I put one of my skirts over the pillow and finally, after tossing and turning for an hour, fell asleep, only to be awakened by the sound of laughter. It was just Mother darling and Cory, but they made enough noise for a half-dozen people. I heard Cory say, "Told you this would be easier here."

"I'd better check on Robin and be sure she's come home," Mother darling told him.

I decided to pretend I was in a deep sleep. She opened the door and stood there so long, I thought she didn't believe I was asleep. Finally, she closed it. I heard them giggling and then, a little while later, I heard them in his bedroom. It wasn't hard to realize what they were doing. Mother darling kept trying to get him to be quieter.

"What for? Robin Lyn surely knows what it's all about, and if she don't, it's time she did," he said.

I tried burying my head in the pillow, but the odor of cigarettes was too much to endure. It wasn't until they fell asleep that I did. I was up ahead of them in the morning, which suited me fine because I was able to take a shower and get dressed before Mother darling and Cory woke. At least, that was what I had hoped.

I was positive I had pushed in the little button on the doorknob that would lock it, but just a few seconds after I had gotten under the water in the tub shower, I heard the door opening and screamed at the sight of Cory, naked himself, stumbling his way toward the toilet. For a moment I thought he didn't even realize I was there, despite the sound of the shower and my scream. He just began to urinate.

I pulled the flimsy shower curtain around me.

"I'm taking a shower!" I screamed.

"You gotta go when you gotta go," he mumbled.

When he was finished, he turned to go, but paused at the door and said, "Don't forget to wash behind your ears." He closed the door on his laughter.

Flushed with embarrassment and anger, I turned off the shower and dried myself. As soon as I was dressed, I charged out of the bathroom. They were both still in bed.

"Mother!" I called at the closed door. There was a long moment of silence and then I heard, "Call me Kay, damn it."

"Kay, I need to see you right now."

I heard her groan. I waited and waited until she finally opened the door and peered out at me.

"What?"

"I was in the bathroom. I had the door shut and I thought locked and he just came in while I was in the shower and . . . and went to the bathroom."

"Next time be sure you lock the door," she said.

"It doesn't work and he saw it was closed and I had the shower running. He had to know I was in there."

"He had to go," she told me. "Don't make a big deal of it," she said. "We have to get some sleep. We've already gotten a job and we start tonight," she added, and closed the door.

My face felt like my blood was boiling just under my skin. I started toward their bedroom door again and then stopped and returned to my room to fume. After a few minutes, I came out and saw that Cory and she had been quite wild and drunk last night. Clothes were strewn everywhere in the already disheveled-looking living room. I thought for a moment, and then I went to his pants and pulled out his wallet. There were three twenties, a ten, a five, and five singles in it. I took the three twenties and put the wallet back.

"That's your fine for being disrespectful," I muttered at the door, and left the apartment.

I didn't get too far before I heard a door open and my name called. Kathy Ann was standing in the doorway of her family's apartment. She was dressed in a robe, and her hair looked like a family of rats had run through it. I debated just ignoring her, but she kept beckoning. As I approached, she stepped out of her apartment and closed the door most of the way.

"What happened to you last night? I didn't even know you had left. How did you get home? I had a great time," she told me before I could offer a single answer.

"Good for you," I said.

"Axel can speak a little Spanish. His family has a Spanish maid. He was impressed with what I already knew."

"Sounds like a match made in heaven," I said dryly, but she was on a happy roll and either ignored or didn't see my disinterest.

She looked at me with a smile smeared across her lips like cake frosting.

"What?" I finally asked.

"We did it," she said. "I mean, I did it."

"It's not like running the four-minute mile or something, Kathy Ann. You don't get a medal."

Her smile faded.

"Don't you want to hear about it?" She looked like she was going to burst into tears.

"All right," I said with great effort. "What happened?"

"He was very gentle and considerate and first announced and showed me he had protection."

"I'm glad of that," I said.

"Still, I was afraid. He told me he understood, that it was like the first time he had to be a linebacker on a college football team and had to bang heads with a guy just as big as he was if not bigger. He said it was like knowing you were going to run into a wall, but you had to go ahead anyway."

"Yeah, that sounds just like making love," I muttered.

"He meant every time you do something new, you are nervous. I thought that was sweet, his sharing his fear with me. He's so big and strong, it was hard to believe anything could frighten him."

"It is hard to believe," I said.

"Anyway, I closed my eyes and held my breath and it was just as wonderful as Charlotte Lily told me it would be. After a little pain, I mean. Axel said he would call me every time he comes into the city." She leaned toward me to add in a whisper, "He's really not supposed to be so wild and active. He's in training."

"It's nice of him to put you before football."

"I thought so," she said.

I stared at her. Are we all like this at one time or another? I wondered. Do we all wear blinders, deliberately ignore the truth just to hold on to one of our fantasies? Is that what was happening to Mother darling, still happening? What can be the final result? Only a great fall, I thought, great disappointment, and from that, bitterness and cynicism. We would be like the fox in the story one of my teachers told, the fox who couldn't reach the grapes and then said they were probably sour anyway. Sincere happy smiles would become

so rare, we would wonder if it was our faces we saw
reflected.

"Where are you going?" Kathy Ann asked.

"I'm going shopping," I said. "I need some new
clothes."

"Can you wait? I'll go with you. I love shopping,
even when it's someone else doing it."

I'm not sure what department store to go to anyway,
I thought. She would know.

"Okay, but don't take too long."

She hurried back into her apartment and I went to the
faded brown bench that was near the empty swimming
pool. I heard another door close and saw a woman holding the hand of a little boy and a little girl. They looked
close enough in age to be twins. The woman paused to
fix the little boy's collar, and then she kissed him on the
cheek and he smiled. As if she could sense her daughter's envy, she turned, brushed her hair, and kissed her
as well. Then the three walked to the parking lot, an
aura of happiness and contentment surrounding them.

That's what love really is, I thought, a thick cocoon
that helps you feel safe, secure, and most of all, cherished.

For a moment I actually missed Grandpa and
Grandma. Despite his hard, critical eyes, there were
moments when the three of us sat and watched television or ate a meal together and I felt like I belonged to
a family. Grandma was so gentle and loving that she
softened him, and he would go on about some adven-
ture he had when he was about my age. For just a little while, a door had been opened and I could look in
and see enough to make me understand what it was
that connected me to him, to Grandma, to this idea of
family.

But then Mother darling would come home or say something and the door would slam shut again.

I heard a door slam shut and looked up to see Kathy Ann practically bouncing toward me.

"Let's go," she said. "I want to buy something for Axel, something to give him the next time he calls."

"Where should we go?"

"Let's go to Dillards," she suggested. "C'mon, we'll catch the bus. So, why did you leave Charlotte Lily's house like that?"

"I had to be home by eleven, and it was already close to midnight," I said.

"Oh. How did you get home?"

"I took a taxicab," I said, instinctively deciding not to reveal Keefer Dawson.

She believed me and then spent the rest of our travel time talking about Axel. From the way she spoke about him, I thought it wasn't only the first time she had made love, it was the first time she had been with anyone. She went on and on about the promises he had made to her concerning their future, how he was going to make sure she had tickets to all the home games, and how he would take her to dances and parties.

"Promises can be like balloons," I told her. "They look and feel good when they're pumped up, but they all leak and eventually fall to earth."

"Not my promises," she vowed. "And when my daddy makes my stepmother a promise, he always keeps it."

"Goody goody for her," I said.

"And he keeps the promises he makes to me most of the time. Didn't your father do that, before he was killed in the plane crash, I mean?"

I gazed out the window without replying.

"I'm sorry," she said. "I know it's painful for you to think about it. Let's just think about good things. I know, I'll practice my Spanish. How's that?"

"Whatever," I said, and she began a catalogue of Spanish words for common things.

After a while I didn't hear her anymore. I felt tight inside, like my stomach had been tied into a knot and everything in it and around it was being squeezed. No, I didn't have a father to even break his promises to me, and now, now I wasn't permitted to have a mother. I was the balloon I spoke about. My life was just full of hot air, and I was leaking badly. Soon, I would fall to earth.

When we arrived at the department store, Kathy Ann went to the men's department to search for a gift for Axel. I went to the women's clothing area, and after a while, I found a young-miss skirt and blouse I really liked. I thought about Keefer Dawson and how he would appreciate seeing me in the outfit. The skirt was nearly sixty dollars, however, and the blouse was another thirty. One wouldn't be good without the other.

The saleslady was a little overwhelmed, which gave me the opportunity to take the skirt and the blouse into the fitting room together. I had done this before, so I felt confident about it. I put the blouse on under my blouse and made sure it was well hidden. Then I came out with the skirt and told the saleslady I wanted to buy it.

She glanced at me quickly and asked me to wait until she was finished with the customer ahead of me or else go to another register. That was even better, so I went toward the front of the store and placed the skirt on the counter. The cashier ran it through the register, and I paid her with Cory's money. Now that I had what I wanted, I wanted very much to get out of the store and away, but I didn't see Kathy Ann anywhere. Nevertheless, I thought it would be wiser to leave, so I did.

Not more than a minute after I left the store, a tall, dark-haired man in a suit and tie seized my left elbow, squeezing it hard enough to make me wince.

"Hey!" I snapped at him. "What do you think—"

"Where do you think you're going, young lady?"

"I'm going home. Who are you?" I demanded.

Some customers going in and out paused to watch the exchange, and I thought I would start to scream any moment to draw more attention and frighten whoever he was away, but he surprised me by opening his wallet and showing me a badge.

"I'm the store security man, and you, young lady, are under arrest for shoplifting. Now, turn around and head back into the department store," he ordered.

"I paid for this!" I cried, and showed him the slip.

He smiled.

"What about what you're wearing underneath your blouse?"

How could he know that unless they had some sort of camera or peep hole in the changing room? I wondered.

"Do you want me to make you take it off out here, or what?" he asked.

I thought about running, but the small crowd of onlookers had built considerably and was now surrounding us.

"Well?" he demanded.

I turned and headed back toward the entrance of the store. As we approached, Kathy Ann came out.

"Where were you? I've been looking all over for you. Why did you go out without telling me?"

"Step aside," the security man told her.

"What?"

"Go home, Kathy Ann," I said, "and tell my sister I'm in trouble."

"For what?" she asked, looking at the security man.

"For shoplifting," he said.

Her mouth dropped open. The security man put his hand on my back and pushed me toward the store entrance.

He took me to an office at the rear of the store where the store manager waited. He was a small, baldheaded man with deep wrinkles under his eyes and thick, wet lips. I could see from the way he was nodding and smiling that his day had been made.

"You juvenile delinquents think you can come in here anytime you want and just rip me off," he said. "This time you were fooled, eh."

I didn't say anything.

"Well? What's your excuse? C'mon, let's hear it. Maybe you have something new."

"I just forgot," I said.

"Oh," he groaned, and sat hard in his seat. "She's not even a little original. I've already called the police. We're going to press charges against you to set an example. We know you kids have been coming in here and pulling these stunts all year long, and we've grown sick and tired of it. The only way to stop it is to see to it that when you're caught, you pay the price, and I don't mean the price of what you stole, either."

I was hoping he was saying that just to frighten me. I was afraid, but something in me kept me from milking it. I couldn't even cry. The rage and tightness I had felt on my way here were still strong.

"What's your name?" he demanded.

"Puddin' Tame," I said.

"Oh, I see, a smart-ass. All right, we'll leave it all to the police and the courts. Sit," he commanded, pointing to a chair.

I looked at it, at the security man and the door, and then sat.

"She had a friend with her," the security man told the manager.

"And?"

"She was clean, as far as I could tell."

"Sure, they come in pairs. One distracts while the other pilfers."

"That's not true," I said. "She has nothing to do with this. She wasn't even with me in that department."

"What's her name?" he asked.

"Pippi Longstocking," I said.

He sat back and rubbed his hands together like someone anticipating a great feast.

A few moments later, the door opened and a policeman entered.

"This is our thief," the manager said. "She's wearing the stolen item under her blouse. You've got your evidence. Book her," he told them.

"Stand up," the policeman told me. He took out a pair of handcuffs. This had never happened to me in Ohio. The sight of them did stab me with a cold blade of fear. I know my arms trembled as he snapped the cuffs around my wrists.

"Let's go," he said firmly.

Marching through the store again, this time with a policeman right behind me and me wearing handcuffs, I drew more curious faces, some heads shaking with disgust. When we emerged, I looked for Kathy Ann, but I didn't see her anywhere.

"Move," the policeman said, poking me toward the patrol car. There was a policewoman waiting beside it. She held the rear door open.

"Watch your head," she said, putting her hand on top of my head as I leaned in to sit on the caged rear seat. "What do we have?" she asked the policeman.

"She's wearing a blouse under her blouse."

The policewoman smiled and shook her head at me.

"Honey," she said, "you just put yourself in a whole can of worms."

They got into the patrol car and we started away. I looked back at the people watching from the entrance.

At least I made someone's news of the day, I thought.

6

Strike One

I had been in a police station before, but I was two years younger then, and although everyone had been serious, I'd had the sense that my youth would provide a parachute. This time when they brought me into the station, I saw no one remotely close to my age. All of the other prisoners looked hardened and experienced.

The policewoman took me into a private room, where I removed the blouse I had taken. She folded it and then brought me back to the desk sergeant, where they took down my name and address. I had a picture ID from my school back in Ohio. Then I was fingerprinted and put in a holding cell with two other women. One looked like she was still coming down from a drug she had taken. The other was talking to her, but I didn't think she heard a word. I gathered they had been arrested for soliciting sex on the street. I was actually happy they showed no interest in me.

I sat on the bench and waited nearly three hours before Mother darling appeared.

"Robin Taylor," I heard, and stood up. The policeman unlocked the door. "Come with me," he said. I looked back at the two women, who were both asleep now, one leaning on the other. In the lobby Mother darling and Cory were standing and talking with the policewoman who had brought me to the station.

They all turned to me as I was brought along.

"I don't even want to hear your excuses, Robin," Mother darling said. "Cory and I have guaranteed your appearance in court. Just walk," she said.

I glanced at Cory, who had a twisted smile on his face.

"Told you not to sin, Robin Lyn," he quipped as they followed me out of the station.

"Don't joke with her, Cory. She knows she's in deep trouble with me. The whole Nashville world can find out I'm really her mother and not her sister," she said, and I spun on her.

"That's what bothers you the most?"

"No, what bothers me the most is your not keepin' your promise not to get into any trouble here. I told you this was a strange, new place. Luckily, Cory knows one of the policemen, and he helped arrange your release, but now we got to think about gettin' you a lawyer and that costs money. How could you do this?"

I got into Mother darling's Beetle and sat in the rear. Cory was driving.

"When that girl, Kathy Ann, came huffin' and puffin' up the stairs to tell me you were arrested for shopliftin', I nearly fainted with disappointment. They said you paid for this," she added, showing me the bag that contained the skirt. "Where'd you get the money for it, Robin, or did you somehow fool 'em?"

"I had some saved," I lied.

"I don't want you goin' anywhere until I say it's okay, hear me? You stay right around the apartment complex. Hopefully, you can't get into any more trouble doin' that. You know they could send you to jail for this? They do send sixteen-year-olds to jail, Robin. You're just lucky they don't know about your record in Ohio.

"They keep the juvenile records secret," she told Cory.

"How many times did she get in trouble like this?" he asked.

"Enough to have her called a kleptomaniac. I had her see a therapist, too."

"That did a lot of good, I see," he said.

"Now you see how hard it is to work on building a career and bring up a child," she told him.

"I'm not a child."

"You sure behave like you are," Cory said.

"At least I don't bust in on people when they're taking a shower."

"Oh, save me," he said. "Next time I'll do my business in a beer bottle. No, maybe I better not do that. Del might drink it by mistake," he said, and laughed.

Mother darling laughed, too.

"Oh, Robin," she said, shaking her head, "with me startin' work in a real club tonight, too. Don't you realize how good our lives could be?"

I folded my arms under my breasts and stared out the window. It was always Mother darling who was disappointed, always Mother darling who had to be protected.

The moment we drove into the apartment complex, Kathy Ann, who was obviously sitting by her window waiting, came charging out of her apartment.

"What happened?" she asked.

"What happened? I'll tell you what happened," Mother darling replied. "She was booked, finger-printed, and given a court date where she could be sentenced to jail. That's what happened. Go on upstairs, Robin. You sit and contemplate what you've done."

I hurried ahead and went into my bedroom, slamming the door closed behind me. Then I threw myself on the bed, became aware of the stench in the sheet and blanket again, and sat up quickly. I thought for a moment and went to the door. They were sitting in the living room, feeling sorry for themselves. Cory was saying how grateful he was that he never got married and had any children. The ones who should be grateful are the children, I thought, who never had him as a father.

"Can I go down to the laundry room and wash something at least?" I asked.

"What?" Mother darling wanted to know.

"The smelly old sheet on this bed and the blanket and the pillowcase. I can't sleep on it! It all stinks from cigarette smoke," I moaned.

"It's better than what you'll have in jail," Cory called back.

"Can I?"

"Just the laundry and back, Robin, and I mean it. You better not run off."

"Unless you want to keep going," Cory added, and then laughed.

"I wish I could," I muttered, returning to the bed to strip it and roll up the sheet, blanket, and pillowcase. Then I started out.

"Don't you need money for that washing machine and dryer?" Mother darling asked Cory.

"Yeah, you have any change?" he asked me.

"No."

He reached into his pocket and then he pulled out his wallet.

"You can get change for a dollar. They have a change machine," he said, and froze, his eyes blinking rapidly as he fingered the bills. "Hey." He looked up at Mother darling and then at me. "I had eighty dollars in here. Now I have only twenty."

"Robin, did you take Cory's money?"

"No," I said.

"She's lying. You can see it in her face."

"Robin?"

"No," I said. She shook her head.

"I'm so sorry, Cory. I'll give it to you," she told him.

"I didn't take it. You don't have to give it to him."

"You see what I've been livin' with," she told him.

"I have some money left over from what you gave me," I told her. "I don't need anything from him."

Before either of them could say another word, I left the apartment and went down to the laundry. All I could think was Kathy Ann spent her whole time at that front window because she saw me and came over to the laundry a second or two after I began to load in the sheet and blanket.

"Tell me what really happened," she said.

"Just what my sister said."

"Why did you do it?"

"I wanted it and I didn't have enough money for it. You never stole anything?"

"Not like that," she replied, shaking her head. "I'd be too scared. I was amazed at how you stole those cigarettes last night. Were you ever caught before?"

"Not often," I told her. "I should have kept some of those cigarettes. You have any?"

"Sure," she said, and dug one out of her shirt pocket. She lit one for herself too, and we sat there watching the washing machine churn away. "How is your sister punishing you?" she wanted to know.

"I'm not supposed to leave the apartment complex until she says it's all right."

"Oh. That's too bad."

"But she's going to be busy nights, singing with the band. They have a job or a gig, as they call it."

"So you'll sneak out anyway?"

"What do you think?"

"Wow," she said, and looked at me as if I was some sort of celebrity myself. "Where are you going to go?"

"I have to have a dent in my head fixed."

"Huh?"

"I didn't tell you the truth when you asked me how I had gotten home last night. I went to see Keefer Dawson and he drove me here."

"You didn't?"

"All right, I didn't."

"Wow," she said again.

Yes, I thought. Wow.

She sat with me until I was finished with my sheet and blanket and pillowcase. Now that she knew more about what had happened, she had a laundry list of questions to ask about my life in Ohio. I told her as much as I could. I wanted her to think I was taking her into my confidence because I had a favor I needed from her.

"You weren't going anywhere tonight, were you?" I asked her.

"No. Why?"

"Can you do me a little favor?"

"Sure," she said, excited that I was taking her into my confidence.

"Come up to my apartment to hang out."

"Oh, sure. I'd like that."

"And when my sister calls to see if I'm there, if she should, tell her I'm in the bathroom. As long as you answer the phone, she'll believe it."

"You mean you won't be there?"

"No, silly," I said. "I'll be fixing my dent."

She made an O with her mouth and nodded, and then she smiled at me.

"Wow," she said.

Maybe that would become my new name, I thought. Wow.

After I made the bed with the fresh sheet, pillowcase, and blanket, I joined Mother darling and Cory, who were eating take-out Chinese Cory had had delivered. Mother darling was not much of a cook. I was a better cook than she was, in fact, because I was around Grandma more when she made our meals, and she taught me. "Your mother was never interested in learning any of this," she said. "All she wanted to do was sing and hang out with nobodies."

I smiled to myself, remembering that.

"You better sit down and eat 'fore it gets cold, Robin," Mother darling told me.

I plopped onto a seat, petulantly. Cory was feeding his face as fast as he could scoop the noodles, chicken, and shrimp into his mouth.

"You're really in serious trouble now, Robin. I hope you appreciate the situation and behave."

I picked up a fork and started to serve myself some food. Cory glanced at me and then burped.

"What she needs is a job," he said, "but with her history, I don't know nobody who'd hire her, except a pickpocket."

"He's right, Robin. That's somethin' we should think about. You have weeks and weeks yet before school starts here."

"I can't look for work if I'm locked up in the apartment, now can I?"

She thought a moment.

"We'll buy a paper and see what sort of work's out there and then we'll see about how to apply."

"I won't hold my breath," I said.

"Damn girl, if you was my daughter . . ."

"I'd commit suicide," I finished, and he sat with his mouth open for a moment and then shook his head and got up.

"I'm gettin' ready to go," he told Mother darling.

"Why are you so mean to him?" Mother darling whispered. "Don't you realize we'd have nothin' and be nowhere if he wasn't helpin' me? The least you can do is show him some respect and appreciation, Robin."

"What? He—"

"Don't start," she snapped. "If you can't be nice, then just don't be anythin'. Just keep your mouth shut, hear?"

I pushed the food away and pouted.

"I don't have time to baby you now, Robin. I've got to make a career happen. You're just goin' to have to grow up or suffer the consequences. Meanwhile, you clean up," she declared, and left to follow Cory.

I sat fuming until I heard them come out of their bedroom.

"I'll be callin' you first break I get, Robin," Mother darling said. "Least you could do is wish me luck."

"Good luck," I spit back at her.

After they were gone, I cleared off the table and washed the silverware and dishes. I began to think

Kathy Ann wasn't going to come up to the apartment, but she finally did appear.

"When are you coming back?" she asked.

"I'll be back before midnight," I said. "I won't forget this favor."

"Can't you be arrested for leaving the apartment?" she wanted to know.

"No. You're not guilty of anything until the court says."

"I was never in a courtroom," she told me, as if she had been denied some pleasure that all girls our age had already enjoyed.

"Lucky you," I said.

"Does Keefer know you're going to see him?"

"Not exactly," I said.

"I told Charlotte Lily about you. She was very interested."

"Like I care," I said.

"Bring me back a chocolate bar with nuts. My stepmother threw every piece of candy out of the house today."

"Axel will like you more if you lose weight."

"That's not what he said. He said he likes a woman with something to grab on her."

"Okay," I said. "One chocolate bar with nuts."

I was getting away cheaply, I thought, and after I put on the skirt I had bought with Cory's money and found a blouse that came close to the one I had stolen, I went to the bathroom to fix my hair and put on some lipstick. Then I started to leave before Kathy Ann could change her mind. Fortunately, she was already hooked on a television program.

"Call me," she said as I started toward the front door, "and let me know what's happening."

"Will do. Don't forget. I'm in the bathroom, and if she calls again, say I've got the runs. She'll believe that."

"I bet you've been lying all your life, haven't you?"

I thought a moment.

"No, my whole life's been a lie," I told her. She smiled in confusion.

"Huh?"

"Thanks, Kathy Ann. I owe you," I said, and left quickly.

I had to wait longer for the bus and at one point wondered if I should try hitching a ride. Finally, it came. I went directly to the shop, but stopped dead in my tracks when I turned the corner and looked at the building. There were no lights on like there had been the night before. Disappointment settled over me like a leaden cape. I felt like crying. Then I remembered Keefer saying he had an apartment behind the shop.

I went around the building and saw a small window with a light on behind it. What if he was with someone? I thought. It would be very embarrassing for both of us. I should have called him first. Feeling timid now, I went to the window and peeked through the flimsy curtain. I saw it was as he had described: a single room with a pullout sofa, a small stove and sink on the right, and a television set across from the sofa. There was a table with two chairs as well. The walls were bare. The truth was, it looked more like some sort of a storage room that had been converted into a living space. The floor was bare, and the only light came from two lamps. How depressing, I thought.

"See anything you like?" I heard, and nearly jumped out of my skin.

I turned, holding my breath. There was Keefer, a bag

of groceries in his arms. When he saw it was me, he broke into a big smile.

"Robin, what the hell are you doin'?"

"I was just seeing if you were in, or if you had any company," I explained.

He nodded.

"Company? Here? It's just me, myself, and I," he told me. "What are you doin' here?"

"I had to get away from my place," I said. "I got into trouble today."

"Oh? C'mon inside then and tell me about it. I love to hear about trouble."

He opened the door, and I followed him into the one-room apartment. He had a very small refrigerator, actually more like a portable thing. He had to bend down to put his food in it. He took two quarts of beer out of his bag and put one in the refrigerator.

"Beer?" he asked.

"Sure."

Now that I was inside, I felt even more depressed. The walls seemed to close in, and I could hear what sounded like a leaking pipe in the wall.

"There's a couple of rats livin' here, too," he said, seeing how I was listening. "Friendly. I even put out some cheese for them."

"Keefer!"

"I'm just kiddin'. That's the hot water heater. So, tell me about your trouble," he said, pouring me a glass of beer. He sat beside me and I described it all. He went from a smile to a serious face and then a very pensive look.

"I doubt they'd send you to jail," he said, "but you will get some sort of probation. You don't need a lawyer. Tell your sister to just throw you on the mercy of the court."

"How do you know so much about it?"

He poured himself another glass of beer, filled mine again, and smiled.

"I wasn't exactly an Eagle Scout myself." He stopped smiling. "Only when I got home, my daddy didn't just tell me to stay put. He took his belt out and gave me welts that lasted for a month."

"What had you done?"

"Stole a car," he said nonchalantly. "Just for a joyride."

"Was that when you had your fight with your father?"

"Who told you about that?"

"Kathy Ann."

"Yeah, I had a real fistfight with my father. I didn't do well. He nearly broke my cheek bone, in fact, but I wouldn't stop until he backed off. He knew he had to kill me to get me to stop, and that's when he told me to get out and stay out, which is just what I did. He never wanted me anyway. I wasn't just an accident, I was a train wreck as far as my father was concerned."

He finished the beer in his glass and poured another. I stared at him long enough for him to widen his eyes and say, "What?"

"I'm living a lie here," I said.

"What do you mean?"

"I'm not here with my sister. I'm here with my mother. She makes me say she's my sister because she wants music people to think she's younger than she is."

"Oh. Then that story about the plane crash . . ."

"I just made that up on the spur of the moment to tell Kathy Ann something."

"Well, what about your father?"

"Your father could be my father for all I know," I

said. His eyes widened more. "No, I'm kidding, but not as much as you think. My mother can't be sure who made me. She was high on something at a wild party, and she says she was with more than one man the same night."

"Wow," Keefer said.

"That seems to be a popular word around here, or maybe just around me."

"Huh?"

"Never mind," I said. I finished my beer. "I guess you and I are more alike than I first thought, only you're lucky. You got away."

"Got away? To this?" He looked around the room. "No, ma'am, this isn't luck. It's a stopover on the way to something better, I hope."

I held out my glass and he filled it again.

"What made you want to come to see me after all this?" he asked.

I shrugged.

"You mend things that are banged around, dented, and broken, don't you?"

He laughed, and then he looked at me long and hard before leaning over to do what I wished he would from the moment I saw him sitting in a pool of sparks.

He kissed me.

And I kissed him back, harder and longer than I had ever kissed anyone.

In my mind the sparks were flying all around us.

7

Honeymoon Fantasies
and Strike Two

❧

"**Y**ou sure you want to get mixed up with the likes of me?" Keefer asked before he kissed me again.

"I could ask you the same question," I replied. He liked that.

"Girls like Charlotte Lily always make me feel small, feel like something disposable."

I saw how angry he became just thinking about it, so I leaned forward and kissed him softly on the lips.

"I'm not Charlotte Lily," I told him, and the smile returned to his face.

"You sure ain't," he said, put his beer glass down, and kissed me on the cheek, the neck, and the lips while he turned me in so he could embrace me more easily. I felt his hands move down to the zipper on my skirt.

"I don't want to get pregnant," I said.

"Don't worry, you won't," he promised. He paused, took out his wallet, and then took out a contraceptive.

He held it up as if he was showing off a diamond in the lamplight. My heart was pounding. He thinks I've done this before, I thought. I was going to tell him I hadn't, but he kissed me again and then began to slowly undress me, kissing every naked part of me he uncovered until he stood up and undid his pants while he looked down at me and said, "You're really beautiful, Robin."

My heart was pounding so, I could barely breathe. When he was beside me, I finally confessed. He hesitated so long, I thought he was going to stop, but then he smiled and said, "You'll never forget me then. Women never forget the first man."

A part of me was disappointed in myself. When I had learned the facts of life, I used to fantasize my first lovemaking. It was always on some glamorous island during a wonderful honeymoon with music in the background and stars blazing above. Instead, here I was in some thrown-together, makeshift, dingy one-room apartment on a sofa that could have been rescued from a junkyard, both Keefer and I tasting the beer on our lips.

There were no shooting stars, no tinkling bells, no angels with magic wands around us. I was uncomfortable with my excitement, sensitive and nervous, moaning under his pleading to relax. Instead of being as soft and downy as a cloud, I was a tightening guitar string, stretched to the point of breaking, every nerve in my body cracking and snapping like a shorted electric wire.

"It gets better," Keefer assured me when we were finished. He lay there, catching his breath, his head against my naked breast, listening to the thumping of my heart. "Are you all right?"

"Yes," I managed.

He lifted his head and kissed each of my nipples before pushing himself away.

"Be right back," he said, and went to the bathroom.

I sat up and began to dress. When he came out, we heard the phone ringing in the shop.

"Who the hell is that?" he wondered aloud. "Be right back," he said, and went to the door that opened on the shop.

I continued to dress.

"Got a message for you," he said, returning. "That was Kathy Ann. She says your 'sister' called and said she was calling back in fifteen minutes and if you weren't there to answer, she was going to call the police herself and report you."

"She would, too, I bet," I moaned.

"C'mon," he said. "I can get you back there in fifteen minutes."

He pulled on his jeans, slipped into his shoes, and grabbed his shirt as we started out.

"Hold on," he told me after starting the engine. I had barely closed the door.

The rear wheels spun and kicked up gravel, and then he turned sharply into the street and accelerated. He wove in and out of traffic, cutting someone off at one point. The driver leaned on his horn. Keefer laughed and just accelerated again, turning abruptly down a side street.

"I know a little shortcut," he said, gunning the engine.

He went through a stop sign and then made some sharp turns again, throwing me from one side of the seat to another. I screamed and he laughed. I couldn't remember feeling more excited and afraid at the same time. Then, when he made a final turn into the street I knew brought us to my apartment complex, he side-swiped a small sedan we passed.

"Damn," he yelled. "I ain't stoppin'. I'm not supposed to be drivin' this truck. Izzy will throw me out."

The driver of the car laid on his horn and followed us as best he could, but Keefer outran him and then bounced into the parking lot of my complex. I caught my breath, not knowing whether to cry or laugh.

"Get movin'," he ordered.

I jumped out of the truck and ran up the stairs. Just as I reached the apartment door, I heard the phone ringing inside. I threw it open and charged in. Kathy Ann had just picked up the phone.

"Here she is," she said, a look of shock and surprise on her face.

I swallowed down a throat lump that would choke a horse, and as calmly as I could manage, said, "Hello."

"What's wrong with you now?" Mother darling asked.

"I think the Chinese food was bad."

"It didn't bother Cory or me."

"Maybe I just had a nervous stomach."

"Well, I'm glad you're listenin' to me for once at least. We're doin' real well here. The owner knows people who he says he's goin' to invite to hear us now that he has heard us more, especially me. I really think I'm goin' to make it, Robin."

"Good for you, Mother darling."

She was quiet.

"I was hopin' you'd change your tone and your ways."

"I am," I said. "That's a promise."

"Okay, Robin. I'll see you later."

"I'll be asleep, I'm sure," I said, and hung up.

Keefer was standing in the doorway. I nodded, and then I laughed and he laughed.

"How'd you get here so fast?" Kathy Ann asked.

"We took the bus," he said.

"The bus?" She looked at me and then at him. "You liars."

We laughed again, and then Keefer heard something and turned to look down at the parking lot.

"Oh, no," he said.

I stepped forward and looked down with him. There was a Nashville police car, its bubble light going, parked right behind Keefer's boss's truck. The two policemen got out, and one directed a large flashlight at the right front area of the truck. The other turned and looked up, so we backed into the apartment and closed the door quickly.

"What's happening?" Kathy Ann asked.

"Shut up," Keefer said. "Put out the lights, quick."

"Why?"

"Just do it," he said, and she and I went to every lamp and switch and turned off the lights.

We stood waiting, no one speaking, but the sound of my breathing and Keefer's loud enough for us all to hear. Moments later, we heard footsteps on the second-story landing. We held our breath.

"Who is it?" Kathy Ann asked.

"Shut up," Keefer snapped.

We waited.

There was a very loud rap on the door, a rap made with a police stick for sure, I thought.

"Open up, it's the police," we heard.

"Oh, my God," Kathy Ann whined.

"Jesus," Keefer said.

"We're going to have that truck towed and impounded

if you don't open this door," the policeman threatened.

"Damn it," Keefer said. "Okay, put on the lights," he told Kathy Ann. She was too terrified to move, so I did it. Then he opened the door.

"That your truck below?" the policeman asked him immediately.

"No. It belongs to my boss," Keefer replied.

"Step outside, please," he said. He looked in at us. "You, too, ladies," he added.

"Why?" Kathy Ann whined.

The policeman just stepped aside for us to come out and we did. The three of us stood on the landing with both of the police officers.

"You were driving that truck a few minutes ago, then?"

"Yes," Keefer said.

"Which one of you was in the truck? C'mon," he said, "the man lodging the complaint saw two people."

Kathy Ann was actually trembling.

"I was," I confessed.

"You know it is a serious offense to leave the scene of an accident?" he asked Keefer.

"What accident?"

He smiled.

"You're not going to stand there and tell us you don't remember hitting another vehicle, are you? The other vehicle's paint is on the truck."

Keefer looked at me.

"I told you I thought I might have hit something," he said.

"I didn't think you had," I said.

The two policemen stared at us a moment.

"Let me see your license," the first policeman asked Keefer. He took out his wallet and produced it.

"This your apartment?" he asked Keefer.

"No."

"Whose is it then?"

"My sister's music partner," I said. "We're living here temporarily."

"Where are your parents?"

"They're dead," I said, glancing at Keefer, who tried to hide his eyes.

"And where is your sister now?"

"She's performing at a dance club."

"What's the occupant's name?" the second policeman asked.

"Cory Lewis," I said. I could feel cold tears coming into my eyes.

"And your name, miss?"

"Robin Taylor."

"All right. For now, we'll take Mr. Dawson here and you, Miss Taylor, to the police station."

"Can I bring the truck back?" Keefer asked.

"Not until the matter is settled," the policeman said.

"Well, why do you have to take her, too? I'm the one who was driving," he said.

"Procedure," the policeman replied. "She was a witness to the events. Maybe next time you'll think about all the ramifications that occur when you break the law. Let's go," he said. Then he paused. "How old are you, miss?"

"I'm sixteen," I said.

The second policeman took his cell phone off his belt.

"Where is your sister performing?"

I started to speak and then realized I didn't know. I really didn't know. They never had told me.

"I don't know," I said. "She forgot to tell me."

"I would think," the first policeman said, "that you

would have realized by now how serious this situation is."

"I'm telling you the truth." I turned to Kathy Ann. "Did she tell you where she was working when she called earlier?"

She shook her head like someone who was incapable of speech.

"All right, come along," the policeman said.

Kathy Ann remained in the doorway.

"What should I do?" she called after us.

"Go home," the policeman told her.

She nodded and quickly closed the door behind her. She remained far behind us as we walked down to the parking lot.

"I won't go anywhere," Keefer told the first policeman. "At least let me take the truck back."

"You can do that later if you're not incarcerated," he said.

They put us into the patrol car. This was the second time within a twenty-four-hour period that I had been in a Nashville police car. The fact didn't escape me, nor would it escape Mother darling when she found out.

At the police station, Keefer confronted the owner of the vehicle he had hit. He was a short, plump man, a chef in one of the local restaurants. Keefer apologized and told him he was an auto body repairman and he would fix whatever damage he had done.

"I'll get on it immediately," he promised. He explained we were in a big rush, and he apologized again.

In the end he decided not to press charges against Keefer. We were there almost two and a half hours. I saw the policeman who had been talking to Mother darling and Cory. He looked at me for a long moment, went to the desk sergeant to find out what it was all about, and then shook his head and left.

The police brought us back to the apartment complex so Keefer could get his boss's truck. It was nearly two-thirty in the morning.

"You'd better keep your nose clean," the policeman told him when we got out.

We watched the patrol car leave.

"Sorry about all this," Keefer said. "Trouble just seems to enjoy my company."

"It was my fault. If you didn't have to rush me home, you wouldn't have hit that car."

He shrugged.

"I guess we're both good and screwed up," he said. "You were right. We're a pair."

We looked at each other and laughed. It was more a laugh of relief than anything else, but it felt good, and then we embraced and I started up to the apartment. I glanced at Kathy Ann's apartment and saw the lights were all out. At least she wasn't hovering at the front window this time, I thought.

As quickly as I could, I undressed and got into bed. Despite all the excitement, I was so exhausted, I fell into a deep sleep, almost a coma, moments after my head hit the pillow. I'll worry about everything tomorrow, I told myself. I'll be Scarlett O'Hara in *Gone with the Wind*.

But I wasn't that lucky. My life was a totally different movie.

A little after four in the morning, Mother darling threw open my bedroom door and screamed my name so loud, she surely woke everyone in the entire apartment complex.

I groaned and reluctantly forced my eyes to open. She was at the foot of the bed.

"Tell me it's a lie. Tell me it isn't true. Tell me they made a mistake and thought you were someone else."

"It's a lie. It isn't true. They made a mistake," I said, and dropped my head back to the pillow.

"You ain't gonna be able to do this, Kay," Cory said from behind. "You can't concentrate on making music, writing new songs, getting better and better if you have that lead weight around your neck."

"I know," she said sadly. I heard her sniff back some tears, but I kept my eyes closed and pretended I had fallen asleep again. "Let me think on it," she told him. "You're impossible, Robin Lyn," she threw back at me, and then she left and closed the door.

I slept into the next day almost as long as they did. I had just made some coffee and was sitting and sipping it in the kitchen when Mother darling shuffled in, her hair wild, her eyes bloodshot.

"I didn't sleep much last night, Robin." She poured herself a cup of coffee and looked at me. I was staring down at my own coffee cup. "Talk," she said. "Cory's policeman friend told us you were brought to the station, that you were involved in a hit-and-run accident. How could you be? I spoke to you here, didn't I? Well?"

"I went for a ride earlier," I said, "and we hit a car and didn't realize it was serious."

"Who's we? Who was drivin'?"

"A friend of mine," I said.

"How can you have so many friends so fast?" she asked.

I looked up.

"I guess I'm a naturally sociable person. Look, nothing happened. My friend is taking care of it all. No one was arrested. It was all settled."

"But didn't I tell you not to leave the apartment?"

"I can't stay cooped up in here. It's too small. The television set hardly gets anything. I hate it here!" I screamed.

"I really don't know what to do with you," she said.

"Trade me in for a new guitar," I shot back.

"Sometimes, I wish I could," she said.

"I always wish you could."

I got up and went back to the bedroom. I heard her bring Cory a cup of coffee.

"She's just a spoiled brat," I heard him tell her.

Yes, I'm a spoiled brat, I thought. I'm spoiled because I don't have any real parents or a real home or a real family. I'm spoiled because my mother sees me as a burden, and always did. I'm spoiled because my grandpa thought I had inherited sin. I'm so spoiled the angels close their eyes when they fly near me.

Later that afternoon, Keefer called.

"How are things?" he asked.

"Status quo. I'm as unwanted as ever, maybe a little more than ever."

"You won't believe it, but this guy I hit is my new best friend. I told him I would take out all of his dents and nicks and make his car look new. Izzy wasn't happy, but I can fix that too, and since it didn't cost him anything, he's just a little upset. He knows he's getting a day and a half and sometimes two days' work out of me a day, and for what he pays me, he's not about to throw me out. I'll be leaving under my own steam," Keefer vowed.

"Take me with you," I said half jokingly. He was silent.

"Maybe I will. I have a plan, and one of these days,

I'll talk about it with you. If you're still interested in me after this, that is."

"I'm more interested, not less," I said, and he laughed.

"Okay. Tell you what. Tonight, I'll come to you. I have this extra work, but figure me for about ten. What time does your mother and Cory get home?"

"Sometime after two, I guess. I gather they calm down by having a few drinks and hanging around or going somewhere else."

"I'll be there."

"In Izzy's truck?"

"No. I'm layin' off it for a while. I have another customer's car at my disposal."

"Does he know?"

Keefer just laughed.

"What he doesn't know . . ."

"Won't hurt him. I know, I know," I said.

Knowing he was coming took the shadowy cobwebs of gloom out of my mind. Mother darling watched me with suspicion as I went about straightening up the apartment and doing some cleaning.

"What are you up to, Robin?" she asked finally.

"Nothing. I'm bored, that's all."

"Then you should get a job. If they don't send you to jail, that is. Cory and I will talk to some people tonight. He knows the manager of a supermarket. Maybe you can get a job as a packer."

"Right. That's sure to cure boredom."

She glared at me a moment, and then she shook her head and went off to fix her hair and prepare herself for another night of performing. She and Cory were going to eat out tonight. I told her not to worry about me. I had found some pasta that was less than a year old.

"You're always so smart, Robin, so quick to be sarcastic. Why don't you put that to good use and do somethin' constructive with yourself."

"I am. I'm writing a song for you," I told her.

"You are? What's it about?"

"About a girl like me who finds out her sister is her mother."

"Very funny."

"Wait," I said as she started away. "It gets better. She find out her brother is her father."

She slammed the door of her bedroom. Cory, who was reading a motorcycle magazine, looked up at me.

"Robin Lyn, what's your sin for today going to be?"

"Living with you," I shot back. His smile wilted as I strutted back to the kitchen to wash down the refrigerator. Grandma always said, "You can't be clean on the inside if you're not clean on the outside."

I wondered what she really meant.

8

Drifting Deeper
into the Abyss

~≫~

Every night for the rest of the week, Keefer came to visit me. I really had little to do with anyone else. Kathy Ann's parents had heard about the truck accident, either from her own mouth or from some other gossips in the complex who witnessed it, and they told her to stay away from me or she would be grounded until school began again. She came into the laundry to tell me.

"Of course, I can meet you downtown sometimes," she said, "but I can't come up to Cory's apartment or anything like that."

"Don't worry about it. Oh," I said, "how's Axel?"

She looked down.

"Nothing bad happened to him, did it?"

"He hasn't called me since that night, and I went and bought something for him, too," she complained.

"Well, football players are like that," I said as if I had all the experience in the world with them. "Maybe he got hit in the head since then," I offered. "How's Charlotte Lily?"

"All right, I guess." Her face brightened. "I told her about you and Keefer and all and she sounded jealous."

"Why? She was the one who told me he wasn't worth her time."

Kathy Ann shrugged, glanced out the window nervously, and then said she would try to see me later. She hurried away.

Now, I thought, I'm like a leper here. Mother darling, if you're going to be a success, you'd better be one soon and get us somewhere nicer to live.

What Mother darling and Cory did manage to do was get me an interview for that job in the supermarket. She was excited enough about it to get herself up early so she could drive me to the supermarket to meet the manager, a man named Al Ritter. He was lean and dark, with a very black mustache and the deepest cleft chin I had ever seen. His office was cluttered with postings on the walls, and his desk was buried under forms and mailings.

He began by asking me to fill out an application. There was a question that asked if I, the applicant, had ever been arrested. Since my court date was coming up the following week and if I got the job, I would have to ask for time off to go to it, I decided to tell the truth and I checked yes. At first I thought it really didn't matter. He glanced over the application so quickly, I decided he had already told Cory or Mother darling he would hire me.

He began by telling me he usually hired only college-age kids because they needed the money desperately and were mostly reliable. Then he picked up the application again, perused it, and paused. His eyes lifted slowly.

"What were you arrested for?"

"Shoplifting," I admitted.

"Where?"

"Here in Nashville. I have to go to court next week," I said as casually as I could.

"I see," he said. "Well, why don't we wait until we hear what happens to you then."

"Whatever," I said, shrugged, and left the office. Mother darling was waiting in her car, her head back, her eyes closed, but one of her tapes playing.

As soon as I opened the door, she sat up and said, "Well?"

"He wants to wait to see what happens next week," I told her.

"Next week? Why next week? What's supposed to be happening?"

"My court appearance, remember?"

"Huh? Well, how did he . . . you told him you were arrested?"

"There was a question about that on the application. At the bottom of the form it says if you deliberately put in false information, you can be summarily dismissed, which I believe means fired on the spot."

She stared at me, her eyes small, dark.

"You did that deliberately, Robin. You made sure he wouldn't hire you, and after Cory had asked him to do us a favor, too."

"Did you want me to lie, Mother darling? That's no way to start a career in the supermarket."

"Oh you . . . you . . ." She mumbled under her breath and started the engine. "I half hope they do send you to jail next week," she said.

I didn't say anything. She looked like she was wiping away a tear before we returned to the apartment complex. Cory was still asleep.

"I don't know what you're going to do with yourself, Robin, except get into more and more trouble," she told me after we entered the apartment.

"I'll keep house here," I offered. "If you like, I'll make dinner whenever you can eat at home."

She studied me closely to see if I was serious and then nodded.

"We'll see," she said, and went quietly into the bedroom, closing the door softly behind her.

"Thanks for making a fool out of me," Cory said after he had heard the story and risen. He opened the refrigerator, took out the orange juice, and drank right from the bottle, making it far less appetizing for anyone else to drink from it now.

"That's something you can do easily yourself," I said.

He glared at me with such rage, I thought I had stepped over the line and he would lunge at me. I actually braced for it, but he calmed down when I added, "I didn't think I should lie to a friend of yours. It would make things even worse."

He frowned.

"If I was hired and I needed time off to go to court, don't you think he would be slightly suspicious and then annoyed that you never told him about me?"

"You coulda just called in sick."

"People gossip," I said.

"That's it," he said, raising his hands, palms to me. "I'm finished. You're not my responsibility."

"Who ever said I was?" I asked, not to be smart, but to see if Mother darling had somehow convinced him he had to look out for the both of us and not just her.

"Nobody, and I thank my lucky stars for that," he told me.

I rose and left him in the kitchen. Lucky stars, what do they look like? I wondered.

The following week Keefer offered to go to court with me, but I didn't think Mother darling would like that, and the truth was, I was a little embarrassed about it and how I would look there. I told him I'd much rather he didn't.

"Fine," he said. "If you need me for anything, you just call."

I thanked him. Despite my brave front, I was trembling inside the moment I awoke on the morning of the court date. Mother darling was complaining from the get-go about how she had to get up early after a hard night of singing.

"It's not easy looking fresh and young when you don't get any sleep," she whined.

"So don't go. I'll go myself," I said.

"Oh, sure. Lucky we were able to get you a public defender. You just dress neat and conservatively, Robin Lyn, and you keep that smart mouth shut, if you know what's good for you."

I was not the first defendant at court. In fact, we had to wait almost an hour to go in. The judge, Judge Babcock, was a woman with short salt-and-pepper hair. She looked like she had last smiled on her first birthday. Her thin lips were so tightly pressed together as she read the report on me, it looked like she had a zipper where her mouth should have been. When she finally lifted her eyes and looked my way, I felt like she was burning two holes in my face.

"Your client is pleading guilty?" she asked our public defender, a very plain-looking, light-haired man named Carson Meriweather, whose suit hung on his body the way it would hang on a clothes rack. It was as if he was all head with a skeleton beneath.

"Yes, Your Honor."

"Do you understand what this means, Miss Taylor?"

"I guess," I said.

"You guess? Either you understand that you are pleading guilty to shoplifting or you are not. This is not some game. Which is it?"

"Guilty," I said before my throat closed.

"Unfortunately, too many young people have reached your age with a warped sense of right and wrong. There was a time when morality was taught in the home, but," she said with a sigh, "it's becoming more and more the responsibility of the court."

She turned to Mother darling.

"Mrs. Taylor, how have you dealt with this situation in your own home?"

"I . . . we just moved here recently, Your Honor."

"Yes? So?" she asked when Mother darling apparently thought that was some sort of an answer.

"I told her she wasn't to leave the apartment complex. She was grounded."

"I see. Did you take the time to explain to her how people are working to make a living, how the employees of this department store depend on the department store succeeding, and how robbing and stealing hurts everyone, that if we didn't stop it, someone could rob her as well and we would have anarchy? Well?"

"I did, Your Honor. I've been asking her to behave herself for some time."

"Oh?"

"I've even had her see a therapist back in Ohio when we lived there."

"I see. And how long do you intend to remain in Nashville, Mrs. Taylor?"

"Oh, I'm here for good, Your Honor. I'm a singer and . . ."

"Then you had better be sure your daughter understands our laws and what we expect of our citizens," she snapped.

"Yes, Your Honor."

Judge Babcock sat up and tapped her pen on the documents before her. It was a long, nerve-wracking pause. She really looked like she was debating whether or not to send me to the gallows.

"My best instincts tell me I shouldn't do this. I should deal with you as severely as the law permits, but I am going to place you on two years' probation and return you to the custody of your mother in the hope that this experience has made an indelible impression on you. Understand, so you won't have to guess, that should you be brought in here for any other offense, I will not hesitate to send you directly to a juvenile detention center, unless," she said, leaning over her desk, "your new crime is so heinous as to have you tried as an adult. In such a case, you would not be sent to a juvenile center. A juvenile center would be like a nursery school compared to where you would be sent. Am I making myself clear, Miss Taylor? You don't look like you're listening."

"I'm listening," I said, a little too petulantly. I knew that the moment I uttered the words, and then I held my breath.

She glared hard at me for a long moment before she turned to Mother darling.

"You have a serious parental responsibility here, Mrs. Taylor. I hope you are impressed with this fact and you will devote more time and energy to your daughter's upbringing and behavior."

Mother darling nodded. She looked like she was going to burst out in tears any moment. I wanted to poke her with my elbow and make sure she didn't embarrass us both. She bit down on her lower lip and nodded again.

"Very well. The matter is resolved for now," Judge Babcock said.

The public defender, who had done little more than instruct me to plead guilty and be polite to the judge, smiled at us and indicated we could leave.

I heard another name called and saw a boy who didn't look much older than ten being brought in with a man who had his hand firmly around the back of the boy's neck. I thought, if that's his father, he would be better off being sent to a juvenile detention center.

"I hope you appreciate the break you just received, young lady," the public defender said.

"She doesn't, but I'll make sure she does," Mother darling told him.

"You don't want to come back here," he said. "That's one hard judge."

Mother darling thanked him, and then she hurried us out of the courthouse.

"I swear," she muttered as we drove back to Cory's apartment, "I don't know where you get that belligerent streak that's in you."

"Maybe from my mysterious father," I suggested. "Hey," I said, nearly bouncing on the seat, "that's how you can tell who my father was. Which of the dozen or so men you slept with that night was most like me?"

She looked at me as if she wasn't sure whether I was being serious or not, and then she smirked and shook her head.

"Keep it up, Robin. Keep punishing me for your own failin' and faults. See what it gets you in the end."

"You mean this isn't the end already?" I retorted.

She tightened her face and drove the rest of the way

in silence. Inside, I felt like brittle china that had just been hit hard and was full of deep cracks. It would take only a small nudge to have it fall completely apart.

Cory seemed only vaguely interested in what had happened to me in court. He said, "Kids her age get away with murder these days." The judge's decision only reinforced his views. Anyway, he didn't want to spend any time talking about me. He had a big announcement to make to Mother darling.

"Bill Renner, a scout for Reliable Records, was at our club last night. I just got a call. He liked your song, 'Ridin' on a Dream.' He wants us to go down to the studio to talk to him about cuttin' a record. I already told Del and Ernie. You go in and put on your best outfit," he continued. "Fix yourself up real good, Kay. I want him to see the possibilities for photos, covers, advertisements immediately."

Mother darling squealed with delight and then ran into his arms. He spun her around. They looked like two happy kids. I couldn't prevent the soft smile that came to my lips, but then, thinking about where I had just been, I couldn't help feeling even more like the lead weight around Mother darling's ankles Cory accused me of being. This was their success, not mine, their dreams coming true. There was no room in that for me.

How I envied them both for the looks of joy and elation on their faces. Mother darling's eyes brightened like a little girl's. Her face blossomed before me, and Cory looked really satisfied with himself.

"Do I know what I'm talking about or don't I?" he asked her.

"You know, Cory, oh, boy, do you know."

She paused to look at me.

"Oh, be happy for us all, Robin. This is a very big opportunity, and it's one of my songs, my songs!"

"I'm happy," I said. "I'm so happy, I could turn into a bubble and burst."

Her smile froze. Cory curled his lip.

"Good luck," I said, and went to my bedroom.

"Forget about her," he said. "We've got to concentrate on this chance and put all our energy toward it."

I could hear their happy voices as they dressed and prepared themselves in the next room. I lay on the bed staring up at the pale white ceiling and tried to think of a dream for myself. Where would I go someday? What would ever make me that happy? Maybe people who are in limbo like me never have any dreams. We just float from one boring moment to another.

I must have dozed off for a while because when I opened my eyes, it looked like twilight. My bedroom door was open, but I heard no one. I listened hard, then I looked at my watch and saw it was already after five. They had to have left. Mother darling probably had stopped by to show me what she looked like and she found me asleep. I was sure she had dressed in that frilly short skirt and sequin-covered blouse that had a matching hat and boots. It was her favorite outfit, and I had to admit she looked like a star in those clothes.

There was a note on the refrigerator.

I left you some money on the kitchen table. Get yourself a pizza or something. I'll call later.
                                                    Kay

She couldn't even sign it "Mother." Was she really afraid someone would see this and know? I crumpled it up and threw it in the garbage. Then I scooped up the money and marched out of the apartment. When I walked out of the complex, I looked to the right and saw Kathy Ann peeking out between the curtains of her front window. Deliberately, I waved vigorously at her and the curtain closed instantly.

Laughing, I hurried down the street and took the bus downtown. All I could think of was Keefer. For now he was my dream and I was happy only when I was with him. The lights in the body shop window were like the lights of a lighthouse beaming protectively into the darkness of my world. The only safe harbor I had was within his embrace.

I entered the shop. Tools were out on the floor. The radio was blasting at its usual volume, but I didn't see him.

"Keefer?"

I looked at the small office, but it was dark. I walked around the cars that were there for repair and then I started toward the door to his apartment. Where else would he be? I thought, and realized he might have stepped out to buy some beer or something.

When I opened the door, I heard a groan. My first thought was that something terrible had happened to him. Either he had gotten hurt in the shop or his drunken father had come looking for him and beaten him up again.

Then I heard her laugh and saw her rise up on the sofa. She was half-naked, her breasts gleaming in the light from the small lamp. She saw me and cried out. A second later, Keefer appeared and they both looked at me. My surprise and shock had nailed my feet to the floor, even though all I could think of doing was turning and running.

"Why, look who's here, Keefer. Robin. You come to have Keefer fix somethin' for you, honey?" Charlotte

Lily teased as she reached for her blouse and slipped it over her head.

Keefer pushed her off him, buckled his pants, and stood.

"No, looks like you're the one getting fixed tonight, Charlotte Lily," I said, the tears burning under my eyelids because I refused to let them emerge.

She laughed.

"I thought he wasn't worth the time of day," I said, my anger now replacing my shock. "Slummin' tonight?"

She laughed again, but with less confidence. Keefer glanced at her and then took a deep breath and started toward me.

"I'm sorry," he said.

"There's nothing to be sorry about, Keefer, unless she was a big disappointment. That's probably most likely," I added, threw her a cold smile, and then turned and left the apartment, closing the door hard behind me.

I heard her laugh again and then Keefer tell her to shut up.

When I was outside the shop and on the street, I permitted my tears to escape. I flicked them off my cheeks and walked quickly away.

I kept walking, at first in no particular direction, and then in the direction of the apartment. It was a long walk. Cars rushed by me, sometimes the drivers sounding their horns because I was too far in the street. Every once in a while, I felt like throwing myself in front of one, but the prospect of all that pain without being killed right off frightened me.

Somewhere in the city behind me, with all its lights blazing excitement, the music rolling out into the streets, people laughing and joking, enjoying their vacations or their evening with friends, somewhere out there, Mother darling was singing her heart out, reaching for her dream.

I was as far from her thoughts as I could be, so far, in fact, it was as if I had never been born.

Maybe I wasn't, I thought. Maybe this is all just a bad dream, and I'm still sleeping in that never-never land where souls exist until they are chosen to be born. I was like an orphan passed over time and time again. Not this one, she's not ready to be in the world, I heard the angels say.

"Just keep dreaming, honey. Just keep dreaming. We'll tell you when it's time to wake up."

Even promises in heaven are broken, I thought.

9

Always Us
Against Them

~~~~~~~

After marching along the highway for nearly half an hour, I felt a pair of headlights remain on me.

Here I go again, I thought. The police. Someone probably complained about a young girl walking on the highway. I heard the horn, and then I stepped aside and turned in anticipation.

It was Keefer in Izzy's truck.

"Get in, Robin," he said.

"No."

"Just get in. I need to talk to you. You've got a ways to go, and you're in the middle of all this traffic. Don't be stupid."

"Why should I change now?" I replied. "Seems all I do is stupid things."

"Stop it. Get in. I need to talk to you."

A car came up behind him, and the driver leaned hard and long on his horn.

I could see Keefer wasn't going to move and that might soon create even more trouble, so I got into the truck and he drove on.

"I'm sorry about what happened back there, but I never told you I was a saint, Robin. Did I?"

"No."

"And I never thought you were one, either," he said.

That made me laugh.

"There are a few people who would agree with that," I said.

"The truth is, I got drunk and she came in, teasing me like she always does. I feel bad about it because I know she did it because she was jealous and just wanted to hurt you, and I let her do it."

"You didn't even call to see what happened to me today," I fired back at him.

"I know. I was thinking of it, but I got drunk."

"Why did you get so drunk during the day?" I asked. From what I could see, Keefer was usually very reliable when he was working. He was good at what he did and he took pride in the results.

"Izzy gave me some bad news today. He's selling the shop. The new owner is going to take over in about a month, and I'm out. He said his wife was tired of them livin' here, and he was going to work with his brother in Florida."

"So? You were planning on leaving someday anyway, weren't you?"

"Yeah, but after I had some money saved. You don't just pick up and go without enough money. I might not get a job that quick, and you need to put down money for rent or a hotel, and you got to have travel money."

"What about your sister?"

"I can't ask her for anything. She's just getting by as it is. I can tell. Besides, I don't want to live off someone else. I want to be on my own."

"I don't have any money, or I'd give it to you," I said, and I meant it.

"Thanks. I believe that."

We were both quiet for a while, both staring ahead at the traffic.

"I'm really sorry about Charlotte Lily. We went together once. I always knew she was toying around with me. She can't be serious about anyone. Her family is well off and she lives in a nice house and all, but she's always unhappy and always out to make someone who is happy unhappy.

"Talk about being stupid, that's me. I let her manipulate me. She's like a devil or somethin', comin' in just when I'm feelin' sorry for myself," he said. "And then the luck of it all with you poppin' over just at that time. Damn."

"I guess I have no right to think I own you or anything, Keefer. We made no promises, and as to finding you with her, well, I'm not one to think she can judge someone else. However," I added after a short pause, "I will confess it hurt."

"I know. I'm sorry. Really," he said. "I ain't never gonna have anything to do with her again. She might have nice clothes and jewelry and all, but she's a tramp compared to you."

"I won't go that far," I said, and then shook my head, "but I'll let you."

He laughed.

"So, tell me what happened today. You're out on the street, so I guess they didn't sentence you to prison."

"I'm on two years' probation."

"Ah, that don't mean nothin'," he said. "Half the city is on probation. You hungry?"

"Starving," I said.

"Let me take you to a great place," he said, and whipped the truck down a street on the right. A few minutes later, we bounced over a gravel driveway to park at a restaurant with a pig lit up in pink lights. The place was called Porky's Hideaway. "Best ribs in town," he said.

The restaurant was one big room, with a band playing what I called hillbilly music, but which Keefer said was really more Cajun style. The food was out in a buffet, and for ten dollars you could eat all you wanted. Besides the ribs, there were Buffalo wings, chicken legs, fish sticks, potatoes, vegetables, all sorts of breads, and a variety of desserts. My stomach churned in anticipation.

We piled our plates high and found a table. The restaurant was nearly full and the good food, music, and party atmosphere drove away my doldrums.

"Before my mother got sick with depression, she used to tell me the only real cure to sadness is a good-tastin' dinner. That's why people serve so much food after a funeral," Keefer told me. The music was so loud we had to shout to hear each other even at the same table.

There must be some truth to that, I thought, because I ate way more than I usually did. Afterward, I sat back and watched some of the people dancing.

"Funny," Keefer said, "Nashville is a place full of music and good times, but I don't often see it. I guess you got to be happy with yourself first before you can go out and have a good time."

I felt sorry for him and wished there was something

I could do. At least I had Mother darling. He had no one but himself, and that had to be pretty scary most of the time.

After we left and we were in the truck heading to Cory's apartment, Keefer asked me if I was really serious when I told him I wouldn't mind running off with him.

"Yes," I said.

"What about now? I mean, considerin' what you saw and all, are you still feelin' the same way about it?"

I thought a moment. I knew he was asking me to forgive him completely for being with Charlotte Lily. Neither of us is a saint, I concluded. If we can't forgive each other, no one will forgive us for anything we do.

"Yes," I told him, and he smiled.

"Great. I have a plan. My father threw me out of our house before I could get to all my things. He never knew it, but I saved all the money I received as birthday gifts from relatives and friends. I was a little miser, in fact. I stuffed it all in this piggy bank my mother gave me when I was about three, I think. It was a giveaway from some hog farm she had been at one time or another. Anyway, I think I've got over four hundred dollars in it, and I want it. It's mine. Only, I don't think I can just walk up to the door and ring the bell."

"Why not? Your mother isn't mad at you, is she?"

"She's not going to go against him," he said. "Never did. Never took my side, ever, or my sister's." He was quiet a moment. "My sister was . . . I guess they call it abused nowadays. Softens it, I suppose, but it ain't softened for her. I know she told Mama, but Mama thought she made it up to get back at him. She just wouldn't believe it."

"Maybe she did, and that was what made her like she is, Keefer."

"Maybe. It's more reason for me to hate him. I just don't want to see him."

He looked at his watch.

"There's a good chance he ain't home. I know how to get into my house without going through the front door. I just want to get my piggy bank and get out. Want to help?"

"What can I do?"

"You just stay in the truck and be the lookout," he said. "If a car drives into the driveway, you sound the horn. Do it at least five, six times, and I'll know to get out of there fast. No tellin' what would happen otherwise. He'd kill me or I'd somehow kill him. Okay?" he asked.

"Okay," I said, but my heart was thumping like an old-fashioned steam-engine train pounding the tracks.

"Good," he said. "It won't take long. Don't worry."

He turned the truck around and headed back toward the downtown area, but before getting there, turned again and wove his way through residential streets until we came to a house that looked hidden from the road behind sprawling old oak trees and untrimmed bushes. With the moonlight peeking through clouds, I could see the lawn was spotted with dry and bare patches. The house was completely dark.

"Usually there's a light on somewhere," he said after we pulled to the curb. He sat there, looking worried.

"Can't you tell any other way if there's someone home or not?"

"He's not home. He doesn't park his truck in the garage. It's full of tools, his work bench, and a table saw. Okay," he said. "The window in my room has a broken lock. I'm going in that way. Get behind the wheel here and hit the horn if a truck pulls in."

"Be careful, Keefer."

How strange, I thought, to have to break into your own house.

He got out slowly, hesitating as if he expected his father to pop out from behind a tree or something, and then he hurried over the lawn and around the right corner of the house. A few minutes later, a light went on. I could see the glow of it on the bushes at the side of the house.

When a pair of headlights appeared ahead of me, I held my breath and placed my hand on the horn. It turned out to be a car, which passed by quickly. Once again, the street was dark. I looked toward the house. Why was he taking so long? Surely, he knew where his piggy bank was. Another set of headlights appeared, and again it was only a car going by. After it had, I looked toward the house and saw the light was out.

I spotted Keefer. This time he wasn't hurrying along. He was walking very slowly, his head up, his hands clutching something. I wished he would hurry. He came around the truck and I opened the door. He just stood there in the street looking in at me.

"What is it?" I asked.

He extended his hands. In them were the broken pieces of what I supposed was his piggy bank. I shook my head.

"I don't understand."

"He took my money. He took my savings, my birthday savings."

"Oh, no," I said.

Keefer spun on his heels and heaved the pieces at the driveway.

"That's not all," he said, moving to get in. I slid over on the bench seat.

"What else?"

"My mother wasn't there. I went looking for her to see if she was in bed, asleep."

"Maybe she was out with him."

"I doubt that." He started the engine. "The lamp beside her bed was on the floor. I put it upright, and then I turned it on, and there, on the floor in the bathroom, was . . ."

"What?" I asked, hardly able to breathe.

"Blood," he said. "Lots of blood."

"Blood?" I gasped.

He drove away. I felt like I had stopped breathing and I was leaving my body. That was how numb I had become.

We drove to the apartment complex, and Keefer came up with me.

"If something terrible happened, wouldn't someone tell you?" I asked him.

"It looked to me like whatever happened wasn't all that long ago," he said.

I stared at him. What could have happened? His eyes were filled with all the horrible possibilities, and my mind began to roam through Horror Hotel. Could his father have done something terrible to his mother and then taken her body off somewhere?

"Should we call the police?"

He thought for a moment. Then, he nodded and walked to the phone like someone who wanted desperately not to use it. I watched as he punched in 911 and then told the dispatcher his address and what he had found.

"I'm her son," he said.

"She's transferring me to someone who might know something."

I nodded and waited, embracing myself. Before I could say anything, he raised his hand.

"Yes," he said. "Yes, I'm her son. I was just at the house and . . ." He listened and as he did, his face lost color. "Okay," he said. "Thanks."

He hung up and stared at the phone a moment. Then he sucked in his breath and turned to me.

"She tried to commit suicide. She's in the hospital," he said.

"Oh, Keefer, I'm sorry."

"I'm gonna go."

"Should I go with you?"

He thought a moment, and then he nodded.

"Sure, that'd be great."

Mother darling wanted me home, of course. She might have already checked to see if I had listened to her, but that didn't matter to me now. None of that mattered to me, and maybe, it never had.

Besides, I thought as we charged down the stairs and to the truck, I'm sure Kathy Ann is watching and could tell Mother darling everything anyway.

After we parked at the hospital, we went to an information desk and found out where Keefer's mother was located. It turned out she was still in what they called an intensive care unit. Only the immediate family could go in, and only for a little while. I waited outside. I was very nervous because we didn't know if his father was in there already, and what sort of a scene he would make as soon as he set eyes on Keefer.

Fortunately, he wasn't. Keefer came out after ten minutes.

"She's still alive," he said, "but she's lost so much

blood, she's in a coma. All the nurse would say is, 'We'll see.' "

He sat, and I held his hand.

"She looked so small in there. It was like she had shrunk or somethin' from losin' all that blood. I tried talkin' to her, but her eyelids didn't even twitch. It was like talkin' to a corpse."

"Oh, don't say that, Keefer. She can get better."

He nodded and looked around.

"I wonder where the hell he is. It doesn't surprise me that he's not here."

"What do you want to do?"

"In an hour I can go back in again. You mind waitin'?"

"No, of course not," I said.

He leaned back against the sofa.

"You want a soda or somethin'?"

"No, I'm fine," I said. He nodded and closed his eyes.

I couldn't help wondering how I would feel if that was Mother darling in there instead of Keefer's mother. Would I be worrying about her or about myself? She was all I had now, all the family in the world to me. Most of my life, she did her best to pretend I wasn't there. Sometimes I thought that was what bothered her the most when Grandpa complained about me: he reminded her I was her daughter and her responsibility.

I supposed I had never made things easier for her. Not only didn't I think I should, but I resented her placing herself at the top of the list of who was important and what was important. Her career was the end-all. If it meant sacrificing my advantages, my time, my opportunities, that was all right. The excuse was always that she was doing it for both of us. All I could think was, if she ever did make it in the music business, I would fall even further down the list until I did what she wanted: disappeared.

And yet, imagining her in there like Keefer's mother with Death standing at the foot of her bed looking covetously at her thin grip on life, I couldn't help feeling sorry for her and sad. The few good times we had together returned to memory. I recalled once when she had sung successfully at a county fair and she had me dressed in a cowgirl outfit. She brought me on the stage with her and I sang a chorus. Everyone thought it was cute and she hugged me. Afterward, we had a good time on the rides. We ate cotton candy and had hot dogs and she won a stuffed puppy on the wheel of fortune game.

I left that back at the farm.

It was part of a dream now, something unreal.

"You got a helluva nerve bein' here," I heard, and opened my eyes to see a stocky, six-foot-three-inch man with the shoulders and arms of a logger standing before us. His black hair looked like it was in revolt, the untrimmed strands going every which way, some stuck on his sweaty forehead and looking like streaks of ink. He had big facial features, but I could see Keefer's jaw and eyes.

He wore a faded plaid shirt, the sleeves rolled over his thick forearms, back to his elbows, and a pair of greasy, stained jeans and black shoe boots.

"You're the reason she's in there," he said, pointing his thick forefinger down at Keefer. The rest of his hand was clutched in a fist, making it look like a pistol.

I looked at Keefer. He didn't move, but he didn't flinch or look frightened either.

"Me?" he said. "You got that backwards. You're the reason she's in there. What happened? What did you do to her to make her do this?" he fired up at him.

His father's face ripened like an apple in an instant.

"You ungrateful little bastard," he said, and reached down to seize Keefer, who pushed his hand away and shifted to his right.

I couldn't help it. I screamed. It seemed to snap his father out of his monomaniacal drive. He turned and looked at me.

"Who's this little tramp?" he asked.

"Shut your mouth," Keefer said. He moved farther to the right and stood up.

Now they were facing each other, and the one-sidedness of the pending battle was clearly evident. It looked like David against Goliath.

"Keefer, no!" I cried. "Don't get into any fights here!"

"You'd better listen to her and get out. Crawl back to whatever hole you're livin' in."

"I'm not the one who should be crawlin'," Keefer said. "You stole my money. You went and broke my piggy bank and took my money."

His father smiled coldly.

"Ain't nothin' in that house belongs to you, boy. You were livin' under my roof, and you owed me for all the things that got broke throwin' you out."

"You're just a common thief and a pervert," Keefer accused.

The rage rose like steam in his father's face, but before he could act, a nurse emerged from the intensive care unit and asked for Mr. Dawson.

They both turned to her.

"Yeah, that's me," Keefer's father said.

"I'm sorry," she said. "Your wife's heart just gave out. The doctor did everything he could."

The words hung in the air a moment, and then Keefer made a terrifying animal scream and charged at his father like a football tackler, hitting him in the right side with his shoulder and driving him back and onto his rear end. The nurse gasped and I screamed. Keefer looked at me and then charged down the hallway.

"Little bastard," his father said, getting to his feet.

"You can come in now," the nurse told him, her eyes still wide and her face still a bit white.

He looked in Keefer's direction, nodded, and followed her into the intensive care unit.

I went hurrying after Keefer. At first I didn't see him. He wasn't by the truck. Then I spotted him at the end of the parking lot, walking in a small circle and raving, his arms flying up. Slowly I approached.

"I'm sorry, Keefer," I said. He continued to circle and then stopped and looked at me.

"He killed her, you know. He should be arrested and tried for murder. He as good as did it himself."

"I know," I said.

"Someday . . ." His threat trailed off into the night.

I went to him and embraced him. I could feel his rage cooling down, and finally he held me and started to sob. He realized it and pulled back.

"I gotta get outta here," he said, marching toward the truck.

I ran after him.

"What are you going to do?"

"Just go back to my hole and maybe drink myself to sleep," he said. "C'mon. I'll take you home first."

I thought a moment.

"No," I said.

"What?"

"I want to be with you."

He stared for a moment.

"Are you sure?"

"Positive," I said, and I got into the truck before he did.

10

From the Frying Pan into the Fire

Most of the night, I was just a good listener. Keefer sat drinking hard liquor instead of beer. Izzy kept a bottle of bourbon in his office, and Keefer brought it back to his one-room apartment. I sat on the sofa bed, and he sat on the floor and talked about his early life, the happier days when he was too young to realize how bad things were for both his mother and his older sister.

"It wasn't until I was about nine," he continued, lying back on the floor and looking up at the cracked and pealed ceiling, "that I understood how horrible it was for Sally Jean. I came into her bedroom one night because I heard her sobbin'. My mother drank with my father often those days, and they were both sunk in a stupor. Only before he had collapsed, he had gone into Sally Jean's bedroom to tell her one of his bedtime stories. That's what she said he pretended to be doin'."

Keefer formed a wry smile.

"It began with that 'Three Little Pigs,' " he said. "You know, where he would run his fingers up her side to tickle her."

"Oh, Keefer," I said. It not only frightened me to hear such a sick story, it made me nauseated.

"He was still tellin' her the same story, only the pigs . . ."

"Keefer, stop!" I pleaded.

He looked at me.

"Yeah, it's better not to hear about it. No one wants to hear about it. I bet my mother put her fingers in her ears half the time. Well, she don't hafta do that anymore, huh? She's better off."

"No one's better off dead, Keefer."

"Right," he said, and took another long drink of the bourbon.

"Why don't you lie down here for a while," I suggested. "Get some sleep."

"Sleep," he said, as if it was an impossibility.

"C'mon," I said. "I'll hold you."

He looked up at me and then he rose slowly, put the bottle on the floor on his side of the sofa bed, pulled off his shirt, dropped his pants, and crawled under the blanket. I stroked his hair, kissed his cheek, and got undressed to lie beside him.

We kissed. I could feel his tears, the ones he couldn't stop, and I kissed them off his cheeks. We held on to each other and our passions grew. He made love to me with a desperation I welcomed. I never felt more giving, even when I sensed anger had slid alongside affection and actually had taken command. He was rough with me, and at times I tightened my arms around him to calm him down as much as to keep myself from screaming. He realized it and became more loving, whispering how sorry he was and how much he cared for me as he kissed and stroked my hair, all the while still inside me.

We made love longer than we ever had, and when he reached his climax, he cried out like someone falling. I brought my mouth to his and we kissed so hard, it was nearly impossible to breathe. When it was over, we rolled on our backs, gasped, and waited to speak.

"Are you all right?" he asked me.

"Yes," I said.

"Thanks for bein' with me," he said, and closed his eyes. I tried to stay awake a little longer, but the day's events took on their full weight and soon, I was just as deeply asleep as he was.

A very loud rapping on the rear door woke me first. Keefer groaned, but did not awaken. I had to shake him.

"Someone's at the door," I whispered.

He opened his eyes, but he was totally disoriented and confused.

"Whaaa."

"Keefer, you better wake up," I urged, looking for my blouse and jeans.

"Open up!" we heard. "It's the police!"

"Oh, no," I cried. The door was rattled hard, and I had just managed to slip my jeans on when it was thrown open, the lock giving way.

Because we had no lights on and the night was overcast, the policeman turned on a large flashlight and searched the room, washing the illumination over Keefer, who was sitting up and rubbing his face with his palms, and over me, who was standing at the side of the bed, barefoot, buttoning up my blouse.

"Put on a light," the policeman commanded.

"What is this?" Keefer asked.

"Put on the light!" the cop repeated in a louder, more demanding tone.

Keefer fumbled for the switch on the lamp and got it on.

Two policemen stood in the doorway, looking in at us.

"You," he said, pointing the flashlight at me even though there was enough light to see everything now. "You're Robin Taylor?"

"Yes."

"Your mother called 911 and reported you missing." He turned the flashlight toward Keefer. "You know how old this girl is?"

"It's not his fault!" I cried. "His mother died tonight. I stayed with him to comfort him."

"Comfort him?" the second policeman said, smiling. "That's a good way to put it. Get your things together and come along," he added.

"I'll go home myself," I said.

"Hey," the first patrolman said, stepping closer. "Don't you think we have better things to do than baby-sit some juvenile delinquent? I should take this guy down to the station and have him booked for corrupting the morals of a minor."

"You'd better go with them," Keefer urged.

"She didn't have to do this."

"No, she didn't. If you would behave, she wouldn't have to call us, now would she?" the second policeman asked.

I slipped on my shoes.

"I'll call you," I promised Keefer.

"If I were you, cowboy, I would tell her to stay away. This girl's mother might still press charges against you," the first patrolman told Keefer. "If she does, we'll be back. You can bet on that," he said.

Keefer looked at me and then urged me to go.

They put me in the rear of the patrol car, and I felt helplessly trapped again. Once we were on our way, the two policemen seemed to forget I was in the car, too. They got into a discussion about baseball and began to argue about the ability of a player. I didn't have to wonder how Mother darling had discovered my whereabouts. I was positive she had gone to Kathy Ann, who surely told her everything she knew.

That was confirmed for me when we drove into the parking lot and, despite the lateness of the hour, I saw her peering between the curtains. I knew she couldn't see my face, but I looked her way with contempt. I couldn't wait to tell her off.

Mother darling was in her bathrobe, waiting, when the police brought me up to the apartment. Cory was in bed.

"She was where you thought," the first patrolman told her. "Do you want to do anything more about that?"

I looked at her, terrified.

"No," she said. "Thanks so much."

"All right. You'd better behave yourself, young lady. You're on thin ice," he warned, and left.

"You're just determined to sink my ship, ain't you, Robin? You're just not goin' to be happy until we're both in so desperate a place, we got to call my father for help, huh?"

"No," I said. "You don't understand what happened."

"No, I don't understand. I guess I never will. Just go in and go to sleep. I'm exhausted, and so is Cory. We've been hired to play at a much more respected place. It's taken a big effort and a lot of concentration, but that's what responsible people do. They try their best. I'm warnin' you for the last time, Robin Lyn, you're not goin' to ruin my chances. Now go to bed."

"Don't you even want to hear anything?"

"No," she snapped. "But I will tell you this. The next time you disobey me, I'll call the police and I won't come to the courthouse with you."

She went into their bedroom and closed the door.

I was too tired to cry or to care. I went to bed and slept longer than they did. When I opened my eyes, I could hear them having their breakfast. The radio was on. I lay there, hoping they would get up and go out before I rose. Finally, she opened my door and stepped into the room. She was dressed.

"Well," she began, "I suppose you're proud of yourself."

"Are you going to listen to me?" I asked.

"You can't tell me anything that will justify your behavior since we arrived here, Robin. I told you when we left that I was goin' to need you to be a responsible person because I would be too busy to watch after you as if you was a child. I thought I was doin' you a favor takin' you away with me. I thought you'd want to be part of my life, not a burden."

"I'm not trying to be a burden, but I have this friend, Keefer Dawson, and . . ."

"I know all about him," she said.

"You don't know anything about him, Momma."

"Oh, I'm Momma now, not Mother darlin'?" she said, smiling.

"Will you just listen. He's a very nice person. It's not what you think or whatever that jealous Kathy Ann told you."

She sighed and looked at the ceiling.

"Okay, you listen," she said. "Cory went back to his

friend at the supermarket, and he had a nice talk with him about you. His friend is willing to give you a chance, despite what you've done. This would help you a lot, too, Robin. The court will be pleased you're doin' somethin' worthwhile and respectable. You'll be able to have some expense money and you won't be idle and gettin' yourself in trouble.

"You go back there today and ask to see Mr. Ritter. We said you'd be there before two and you could start today. You better not screw this up, Robin. This is absolutely the last time anyone's gonna do somethin' to help you.

"We're goin' off to Del's garage to work on our music for tonight. I want you to come right home after work. If I hear you went back to that boy, I'll do what the policeman told me to do. I'll have him arrested. You understand me? Well? Don't just lay there glarin' up at me, Robin. Do you understand?"

"Yes," I said coldly. "I understand you real well, Mother darling."

She flared her eyes, spun on her heels, and walked out, closing the door sharply behind her. I remained in bed until I heard them leave the apartment. I was certainly in no mood to see Cory and hear his sarcasm.

As soon as I could, I called Keefer.

"I've been afraid to call you," he said. "What happened?"

I told him everything.

"We'd better be careful."

"Did you call your sister and tell her about your mother?" I asked.

"Yeah, but she doesn't want to come back for the funeral. She doesn't want to see him under any circumstances, and she can't do our mother any good anyway, she says. I guess I can't blame her. I told her I'd see her someday, and I will."

"You're not going to just pick up and go without telling me, are you, Keefer?"

He was silent.

"Keefer?"

"No. I have some things to plan out yet," he said.

"I'm going to see you no matter what my mother threatens. She won't do anything anyway, because that would expose her even more and she's too nervous about spoiling her chances to be a big country singing star."

"Well, be careful," he said.

I told him what they had arranged at the supermarket.

"Where's that market?" he asked. After I told him, he was silent again and then he said, "That might be good."

"Why?"

"I'll tell you later when I see you," he promised.

"When is your mother's funeral?"

"It looks like it's tomorrow. He's just tryin' to get it all over with fast as he can so he can get back to his miserable ways. I wouldn't a known anything if I didn't call my cousin Charlie. He's the only one on my father's side has anything at all to do with him and only because he's almost much of a drunk."

"I'd like to be there with you," I said.

"I know, but maybe it's better you stay away for a few days. I'll find a way to get in touch. Sorry about all the new trouble I got you in," he added.

"You didn't get me into any trouble, Keefer. I get myself in trouble. That should be my middle name. My grandpa used to say he knew exactly who my father was. 'He's Old Scratch.' "

"Who's that?"

"The devil," I said, and laughed. "Maybe he was right."

"Well, if all his daughters are as pretty and as nice as you are, he's not so bad after all," Keefer said, and we both laughed. "Be seein' you," he said. His voice, small and hopeful, lingered in my ear after we hung up.

I didn't have much of an appetite, but I made some fresh coffee and then had some toast and jam. I really didn't want to go to work in a supermarket, but I had to agree that Mother darling was right about my earning some expense money, altough I wasn't thinking of having it for incidentals and recreational expenses. I was thinking I would work awhile and save up enough to go off with Keefer some day, just as he dreamed. The idea became more and more exciting and possible. I couldn't wait until we were together again and we could make some real plans. I would convince him to find some other work here in the meantime. With the two of us earning, we could have enough to travel and find a new and happier life someplace. Why not? Mother darling would probably be grateful. She probably wouldn't even report my leaving to the police. As long as I wasn't around and couldn't hurt her reputation and spoil her chances, why would she care?

With new motivation and energy, I dressed and started out to make the best impression I could on Mr. Ritter at the supermarket. Before I left the complex, I stopped at Kathy Ann's apartment. For once, she wasn't planted in the window, watching for me or anyone else to fill her boring life with new gossip. But I was still fuming.

She opened the door, surprised and then immediately frightened by the look on my face.

"I'm not supposed to hang out with you, remember?" she said, and started to close the door. I put my foot in the way to stop it.

"I know you told where I would be last night. I know it was because of you that the police arrived."

"I couldn't help it," she wailed. "Your sister came down here and begged my mother to let her speak to me. It was so late and my mother was very upset. My father was still asleep, thank goodness, or it would have been worse."

"Why did you do it?"

"My mother called me out and she said if you know something to help this woman, you had better talk now, Kathy Ann, or I'll see to it you're punished for the rest of the summer."

"You were just jealous," I accused, my eyes fixed on her so firmly, she couldn't look at me. "Charlotte Lily said you had a crush on Keefer and you were just a bitch, weren't you?"

"No."

"You know what I'm going to do? I'm going to tell Charlotte Lily what you did so she can tell every person who knows you what a creep you are to betray someone. No one will ever trust you again," I vowed.

Her eyes filled with tears, and she shook her head.

"I couldn't help it."

"Me neither. I can't help it, either," I said. "Go have something else to eat. Maybe they'll take you in the circus some day," I spit at her and walked away.

She closed the door behind me. I was sure she would be trembling all day and what she would try to do now was call everyone she knew and explain what happened. That, I thought, would create more problems for her, because I really didn't intend to bother talking to

Charlotte Lily. I couldn't care less if she had any friends or not, but once she started to talk about it, they would wonder why she was being so defensive and that would be just as effective.

I left for the supermarket and arrived there about twenty minutes later. Mr. Ritter made me wait for nearly as long and then finally called me into his office.

"Well," he said, "I try not to hire anyone with a history that would make me think twice about having them around money in my store, but I'm going to make an exception with you. You have a good friend in Cory Lewis," he added. "I hope you appreciate that."

It took all my effort to smile and swallow down the words I wanted to say, but I did and nodded.

"Even so, I want you to understand you're on probation here, a test of sorts. I don't expect you to ever, ever be late for work, understand? The floor manager, Tammy Carol Allen, will show you around, describe your exact duties, and tell you when you take a break and what's expected of you. Don't come here wearing makeup like a clown or wearing anything that might be inappropriate. You don't smoke in the store, and I don't want to see you chewing and cracking gum in your mouth, hear?"

"Yes, sir," I said.

"Always be clean-looking and neat. People expect to see the employees looking that way. We're handling food here. Never sass a customer, no matter what. You're always polite and helpful. We pride ourselves on service. Always be sure to ask if the customer wants assistance with his or her packages, hear?"

"Yes, sir."

"Okay, I have your information on the application you filled out. You go see Tammy Carol and she'll give you your assignment. Mind," he said when I stood up and turned to go, "you break any of my rules, there's no second chance. You're out. Hear?"

I wanted to say I hear fine, but I just gave him a plastic smile and nodded.

He kept his stern face, and I left.

Tammy Carol was a woman in her late twenties who looked ten to fifteen years older. She was the sort of person who enjoyed even an iota of authority. She let me know that on the floor, she was God, Jesus, and the Holy Ghost. She made me stand and observe other grocery packers for nearly half an hour before giving me a shopping center apron and assigning me to a cashier.

"You be sure to ask paper or plastic before you start," she emphasized. "And you smile until your face hurts."

I was tempted to say, "I guess yours never does, then," but I nodded again and put on the apron.

All the while I kept one thought at the top of my mind: You're doing this to be free. As soon as you can, you will be gone and this won't even be a memory.

I wished I could treat the rest of my past life the same way and yet still have a future. Those who saw no tomorrow for themselves, I realized, would be forever stuck in their yesterdays.

That wasn't going to happen to me.

11

The Best-Laid Plans

Whenever there was a lull in the supermarket, Tammy Carol was right behind me, assigning me to other duties, which included washing down the freezer areas, mopping floors, and stacking canned goods. Everything I was told to do, I was told as though it was as important as doing brain surgery. The cans had to be turned just so. The mop had to be moved from right to left in perfect squares. When I wiped down the glass cases, I had to use a circular motion, not making my circles too large or too small. I could feel her breathing over my shoulder, making sure I did it as she instructed, and from time to time, Mr. Ritter appeared to scrutinize my work.

It was constantly on the tip of my tongue to tell them where they could put this job, but I swallowed back the urge to scream and kept my plastic smile until it did exactly what Tammy Carol predicted it might: hurt.

Finally, it was quitting time. Mr. Ritter was there at the front door to watch me leave.

"You've passed muster this first day," he said. "If you behave yourself accordingly, we'll get along fine and you will work here for the remainder of the summer. If you're really good, I might consider you for weekend work once you return to school," he added as another incentive. He spoke down to me as if he was on a high throne and I was kneeling at his feet.

"Thank you," I said.

I didn't realize how tired I was until I was outside, walking to the bus stop. And then, as if my body wanted to take revenge on me for what I had put it through all day, I felt cramps beginning and realized I had forgotten the time of the month and I hadn't brought any protection along with me, not even thinking about it when I passed the sanitary napkins and tampons on the store shelves earlier. I was in a small panic that grew more and more intense as the bus made stop after stop on its way to my station. By the time I arrived, I felt the beginning of staining and hurried out, practically running down the aisle.

I was surprised that Mother darling and Cory were home. I didn't know that they weren't starting this gig at their new and better place until later in the evening. They were now the principal act, and that meant they wouldn't begin until about ten. When I came charging through the door, they both looked up in surprise.

"Well, at least she knows what come right home after work means now," Cory quipped.

"How did you do?" Mother darling asked.

"I gotta go to the bathroom," I said, and hurried on. When I got in there, I saw my tampons were gone, removed from the area under the sink where I had placed them. I opened the door and screamed, "Mother, where are my tampons?"

"You don't keep things like that in the bathroom," Cory replied for her. "I don't like looking at them."

"They were under the sink."

"Next to my stuff," he shouted back.

"Where are they?"

"They're in your room," Mother darling said. "Calm down, Robin."

She brought them to me. I took them from her and slammed the door. I could hear Cory's laughter.

"He's a sick person," I yelled.

"Yeah, right. I'm not the one stealin' and sleepin' around. I wouldn't be so quick to call anyone else a sick person. Besides," he said when I came out of the bathroom, "we just wanted to be sure you weren't pregnant, right, Kay?" He grinned at me.

I looked at Mother darling.

"That's all I'd need now," she said.

He kept grinning at me.

"Maybe you're not sick," I said. "Maybe you're just ignorant."

Before he could reply, I went into the bedroom and closed the door. I hate it here, I told myself. I hate it!

"That's a fine way for her to behave after I go and beg Al to give her this job. And you're eatin' and sleepin' in my home!" he shouted.

"Not for long," I said in a loud whisper. "Not for long."

After they had left, I called Keefer, but no one answered at the shop. There was an answering machine, so I left my name and told him I would be home. I didn't think he was going to call. It was nearly midnight and he hadn't. I fell asleep curled up on the sofa watching television on that small set of Cory's. Every once in a while, something would interfere with the reception. It sounded like someone on a two-way radio. Finally, the phone rang and I jumped up.

"Can you talk?" he began.

"Yes. They're at work," I said.

"I was with my cousin Charlie. He called to tell me my father had gotten dead drunk and he dropped him off at the house. I told him I wished he had dropped him off a bridge, and then he decided to come downtown and meet me at the Giddup Saloon. We sat and talked for hours about my mother. He's ten years older than me and remembers her as a young woman. He said she was quite a dancer. Imagine that," Keefer said. "I don't think I ever saw her dance."

"Are you all right?"

"Me? Yeah. So, how was your first day on the job?"

"Hard," I said. "They had me do everything but sweep the sidewalk outside, but I think that's coming."

"Don't you work with a cashier?" he asked quickly.

"Oh, yes, most of the time. But if it gets slow and they have enough packers, they put me on stacking goods or cleaning."

"When the cashiers are through with their shifts, they have to prove—check out—their registers, right?"

"Yes, why?"

"I have an idea. I'll talk about it when we see each other again, if we ever do," he added.

"Don't be stupid. I'm saving almost everything I make so we'll have money to get out of here together."

"You are? That's great," he said. "What time do you work tomorrow?"

"Tomorrow I'm twelve to eight."

"Okay. I'll stop by about eight."

"Let's meet outside," I said. "The manager is Cory's friend, and he might tell him he saw you."

"I'll be in a blue Chevy with a bashed-in right front."

"Keefer, how do you know these cars are safe to drive?" I asked, laughing.

"They're safe. Don't worry. The funeral's tomorrow morning," he added. "That's why he got dead drunk tonight."

"Oh. I could be there maybe."

"No. It's not going to be long."

"Don't get into any fights with him, Keefer."

"I won't. Charlie will keep him away from me. It'll be all right."

"I'm anxious to see you," I said.

"Same here. I'd better get some sleep. You too. Take care, Robin," he said.

I wanted to say more, but he hung up. I really was so tired and achy with cramps that I looked forward to falling asleep. It didn't take long. I was in such a deep sleep that I didn't hear Mother darling and Cory come home from their show. It surprised me to wake up with sunshine spilling over my face. At first I thought they had not yet returned. I imagined they had gone partying to celebrate their continued success, but when I stepped out of the room, I saw Mother darling's outfit on the sofa, her boots on the floor. I had slept until almost nine-thirty myself and I didn't hear a peep coming from their bedroom.

Taking care to make as little noise as possible, I made some coffee and had a small bowl of cereal. Afterward, I took a quick shower, dried myself and then went to change my tampon. I was so lost in thought about Keefer and his mother's funeral, I didn't at first realize the bathroom door had been opened. I looked up and saw Cory standing there, gaping at me, and I screamed, this time so shrilly and loud, he actually winced and jumped back, closing the door quickly.

I dressed as fast as I could, the rage keeping me hot and frantic. Cory had retreated to his and Mother darling's bedroom, but that didn't matter to me now. As soon as I was dressed, I opened their door and shouted, "That was disgusting. You knew I was in there."

Mother darling was still in bed, her eyes closed. She turned and her eyelids fluttered open. Cory was standing at his closet. He was in his underwear and choosing a pair of jeans to wear.

"Whaaa? What is it?" Mother darling asked.

"He did it again. He just burst in on me and after he saw I was in there, he didn't close the door. He just stood there gaping at me," I accused.

Cory smirked.

"That's a lot of crap. You didn't give me a chance to close the door. You just went hysterical."

"Did you enjoy the view? Are you interested in women's hygiene that much?"

Cory looked at Mother darling.

"Can you do something about her?"

"Robin," she began, sitting up and letting the blanket fall to her waist. Her nudity never shocked me, but her nudity with a man in the room did. I turned away. "I'm sure it was just an accident," she began.

"Right," I said. "An accident. That's exactly what he is, an accident. I bet his mother collected on collision insurance or something when he was born."

"Very funny."

"Robin."

"Forget it," I said. "I'm going to work."

I slammed their door and rushed out of the apartment, my steps pounding the stairway and clicking over the walk. There wasn't a bus for quite a while. I grew impatient and walked toward the next station. With the way my nerve endings were twanging and my stomach was churning, I couldn't just sit and wait with the other people. It was a mistake because the bus arrived only five minutes later and passed me up on my way to the next stop. I ran, but I didn't get there in time. Tired and disgusted, I flopped on the bench and waited again. This bus seemed to make more stops. By the time I arrived at the supermarket, I was just a minute or so late. Mr. Ritter jumped out at me the moment I entered.

He didn't speak. He pointed to his watch.

"I missed the bus," I began. "And the next one wasn't as fast and . . ."

"You have to anticipate such things, young lady. The trick is to start earlier, understand?"

"Yes, sir."

"My policy is if you're a minute late, you are still docked for an hour. My advice to you is be here early tomorrow to be sure you're not late. If you were a minute or so more, I'd fire you, so count your blessings."

I mouthed a thank you and went in to get my apron. Everything made my cramps more intense this particular morning. People thought I was smiling, when I was really grimacing in agony. My bad luck continued. It turned out to be one of the busiest days of the week. I never stopped until my break for lunch.

Instead of joining the other employees, I went outside and found a bench upon which to sit and eat one of the ready-made sandwiches the store sold. It was to be subtracted from my salary, of course. I ended up feeding most of it to the birds.

When a lull came in the afternoon, Tammy Carol had me working at the frozen food freezer. She wanted everything taken out and rearranged neatly. It was hard because it was so cold my fingers became numb. If I paused too long, either she or Mr. Ritter was there to tell me I couldn't leave the items out of the freezer too long. Get with it.

My last shift as a packer was the hardest. I was so tired and cranky, I dropped a bottle of cranberry juice, which shattered at my feet.

"That will come out of your salary," Mr. Ritter told me instantly. "I want this cleaned up immediately. First, get our customer another bottle so she is not delayed another unnecessary second. Go!" he shouted.

I hurried, clinging to this bottle for dear life, and returned. Then I started to clean up the mess. I cut my finger on a piece of glass, which enraged him even more.

"Dropping blood everywhere now. Go in the back and use the first-aid kit. I should have my head examined. Cory owes me big time," he eagerly announced.

Finally, eight o'clock came and I punched out.

"Remember," Mr. Ritter said as I was leaving, "get here early tomorrow."

I nodded and left. I was in such a daze that for a moment, I had forgotten Keefer was going to be there. He actually had to sound his horn. I turned and saw him waving from the battered vehicle. Never so glad to see him, I ran to the car and he got out to embrace me.

"Hey," he said. "You look worse than me."

"I had a terrible day," I said, and rattled every moment off in minutes. Then I remembered what his day had to be like and asked him how it went.

"It was hard. My father was in a stupor, which was

good. He actually looked like he didn't know who I was. Charlie was great. I stayed after everyone left and had my last conversation with her," he added, his eyes getting glassy. He took a deep breath.

I kissed his cheek and squeezed his arm gently. He shook his head.

"I can't stay here," he said. "I thought I could work it through, get another job for a while, but I just want to get away."

"Me, too," I said. "I'm miserable back at that apartment, and they really don't want me around." I told him what a creep Cory Lewis was and how I was devastated by my mother always taking his side no matter what.

"She's dependent on him now." He looked back at the supermarket. "You have an idea about how much money the cashier checks out when the shift is changed?"

"I don't know. I think about twenty-five hundred or so. Why?"

"I'd like to borrow it," he said.

"What?"

"It's an easy robbery. I thought about it even before you began to work for a supermarket."

"Really?" My heart began to thump.

He shrugged, and then he reached under the seat and brought out a pistol. I thought all the breath left my body. It was one thing to shoplift—some of my friends back in Ohio actually thought it was a game—but a gun!

"Where did you get that?"

"It's Izzy's, but he doesn't even remember he has it half the time. Don't worry. There are no bullets in it, but no one would know, of course. What I want to do is walk in just as the cashier finishes checking her receipts and do it and walk out. We'll leave right from there."

"But I can make enough money in a month or so and—"

"I don't want to wait," he said sharply.

"But didn't you say Izzy wasn't selling for a month and—"

"You don't have to be part of it if you don't want to, Robin. I'll understand. Just pretend you don't know who I am."

I stared at him for a moment, and then I looked at the gun and sat back. He waited as I thought.

Could I do this? Should I? What would life be like here after Keefer left? How long could I stand it, anyway? What was I leaving? Mother darling had a new family: her band and all the people who would be involved in her career. I would always be on the outside or sitting in some dark corner waiting for her to remember me, and when she did, it wouldn't be a memory of joy; it would be a memory of obligation. All I did was remind her of one of her big mistakes in life.

I nodded slowly and then turned to him.

"Okay, Keefer. Let's do it. Let's get as far away from here and everything that is here as we can."

He smiled.

"Okay, here's my plan. Don't cause any undo suspicion by packin' a bag or somethin'. Choose whatever is so important to you that you can't leave it behind and let's get it out tonight so you leave for work lookin' just like you did this mornin'. We'll have enough money to buy you whatever you need along the way."

"There's nothing I want," I told him, "nothing to get tonight."

"Same here," he said, nodding in understanding.

Then he got excited again. "We've got this SUV that was in a multiple-car accident two days ago. The back end is smashed in so that the door can't be opened, but the taillights still work and there's nothin' wrong with the engine. It's perfect. The owner left for a meeting and a few days' vacation in Florida. We'll use it and dump it somewhere. I know exactly how to do all this, so don't worry," he assured me.

"But you've never robbed anyone, Keefer, have you? How do you know what to do?"

"It's not that hard, and it will only take a few minutes at the most. In and out, and then we're gone," he added, "gone for good. Believe me, it's easy."

"I believe you, but I don't think I'll sleep tonight just thinking about it," I said.

"Yeah. I know what you mean. I wish we could be together, but that would set off all sorts of alarms and make tomorrow impossible. I won't even take you all the way back now. I'll let you out about a block or so from the complex. Do exactly what they want you to do so you don't cause any suspicions or concern, okay?"

I nodded.

He kissed me and then we both looked at the supermarket a moment. Suddenly, the place I hated more than anywhere was the source of new hope.

"I guess you'll feel a little funny takin' their money, huh?" Keefer asked.

I laughed.

"Are you kidding? There's no one I'd rather rob from than that manager. I can't wait to see the look on his face."

Keefer smiled, started the engine, and drove off. We were both pensive until he reached the block where he thought I should get out and walk the rest of the way.

"All we need is Kathy Ann to see us together and blab," he said.

"She'll have plenty to blab about when it's over."

We looked at each other silently.

"If you change your mind for any reason . . ." he began.

"I won't. Don't worry about it." I leaned over to kiss him, and then I got out of the vehicle. He remained there looking after me as I walked away.

My heart wasn't pounding anymore, but it was acting strangely—ticking like a time bomb. My whole body felt strange, in fact. I thought I had lost all my weight and would soon start to rise off the sidewalk and float with the wind like some balloon that was released.

Off I would go into the distance, growing smaller and smaller until I became a thin memory, easily forgotten.

By now I was sure Grandpa had forgotten me. Good riddance to that child of sin, he probably thought, and went about his work with a sense of relief. He no longer had to worry about the devil moving in and out of his home, threatening his precious pure soul.

And Mother darling . . . she would surely turn my running away into a song.

Off she went into the night, thinking there was
nowhere she belonged,
My accidental daughter who came and went like
a dream to be remembered only when dark
clouds warned us of another storm.
My accidental daughter.

That's not bad, I thought as I strolled slowly back to the apartment.

Maybe I'll just write it down and leave it for her so she would have something from me she could use.

It was already something of far more value than anything I would take from her.

12

Strike Three

As I had predicted, I couldn't sleep. First, I tried tiring myself further by watching television until nearly one in the morning. My eyes did close and open, close and open. I thought I had dulled my teeming brain enough and finally rose, turned off the set, and went to bed. For a few minutes, I actually did sleep, but then I woke with a twitch that nearly sent me flying off the bed. My eyes snapped open, and all the thoughts, plans, and words Keefer and I had exchanged came flooding back. My heart started to pound.

Hours later, I heard Mother darling and Cory return. They were both obviously drunk. They didn't seem to care how loudly they talked. I heard their great excitement. Mother darling's songs and the band had gone over exceedingly well, I gathered. I heard her keep saying, "Ten weeks! We have a guaranteed ten weeks there!"

"Next stop, the Grand Ole Opry," Cory cried, and they clinked bottles of beer. Then they broke out in one of Mother darling's songs:

"My heart is a prison and you've got the key,
But darlin' there's no prisoner I'd rather be."

I couldn't help lying there and envying Mother darling's happiness. Everything I heard her say was about her and Cory and the band. There was no mention of me. It was truly as if I wasn't there; I never existed. I buried my face in the pillow and tried to shut out their cries of joy. They were up celebrating for at least another hour or so before they finally collapsed in bed. Their laughter lingered in the silence. I fought harder to get some sleep, and some time just before the first glittering rays of morning, it came.

I woke up and groaned and turned over and fell asleep again, this time not waking until nearly eleven. Panic nearly froze me in bed. I leaped out and dressed as quickly as I could. It had been my intention to review all my possessions, despite what I had told Keefer, so I could decide if there was anything dear to me. Now, all I could do was throw some cold water on my face, run a brush through my hair, and hurry out to make the bus. If I was late today, Mr. Ritter would surely do what he threatened and fire me on the spot. That would mess up Keefer's whole plan.

For a moment or two, I hesitated at Mother darling's bedroom door. I was leaving without saying any sort of good-bye, any final words. We might not speak to each other for some time, I thought. How would she really react? Would she breathe a sigh of relief and go on happily with her developing music career? Would she spend a few hours worrying about me or regretting how I had been treated? I imagined Cory telling her not to waste any time thinking about me. I wasn't worth it, not after all they had done for me. Like that was anything significant.

Neither she nor I had called Grandma and Grandpa to tell them we were fine. I knew she believed they thought good riddance when they thought of us, but I couldn't believe that completely. Grandma surely worried, and despite his harsh, cold ways, Grandpa had to give us some thought. People, family people, surely just don't dispose of each other like empty milk cartons or something, do they?

Maybe they do, I thought. I couldn't be more confused when it came to all that. All that seemed concrete and sure to me at the moment was Keefer's devotion, Keefer's dreams and plans, because everything included me. I was made a big part of it. I was important to someone finally, someone who needed me about as much as I needed him. That's a gift, I thought. That's a stroke of luck that's come my way, and I can't just toss it aside. For what would I give it up, anyway? This?

I looked around the disheveled apartment with their clothes strewn about, the empty beer bottles on the table and floor, Mother darling's boots staring at me. That's it, I realized. I'll take those. At least, I'd have something of hers. I scooped them up and left the apartment, closing the door softly behind me.

Stay asleep, Mother darling. You're better off, I thought, and hurried down the stairs.

I was lucky with the bus and made it to the supermarket ten minutes early. Now came the hard part—working until the first cashier shift ended. I had to keep up that plastic smile, look calm and innocent. Despite that, I couldn't help but gaze out the window, anticipating Keefer's arrival. When I finally did see him pull up to the curb outside, I think my heart stopped and started. The blood drained from my face, and I fumbled with the groceries

"You all right?" the cashier, Betty Blue Nickols, asked. I had worked with her before and found her to be pleasant. She was an older woman, close to fifty, I thought. The regular customers knew her by name and obviously liked her. Many exchanged small talk with her as she worked, talking about their children or their other family members as if she really knew them. It brought a warmth to an otherwise very cold and impersonal world, I thought.

"I'm fine," I said quickly.

My eyes went to the big clock on the left wall. In ten minutes, Betty Blue would be closing out her register. Keefer was sitting in the battered SUV, watching me through the window, waiting for my signal. Every minute that clicked off brought more blood to my face. My skin felt like it was on fire. Did I have a fever? The inside of my throat became dry as well. My hands trembled around the groceries I packed. At one point Mr. Ritter came around and looked hard at me, his eyebrows turning in like two annoyed caterpillars. I held my breath, and then he walked off to help a customer.

Betty Blue closed her register and put up her sign to indicate her aisle was shutting down. Then she opened her register again to begin to count her cash. I turned slowly, and looked out at Keefer. This was the moment of decision. If there was a good angel on one of my shoulders, he or she was asleep. I nodded emphatically and he got out of the SUV and strutted toward the supermarket entrance.

I was supposed to move over to the next cashier, but I hesitated long enough for Keefer to come in and approach Betty Blue, who looked up with surprise.

"I'm closed," she said, and then grimaced at the realization he had no grocery cart or groceries to check out anyway. Keefer glanced at me and then pulled the pistol out of his jacket.

Betty Blue gasped.

"Just put the cash into a paper bag."

Betty Blue froze. Keefer's eyes registered a sense of panic. I was afraid of what would happen next if she didn't move quickly, but she was in shock.

"Robin, do it," he said, and I pushed her back and began to take out the cash and drop it in a bag.

"It's all there," I said.

"Let's go," he snapped.

I knelt down and grabbed Mother darling's boots where I had hidden them under the counter.

"Hurry up, Robin," he ordered.

A customer coming up saw the gun in Keefer's hand and screamed. Mr. Ritter came around one of the aisles and dropped his jaw, his eyes nearly popping out.

Keefer and I ran to the exit and out, me clutching the bag with one hand and Mother darling's boots in the other. We got into the SUV and he started away. I didn't look back. I didn't think I could move my head. I was that frozen.

"Count the money!" Keefer screamed. "Let's see what we've got."

I nodded and then began. We had just a little over two thousand dollars. He was pleased.

"That's great. It'll be enough to start." Then he smiled. "It was easy, easier than I thought, huh?"

"Yes," I said.

"Hey, what's with those boots?" he asked. I was clutching them again. I hadn't even realized I was.

"They're my mother's," I said.

"You're the same size?"

"No," I replied.

He shook his head, his lips twisted in confusion.

"Then . . . why did you take them?"

"I don't know," I said. I looked at them. "I don't know."

"Forget about it. You'll have a nice new pair that fit you soon."

"I don't care about boots."

He laughed and shook his head. We were driving fast, slipping under streetlights before they turned red and weaving around slower traffic.

"Do you know where you're going?" I asked.

"Absolutely," he said. "I've been planning carefully on this getaway."

He let out a whoop.

"We're outta here!" he cried.

I tried to smile. Were we? I looked ahead and relaxed a little. Maybe it would be wonderful. Maybe it would be great, I thought, and closed my eyes to wish hard.

Then I heard Keefer's guttural cry and I opened my eyes to see a police patrol car ahead. At first I thought it was just there, waiting for speeders, but suddenly, it pulled out and planted itself right in our way, its bubble light going. Keefer hit the brakes and turned to back up, but there behind us, coming up fast, was another police patrol car. He started to turn and then stopped. A third patrol car was coming too fast down the other lane.

He turned to me.

"Bad luck," he said, and shrugged. "They must have

been just close enough to get the call and cut us off. And we were almost to the open highway. Damn."

Blood drained from my face at the sight of two policemen, their guns drawn and pointing at us. They were crouched behind the doors of their vehicle. Another policeman screamed through a bullhorn behind us, ordering us to come out of the truck with our hands raised high.

"I'm sorry," Keefer said.

I began to cry. With Mother darling's boots still in my hands, I stepped out of the truck when Keefer did. His hands were up and so were mine.

It occurred to me as the police drew closer that Mother darling might still be sleeping.

We were separated almost immediately at the police station. I thought I would be placed in a prison cell, but I was brought to a room with a long table and two chairs. There was a mirror on one wall. I sat there for a long time, staring at myself and wondering what was going to happen to me next. Finally, a woman with very short dark hair, wearing a gray skirt suit, entered. She looked about thirty or thirty-five to me. She didn't smile, but there was something warm about her soft brown eyes. She opened a briefcase and took out a long pad and a file.

"I'm Lou Ann Simmons from the district attorney's office," she began. "There is someone coming over from the public defender's office. I guess it's someone you know fairly well, Mr. Carson Meriweather. It's not all that long since you and he were in court," she added pointedly. Then she smiled again and continued. "You can wait for him to arrive, if you like, or you can tell me your side of this."

"My side?"

"What was your role in the robbery exactly?"

I wasn't sure what she meant by exactly. I shrugged.

"I put the money in the paper bag. Is that what you mean?"

"You were in on the planning, too, weren't you?" she followed, obviously pleased I was responding.

"Yes."

"You were supposed to give a signal or something, which you did?"

"Yes."

The door opened and Mr. Meriweather entered quickly. He looked at Lou Ann Simmons.

"Have you been questioning my client?"

"She was asked if she wanted to wait for you," Lou Ann Simmons replied. The warmth in her eyes was gone. I had the feeling it was something she could turn on and off at will.

"She doesn't understand what's happening here. She's a minor."

"She was involved in an armed robbery. That status might be denied."

"All the more reason for you not to have gone ahead without me," he fired back.

I felt like I was an observer in an argument that involved someone else besides me.

"She's confessed to her active participation in the event. I can ask her the same questions with you present."

"I want to speak to my client alone," he said sharply.

"I think the best thing you can do and convince her to do is cooperate with me. Keefer Dawson will not be tried as a minor, and he is responsible for bringing her into the act. I hope you're not going to make this complicated," she added, put her notebook and the file back in her briefcase, and left.

"I would have thought you would know enough not to speak to anyone without your attorney present," Mr. Meriweather chastised before sitting in the seat she had taken.

"I didn't know what to do."

"With your past record, I would have thought you would," he said dryly. "Don't you realize how serious this situation is? You were on probation."

I tried to swallow, but couldn't. All I could do was nod.

"She's not bluffing. They could have you tried as an adult. You'll go to a hard penitentiary. And for years!" he emphasized.

"Was my mother called yet?"

"Your mother can't save you now," he muttered. "This man, Keefer Dawson, talked you into participating in this robbery, didn't he?"

"He didn't talk me into it."

"He talked you into it," Mr. Meriweather insisted. "You didn't have any idea he would have a gun?" he said, seemingly as a question, but more as an answer he wanted to shove down my throat.

"Yes, I did. I saw it before, but he told me there were no bullets in it."

"That would make no difference. How would anyone being held up know there were no bullets in it, and how do you know for certain that there were no bullets in it?"

"He told me," I said.

"Then you did not know for certain," he concluded.

"You see how complicated this can be and how much trouble you can be in?"

I nodded.

"All right. Just sit here and don't—don't—ever talk to anyone about this without my being present."

He got up and left the room. To me it felt like nearly an hour had gone by before the door was opened again. This time it was Mother darling. She just stood there for a few moments and looked in at me. I thought she was going to back up and close the door. Finally she entered. I saw her eyes were bloodshot from crying. She sucked in her breath and sat.

"There were many times," she began, "when I thought my father was right. I didn't know why it should be, but evil, like some pollution, seeped into me and then into you. That was a big reason why I wanted to leave home. I wanted to get away from his eyes, from his way of lookin' at us, remindin' me all the time of the mistakes I had made."

"Me, especially," I said.

She stared.

"Yeah, I suppose I always thought of you that way, Robin. I'm not denyin' it. It's no secret I never intended to be pregnant, but I really believed that somehow, some way, because of my music or through it, I'd make things right. I guess I never got that across to you, no matter how many times I tried gettin' you to see it."

"It's your career, not mine," I snapped back at her. "You're the star, Mother darling."

She shook her head.

"I don't blame you for hatin' me, I guess." She smiled. "Remember that song I wrote years ago: 'I want to love you but I can't help hatin' myself for wantin' that.' "

"I'm not the reason for a song, Mother darling. I'm a person," I told her.

She nodded.

"Yep, I guess, but what sort of a person have you become? I'll take as much blame as goes around, of course, but that's not goin' to help us much now."

She turned and looked at me.

"Mr. Meriweather says Keefer Dawson is tellin' the district attorney that he talked you into this, that you didn't know he was goin' to have a real gun."

"It's not true!"

"It's somethin' that will help you, Robin. Mr. Meriweather sent me in here to convince you not to contradict Keefer. Keefer should do this. He had no business bringin' you into it."

"He didn't bring me into anything. I wanted to do it," I practically shouted back at her.

"You want to go to a real terrible prison where ugly things happen to girls your age and you want to go there for years and years? Is that what you want?"

"No, but—"

"But that's what's goin' to happen to you if you don't shut your trap, Robin. You nod when you're told to nod and you shake your head when you're told to shake it, understand? Otherwise, there's no tellin' what that judge is goin' to do to you. Mr. Meriweather is tryin' to work somethin' out with that assistant district attorney. If you will sign the statement agreeing with what Keefer Dawson is tellin' them, she'll consider a recommendation to the judge that will help you."

"I don't want Keefer taking all the blame," I said.

"He would have done somethin' like this with or without you, wouldn't he?" she asked.

I thought about it.

"Probably," I said. "His mother just died—committed suicide—and his father hates him and he lost his job."

"That's all for his lawyer to tell, Robin. There's no point tyin' yourself to someone else's troubles."

"It is if you care about him," I told her. "That's something you wouldn't understand, Mother darling. You never cared about anyone more than you cared about yourself."

"That's not fair, Robin. I did care about you. I do."

"Then how did you bring us—bring me—to live with that horrible Cory Lewis?" I cried.

She stared

"I didn't just come to Cory with you because he was involved in the music business, Robin. There was a chance—there *is* a chance," she corrected, "that he is your real father."

I felt as if lightning had snapped over my head.

"No," I said. I shook my head vigorously to throw the words back out of my ears.

"As I told you, there was more than one, but he was there that night and we . . . we were lovers that night."

"No," I insisted.

"It doesn't matter. Cory wanted to do somethin' for us because he thought it might be true."

"If it is, I wish I was never born," I said. "Almost as much as you wish it."

"I don't wish it anymore, Robin, but I don't expect you to believe that. I really was hopin' you'd be part of my success and be happy."

"Good title for a new song. Start writing it," I snapped, and she bristled.

"I'm tellin' that lawyer you'll do what he says,

Robin. If you don't, you're goin' to be one sorry girl."

She rose.

"You don't help him by hurtin' yourself," she added.

I looked up at her. It was the first thing she had said that I thought made any sense at all.

And something I wished she would turn into a song.

13

Caged Birds
Sing Sad Songs

~

"This is the story," Mr. Meriweather said, with Mother darling sitting beside him. "We can keep you out of prison, keep you from being tried as an adult, even keep you out of a juvenile detention center."

I held my breath and looked from him to Mother darling and then back to him.

"How?"

"There is a special school for young girls who, shall we say, have exhausted all the traditional means of correcting their behavior, or rather, their misbehavior. Their parents are totally defeated, as is your mother."

I glanced at her, and she shifted her eyes guiltily away.

"What sort of special school?"

"It's a school run by a specialist in behavior modification, and for many, a school of last resort. Now before I go any further in my explanation, let me make clear to you that once you go there, you do not have the privilege of deciding you don't want to be there. You're there until it is decided you can return and behave in a reasonable manner, and you would still be on a term of strict probation. Should you attempt to escape or run away from this school, you would be immediately returned to court and sentenced to a real prison—sentenced, in your case, as an adult. It's part of the agreement we will sign."

"But how long am I at this school?"

"You can be there months; you can be there years. It's entirely up to you. That's the beauty of it, if we can say there is any beauty. You're in control of your own destiny. In a real prison, you're lucky to be in control of your own bowel movements," he said, his lips taut, his eyes ice-cold.

"It's just another school?"

"No, I'm not saying it's just another school. It's a special school. There are different rules, different activities. Its purpose is to change your behavior, change your miscreant ways, and make you a productive member of society. You sign a contract to turn yourself over to the school. Your mother signs as well," he added, looking at her.

Something in her face told me she wasn't happy to be doing it, even though Mr. Meriweather had made it sound like a way out of a horrible prison experience. It made my heart flutter.

"I don't know," I said.

"You can have a little while to discuss it with your mother. Then I have to inform the assistant district attorney, and together we will confer with the judge. This is the last breath of mercy you will find in this court," he added, and rose. "One more thing. It's normally very, very expensive to go to this special school. It's privately run, but an anonymous benefactor has provided what we can best describe as scholarships for girls whose families cannot afford it, but who need it desperately nevertheless. That, for you, is another stroke of luck just when you need it the most."

He looked at Mother darling.

"I'll be back in a little while," he said, and left us.

"What is this all about?" I asked.

"Just what he said. I didn't even know it existed. Even though we said you would sign the statements, the judge was not persuaded to consider you a minor. The gun made all the difference. You're headin' for some hard time in a hard place with women who have done some terrible things and will see you as a ripe piece of fruit. Virgin fruit," she added in practically a whisper.

"Do you know anything about the school?"

"Just what you heard."

"Where is it?"

"I don't know."

"You don't know? What do you mean, you don't know?"

"They don't want the parents to know where it is. They don't want parents to change their minds and go fetch their children."

"But what if I call you and tell you where I am?"

"You can't call anyone, Robin."

"But . . . that's worse than jail, isn't it? Don't prisoners get the right to call people?"

"Not right away. I think you can call after a while. I don't know everything."

I stared at her.

"You don't know anything, do you, and you don't

care. It's a way to get rid of me. That's all you know."

"That's not true. I don't want you goin' to a real prison and . . ."

"And what?"

"I haven't been a good mother, and I probably won't ever be," she admitted. "It's true what he said. I'm not capable of doin' what has to be done. I need help. Look at this," she said, unfolding a paper. "I was asked to check off what applies to you."

> *Does your teen struggle with basic family rules?*
>
> *Has your teen ever been expelled? Been truant? Failed subjects?*
>
> *Is your teen verbally abusive?*
>
> *Does your teen associate with bad peers? Have problems with the law? Lack motivation?*
>
> *Lack self-worth? Have problems with authority? Has your teen been sexually promiscuous? Been manipulative and/or deceitful? Stolen money or other valuables from your home?*
>
> *No matter what rules and consequences are established, does your teen defy them?*
>
> *When dealing with your teen, do you often feel powerless?*

I put the paper down.

"You see, I had to check everythin', Robin."

"Big deal," I said.

"Yes, it is a big deal. I'm signin' the paper."

"I don't care," I said. "Sign it."

"You'll thank me someday."

"I can't wait," I said.

She rose and walked slowly to the door.

"They're goin' to take you directly from here, Robin. We won't have a chance to say good-bye."

"We said good-bye a long time ago, Mother darling," I told her. I said it firmly, but my eyes were clouded with tears.

She nodded.

"I'm sorry, honey. I'm sorry I hurt you. No matter what you think, I'll never stop lovin' you. I hope you come back."

"To what?"

"To me," she said, and opened the door. She hesitated, and then she closed it.

It wasn't a loud noise, but to me it was like a gunshot.

A few minutes later, a policewoman came in.

"You'd better go to the bathroom," she said. "You've got a long trip ahead of you."

I did what she suggested. When I came out, she was waiting for me.

She took me down a hallway to a door where a police vehicle was parked. A patrolman opened the rear door and I got in. It occurred to me that I had nothing but the clothes on my back. I was going to say something about it, but no one seemed interested in anything I had to say, so I kept my mouth shut.

I looked back when the car pulled away. I don't know why. Something made me do that.

I saw Mother darling standing on the walkway, clutching the boots I had taken.

She held them as close to her as I had held them to me.

It was all we shared at the moment.

But it was enough to free the tears locked in my heart.

PART TWO

TEAL

1

Suspended

As soon as our English teacher, Mr. Croft, took off his sports jacket and draped it over his desk chair in front of the classroom, I knew I was going to laugh. The laughter rose in my chest in waves, rolling freely upward. Mr. Croft turned to write the first grammar exercise sentence on the board, and I saw his shirt partially out of his pants. It really wasn't anything all that unusual. He was not a very neat dresser. However, everything had struck me as humorous this morning, from the security guard at the front entrance looking at me with grouchy, suspicious eyes, to the snob birds in the bathroom who nearly exploded with shock when I plucked my silver flask out of my purse and took a sip.

"What's that?" Evette Heckman asked.

"Orange juice and vodka," I replied, smiled, and drank some more. When I offered it to them, they fled as if I was offering them a drink of poison.

In class my laugh came out with a sound that resembled someone spitting up a drink first, and then I went into the giggles. Mr. Croft turned with confusion on his face and raked the room with his eyes, finally settling on me. His grimace of bewilderment changed to a smirk of annoyance, and that made me laugh even harder.

I knew the vodka I had taken from my parents' bar to mix with the orange juice had most to do with my inability to contain myself. This wasn't the first time, and something told me it wasn't going to be the last, no matter what happened this particular morning.

"What do you find so funny, Miss Sommers?" Mr. Croft asked. "Surely not restrictive and nonrestrictive clauses, although the results of your quiz yesterday might suggest you're not taking this very seriously."

Everyone's eyes were on me. Some of the snob birds looked angrier than Mr. Croft, probably to win favor or maybe because they really did think I was interrupting their precious private-school educations. The idea was, if you paid more for it, you would take it more seriously. At least, that was the theory my parents believed or, should I say, hoped was true, especially for me. I had all but failed tenth grade the year before in public school. I had been suspended three times there and put in detention so often, there was a joke that I would get a degree in it. After I was caught vandalizing the girls' room, which cost my father nearly a thousand dollars, my parents thought a strategic retreat to a private school would be the solution. I would be less apt to be influenced by bad seeds. The truth was, I was the one doing the influencing.

Mr. Croft brought his hands to his wide waist and glared at me. His nostrils were as big as a cow's when they flared. He turned his lips inward, outlining his mouth in two thin white lines of rage, and clenched his teeth.

"Well?" he demanded, speaking through the wall of cigarette-stained enamel.

I laughed harder. I couldn't help it, even though my stomach was hurting and I was gasping for breath.

He sighed.

"I think it's best you get up and go to the principal's office, Miss Sommers," he said in a tighter voice.

I continued to laugh.

"Teal Sommers!" he screamed, stepping toward me. "Get up and get out this minute."

He pointed at the door so vigorously and sharply, the button on his cuff undid and his sleeve sagged like a torn curtain. Someone gasped, but that just widened my idiotic grin. He saw what happened and lowered his arm, pointing more gracefully with the other arm and hand toward the door.

"Go. I will intercom the office to let Mr. Bloomberg know you are coming," he assured me.

I caught my breath and let my head fall back a moment. I was looking up at the ceiling, watching the lines of the tiles wiggling. Mr. Croft walked all the way down the aisle to my desk. By this time his rage was building like milk boiling in a pot. Any moment he might seize my arm and pull me out of my seat, I thought.

"What is wrong with you, young lady?"

"Smell her breath," one of the snob birds cried out. I wasn't positive, but I thought it was most likely Ainsley Winslow. Always full of herself, she'd hated me from the moment I told her that her nose job was poorly done, was too pointed, and made her resemble a chicken.

Mr. Croft looked in her direction and then down at me with more intense scrutiny.

"Is that true, Teal? Have you drunk something you shouldn't?"

"No, sir," I said, and then I covered my mouth with both of my hands quickly because my stomach was starting to send up more than laughter. It took two hard swallows to keep it down, my eyes bulging with the effort.

"Go!" he commanded with a sense of panic as well as anger in his voice.

I rose much too quickly and awkwardly and fell against him. He jumped back as if I was on fire. As fast as I could, I scooped up my books and charged toward the door. Behind me I heard the rest of the classroom laughing. I fumbled with the knob and went out, closing the door behind me. The churning in my stomach stopped for a moment, but the corridor seemed to turn on its side and then right itself. I hiccuped so loudly, the sound bounced off the walls, echoing all the way to the end of the corridor. With one hand against the wall to steady myself, I started down the shiny tiled floor.

The librarian, Ms. Beachim, came out of the faculty room and paused to look at me. She lowered her glasses over the bridge of her bony nose and peered.

"Are you all right?" she asked.

"No," I said. "I feel like I'm inside out."

"Pardon?"

"Like a sock when you take it off," I told her. Then I laughed, and she stood there gaping at me with her hands pressed against the base of her throat.

I straightened my shoulders and tried to walk a straight line, but I guess I had drunk more orange juice and vodka than I normally did, especially in the morning. The world would not stop swaying. I was getting more and more seasick.

Finally, I reached the principal's office. When I stepped in, I paused, or at least I thought I had. Even though my feet were planted, somehow it was as if I was still moving.

Mrs. Tagler looked up from her desk. As soon as the principal's secretary set eyes on me, her eyebrows lifted and her lips went into a crooked smile. She had a hairdo and a face that reminded me of a praying mantis, especially with those long, thin arms she kept bent at the elbows and those hands with fingers curling inward.

"Now what?" she asked.

"I thought he was going to call and lodge a complaint," I said.

"Who?"

"Mr. Croft's shirt is out of his pants," I said.

"What?"

"He's a mess."

I giggled, and she let her jaw drop enough for me to see the gold crown in the back of her mouth.

"You were sent to see Mr. Bloomberg?"

"No, I was asked to pay him a friendly visit," I replied. "To see how things were going and if there is anything I can do to help improve the school," I added, and, before I could stop it, hiccuped.

She nodded knowingly.

"Sit down," she ordered as she rose like a gusher to her full six feet of height. Her husband, I was told, was only five feet five and had to be careful he didn't get poked in the eye by one of her breasts. She always wore those stiff pointy bras that looked like they had been borrowed from Madonna's costume closet.

Mrs. Tagler went into the principal's office, closing

the door behind her. Only seconds afterward, the door was thrust open and Mr. Bloomberg stood there glaring out at me. Something in my face told him the whole story. His bushy rust eyebrows curved downward when I hiccuped again.

"I don't want to talk to you in the state you're in," he said. "Go directly to the nurse's office. I'm calling your mother." He turned to Mrs. Tagler. "See that she goes to Lila's office," he said, and she nodded.

"Come along, Teal," she said, her voice softer now.

I stood, remembered my books, and reached down, knocking them every which way.

"Oh, forget them," Mrs. Tagler said. The phone was ringing. Mr. Croft had finally gotten himself together enough to call, I thought. She picked up the receiver and listened.

"Yes, he knows," she said. "Thank you."

She considered me, wavering before her. She seemed to go in and out of focus, and that made me smile. Then came another hiccup, and another.

"Go on, Teal," she ordered. "I have more important things to do than baby-sit a sixteen-year-old girl who should know better."

I left the office and, with her walking beside me, went to the nurse's office, which fortunately was only two doors down.

Mrs. Miller looked up from her desk. She was completing one report or another. That's all she ever seemed to do in this place, I thought, complete reports or coddle one of the snob birds who was having a bad monthly, as she referred to it.

"What is it?" she asked, staring up at me, her eyes glittering with suspicion.

"Our Miss Sommers has had something alcoholic to

drink, apparently. She needs to sleep it off until her mother arrives. She was sent to the office but Mr. Bloomberg doesn't want to see her in this condition."

Mrs. Miller was up and around her desk. She took a long look at me and then directed me to one of the small rooms in which she had a cot-size bed.

"How are you feeling now?"

My hiccuping had finally stopped, but that didn't help all that much.

"Nauseated," I said.

"Lie down. If you have the urge to regurgitate, use this," she said, putting a basin next to the bed. There wasn't any sympathy in her voice, just firmness. "Why do you do this?"

Instead of answering her, I closed my eyes. The question seemed to reverberate in my brain: Why do you do this? Why do you do any of these things, Teal? Who do you think you're hurting? Where is your appreciation for all the wonderful things you have and all the wonderful things we're doing for you? Blah blah, I thought. It was like a broken CD or like being locked into an echo chamber.

I felt my stomach settle down, and moments later, I was asleep.

"What have you done?" I heard someone shout through the walls of my pleasant cocoon. I groaned, opened my eyes reluctantly, and looked up at my mother.

I never fully appreciate how tall she is, I thought, or how bony her shoulders are, even through her stylish designer suit. My father accused her of being anorexic, but somewhere, at one of her spas, no doubt, someone told her if she stayed thin, she would never look old. To me, just the contrary was happening. She was in her late forties, but looked ten years older. Her skin seemed so taut over those high cheekbones she prized, and the effect of that was to emphasize her jawbone. In dim lighting, with just a glow on her face, she looked like a skeleton. I told her that once, and she nearly took off my head with a sharp slap. Despite the miles and miles of skin creams she had available on her vanity table, her hands were never soft to me. I couldn't remember them ever being soft, and of course, she had perfect nails always. She once missed an important gynecological exam because it conflicted with her manicure.

"Well?" she demanded. She swung her purse toward me in an aborted move to club me into attention. It hovered over my face a moment, and then she brought it back toward her.

I scrubbed my cheeks with my palms and, unfortunately, burped.

She stepped back as if I was truly going to explode.

"You're disgusting," she said, pulling the corners of her mouth down.

I sat up.

"Is it morning already?" I teased.

My mother's eyes were truly her best feature. They were normally big, luscious-looking hazel-green, with naturally long eyelashes. She could widen them to almost twice their size when she wanted to show her rage or surprise. For a moment she looked all eyes to me, like some sort of extraterrestrial creature.

"You're not funny, Teal. Do you know how much your father is spending to have you attend school here?" she asked.

I always thought it was odd how she referred to any expenditures the family had as purely my father's. She was obviously not one of those wives who believe half of everything their husbands own belongs to them. Sometimes, she gave me the feeling that she was as much a tenant in the home as my older brother, Carson, had been, and I still was.

"I forgot, Mother," I said.

"Fifty thousand dollars," she said, tapping her foot after each word for emphasis. To me she looked like she was keeping beat to music. "If we add that to all the money he's spent on psychotherapy, tutors, fixing the things you've broken, paying off people who have lodged complaints against you, and everything else I can't think of, he's spent as much as some third world countries spend over a year!"

"Maybe he should ask the UN for help, then," I said.

"Get up," she snapped. "You've embarrassed me again and again. Don't you have any concern for this family and its reputation? Oh, what have I done to deserve this?" she asked the ceiling.

"Forgot your birth control pills sixteen years ago?" I offered.

She turned a shade darker than blood red and looked out toward Mrs. Miller's desk. In front of other people, my mother was always stylish, elegant, and able to manage her rage. She rarely, if ever, had a strand of hair out of place, and when I was little, I used to believe that creases were terrified of forming in her clothing. She would have them ironed to oblivion.

"I suppose this is really all my fault," she said, not really sounding like she was taking the blame, "for having you so late in life."

I did actually agree with that diagnosis. My parents made me on a hot summer night after they had both had too much to drink. My father let that little detail out once when they were arguing over something stupid like how much of his money my mother spent on fresh flowers, especially in the winter. I happened to overhear it.

"Maybe I was just dying to be born, and there was nothing you could do about it," I offered dryly.

She pulled herself up, primping like a proud peacock. Then, as cool as a brain surgeon, she stepped out of the little comfort room and spoke to Mrs. Miller.

"Do you think she is in any sort of condition for a meeting with the principal?" she asked, hoping to hear no, of course.

Mrs. Miller rose and came to the room.

She grabbed my shoulders and turned me to her as I stood, and then she shook her head.

"What gets into you kids these days?" she asked.

"Aliens?" I responded. "Through our belly buttons, I think," I added.

Mrs. Miller nearly smiled.

"She's fine, Mrs. Sommers. She'll probably have a good headache all day. Give her some Advil at home."

"I think it would be better if she suffered all day and appreciated the damage she is doing to herself," my sweet, loving mother replied.

Mrs. Miller looked like she agreed.

"Come along, Teal," Mother said, and I started out.

"Your books," Mrs. Miller reminded me. "Mrs. Tagler brought them in after you arrived."

"Oh. Sorry," I said. I really meant sorry she had brought them in, but Mrs. Miller smiled and handed them to me.

I continued after Mother, who tapped the corridor floor tiles with the sharp heels of her shoes like some drum roll as she reluctantly led me back to the principal's office to be executed in red ink. I remained a good yard or so behind her, imagining an invisible rope tied to my neck, which was used to tug me through life itself.

"How is she doing?" Mrs. Tagler asked my mother when we entered.

"Rather badly, I would say, wouldn't you?" Mother replied, her lips slicing a thin red line in her face. I always thought that for an expert on cosmetics, Mother wore her lipstick too thick.

Mrs. Tagler rose without speaking and went into the principal's office. Mother turned to me, shaking her head.

"I was on my way to have lunch with Carson," she said. My brother, who was nearly fifteen years older than me, was already running the business affairs division of my father's real estate development company. He had his own townhouse and was practically engaged to the daughter of a wealthy banker.

Carson was everything they would want me to be, I thought. He is Mr. Briefcase, a suit and a tie with a perfectly designed manikin within, Mr. Perfect who uses a Waterpik after every meal. I called him my father's second shadow, especially when it came to business.

Our father specialized in malls and entertainment centers, and it had made him—us—very wealthy, millionaires a few times over. At the end of the fiscal year, Carson liked to break it down to how many dollars were made per minute. I suppose in my case it was how many dollars were wasted every minute.

We lived in a full-blown estate house with nearly twelve acres, an Olympic-size swimming pool, and a clay tennis court, which only Carson used occasionally. The property was walled in and gated.

"I'm sorry I spoiled your day," I told my mother.

When Mr. Croft asked for examples of understatement once, I raised my hand and said, "My mother favors my brother over me." *Worships* would have been more like it.

"My day?" She laughed. "It's more than one day you've spoiled, Teal," she added.

I looked up at her sharply and felt tears trying to introduce themselves to my eyes. Only my own ever-present boil of rage kept that from happening.

The principal's door opened before I could say anything, and we were ushered in. Mr. Bloomberg did not get up when we entered, and I could see that bothered my mother. He was trying to make a point, however. The point was, this was definitely *not* a social occasion.

"Please have a seat," he said, nodding at the chairs Mrs. Tagler must have just placed directly in front of his marble-topped, immaculate-looking desk. Everything was so neatly organized, I felt like wiping my hands through the piles of papers and files before sitting and knocking them all about. Of course, I didn't.

"I am sure you realize, Mrs. Sommers, that this is Teal's fourth appearance before me generated by her misbehavior in three months."

"Yes, of course. I'm very, very upset about it, Mr. Bloomberg."

"We pride ourselves on how well run our classrooms are and how professional our staff is. To waste all that over this sort of thing is more than just a breach of our school rules; it's a veritable sin."

"Oh, I agree," Mother said. He could have said, "Let's hang her at dawn," and she would have nodded. As long as it didn't conflict with her hair appointment, of course.

"Alcoholic beverages, drugs of any kind, weapons of

any sort, all those are grounds for expulsion after only one incident, Mrs. Sommers, much less three or four. I have," he continued, reaching for a document on his desk, "asked Mrs. Tagler to retrieve your contract with us. Both you and Teal signed the document when she entered the school, you will recall. I have underlined the stipulation that if and when Teal should be asked to leave the school as a result of repeated misbehavior, you forfeit your tuition."

He handed it to Mother, who pretended to read it with interest and then handed it back to him, nodding.

He then sighed deeply and looked at me.

"Is there any possibility you will change your behavior, Teal?" he asked.

Mother turned and glared through me.

I shrugged. He knitted his thick, dark brows together and leaned forward.

"That's not quite the response I was looking for," he said.

My mouth felt so dry. That was all I could think about, and I was on the verge of asking for a drink of water. He turned to Mother.

"If she is sent to this office again for any reason, no matter how small the violation, we will have to ask her to leave the school. For now, she is suspended for three days. I hope you and your husband will impress upon her how serious this has become, Mrs. Sommers. We're not a public school. We don't have the time or the inclination to reform disrespectful young people. Anyone who attends this school should know the value of the education he or she will receive."

I wanted to put my fingers in my ears, but I didn't dare. Most of the time, actually, I wanted to put my fingers in my ears. I guess drinking booze was just another way to do it, especially at this school for penguins and canaries, I thought.

"I understand," Mother said. She glared at me. "We'll have a good talk."

He nodded, firming his lips and looking at me skeptically. Our eyes met, and he knew the clock was ticking on my expulsion. He could also see how little importance I was placing on it.

"Very well," Mr. Bloomberg said in a tone that clearly indicated the meeting had ended.

Mother rose, and I followed her out. Mrs. Tagler looked up at us as we passed through the outer office. She and my mother exchanged looks of sympathy as if I was more like a disease than a child.

"Your father is going to go ballistic over this, Teal," she said as we left the building and headed toward Mother's big Mercedes.

I knew what was coming. Mother had a set lecture. I really believed she had written it all down and memorized it. It always began with how much my father had done for me. The lecture started as soon as we were in the car and she was driving out of the school parking lot. She should have recorded it and put it on a CD she could just play, I thought.

"Look at what you have, Teal. A beautiful home. Your own suite, your own telephone and a computer, clothes that rival any princess's wardrobe, clothes you don't wear, I might add. Any toy you wanted as you grew up, you got. You have servants waiting on you, a car and driver to take you wherever you want to go, and if you behaved, you would have your own car. Why, why are you like this? What do you want?" she asked, a little more hysteria in her voice than usual.

I looked out the window.

What did I want?

Should I tell her? Could I ever tell her? How do you tell your own mother that what you want the most is simply to be loved?

2

Grounded

It wasn't a surprise to me that I often imagined myself locked in some echo chamber. My big house was filled with words that bounced around me, repetitions of threats, lectures, and ever-changing rules. In other homes, I suspected the walls lovingly absorbed the words spoken between mothers and daughters, fathers and daughters, brothers and sisters, but not in mine. The warmth in our home came from central heating, not from smiles and kisses, hugs and loving caresses.

A few years ago, I sat and thumbed through the pile of family albums we had in the den. I was more fascinated with my brother when he was younger and his relationship to my mother and father than I was with anyone else. One of my therapists once accused me of being a little paranoid about it. He was referring to the way I described my mother smiling at Carson or holding Carson's hand, or the way my father held him when he was a little boy, and the way they held me or looked at me when I was his age.

First, there were three times more pictures of Carson than there were of me. Mother's explanation for that was my father became more successful during my early years and was far busier than he had been when Carson was growing up. Therefore, there wasn't as much time to recreate. As he became more important in the business world, they moved up the social ladder, and Mother had the added burden of presenting him and herself to the substantial world, as she liked to call it. She became a social bird who primped her feathers and held court at dinners and balls, making sure her face was pasted on the society pages and in the slick community magazines. If I even approached what some might consider a complaint about how little we did together, I was told the sacrifices were all very important and good for the family, which of course included me, so I shouldn't feel I was neglected.

I had three nannies in my first ten years, two of whom, according to my father, demanded battle fatigue insurance. I suppose the worst thing I did before I was nine was knock over the perfumed candle in Mother's bedroom after she and my father had left for a dinner with the mayor. It was my misfortune or my intention, depending on who tells the story, that the candle remained burning. Its tiny flame managed to lick the sheer nightgown my mother had on a hanger by her closet door. That triggered a bigger fire, which spread into the walk-in closet.

We had a sprinkler system in the house. Naturally, we would, Daddy being a developer and up on everything that was possible and necessary. The flames set off the sprinkler, which then soaked Mother's wardrobe, ruining, she claimed, one hundred fifty thousand dollars' worth of clothing. My father actually fired the nanny I had at the time. I knew that if he could have, he would have fired me.

"You're finished here as my daughter," he would have said. "Get out. Go to some orphanage!"

I actually dreamed such a scene and woke up crying. Carson, who was twenty-five at the time and still living at home, was the only one to come to my bedroom to see what was going on. I told him I had a nightmare.

"My advice to you," he said, "is to stuff it back into the pillow. That's what Mother used to tell me to do when I had a bad dream, and it works."

It was something she had told him when he was only four or five, I was sure; but at least she had come to his room when he had cried. My tears made her nervous because she was older and more apt to get nervous, and making her nervous was forbidden because "nervousness leads to wrinkled brows and palpitating hearts."

"I didn't mean to start the fire," I said. Vaguely, I wondered if I did. It was during the period I was seeing a therapist and was told that sometimes we don't realize ourselves what we secretly want to do. Now I know he meant subconsciously, but I was too young to understand that, so he called it my secret self. He had me so convinced I had a secret self that I often paused quickly in front of a mirror to see if another me would be visible, perhaps caught unaware.

My brother Carson grunted after I protested my innocence. He has my mother's nose and mouth, my mother's eyes, but my father's bulky upper body and my father's dark brown hair. From the rear, especially from a distance or when there isn't much light, it's hard to distinguish who it is, Daddy or Carson.

"You know what Daddy says about apologies," he reminded me. "They are always too little too late and might as well not be uttered. Usually they serve only to remind the injured party he or she has been injured."

He stood there stiffly in the middle of the night and lectured me just the way our father would. I couldn't remember anyone speaking to me as an adult would speak to a child. We were all always adults in my house. Whether I liked it or not, I was never classified as an infant or an adolescent, or even a young adult.

"In my house we all take responsibility for our actions," my father preached. "You are told or shown what is right and what is wrong and you are in charge of your own behavior accordingly. No one can look after you better than you can yourself, and you shouldn't expect it or depend upon it."

Carson was the one who came up with the idea to keep a profit-and-loss statement in relation to me. Everything I broke, accidentally or not, every bit of damage that could be calculated, was placed on the loss side. Someday, I would do something to earn a living and then he would then calculate the assets and work out the profit and loss. Daddy thought he was so clever and even suggested he submit his idea to some business magazines.

I told Carson it made me feel good to know I provided some amusement to them. He either didn't understand or deliberately misunderstood my sarcasm. I suppose I always felt like an outsider, and they had always treated me as one. It shouldn't have come as such a surprise to my mother that I was nothing like her.

Especially now, during what she saw as my debutante years, she puzzled over why I was such a mystery to her. Why didn't I want the same things she always wanted? Why did I insist on wearing torn jeans instead of the expensive designer jeans she bought for me? Why did I put a ring in my nose and on my belly button occasionally? Why did I listen to that terrible music, and especially, why did I still want to hang out with friends who were, in her words, "beneath us"?

There was never any doubt in my mind that if I, as I was, were not her daughter, I would be beneath her as well. She never really looks at me, never sees me for who I am, I thought. Maybe she is afraid of what she helped create. Maybe my father has the same fear. I just remind them of their biggest mistake.

My father wasn't even there for my birth. He was away on a business trip. My mother accused him of deliberately scheduling it for that time. Finally, she got him to admit that he felt my being born was chiefly her responsibility.

"How come?" she asked.

"The woman," he said, "is the one primarily responsible for preventing pregnancy, not the man."

The way he described it, the man was an innocent bystander.

And so Mother was to be in charge of my upbringing. When I had all that trouble in public school, I overheard them arguing about it.

"I know what we agreed," she told him, "but I'm too old for this sort of thing, Henderson. She's rushing me into old age. The stress shows. You don't have the full brunt of it. You're off doing your projects."

He was quick to remind her that those "projects" paid for the big home, the expensive cars, expensive vacations, miles of clothes in her walk-in closet, on and on.

That was when she convinced him to spend the money to send me to this wonderful private school.

"We've got to get her away from this crowd of juvenile delinquents," she argued.

"It seems to me," he replied, "their parents probably want to get them away from her. Maybe we could ask them to contribute to the tuition. They'd gladly do it to get her away," he muttered.

Nevertheless, he relented and wrote the check to get me into the private school. Now, I was being sent home from that one, as well.

"Go directly up to your room and remain there until your father returns," my mother ordered when we had arrived. "And I don't want to hear that music blasting. Just sit and contemplate what you've done and what you've become," she advised.

I marched up the stairway. I was still feeling tired and bored and actually looked forward to getting back into bed. I fell asleep pretty quickly and awoke only when pangs of hunger made me dream about food.

Mother was gone again, so there were only myself and the two maids at home. It took one just to look after mother's things, clean her suite, and do her errands. I could hear the vacuum cleaners roaring away, sucking up every particle of dust. I sauntered into the kitchen and made myself a cheese and tomato sandwich. I didn't realize how hungry I was, which was probably a result of the alcohol I had drunk. I ate two sandwiches and a chocolate-covered frozen vanilla yogurt bar.

Usually, young girls envy their mothers for one reason or another. Most of my girlfriends at public school felt they weren't as pretty as their mothers. It was different at the private school. There, the snob birds I cared to talk to all had no problem with their egos. I don't have the same sort of bloated self-image, but I couldn't say I ever wanted to be just like my mother.

There are things about her I like, but we do seem so
different that I can understand someone wanting to
double-check my birth certificate to have proof she
gave birth to me.

For me the envy was reversed when it came to our
figures. Mother could never understand how I could eat
whatever I wanted, as much as I wanted, and not
become a blimp. She was always on one diet or another,
and she had a personal trainer. A new ounce of weight,
a wrinkle, something sagging, whatever, put her into a
panic. When I was very little and I walked with her, I
noticed how she would often pause to look at her reflec-
tion in a store window. She would never pass a mirror. I
first thought she was checking to see if anyone was following us. I'd turn to look back. It didn't take me long
to realize I was right. Mother was being chased by age.

Now I often caught her looking at me. If envy could
be translated into tears, she would be crying her eyes
out. The only satisfaction she had was in telling me that
if I didn't take better care of myself, I would regret it
someday.

"One day you'll wake up and see fat where there
wasn't any or that firm behind of yours will suddenly
turn into marshmallow, Teal. You've got to do preven-
tive things. You don't exercise like you should. You eat
everything I tell you not to eat. I should know," she concluded. "I had your figure and I discovered how hard it
was to maintain."

Sometimes, being spiteful, I would deliberately add
another scoop of ice cream to my dessert or gorge
myself on a bag of Kit Kat bars right in front of her. I
knew she was dying to eat one.

"Who bought that?" she would cry. "I distinctly left
orders not to buy that."

"I did," I said. "I love them."

She would practically flee from me, or from the desserts.

Go on. Run away. I'll never get like you, I vowed.

After my late lunch, I took my portable CD player and went for a walk. We had a telephone in the pool cabana, so I stopped there and called one of my so-called "beneath us" friends from public school, Shirley Number. I expected she would be home by now, and she was. I told her what I had done and what had happened to me. She thought it was funny, of course, and then went on to talk about some of the things she and the other girls I knew were doing. I really missed being with them.

"Do you see Del Grant?" I asked her. He was a senior I'd had a crush on since ninth grade.

"No," she said. "Don't you remember? Oh, I guess I didn't tell you," she added.

"What?"

"He dropped out of school when his father left them. You know what his mother is like, her drugs and all."

"Dropped out?"

"Yes, he works full-time at Diablo's Pizza in the mall. He says he has to help support his seven-year-old brother and five-year-old sister."

"Oh. Bummer," I said.

"He doesn't seem unhappy, but you know Del. You couldn't tell if he was unhappy anyway."

"Is he going with anyone?" I asked, and held my breath.

"Not that I know of. Selma Wisner has a mad crush on him and practically stalks him, but he doesn't seem terribly interested in her."

"I'll meet you at the mall this weekend," I said. "Saturday, okay?"

"Really? I thought you weren't allowed to hang out with us anymore."

"I'm not."

She laughed.

"Okay, we'll meet for lunch. Are they going to let you out on the weekend?" she asked.

"No, but that hasn't stopped me before," I said dryly.

She laughed again.

"I miss you," she squealed. "Everybody's so . . . everybody," she said. It brought a smile to my face.

"See you soon," I said, and hung up.

I walked some more, thinking mostly about Del Grant now. I suppose what I liked about him the most was that he was a loner. Probably because of his home situation, he avoided making friends with many people. He never had time to be in an extracurricular activity at school, and was absent so often, he barely got by. He kept to himself and wasn't very talkative in school, and whenever I saw him anywhere in the city, he smiled or nodded, but always looked like he was afraid to do much more.

Yet I never thought of him as shy. To me he looked like he knew more and was older than the other boys his age. I had the feeling he thought that the things that were important to them were childish or meaningless. He was clean and neat even though he was poor and didn't have much of a wardrobe, sometimes wearing the same thing for days. But he looked like he took care of what he had. Neal Sertner told me Del's mother cut his hair, when she wasn't drugged out on something or other. When he had it cut, he looked stylish. His mother worked on and off in a beauty parlor, but she had gone through so many, been fired from so many jobs, that people said she didn't only burn her bridges, she burned the roads to the bridges.

I liked Del's dark eyes, the way he tilted his head just slightly when he looked at someone, especially when he looked at me. I saw a strength in him I admired. He wasn't big by any means. He was just about five feet ten and about normal weight for his age. He didn't have big muscles or shoulders, but he looked tight, firm, hardened not by exercise but by life itself, and for me that added a note of maturity I respected.

His nose was perfect, and his lips weren't too thick or too thin. His jaw line was a bit sharp, perhaps, but he had a male model's cheekbones. He walked through the school not so much with confidence as with indifference. His eyes were always fixed straight ahead, and when he sat in the cafeteria or when I saw him sitting in a classroom, he stared down and looked up only when he had to, but he never appeared to be afraid of anything.

The other boys in the school simply kept clear of him. When he walked through a crowd, it was like Moses parting the sea. The other students would step back. They looked like they were afraid of touching him. They glanced at him and then quickly returned to their own conversations as if he wasn't really there. I loved the fact that Del didn't seem to care at all. Their indifference reinforced his.

We're alike, I thought. Someday he'll see that; he'll look at me a little longer, let me talk to him a little more, and he'll understand and he'll smile and he'll want to know me. That was my schoolgirl fantasy before I was abruptly ripped out of public school and sent to Snob Birdland. My biggest fear was that he would think I wanted to be there; he would think I was just some conceited little rich girl.

"Teal!" I heard Mother scream. "What are you doing

outside? Didn't I tell you to stay in your room? Your father is on the way home from work. Get yourself in that house and up those stairs," she ordered.

She had just pulled up in her Mercedes, stepped out, and saw me sauntering along the edge of our gardens. I saw she had a bag with the name of one of her favorite boutiques printed on the outside.

"I needed some air," I said.

"You're going to need more than some air," she fired back. "Get in that house."

I did what she said and went up to my room, where I flopped on my bed and, with my earphones still on, folded my arms and pouted, staring at the door. Soon my father would be opening it, and I had to prepare myself for that scene.

Daddy could be the most dramatic man. I think it came from his business negotiations. He was good at posturing, and no one I knew could fix his eyes on you and burn a hole through you as well as my father. It was probably that and his quick mind that had made him so successful in the business world. Carson had inherited his math abilities. It was like I was completely passed over when it came time to distributing his genetics, as far as mental capacity went. Maybe that was why he and I never got along. If I didn't resemble him in other ways, I would bet he would have accused my mother of infidelity. Even now he often had a look on his face that suggested he thought I was created with a mixture of sperm, his and some lover's my mother must have taken. What else could explain me?

The door opened slowly, and he was standing there staring in at me.

My father never hit me, never so much as raised his hand. I know there are many people who would say I am the way I am because of that. Ironically, Carson says he did spank him and once slapped him so hard, he made his head spin.

I didn't take off the earphones for a long moment. I knew that was only adding fuel to the fire, but I was trying to postpone the inevitable. Finally, I did.

"Drunk? At school?"

I didn't answer.

"I don't even want to hear an excuse. You're so clever with your excuses, Teal. You really should think seriously of becoming a defense attorney. But that would mean taking school seriously and trying to become something, do something with your life other than ruin and destroy and bring static and havoc into everyone else's life.

"I don't want you leaving this house until I say so, understand?"

"Don't leave the house? I don't have to go to school?" I asked.

"You know what I mean, Teal. Of course, you have to go to school, although I don't imagine you will last there much longer. When they kick you out, you will be in a far worse situation, believe me, so if there is any advice you should heed, it's this: don't get into any more trouble. I mean it, Teal. I have reached the end of my patience."

I started to put the earphones back on.

"Just a minute, young lady. Before you withdraw into your own world as usual . . ." he said, and marched across my room to my phone. He unplugged it. "No more private line, and you will not be permitted to make any phone calls on the family lines or my line, understand?"

"Smoke signals still okay?"

He stared at me and for the first time, I did see something more than just impatience and disappointment. His eyes weren't hot with anger. They were cold, deadly, fixed on me like a snake fixes on its prey. It actually put a shudder down my spine. I had to look away quickly.

"You're not going to go on bringing this family down, Teal. Your mother has given up, and I don't have the time or the inclination to baby you and try to convince you how you are wasting your life. Don't push me on this," he warned.

"I hate the school I'm in," I whined. "It's full of snobby girls and boys who act like they're all God's gift to women. I haven't a single real friend!"

"That's not why you're there. You're there to get an education, not to socialize. It's an opportunity other girls your age don't have, and you should make the most of it."

"I hate it," I insisted.

"You're there because you couldn't go to a public school without getting into trouble."

"I got in trouble here, too," I said, and he straightened up.

"Don't do it again, Teal." His eyes were clouding like a sky being prepared for a fierce thunderstorm.

"Now," he said in a softer tone, "I want you to spend your time thinking about your future, thinking about what you've done with your blessings. You and I will sit and talk about what you want to do with yourself."

"When?" I asked, looking up quickly. He had never offered to do that before.

"As soon as you show me I won't be wasting my time," he said.

"Oh."

"No 'oh.' I'll do it when you prove to me you're worth it, Teal. I want to see an improvement in your school work as well as your behavior. I don't want to see you giving your mother any more aggravation. If you show me you're mature and you can behave like an adult, I'll treat you like an adult and talk to you like an adult."

When will you treat me like your daughter? I wanted to reply, but I bit down on my lip and trapped the words in my mouth.

He walked to the doorway, carrying my phone, and then turned back.

"You're grounded now. You don't go anywhere but school and back, Teal. Do you understand?"

Instead of replying, I put my earphones on again and lowered myself to the pillow to stare up at the ceiling. I didn't know how much longer he stood there looking at me. All I knew was when I lifted my head some time later, he was gone and the door was closed.

I was just as alone as ever.

3

Drifting

My three-day suspension did not pass quickly. When you have so much time to spend by yourself with no responsibilities, the clock becomes arthritic, its hands creaking reluctantly along. One of our maids who also prepared our dinners used to tell me that a watched pot never boils. Every time I asked if dinner was ready, she would recite that. I suppose there was some truth to it. I found the more I looked at the clock, the slower it seemed to move.

Without any transportation, I really couldn't leave the house. I suppose I could have called for a taxi or snuck a ride in Mother's Lexus SUV when Mother wasn't around, but there was no place for me to go during the day anyway. All my real friends were in public school. Late the first day of my suspension, a taxicab did arrive, but that was because the driver had been hired to deliver my homework assignments. I could just see my brother Carson adding that cost to his profit-and-loss statement on me. I found out Mother had asked Mr. Bloomberg if I could be given the work so I didn't fall too far behind. I didn't know how to break the news to her that I was already far behind. My report card was sure to be in Christmas colors, with failures twinkling like holiday lights.

Out of boredom more than anything else, I diddled with the assignments, getting slightly interested in the history chapter on the American Civil War. Mr. Croft sent a pile of grammar exercises, more than he was giving the rest of the class, I felt sure. I knew he used homework as punishment or as a means of revenge.

On Friday, I was permitted to return to school. Even though the snob birds looked so self-satisfied about my punishment, I handed in the assignments and sat in class like a perfect little angel. There was a great temptation to chew off their feathers and wipe those gleeful smiles off their faces, but I was operating under the hope that if I didn't get in trouble right away, my father might grant me a reprieve.

At dinner that night, he cross-examined me on my day, and I tried to give him the answers I knew he would like. I had passed a science quiz with a seventy-eight and a history quiz with an eighty-two and showed them to him. He looked them over carefully, studying the grades to be sure I hadn't tampered with them. I had done that before, changing threes to eights and ones to nines.

"Well," he said, tapping the papers, "this is not terrific, but it is an improvement of sorts," he relented.

I threw Mother a mournful look.

"I'm trying," I declared. "The other kids have been

attending this school for years. They're used to everything," I moaned. "It isn't fair to judge me the same way. You've got to get used to new teachers, get used to the building, everything."

He looked like he was softening, so I continued.

"It's always harder when you attend a school or do something you've never done before. It was probably hard for you when you first went to college, wasn't it?"

"No," he practically bellowed back at me. "I had good study habits and I had a determined purpose," he said, continuing to hold on to his steel spine. "Challenges weren't challenges if they weren't hard. You can't be proud of yourself for hitting soft balls, Teal. If you want to survive in this world, you have to toughen up."

"Well, I'm trying," I whined.

"See that it continues," he said, glancing at Mother, whose neck muscles were straining. They always did when there was any sort of tension, especially at the dinner table.

I lowered my head and returned to my seat. Then I looked up as if I had just remembered something.

"Can I go to the mall tomorrow? I'd like to do some shopping," I said. "I need some things."

He continued to eat without replying.

"I'll come right back."

Still he was silent.

"I can't be locked up here like a prisoner!"

"Oh, let her go to the mall," my mother said, acting as if she was now having trouble breathing.

My father glared at me.

"I shouldn't let you out of here. You haven't done enough yet to make up for all the trouble you've caused your mother and me," he said. He paused, shaking his head. "It's a mistake, something I'll regret, I'm sure. Okay, but I want you back here before five, understand?"

"Yes," I said quickly before he changed his mind.

"I mean it, Teal. If you don't get back here by five on the dot, I'll have you locked in your room."

"I will!" I cried even though I had no intention of doing so. I would come up with some plausible excuse. Like he had said, I was good at it. "Can I use the SUV?"

It was the vehicle Mother was supposed to use when she went shopping, but she was still favoring the Mercedes sedan.

He put down his fork sharply.

"I'm glad you asked that. I had forgotten that I just received a serious warning from the police department concerning seven parking tickets I never knew you had gotten when you did use it."

I shook my head.

"I don't remember any parking tickets," I said. I did, of course. I had merely torn them up and thrown them away. My friends at public school thought that was funny. "You know," I added before he could speak, "I heard that for a joke some kids were taking parking tickets off the cars before the owners could find them. I'm sure we're not the only ones the police are giving serious warnings. Call your friends at the mayor's office if you don't believe me. You'll see I'm right," I said.

"You didn't do that, too, did you—take parking tickets off people's cars, Teal?" he asked, his eyes narrowing with suspicion.

"No, Daddy. That's really juvenile."

"I'm glad something is below you," he muttered. "Speeding tickets aren't, however, are they?"

"I haven't had one since . . ."

"And you better not have another, young lady, or driving my vehicles will become prohibited forever, understand?"

"Yes," I said.

He picked up his fork again.

"You can take a cab both ways. You don't need to take the car."

"But—"

"I want you back by five," he repeated sternly, which I knew meant the conversation was over.

"Okay," I said in a small voice. It was never good to argue too much with him.

"We do want so much to give you things, honey," Mommy said, reaching over to put her hand over mine. "We want you to be happy and to succeed in life, but you must improve your behavior."

"I know," I said, nearly whimpering. She patted my hand and smiled.

I could be so agreeable when I had to be. Inside, that second self my therapist used to talk about was laughing so hard, I thought she would break out and dance on the table.

"We have so much," Mother went on, "so much to give you if you will just be kind to yourself first."

I nodded.

"May I be excused?" I asked. "I want to soak in a bubble bath."

Mother smiled. Doing feminine things reinforced her lifestyle, validated it. If I could just be more like her and care about my hair, my skin, my fingernails and toenails, we could go off to the great beauty parlor in the sky together, mother and daughter choosing antioxidants and nail polish. Afterward, there was always lunch at the club with the ladies' auxiliary or some such charitable organization. What else could I possibly want out of life?

"Go on, go on," Daddy said, "but keep everything I've said here," he added, pointing to his temple.

Right, Daddy, I thought. I'll keep it there in your head, not mine.

Off I went, smiling to myself and thinking about Del Grant.

After my parents went to bed, I snuck out of my room and down to Daddy's office, where I called Shirley to determine a time and a place in the mall where we would meet.

"Why don't we just meet at Del's pizza parlor," she suggested, her voice full of giggles.

"Not a bad idea. That's what we'll do," I said, and hung up. I practically floated my way through the hall and up the stairs to my room, closing the door so softly, it was as if a breeze had passed through and nothing else. All the echoes, the lectures, and the threats were left outside.

Then I curled up in bed and dreamed the dreams I wanted.

I slept late and then, when I finally rose, I spent my time deciding what I should wear and how I should style my hair. Mother, passing by, was pleased I had put on the pair of designer jeans she had bought for me last month. They were hipster denim with a sash. They cost four hundred fifty dollars. If Mother hadn't seen the jeans advertised in *Vogue*, she would never have bought them for me. Normally, I wouldn't care, but I wanted to look outstanding and a little older so Del would notice me quickly. With my matching tight-fitting short-sleeved silk blouse, I thought I looked very sexy. I wore a bra because my father went into a small rage whenever I didn't, but as soon as I left the house, I would take it off.

I brushed my hair back and even put on a pair of earrings.

Someone else's mother might have questioned why her daughter was getting so dressed up just to go to a mall, but not mine. She would do the same thing just naturally. She wouldn't leave the house even to go to the post office unless she was prepared to have her picture taken for *Cosmopolitan* or some such magazine. As far as she was concerned, there was only one place where a woman should not have herself put together as perfectly as possible, and that was in her own bedroom. She shouldn't step out unless she was dressed well enough to meet the President of the United States.

I was only interested in meeting Del Grant.

Mother left the house before I did, and Daddy, of course, had long gone to his office. He worked six days a week, sometimes seven.

I started to call for a taxicab and then put the phone down and checked to see if the keys to the Lexus were where they usually were in Daddy's den. They were. I can be back before either of them return, I thought, and snatched them up. It would make more of an impression if Del saw me driving this.

Shirley was at the mall on time with Darcy Cohen, and Selma Wisner beside her.

"So how is life in the clouds?" Darcy asked immediately. She was a tall, thin redhead with patches of freckles on her cheeks and lips so orange, she never needed lipstick.

"I'd rather be in Philadelphia," I said.

"What?" Selma asked, grimacing like she had a toothache.

"That's something my father is always saying when he's unhappy. Someone named W. C. Fields had it written on his tombstone."

"In other words," Shirley told her, "Teal hates it."

"Oh. Well, why don't you just say you hate it?" Selma asked me.

"I did."

I looked through the window and saw Del preparing a pizza. He caught sight of me and paused. I smiled and he nodded. Darcy caught our exchange.

"You know they might take his brother and sister away from his mother," she said.

"Really? Why?"

"She's so drugged out most of the time, they don't even get fed," Darcy said. "His house is such a mess, even the rats are deserting it."

"I feel so sorry for Del," Selma moaned, looking at him. "It's ruining his life."

"I bet you feel sorry," Shirley told her, "so sorry you wished he would ruin yours."

"I do feel sorry, and not for those reasons!" she cried, but stole another quick glance at Del.

"Forget it," I said, pretending to have no interest. "What are you girls doing for fun these days besides painting your toenails and dreaming so hard of lovers you might get yourselves pregnant?"

Selma blanched and Darcy laughed.

"It's been very quiet since you left," she said. "Same old, same old."

"Why? What great things have you done at your precious private school where everyone is prim and proper?" Selma threw back at me.

"Actually, Teal was just suspended for being drunk in school," Shirley announced. The two looked at me.

"Really?" Darcy asked. "Suspended already?"

"Big deal," I said. "This place is so quiet," I added, looking around. I kept stealing glances at Del, who looked like he was stealing glances at me. "I tell you what. Let's play shoplifting."

"Oh, come on," Selma said.

"Scared?"

"No, it's just that we haven't done that since we were twelve, have we, Darcy?"

She shrugged.

I looked at my watch.

"Okay, here's the deal. In a half hour we return here and compare. Like always, whoever has the most expensive thing gets her every wish and command and the rest of us are her slaves for the remainder of the day."

"I hate this game," Selma said. She looked at Shirley and Darcy, who weren't agreeing with her, and then said, "Oh, all right."

"Go," I said, and they fanned out. I watched them for a moment, and then I went into the pizza parlor.

"Hey," Del said. "I thought you moved away or something."

"Something," I said, happy he had started the conversation. He laughed. "My parents forced me to attend this private school where everyone thinks she's better than anyone else."

"You don't have to go to a private school to meet people like that," he said, and returned to the pizza he was preparing.

"I heard you left school," I told him when he drew close again.

I didn't think he was going to respond. I stood there, waiting. He served another customer and then he returned to me.

"I left it years ago," he said, "only I was the only one who knew."

I smiled.

"Where are your friends?" he asked.

"Oh, doing my bidding as usual," I said. His smile widened.

"And what exactly is that?"

I told him our game, and he shook his head and walked off to serve some other customers.

He thinks I'm kidding, I thought. I decided to show him and hurried out. I went directly to Mazel's jewelry store because I had a good plan. Mother had bought a number of pieces there, including the bracelet I now wore on my wrist, and Mr. Mazel knew my father well. Everyone here did. Daddy had built the mall.

Mrs. Mazel was catering to a customer, and Mr. Mazel was in the rear working on repairing a watch.

"Oh, Teal," Mrs. Mazel said, "how are you?"

"I'm fine," I said, smiling. "I'm just thinking about what I'll buy my mother for her birthday this year."

"That's nice," she said, and called to her husband, who came out with a forced smile on his face.

"What can I do for you?" he asked.

"I'm just looking to see what would make a nice birthday present," I repeated.

He nodded and tightened his lips as he perused his own jewelry case.

"Bracelets are nice, especially with matching earrings," he suggested.

I looked into the case.

"Yes. Could I see a few?" I asked.

"Which?" he returned.

"This one, that one, and that one," I said, picking out three randomly.

They looked like they all weighed a ton as he put them on the counter.

"The ones you have chosen are expensive," he warned.

"Oh, and those earrings and those," I said, ignoring him and pointing.

He looked at his wife and then brought them out.

Another customer entered the store. I pretended to really be considering the bracelets, taking each and trying it on my own wrist, holding it up and studying it. To do so I removed the cheaper bracelet Mother had bought for me. When I had the opportunity, I put it in the box containing the one that most closely resembled it and kept the more expensive one on my wrist.

Mrs. Mazel had made her sale and was preparing to wrap the gift box. Mr. Mazel was very involved with his new customer now.

"Thank you," I called out to him. "I have a good idea. I'll talk it over with my father and be back."

"Okay," he said, now looking like he believed I would buy something.

"Thank you," I repeated at the door and left. I hurried back to the pizza parlor.

Darcy was waiting.

"How did you do?" she asked quickly.

"You'll see," I said. "Come on inside. Del wants to see what we've done. Where are the others?"

"There's Shirley," she said, and nodded to our left. She was hurrying along, a smile on her face.

"I'm going to win," she declared.

"We'll see," I said. "Come on inside."

We entered the pizza parlor. Del saw us and meandered over.

"You can be the judge of who has the most expensive thing," I told him. He squeezed his lips in the corners, still skeptical.

We all turned as Selma entered, her brow furled.

"I nearly got caught," she moaned. "I had to pretend I forgot and then I had to pay for this," she said, pulling a silk scarf out of a bag. "It took my whole allowance! Fifty dollars!"

"That beats me," Darcy said. She revealed a fountain pen. "This was only thirty-nine."

Shirley's smile went from ear to ear. I looked nervously at Del, who was shaking his head.

"Voilà!" Shirley said, and produced a PalmPilot from her jacket pocket. "Four hundred and ninety dollars. And it was on sale. It's worth a lot more. It's the newest model."

"Sorry," I said, raising my wrist slowly. Mouths dropped.

"How much was that?" Selma asked, breathlessly.

"Ten thousand dollars," I revealed as nonchalantly as I could while looking at Del.

"How did you do that?" he asked.

"I simply exchanged my cheaper one for this one in the box. There was a close enough resemblance so that Old Man Mazel won't notice until someone else looks at it. Maybe they'll buy it anyway and he won't lose a cent," I added.

They were all speechless.

"That's pretty serious shoplifting," Del said, impressed.

"It's not important," I said.

"It's beautiful," Shirley moaned, practically swooning.

"Big deal. It's just a bracelet," I said, and unfastened it. "Here. Consider it your birthday gift," I told her, and gave it to her.

She didn't move to take it. She looked from me to the other girls to Del and then at the bracelet.

"Really?"

"I'm not impressed by expensive things," I said, my eyes half on Del.

"I am!" she declared, and snatched it out of my hands.

"That doesn't matter," I said. "You've all still lost. Can I borrow a pen, Del?" I asked him.

"A pen, sure," he said, and handed me one.

I took a napkin and wrote a list of things I needed at the drugstore and at the department store, and a CD I wanted for the car.

"Here," I said. "Take this list and this money," I said, handing Shirley five twenties, "and get me these things. Bring them back here while I have a piece of pizza. And hurry," I ordered.

They left, Shirley practically hypnotized by the bracelet on her wrist.

Del laughed. He got me a piece of pizza, and I sat at the counter and picked at it. I really wasn't hungry.

"I guess you have them wrapped around your little finger," he said, standing back, his arms folded.

"I get bored, that's all," I said. I could see he was looking at me harder and with a lot more interest. "Don't you?"

"All the time. That's why I like to work. It keeps me from thinking."

"Sometimes I think I'm years older than all my friends. It takes so little to impress them."

He shook his head.

"That bracelet wasn't so little."

I shrugged.

"It was to me."

"I know a used car I could have bought with it."

"How do you get to work and home?" I asked.

"The bus and some walking," he said.

"I can take you home today. When are you off?"

"Oh, I have another four hours here yet," he said.

"No problem," I told him. "I have all the time in the world. I'm trying to avoid going home."

He smiled.

"You and me both," he said. He went back to work, and I thought he had forgotten what I offered. Later, after the girls had returned, he came over again and said, "Four-thirty."

"I'll be here," I told him, and left the parlor, the girls trailing along.

"What was that all about?" Selma asked.

"Nothing," I said. "I'm just giving him a ride home later. That's all."

"That's far from nothing!" she cried.

I stopped and looked at her.

"Never let a boy think anything is big or important to you. Always make them feel inadequate. That way, when you do show some appreciation or excitement, they will be so grateful. Your trouble, Selma," I added, "is you give it all away too easily and too quickly."

"Me! You just gave away a ten-thousand-dollar bracelet like it was bubble gum."

"That's all it is, Selma. It's just going to take you longer to find out than it took me," I said.

She stopped grimacing and looked at the others, who were looking at me.

Was I really so different after all?

Why, I wondered, do I feel like I'm drifting away from everyone, even the friends I thought I liked?

Where was I drifting to? Where was I going?

Pushing String Uphill

I left the girls a little after four o'clock and waited for Del outside the pizza parlor. He looked surprised I was still there when he was ready to leave.

"You really want to take me home?" he asked.

"Why not?"

"I don't live in the best of neighborhoods. I've seen your house from the outside."

"It's just a house," I said.

"A very big house."

"Forget about my house. Let's go," I said sharply. He pulled his head back as if I had slapped him, but he walked out of the mall with me, a small smile on his lips.

I paused outside the entrance and turned to him.

"I'm sorry I yelled at you. People think it's difficult being poor. Well, it can be difficult being rich, too. Everyone has so many expectations. You're supposed to act this way and do this and be this."

"So you're the original poor little rich girl, huh?" he said, not much moved to be sympathetic.

I glared at him, and then I started to laugh at myself.

"Okay, okay, forget it," I said, and led him to the SUV.

"Nice car. It looks brand-new," he said, getting in.

"It is. My father bought it for my mother to use for her daily errands, but she won't give up her Mercedes. She thinks it makes more of an impression when she pulls up to valet parking in a Mercedes and that's important, even when she's shopping at a department store."

He smiled and looked out the window.

"I always thought there was something about you that was different from the other girls at school," he said, still looking out the window. My heart began to thump harder and faster.

"What do you mean?"

He turned to look at me.

"You seemed . . . older, like you have had more experience, and I don't mean just the kinds of things rich people can do. I guess I'm not that good at explaining things," he concluded when I continued to look at him, keeping one eye on the road ahead. "Forget it," he tagged on, almost angrily.

"No, I like that. I know what you mean, too."

"Yeah? What do I mean?"

"You knew how much I hated being thought of as that poor little rich girl you just accused me of being."

He laughed.

"Maybe, but give me the chance to hate being rich," he said.

He followed that with more specific directions to his house. We drove into the city and to the very run-down neighborhoods. Many buildings looked like they had been condemned. They were obviously empty, their windows boarded or broken. Finally, in the midst of the garbage-laden empty lots, there was a small house with not much of a front lawn left, just some weeds and patches of wild grass. The driveway was broken and pitted. The house was a faded brown, with rust stains from the broken roof gutters streaking down the siding.

"Home sweet home," he said.

I pulled into the driveway. He sat there staring at the house's front windows.

"Looks like my mother's not home," he remarked, and then added, "Damn her."

He got out angrily, seemingly forgetting all about me. I shut the engine off and followed him.

"You oughta just go," he said at the door, waving behind himself as if he wanted to shoo me off. "Thanks."

"It's all right," I told him.

He hesitated, and then he opened the front door. I couldn't help grimacing at the smell. It was a combination of neglect, stale food, something that had burned in the stove, and cigarette smoke that was so embedded in the old, threadbare curtains and worn thin carpets and furniture, it would take a hurricane to wash it away.

There were toys scattered over the small entryway and hallway.

"Shawn," Del screamed. "Where are you?"

A thin, dark-haired seven-year-old boy with sad and frightened brown eyes appeared in the living room doorway. Evidence of a recently eaten chocolate donut was smeared about his lips. His shirt was out of his pants, his fly wide open.

"Where's Patty Girl?" Del asked him.

"In the bedroom playing with Cissy," Shawn replied. Del turned to me.

"Cissy is her imaginary friend," he explained. "Ma's not here?"

Shawn shook his head.

"Didn't I ask you to clean up the house, get all your toys and Patty Girl's back in your toy chests before I got home from work every day?"

Shawn nodded.

"Forgot," he said.

"Well, get going," Del ordered. "C'mon, or I won't be buyin' you anything more."

Shawn began to gather the toy cars and little soldiers.

"Gotta check on Patty Girl," Del muttered, and I followed him to the first bedroom on the right.

There we found his sister sitting on the floor, her overly bleached pink dress spread around her, her feet shoeless, and her light brown hair hanging limply down the sides of her pretty little face. She had Del's hazel green eyes and petite facial features. The moment she saw him she lit up, and when she saw me, she became intrigued.

"Patty Girl, did you leave your toy teacups on the living room floor again?"

"Cissy did," she said.

He swung his eyes at me.

"Well, didn't I tell you to be sure to tell her to clean up every day?"

"She doesn't listen good," Patty Girl said.

"If she doesn't listen, you can't have the toys to share with her anymore."

Her face quickly saddened.

"Go help your brother clean up the hall and the living room and I'll start making your dinner."

"Can Cissy and I set the table?" she asked quickly.

"If you clean up," he told her and she jumped to her feet enthusiastically.

"Say hello to Teal first," he ordered.

She looked at me.

"Hello," she said.

"Hi."

"Are you a baby-sitter?"

"No," I said, laughing.

"I don't need a baby-sitter. I have Cissy," she informed me, but mostly informed Del, and then hurried out of the room, carrying a limp rag doll in her arms.

I looked at the small bedroom Patty Girl shared with Shawn. The wallpaper was pealing. The windowsill looked caked with dust, the windows cloudy. There was a wooden floor with a rug between the two beds, each bed unmade. Clothing was strewn about, over chairs, over the dresser, and on the bed. I could see there were garments dangling awkwardly from hangers in the closet.

"You don't have to hang around," Del said. "Thanks for the ride."

"I don't mind," I said, and he looked at me as if I had gone crazy. "What are you making them for dinner?"

"They love macaroni and cheese, and it's no big deal to make."

"Where's your mother?"

"Your guess is as good as mine," he said. "She'll come home and tell me she was looking for a job and lost track of time or something like that."

He went into the kitchen, and for a moment, I had trouble swallowing. Dishes were piled up beside the sink, which was filled with pots. There was a garbage can with paper, wrappers, stained napkins spilling over the edges and on the floor. Used silverware was on the yellow Formica table, the forks and knives caked with old food. One of the chairs had been pulled near the cabinet, obviously to be used as a ladder by Shawn. The cabinet door was opened, and the box of chocolate donuts was on its side.

"She was supposed to clean this place up this morning," he said, shaking his head. "She probably won't even remember the promise."

He sighed deeply.

"Well, let's get to it," I told him, and rolled up my sleeves.

He turned with surprise as I began to work on the pots and pans. I smiled back at him.

"Maybe if she sees how nice it can be, she'll keep it that way," I said.

"Right. Tell me another fairy tale," he muttered, and went to the cabinet to get the macaroni and cheese.

Two hours later, I was still working on the kitchen. I had to improvise when it came to cleansers and soaps. They had very little in the pantry. While Del prepared dinner for his little brother and sister, I organized their dishes, cleaned the silverware and put it away, and did my best to wash down the broken linoleum floor. I cleaned the front of the refrigerator and the front of the stove as well, scrubbing out the stains with pure elbow grease. Then I went to work on the cabinets, organizing what they had.

I never thought about the time. I saw Del looking at the clock on the counter and realized he was waiting anxiously for his mother's return.

"She doesn't even remember what time I come home from work on days when I go in earlier," he muttered after Shawn and Patty Girl had eaten and were sitting and watching television. "She couldn't be sure I'd be back to take care of them, and she's still not here."

"Where is she, Del? Don't you have any idea at all?"

"She has these friends, barflies. I'm sure she's drunk or high on something somewhere. Someone will dump her off tonight. Usually it's not a pleasant sight, Teal, so I wouldn't hang around much longer if I were you. Besides, don't you have to get home?"

"I'll just call," I said, seeing it was already well after six-thirty. Dinner at our house was promptly at seven. It was Saturday night, and my parents were going somewhere for sure, but by now my father surely must know I'm not home, I thought. He would see my empty place at the table and he would look for the Lexus and as my mother often said, he would "go ballistic."

"Can't use that phone," he said, nodding at the one on the wall. "Our service was shut off three days ago. I didn't know she hadn't paid the bills for months."

"Oh. Don't worry. I have a cell phone in the car," I said.

"Just go home," he said despondently.

"What are you going to eat tonight?"

"I don't know. Eggs," he said sharply. "Who's hungry?"

"I'm hungry. Where's the nearest supermarket?"

"Go home, Teal."

"I'm all right. Really," I said. "Besides, it's Saturday night."

"Some Saturday night," he muttered.

"I know. I'll get us one of those ready-made chickens or something. Where's the nearest place?"

He told me and gave me directions.

"You sure you want to do this?"

"Absolutely."

"Slumming, is that it?"

"What do you think?" I fired back at him, my eyes just as hot and fixed on him as his were on mine. He softened and shrugged.

"I don't think much anymore," he said.

"So don't. Just relax. I'll be right back," I said.

I rushed out and followed the directions he had given. I thought about calling home, but then thought that if I did, my father would just insist I come right home. I was in trouble as it was, I concluded. Why worry now about how much more I'd be in by not calling and not returning?

Instead, I went to the supermarket and bought the chicken, some easy-to-make frozen vegetables, bread, and a big chocolate cake I was sure Shawn and Patty Girl would like. When I drove back and pulled into Del's driveway, I knew something was very wrong. The front door was still wide open, and I could hear the kids crying.

Slowly and now nervously, I carried the groceries to the house and hesitated at the door.

"Del?" I called.

"Get outta here," I heard. "Just go, Teal." His voice was full of hysteria.

I stood there, shuddering, my feet nailed to the concrete step.

"What's wrong?" I cried.

I heard a terrible groan. Maybe I should have turned and run. Maybe my whole life would have been different if I had, but I didn't. I entered the house and looking down the hallway into the kitchen, I saw a woman's feet and legs on the floor. I hurried down and looked at Del trying to lift his mother, who had obviously passed out.

Shawn and Patty Girl were in the corner, cowering and crying.

"What happened?" I gasped.

"She came home dead drunk and then passed out. She's done it before."

"I'll help you," I said, and put the bags of groceries on the kitchen table.

His mother was about five feet eight and stout so she was heavy to lift, especially as a dead weight. Her straggly brown hair was over her face. The blouse she wore was stained and missing buttons. Her breasts sagged beneath the flimsy material. We lifted her and together, practically dragging her, brought her to her bedroom, which, although larger than the bedroom Shawn and Patty Girl had, was almost as disheveled and dirty.

After we lowered her to her bed, she moaned. Her eyelids fluttered, her arm jerked up, and then she blew out her lips and went unconscious again.

"Shouldn't we get her to the hospital?"

"What for? They'd either laugh us out of there or commit her, which might not be a bad idea. Only then, they'd come and take the kids," he said. "She'll sleep it off and in the morning she won't remember any of it, believe me," he said with disgust. "C'mon."

We left the bedroom. I looked back. She did seem dead to the world. He closed the door and turned his attention to Shawn and Patty Girl.

"Stop crying!" he ordered. "She's just sleeping, just like you two have to be doing."

Shawn had his arm around Patty Girl, who clutched herself.

"Oh, Del, they're so scared."

"Tell me about it," he said.

I went to them and helped calm them down. Then he and I put them to bed.

"I've got a beautiful chocolate cake for you two," I told them. "Tomorrow, you can eat it, okay?"

Shawn nodded.

"And Cissy, too," Patty Girl said.

"Of course," I told her. She smiled and then turned over to close her eyes.

One moment they were in abject terror and the next, they were closing their eyes and hoping for a candy-cotton dream world.

Where were they drifting to? I wondered. We weren't all so unlike, despite the difference in wealth. However, there was no denying that this was a more serious case of neglect than any I could ascribe to myself. It made me think I should stop wallowing in my own self-pity.

Del sat at the kitchen table, his body slumping in defeat.

"I don't know how much longer I can keep this up," he said. "They've been coming around threatening to take Shawn and Patty Girl away. Maybe they would be better off. Maybe I should stop pushing string uphill, huh?"

"No, they need you," I told him.

He looked up at me, and then his face softened.

"Hey, thanks for all you did. You're tougher than I thought you were."

"What did you think I was?"

"A poor little rich girl being tortured with expensive clothes and private schools, forced to go on expensive vacations with her parents," he recited.

"You're exactly right, especially the tortured part."

He laughed and looked at the bags of groceries.

"You bought all this?"

"Yes, and I'm still hungry. Help me make dinner," I ordered. He saluted and we began. Somehow, despite the scene of horror we had just gone through, we had fun doing it, and I couldn't remember enjoying a meal more.

Afterward, he helped me clean up and then we sat in his living room and talked. He told me about his father and how he became so disgusted with his mother that he just upped and left them one day.

"I was only twelve when he did it the first time, but I remember thinking he was weak. He moaned and groaned about how she was killing him and how he couldn't stand it anymore. This last time, there was no doubt in my mind he wasn't coming back. 'Maybe after I leave and really stay away, she will see how serious it all has become and then she will straighten out,' he told me. He knew she wouldn't, but he didn't care. I hope he's just as unhappy wherever he is, and I hope it's hell."

What could I say? Could I tell him I often felt as alone? Looking around his home and seeing what he had to contend with, I couldn't imagine him understanding how someone who lived in what was practically a palace and had maids and servants and beautiful things could ever be discontented. In fact, suddenly, despite the warm time we had spent with each other, he glared at me angrily.

"So now you see how the other half lives," he muttered. "You can go home and be thankful."

"For your information, Del Grant, my life is not a bowl of cherries. My parents never wanted me and, despite themselves, can't keep it a secret. My mother and I have little in common, and my father favors my brother and treats me like a stepchild. I practically have to make an appointment to see him. The only thing that gets his attention is my getting into trouble."

"Is that why you do it?"

"Maybe. Maybe I'm just bored," I said.

He smiled.

"Okay. I'll pretend you're just as unlucky as I am," he said.

We stared at each other, and then we both broke into a laugh and he leaned over right in the middle of mine and planted a soft kiss on my lips. It took me completely by surprise, and I stopped laughing. His eyes were so close to mine, I thought we could look into each other's very souls. We kissed again, this time with his arms around my waist. It was a long, demanding kiss that seemed to reach into the center of my heart. A warm glow curled around me. When he lifted his lips, I brought mine back to them. After we parted, he stood up without speaking and took my hand so I would stand up.

We walked slowly to his bedroom. He didn't put on any lights. At the side of his bed, we kissed again and he began to undress me. I stood there like a princess who was dressed and undressed every day by her servant. I was totally nude before he undid a single button of his own. He lowered me to his bed and we lay side by side, kissing softly, his hands exploring my body, making it come alive and tingle until I thought I would go mad with my wet desire.

"Last chance to escape," he whispered.

"My last chance was out there in the living room," I told him, and he laughed and undressed.

Was it reckless to make love like that, to not think of any consequences?

Yes, but I wanted to be reckless. I think that not only surprised him, but frightened him a bit as well.

"Hey," he said. "You're not thinking about tomorrow."

"I thought it was tomorrow," I said with a smile.

He laughed, but he leaned over, opened a drawer, and prepared protection.

He came at me again and we made love and clung to each other just like the two drifting lost souls we were, finding safety only in our lovemaking, in the height of excitement we gave each other. Every cry of ecstasy, every explosion inside us reassured us we had a reason to be.

The darkness we lived in fell away like an old, rotted curtain and left us standing in the light, holding hands, waiting for that tomorrow full of promises to drown our disappointments.

Afterward, we fell asleep beside each other, his arm under my breasts, his face turned to me so that his breath warmed my neck.

I was unaware of how much time had spilled, but like milk, I didn't cry over it.

Of course, I was about to learn that I should have.

5

Brothers and Sisters

"It's two in the morning!" Del announced.

He had woken and turned on a lamp. The light blinded me for a few moments.

"What?"

"We fell asleep. I'm sorry. It's two in the morning. You're probably going to be in big trouble."

"I'm used to it," I said, sitting up and grinding the grogginess out of my eyes with balled fists. I looked about the room, trying to gather my wits. Then I smiled at him. "Hi," I said.

He laughed.

"You're crazy. C'mon. Get up and get dressed before the cavalry arrives."

"Don't worry about it. They would never do that. They couldn't stand the embarrassment of any bad publicity," I told him, but started to dress.

"You haven't done anything like this before, have

you? I mean, stay over a boy's house without their knowing?"

"No, I didn't stay, but I went to a party I shouldn't have gone to when I was in the ninth grade. It was a party for seniors and I got drunk. They found out I was with a senior boy that night, too."

"What happened?"

"I made love or let him. It was my first time, so I wasn't really in any sort of control. I think I was just trying to shock my mother. I even told her what I had done."

"You told her?"

I slipped my blouse over my head and pulled it down.

"Well, I came to her and I told her I thought I might be pregnant. She never paid more attention to me than she did those weeks. Almost every morning she was there to see if I had gotten my period."

"What happened?"

"She almost had a nervous breakdown, and she had me swear and promise that I would not tell my father anything. In the end she set up a secret appointment for me with her doctor and I had to confess I had gotten my period."

"You mean you had and you hadn't told her?"

"Like I said, as long as she was concerned, she was paying attention to me. She was so relieved when I told her. She didn't even care how I had been playing with her."

Del shook his head in disbelief.

"Most of the girls I have known would have done everything they could to keep such a thing from their mothers. They certainly wouldn't brag about being with an older boy and making love when they were only in the ninth grade."

He paused and thought a moment, nodding to himself.

"What?"

"You must really hate her," he said.

That made me pensive.

"I don't hate her," I said. "Just the opposite. I wish I had a mother."

"You and me both," Del said.

He walked me to the door, pausing at his mother's bedroom to listen. It was dead quiet.

"She'll sleep into the late morning and then tell me I'm lying about everything I said happened."

"I'm sorry about her," I said. I really meant I was sorry for him and his brother and sister. He nodded and followed me out to the car.

We kissed and I got in and started away. I was more than halfway home when I saw the police car behind me, its bubble light going. I checked my speedometer. I wasn't speeding. They pulled alongside and waved me off the highway. As soon as I stopped, I heard one of them through the loudspeaker on their vehicle.

"Get out of the vehicle with your hands up," he ordered.

"What?" I cried.

What was going on?

"Out of the vehicle now!"

Heart pounding, I stepped out and kept my hands up.

"Lie down on the road and put your arms straight up," I heard.

On the dirty road? I thought. I started to turn to argue when I saw one of the policemen was out of the vehicle and had his pistol drawn and pointed at me. I practically fainted. I went to my knees and then slowly did what they had asked. Moments later, I heard them beside me.

One took my left arm and brought it around behind me, then took my right arm and did the same. The handcuffs were locked on my wrists, and I was told to stand.

"What is this?" I cried.

"This car was reported stolen," the officer who had put the handcuffs on me said.

"No, it's my car. It's my family's car. I'm—"

"Move," he ordered, turning me toward their vehicle.

"I'm not lying. Check my purse. Check the registration," I pleaded.

Without responding, he opened the patrol car's rear door and guided me into it, closing the door. I watched them search the SUV, and then they returned and got in.

"I'm Teal Sommers. That's my family's car!" I screamed when neither of them made any attempt to let me free. "Didn't you look at my license?"

"Just relax," the driver said. "The car was reported stolen, and that's all we know."

He drove off. I looked back at the Lexus and then slumped in the seat.

What was going on?

At the police station, they brought me to the desk and had me booked as a car thief. I was placed in a cell, and no matter how much I protested, no one stopped or seemed to care. Finally, because I remembered from watching movies, I asked to make my one phone call and I was led to a phone.

I dialed home. It rang and rang. I was calling Daddy's direct line. He always picked up when that line rang, but instead, I got his answering machine.

"Daddy!" I screamed. "I've been arrested for stealing our own car. I'm in jail. Come and get me."

The policewoman hung up the phone and led me back to the cell where I sat waiting. Hours went by and

no one came. Finally, tired from screaming and protest-
ing, I sprawled out on the hard wooden bench and fell
asleep. I woke when I heard the door of the cell rattle.
The policeman said my father had come to get me.

"Finally," I moaned, and walked out.

"Just get in the car," Daddy said when I saw him at
the front desk. "Go out and get into the car. It's right in
front."

"Why didn't you come earlier? Why didn't you call
to tell them I didn't steal the car?" I asked.

He looked at the police dispatcher and then at me
and said, "But you did steal the car, Teal. I told you that
you couldn't have it and you took it. That's stealing.
You don't own that car. I do. Now you're known as a
car thief. Happy?" he asked. "Get in the car," he
ordered before I could respond.

I went out and got into his sedan. When he got in, he
said nothing until we had driven away from the police
station and I asked him why he had let this happen.

"You let it happen, Teal. I am not going to coddle you
any longer, young lady," he said "From now on, whatever
you do, you will pay the consequences that result, no
matter what those consequences are, understand?"

I didn't say anything. I turned away and pressed my
forehead to the window. Right now, I thought, I'd trade
places with Del in a heartbeat.

Mother was waiting in the hallway when we arrived.
She stood there with her arms crossed and her lips
pursed.

"Well, what do you think of yourself now?" she
asked as soon as I entered. Before I could respond, she
cried, "Look at yourself, your hair, your expensive
jeans. You're absolutely filthy. How could you want to
be seen in public like this?"

"She wasn't in public, Amanda," Daddy reminded her. "She was in a jail cell."

"Oh, dear me, dear me," she wailed. "Will it get out, Henderson? Will it be in the newspapers?"

"No, she's still a minor," he said, and looked at me. "I'm afraid she will be a minor for a long, long time, the way she is going."

"Well, we can be grateful for that, I suppose," my mother said, and sighed. "Go up to your room, Teal, and sit and contemplate what you have done and what you are becoming. I have to get to an important luncheon," she added. She made it sound as if, otherwise, she would sit and talk with me.

"Get upstairs, young lady," Daddy ordered. "Don't even think of leaving this house."

I walked up the stairs slowly and just collapsed on my bed. All I wanted to do was sleep, sleep forever. Hours later, I woke, groaned, and stretched. I did feel terribly dirty and decided to take a bath. How would I contact Del? I wondered after remembering his phone had been turned off. I had to let him know what had happened to me. I thought he was the one person who would have any sympathy.

After I had gone down to get something to eat, it occurred to me that Del would be at work. I flipped through the yellow pages and found the number for his pizza parlor in the mall and then called. He answered the phone.

"It's me," I said. "Can you talk?"

"Yeah, there's a lull."

"You won't believe what happened to me," I began, and described it all without taking a breath.

"Your own father had you arrested and left you there?"

"You heard it," I replied.

"Well, you weren't actually convicted of anything," he said, sounding like an attorney, "so he wasn't right that you're labeled now as a car thief. Besides, you're still a minor in the eyes of the law, so no one can hold what happened against you or use it as evidence in any other court proceeding."

"I'm not in the least bit concerned about any of that, Del."

"You should be," he said.

"How are things at your house?"

"My mother was still sleeping when I left the house. I made her some coffee. She sipped it and passed out again. I got the kids up and dressed and came to work," he recited, "just like I do almost every day. I hope she will get up and give them lunch at least. I can't call the house to check on it, thanks to her."

"We should both just run off," I suggested. I was more than half serious, and he heard it in my voice because he was silent for a long moment.

"I wish I could," he said. "I'd hate to think what would happen to Shawn and Patty Girl if I left them with dear old Mom."

"I shouldn't have given away that diamond bracelet yesterday. You could have pawned it and used the money."

"No, I wouldn't have taken it, Teal. My brother and sister and me are in trouble enough. I go to jail, and they go to foster homes in a heartbeat."

"It's not fair," I said.

"I stopped thinking about what's fair and what isn't a long time ago. I got to get back to work. We just got a crowd of teenagers, and they all look hungry."

"I'll try to see you later," I promised. I had no idea

how I would, but I felt I had to hold on to the hope.

"Good," he said, and hung up.

I sat in the kitchen, moping. I was still in a bit of a daze from the night before. I heard the vacuum cleaner go on in Daddy's office. The maid was permitted in there on Sundays only, which meant he wasn't home either. I was glad of that. I didn't want to have another lecture. Lately, that was the sole sum of all our one-sided conversations: sermons on behavior.

Moving like a sleepwalker, I went back upstairs and moped about my room. I had a pile of homework to do, but just starting it seemed like a monumental task. I flipped through some pages and then fell back on my bed and stared up at the ceiling. Prohibited from leaving the house, I felt just as trapped as I had the night before in the jail cell. I kept thinking about Del and our time together.

Suddenly, I heard the door slam downstairs and then heavy footsteps on the stairway. Moments later, there was a knock on my door.

"Who is it?" I called.

The door opened and Carson stepped in. He was wearing a sweater and sweat pants and looked like he had just come from his gym.

"Dad told me what you did last night and what happened," he began.

I sat up.

"He left me there all night."

"You're lucky he came to take you home at all," Carson said. "What is wrong with you, Teal? Why do you keep doing these things? What do you want?"

"I want to be left alone," I snapped back at him.

"You don't want to go to school? You don't want to achieve anything with your life? You just want to party, get drunk, screw around? What?" he shouted at me, his face red, his arms out.

For a moment Del's relationship to his siblings flashed across my mind. He was the older brother and he showed them so much love and affection. Carson and I rarely ever kissed each other, rarely held each other's hands, and rarely hugged each other, even on birthdays. He was so much older than I was in every way that it turned him into a stranger, not a brother. It wasn't hard to see that he really wasn't here this morning for me; he was here because he was upset for our father and mother.

"Just leave me alone," I said, falling back on the bed.

"Daddy thinks you might need some sort of military school, Teal."

"You mean prison, don't you?"

"The last step before it, yes," he said.

Out of the corner of my eye, I watched him wander over to the windows and stare out.

"I guess I should have done more with you," he said in a tone of voice that was softer than ever. It widened my eyes. "Your birth was quite a surprise."

"For me, too," I muttered. He nearly smiled when he turned to look at me.

"I used to resent you," he confessed. I looked up at him. "You came when I was a teenager, and for nearly fifteen years, I had been the center of all the attention."

"As it turned out, you had nothing to worry about, Carson. You still were and you still are," I fired back at him.

"That's not true, Teal."

"What do you know? You were out of this house by the time I was five."

"So that's why you're doing all these things? Just for spite?"

"I'm not doing anything. I needed the car yesterday and he wouldn't let me have it. He was doing that just for spite."

"You were sent home drunk from school! What was he supposed to do, reward you?"

"He loves punishing me. It helps him forget his mistake."

"What mistake?"

"Having me!"

"They're not sending you to the right therapist," Carson decided after a moment. "You do need real help."

"Right. You can go now, Carson. You did your duty. Go make your report to Daddy and tell him I haven't set the house on fire again."

He stared at me.

"I came to offer you help, Teal. I'm willing to listen to you and to give you advice."

"If you want to help me, tell him to stop punishing me so much and treating me like a common thief."

"Give him reason to have faith in you, and he will. You'll see," he promised.

I thought for a moment. There was a line I remembered from a story we had to read for English class. A grandmother told her granddaughter, "You can get more with honey than with vinegar."

"Thanks," I said, and looked up at him. "I really don't have anyone to talk to, Carson. Mother is so involved with her social events and Daddy's always so busy and you're hardly here. None of the friends I have at the new school are nice. They're all so snobby. They hold it against me because I was in public school all this time."

"Really? What creeps."

"Yes, I agree, so I don't try to make friends with them. I'm not happy in the private school. Maybe you can get Daddy to put me back in the public school. He'll save money."

"Um," Carson said, thinking.

"It's not any better. The teachers aren't so great. I heard they don't get paid as well, so the school doesn't get the best possible teachers."

"That's true. I attended a preparatory school, you'll remember, and that wasn't so terrific."

"You know, then."

"I'll talk with him," Carson said. "Obviously, some changes have to be made."

"Thank you, Carson. I feel so helpless sometimes."

He nodded. Honey was working, I thought.

"They took away my allowance. You know what it's like being around those snob birds and not having a cent in your pocket? They don't let me forget it. They flash their fifties and hundred-dollar bills in my face."

He grimaced.

"They do?"

"Oh, every chance they get. They don't buy things. They just carry it to show off or drive the cafeteria cashier crazy by handing her big bills. She doesn't have that sort of change, so their charges get put on a bill and sent to their parents anyway."

He nodded again. I felt like a fisherman pulling in a catch that nibbled, bit, and now was easing onto the hook.

"Can you imagine what it's like for me? And Daddy thinks I'm better off there."

"Okay, okay, I'll talk to him about it all."

"Could you do one more thing for me?"

"What?"

"Just loan me some money, just so I have it on me. I won't spend it," I said. "Daddy won't let me have any, but I dread returning to school tomorrow and looking like a pauper one more day."

He bit the inside of his cheek as he thought.

"It will be just between you and me, Carson. You and I have never had any brother-sister secrets between us. Can't we?"

"Okay," he said, "but you've got to promise not to spend it and not to let Daddy know what I've done, Teal."

"I swear," I said.

He reached into his back pocket and took out his wallet.

"If you have two fifties, it would be great," I said.

He hesitated, and then he gave them to me.

"This is an act of trust on my part, Teal. Don't disappoint me."

"I won't."

"And I want to see you work harder at school until we figure out what's best for you, okay?"

"Yes, I will," I said. "There's my homework waiting on the desk," I added, nodding at the books. "I'm getting right to it."

"Get your grades up. It will make it easier all around," he urged. "That way we can take another look at the situation after the midterm period. Any change would be easier. I know what it's like to be stuck somewhere you hate, believe me."

"Thank you, Carson. This is the first time I've really felt like you were my brother."

I got off the bed and stepped up to kiss him on the cheek. He turned a little red, but smiled.

"We'll get you on the right track," he said. "Dad will be glad we had this talk, too. I promised him I would try, and he was hoping it would help."

I smiled at him, and he went to the door. He stood there a moment and then suddenly smiled gleefully.

"What?" I asked.

"Since we're sharing secrets, I have one for you."

"You do?"

"I'm going to marry Ellery Taylor. I've bought an engagement ring and will be giving it to her this week, probably Wednesday," he said. "So, you will be a bridesmaid at a big wedding this June."

"Congratulations," I said. "I like Ellery."

I didn't. She always looked like she was constipated when she was around me, and she was such a good little audience for Mother, nodding and agreeing with every silly little pronouncement. I wanted to puke, and she saw it in my face and avoided me whenever she could. She would certainly hate the idea of my being one of her bridesmaids. She would be afraid I'd step on the train of her wedding dress or something. Maybe I would.

"I plan on telling Mother and Father on Sunday, so keep it locked up," Carson said.

"My lips are sealed," I told him.

The moment he left, I went downstairs to Daddy's den and called the pizza parlor. There was a great deal of noise in the background, so I knew Del couldn't stay on the phone long.

"I'm sending something over to you," I told him. "A surprise. It's for Shawn and Patty Girl."

"What is it?"

"It's a surprise. Just do what you have to with it," I told him.

After I hung up, I called Daddy's messenger service. Then I put the two fifties into an envelope and wrote "Del Grant" on the outside. The messenger arrived, and I gave him directions. By the time Daddy found out I had used his service, it would be too late anyway and I would have time to think of some excuse like I had to get homework from someone or something.

Then I went back to my room and started my homework.

Of course, I would do better in school, I thought. Honey gets more than vinegar.

6

A Life of Rainbows

Del was angry about the money and called me from
the mall before he left for home. Fortunately, Daddy
wasn't back from wherever he had gone on business so
I was able to take the phone call. I pleaded with Del to
keep the money.

"It's nothing, just pocket money for me. I'll waste it
on some new lipstick and such. Your brother and sister
have real needs and it will help you keep the dogs off,"
I reminded him. "If the social worker comes around and
sees they have what they need, they won't haunt you."

"I don't like charity," he insisted.

"Okay, so consider it a loan. When you're rich and
famous, you'll pay me back."

"Right, me rich and famous. That's a good laugh."

"I'll try to see you this week," I said. Then I heard
the front door open and told him I had to go. It was
Mother bursting in with all the latest social gossip. She

couldn't wait to get to her phone to pass it on. In her world, whoever knew something someone else didn't was the person to envy. She barely seemed to notice me and asked me nothing about how I had spent my day. I almost felt like telling her about Carson's impending engagement just to see the shock on her face that I knew something so socially important before she did, but I didn't want to lose Carson's trust.

I went back to my room and returned to my homework instead.

The next day I discovered that despite the lesson Daddy tried to teach me by having me arrested and kept in jail overnight, no one at school knew anything about it. Del certainly wasn't going to gossip, and I wasn't about to tell anyone, either.

All that week I did as well as I could at school. I was even nice to Mr. Croft and stayed after class to apologize to him for my previous behavior. I knew he liked things that were dramatic, so I concocted a new story.

"Not that it makes what I did right," I told him, "but I had a bad shock at home. A cousin of mine whom"—I made a point of using the correct form, practically humming the *m*—"I was very close to was killed in a terrible car accident. No one wants to talk about it."

"Oh, I'm sorry," he said. "How horrible."

"No, I'm sorry for what I did," I repeated, and assured him I would behave in his class from now on. Then, I asked him about a grammar problem I really did understand, but I let him review it quickly, pretending to grasp it finally because of his extra help, and thanked him.

Every day thereafter, he gave me a nice hello before class began. I could see the looks of confusion, even anger, on the faces of the snob birds, and I smiled to myself. I was actually beginning to enjoy being good. People, I discovered, wanted you not to be a problem so much that they were more trusting and gullible. My grades improved, and then, unbeknown to me, Mr. Bloomberg had all my teachers fill out a behavior report. It was sent home by the end of the week, and at dinner that night, Daddy surprised me by bringing it to the table and announcing what it was.

Mother held her breath as he took it out of the envelope and unfolded it.

Daddy put on his glasses and sat back.

"Apparently," he began, "every one of your teachers has indicated a significant improvement in your classroom decorum and your work ethic."

He lowered his glasses on the bridge of his nose and peered over them at me.

Mother released a deeply held sigh of dread.

"Also apparently, your experience in the real world, namely a jail cell, has awoken you to the potential consequences of your misbehavior. I say 'apparently' because I've been disappointed in you many, many times before, Teal."

"Well, if all of her teachers have only good things to say," Mother interjected, "then certainly . . ."

Daddy held up his hand and she caught her next words in her throat.

"I need to see consistency. I want to see a report like this every week from now on."

He folded the paper and put it back into the envelope.

"I understand, however, that you and your brother had a good heart-to-heart talk about all this and about your future," he said.

"They did?" Mother asked, looking from me to him.

I could see it coming. "Why wasn't I told about that?"

"Carson volunteered the assignment. You'd have to speak to him," Daddy replied.

I winced at hearing my talk with my brother referred to as an assignment. Didn't anyone in this family do anything because they really felt like doing it? Was everything a responsibility, an obligation? Was it the same for all families or just mine?

"Well," she said. "He didn't mention it to me when I saw him today. I'm just surprised, that's all."

"To return to my point," Daddy said clearly, showing he didn't like to be interrupted, "you complained about the private school and apparently won over your brother's support."

"She did? He did?"

"Amanda, please. I don't know if you realize the opportunities and advantages you have attending this school, Teal. Your classes are smaller, aren't they?"

"Some are," I said.

"As you can see from this report, your teachers give you more individualized attention," he added, waving the envelope. "And more to the point, your behavior and achievement at public school have been deplorable. There is nothing I would like more than saving money. I would love you to be able to attend public school and be successful, but you haven't been able to do that, and I can see you'll be watched over more closely here. However," he concluded, unfolding his napkin to indicate the conversation was ending and we were to concentrate on eating, "should you have a successful year and still wish to return to a public school, we'll discuss it. And," he added before I could protest, "you can thank your brother that you even have that. There are other places, not so pleasant, I was beginning to envision you in, Teal. Just continue to watch your step, young lady."

He turned to the maid, and she began to serve dinner. Mother, still upset about being out of the news loop, pouted.

"I just don't understand it," she said, "I just don't. Carson never keeps anything from me. We've always been so close. As close as any mother could be with any child," she added.

I couldn't help the tears that burned under my eyelids. We've never been close, I thought. And then it came. It just burst out of me, riding atop a magic carpet of pain and rage. I couldn't help it.

"He told me he's giving Ellery an engagement ring. Supposedly he gave it to her this past Wednesday," I said, sounding nonchalant about it.

Mother's mouth dropped open so wide, her yet to be chewed pieces of lettuce and tomatoes dripped over her lower lip. Daddy glanced at me, and I knew immediately that he had known. Carson had confided in him, and what he had told me was to be our special secret, our first brother-sister secret, was really not any such thing. It made me feel better about betraying him. I would have an answer when he learned about it.

"A formal engagement? A ring?" She turned to Daddy. "Did you know about this, Henderson?"

He shook his head and went back to his salad.

"First I've heard," he said, but anyone objective who heard him say it would know he was lying. Mother, of course, chose to believe him. She turned back to me.

"What did he say exactly?"

"I don't remember his exact words," I replied.

"Well, not exactly then. What?"

"He just said he was giving her a ring and would tell

you at the end of this weekend. Oh," I said, making it sound like a small added detail, "and they would be married in June."

"June!" She threw down her fork. "There's not enough time between now and June to do a decent wedding."

"Maybe they'll elope," I offered, and she opened and closed her mouth.

"They will not. They most certainly will not. Henderson?"

He shrugged.

"I don't expect they would," he said. I was sure he already knew every detail of Carson's plans.

"This is . . . astounding," she muttered. She had turned a bit white and looked like she was going to have a panic attack. "I've got to get right on the phone with Waverly Taylor." She started to rise.

"Amanda," Daddy snapped. "How can you do that? Maybe Carson hasn't even given Ellery the ring yet. You will have to wait and hear it from him. Sit down," he ordered.

Mother froze and then, as if her body had turned to pudding, poured back into her chair.

"But . . . this is a crisis, Henderson, a true social crisis. Do you know how hard it is to book the club for a wedding, or any decent hall, with such short notice? These things are planned nearly a year in advance, maybe two. You don't know about such things," she lectured him. "You're too busy in the business world. This is my world."

"Nevertheless," Daddy said calmly, "you'll have to wait to see if the event is indeed going to take place. Right now all you have is Teal's report of a conversation she had with Carson."

Mother thought a moment and then turned to me.

"You are telling us the truth, aren't you, Teal? I mean, this isn't one of your terrible lies, is it? Please, be honest," she pleaded.

"It's what I remember," I said practically under my breath, and started to eat. I glanced at Daddy, who was looking at me angrily again. He was sure to run off and tell Carson what I had done.

Mother lost her appetite. Then she said she had a terrible migraine headache and went up to her room. Daddy pounced on me the moment she left us.

"Why did you do that? Why did you tell her Carson's plans?"

"I didn't see how it would matter," I said.

"Of course you knew it would matter. You can be very mean, Teal."

"I'm not mean," I said, my tears now clouding my eyes. "It just came out."

"Your brother obviously meant to present it as a surprise to her. He was wrong to confide in you, and all that you have done tonight is reinforce the belief that you cannot be trusted. Trust is something that has to be earned, and frankly, I can't see how you will have that with anyone," he lectured.

"You hate me!" I screamed back at him.

"Lower your voice."

"You've always hated me, right from the time I was born."

"Don't be ridiculous."

"I'm not being ridiculous, Daddy. You know it's true and I know it's true."

"I don't hate you. How can I hate my own flesh and blood?" he challenged.

"You can. You don't even believe I am your own flesh and blood."

"What? That's enough. You're walking on the edge of a cliff, Teal." He pointed his right forefinger at me like the barrel of a pistol. "If I ever hear such nonsense from your mouth again, I'll . . ."

"Have me burned at the stake. I know," I snapped, and rose.

"You haven't been excused, young lady," he shouted after me. "Teal Sommers."

I kept walking and then charged up the stairway to my room and slammed the door shut. For a few moments I stood there listening. Would he come up after me? I heard nothing and relaxed.

About two hours later, I went downstairs again. I had left in the middle of my dinner and I was still hungry, so I headed for the kitchen to get myself a snack. Daddy was in his den watching television. It was rare that he sat with Mother and me and watched television. He had his own set and liked to watch shows he said we wouldn't appreciate. To ensure his privacy, he actually locked his den door. More often than not, the three of us were like strangers in a hotel, each of us off doing his or her own thing, meeting in hallways, mumbling good night or good morning.

I made myself a sandwich with some of the chicken that had been put away and ate it at the breakfast table. It was nearly nine-thirty now. Del would be getting off work at the pizza parlor in a little over a half hour, I thought. I had spoken to him almost every day, but we hadn't seen each other since I was at his house. He told me that someone from the social services department had made another visit to his house and given his mother another stern warning.

Why was it such a battle to have a family, to be a family? Why did people who should love each other hurt each other so much? All that week I had been fantasizing about us, imagining Del and me together with his little brother and sister, imagining us running off and living happily somewhere by ourselves. We didn't need parents. They didn't want us anyway. We're too much of a burden. We're in the way of their selfish happiness, I thought.

It wasn't really such a fantasy, I told myself. He and I are strong enough to work, to support ourselves and two little children. We could go someplace where no one knew us and where no one would interfere. I was sure that in time I could convince him to do this.

As I made my way back to my room, pouting and hating being under house arrest, I saw Mother had left her purse on the entryway table. She often did when she came home excited about something and anxious to get on the telephone with her girlfriends.

After being sure no one was around, I opened her purse and sifted through it. As I expected, there was money folded, crushed, and crumpled. I took it out slowly and unfolded the bills. I had nearly four hundred dollars in hand. I knew I was taking a very big chance, but I had to see Del. I had to begin to convince him that my fantasy could be a reality for us.

I hurried around to the French doors that opened from the sitting room to the patio on the west side of the house and slipped out, taking care to keep the doors from locking behind me, but making sure they looked locked. Then I ran as fast as I could down the driveway. About a half mile or so down our street, there was a gas station and a quick-stop store. I used the pay phone and called a taxi. Fifteen minutes later it arrived and I had it take me to the mall. I arrived just as Del was finishing his cleanup and closing down the ovens.

"Hey," he said, seeing me, "I thought you were home in chains."

"I was," I said, "but I broke out."

He laughed.

"I'll just be a few more minutes," he said, and I waited for him outside. Because so many of the stores were closed or closing, the mall was nearly empty, with just a few stragglers here and there. I saw none of my old friends, but I wasn't upset about that. I didn't want anything to distract me and Del.

"So," he said, coming out, "how did you manage this?"

"I just snuck out," I told him.

"Oh, no. They're not going to have the police looking for you again, are they?"

"They won't discover I'm gone. My mother is having a social and emotional crisis, and my father is locked in his den. They rarely come to my room when I close the door. I got a cab and came here, so my father can't call the police and claim one of his vehicles has been stolen."

Del shook his head.

"I've got to get home," he said. "I'm worried. My mother was acting weird this morning. I can catch the bus in a few minutes."

"We'll just take a cab. I have money," I told him, and showed him.

"Wow."

"I can get more, Del. We can save it up as I get it until we have enough," I told him as we walked out of the mall.

"Enough for what?"

"Enough to run off together. With Shawn and Patty Girl," I quickly added.

He stopped and looked at me, a small, incredulous smile on his lips.

"Run off? To where?"

"I don't know. We'll plan it out. We can go almost anywhere we want if we have enough money, can't we?"

"If your father went ahead and sent the police after you when you were gone a few hours, what do you think he'll do if you left like that?"

"I don't care. Once I'm gone, he won't care, either." Del shook his head.

"Here's a start," I said, showing him the money again. "I have nearly four hundred dollars here. Take it and hold it safe for us."

"I can't keep taking money from you, Teal. How are you getting it?"

"It's all around the house, like dust," I said. He stared at me. "My mother doesn't even know how much money she leaves about and doesn't worry about it in the least."

"It's still stealing, even if it's from your own mother, Teal, and if I take it, I'm an accessory to the crime."

"It's not a crime!" I insisted. "Oh, Del, don't you see? It's a real chance to be happy."

"You've been with me only once, and you're ready to spend your whole life with me and help me care for my brother and sister?"

"Yes," I said as firmly as I could. "And stop shaking your head. It's true, and it's a good idea."

He walked on, pensive.

"What did you buy Shawn and Patty Girl with the hundred dollars?" I asked.

"Clothes they needed."

"See? It was a good thing, then. Why shouldn't they have what they need? Why shouldn't all of us, you and me included?"

"I don't know," he said.

"Well, I do, Del. We should and we will."

He said nothing. We paused at the bus stop.

"We can take a taxicab," I reminded him.

"The bus is good enough."

"Don't be so afraid to use my money. You'll get home faster, Del. It's better that you get home faster, isn't it?"

He looked up the street. There was no sign of a bus yet, and the street looked desolate and dark. Then he turned back to me. I knew it was painful for him to say it, to admit it, but he did.

"Yes. It's better I get home faster."

I smiled.

"Good."

"But listen to me, Teal. You can't buy love. That's just something that happens on its own. It takes time sometimes."

"I'll wait," I said, smiling. "You're worth it. We're both worth it."

He shook his head again and then smiled.

"Okay, we'll see," he finally relented.

To me it was like being promised a life of rainbows.

We made our way to a taxi stand and left for his house. The moment we arrived, Del knew something was very wrong. The front door was wide open.

We paid the cab driver. Del hesitated after he got out.

"You should stay in the taxi and go right home," Del told me, his eyes fixed on the open door. "You don't want to get involved in anything now, not after all the trouble you got yourself in before."

"It's all right. Let me be sure you and the children are okay first."

Slowly, we both approached the front entrance. We heard some laughter and Del's shoulders relaxed.

"It's just her and her sick girlfriend LaShay Monroe. She's bad news," he told me. "She's connected to some Jamaican drug king and gets my mother smoking pot and doing other things," he revealed. Although he didn't go into detail, I could see from his face that the other things were better not mentioned in any detail.

We walked into the house and looked through the living room doorway. His mother and a tall, thin Jamaican woman were sprawled on the floor with their backs to the sofa. The room reeked of marijuana.

"What are you doing?" Del asked.

They both stopped laughing and looked up at us.

"Uh-oh, it's the voice of my conscience," his mother said, and they both laughed again.

"You're disgusting," Del spit at her. "Where's Shawn and Patty Girl?"

"They're sleeping. Stop being such a long face. You remind me of your father. Who are you?" she demanded, turning to me.

"None of your business," Del told her.

"She looks like someone's business, mon," LaShay said with a smirk, and Del's mother and she went into another fit of laughter.

"For your information, Ma, if you remembered half the stupid things you do, you would remember she helped me lift you off the floor and get you into bed the other night," he told her.

His mother stopped smiling.

"Watch your tongue, boy."

"Couldn't you at least close the front door? Does everyone walking by in this neighborhood hafta know what you are doing in here? You know that could bring more trouble down on us," he chastised.

How strange it was to see the son being more responsible than his mother, I thought.

"Who cares what this neighborhood thinks?"

"You'll care if they call social services," he said.

"See," she said to LaShay. "See what I put up with? Talk about ruining some expensive weed. Just like his father, he can mess up a good time."

LaShay nodded and glared back at us as if it was true that we were the bad ones.

Del shook his head and said, "You disgust me."

He went down to Shawn and Patty Girl's room. I followed, and when we looked in, we saw they were not asleep. They were together, holding each other.

"Hey," he said, moving in quickly. "What's the matter with you two?"

"Bad dream," Patty Girl said. "Screaming for Mommy, but she didn't come."

"Oh, the poor thing," I said.

"You have to go back into your own bed, Patty Girl, or neither of you will get any sleep. C'mon," he said, and tried to lift her away from Shawn, who just looked up at us wide-eyed and held on to his little sister for dear life.

Del turned to me.

"God knows what went on here before we arrived," he told me.

I knelt down and started to reassure Patty Girl.

"I'll stay with you until you fall asleep," I promised. That brought some hope into her little eyes. She loosened her grip on her brother, and Del got him to loosen his on her. I put her into her bed and sat beside her. "I have an older brother, too," I told her, "and he told me that when I have a bad dream, I should push it back into the pillow."

"How?" she asked.

"Just push your head hard into the pillow and then close your eyes and tell your bad dream to get out. Go on," I urged.

She looked at Del, and he nodded. Then she closed her eyes and pressed her head back.

"Say 'get out,' " I urged.

"Get out," she repeated.

"Good," I said. "Just a moment."

I took the pillow out and pretended to shake the dream onto the floor.

"There," I said. "It's gone. You can sleep now." I returned the pillow under her head and she smiled. "Close your eyes and try to sleep," I said.

Del and I sat in the room with his brother and sister and whispered to each other. Outside the door, we could hear his mother and her girlfriend LaShay continue to laugh and smoke.

"Maybe your idea about running off isn't so stupid after all," he said.

"It isn't. By doing what you've been doing, all you are accomplishing is keeping them in a bad situation, Del. I know you don't want to see them separated and sent off to foster homes."

He nodded.

"You're pretty good with her," he said, looking at Patty Girl, who was now asleep.

"I guess I just think about what I wish it had been like for me when I was her age," I said. "Maybe if I had a big sister like me . . ."

My voice and my wish drifted off like smoke.

He looked at his watch.

"You had better get home, Teal. It's getting late, and you could get into bigger trouble."

As quietly as we could, we slipped out of the bedroom. We paused in the hallway. His mother and LaShay had gone into her bedroom and were now talking very low.

"She's going to get her into something very bad," he predicted. "It's just a matter of time anyway."

"We can do something about this, Del. You'll see," I said.

He nodded and smiled hopefully. He looks desperate enough to believe in the tooth fairy tonight, I thought.

"It's not a fantasy," I assured him.

He walked me to where I could get a taxi home, and then we kissed good night.

"Thanks for helping with them," he said.

I felt so sorry for him, so sad when he closed the taxi door and we started away.

He stood there watching me drive off in the taxi and then put his hands in his pockets, lowered his head, and returned to a hell far worse than my own.

7

In a Reckless Mood

I was able to get back into my house and up into my room without being discovered. It reinforced my feeling that I could do anything I wanted if I was just careful and clever enough. I was so excited about the possibilities that loomed ahead for Del and me that it took me quite a while to fall asleep. I imagined us all heading west in my mother's SUV, looking forward like explorers out to discover new worlds, every experience fresh and promising. To live without rules and restrictions, curfews and punishments was truly to be free.

As usual on a weekend, I slept late into the morning. For a while when I was younger, my father tried to get me to rise earlier and take care of my personal chores, like make my bed and clean up my room, but Mommy never liked how I did it and was always afraid someone would look in and see.

"She's deliberately messy, Amanda, because she

knows you'll have the maids do everything if she is," Daddy told her, but it was less stressful for her to have the maids take care of my things than oversee the way I did it. They just had to wait for me to rise and go down to breakfast, and that was that.

Actually, what woke me this particular morning was the sound of Mommy crying. I could hear her sobbing below in the sitting room because the window was open and the window in my room was open. At first I thought it was a baby bird that might have fallen out of its nest.

Seeing and hearing my mother cry was not very unusual. She could shed tears over the smallest, silliest things, such as getting a luncheon invitation days after a friend had gotten hers, or having her name left out of an article on the society pages. What, I wondered, would she ever do if she had even a tenth of the problems Del had? So I didn't rush down to see what was wrong. I showered, dressed, and by the time I got downstairs, she was sitting quietly in the living room and just staring out the window, dabbing her eyes with a handkerchief and jerking her shoulders up like someone with the hiccups.

"What is it now, Mother?" I asked from the doorway, my voice heavy with disgust.

She turned slowly. Then she sighed deeply, so deeply someone might think her heart had cracked in two.

"I confronted your brother this morning," she said, holding her hand to the base of her throat. "He has indeed gone ahead and proposed to Ellery, but what is worse is, everything has already been decided: where the wedding will be held, colors of the gowns, favors, even the menu!"

"Well, that should make you happy, Mother. Why

are you crying? You don't have much to worry about now."

She paused and stared at me as if I had gone completely insane. Then she shook her head and looked out the window again. The sky was overcast and the day looked gloomy, which I was sure fitted her mood snugly.

"Leaving me out of what is the most important day in his mature life should make me happy?" she said. "I feel like my own son stabbed me in the back."

"Don't worry, Mother. I'll be sure to have you make all the arrangements for my wedding, especially the colors of the napkins," I said, and she spun around.

"This isn't funny, Teal. How do I face my friends when they ask about the wedding? Do you know the announcement has already been constructed and sent into the papers? To have accomplished all this so quickly, Waverly Taylor must have known this was coming for some time. My suspicion is your brother gave Ellery the engagement ring long before he even told you he was going to do it and certainly long before he planned on telling me."

That was a sour note for me. She was probably right, which meant I wasn't taken into his confidence to the extent I had thought. I was so desperate to believe my brother was finally treating me like his sister that I accepted it all without any doubt.

"I'm just sick over this, just sick," Mother said. "I have a good mind to just tell them to go ahead and plan the rehearsal dinner, too. That is supposed to be my— your father's and my responsibility. The worst thing about all this is, your father isn't a bit upset and probably wouldn't mind if I did tell them that."

"He's not upset because he knew it all," I blurted.

Her eyes went into that wide mode that revived my memories of ET.

"What are you saying, Teal? I was the only one in this family kept in the dark? Your brother told your father everything, told you, had his future in-laws involved, but left me out?"

My perfect brother Carson, I thought, really messed up. It brought a smile to my lips, which my mother misinterpreted as my being happy she was excluded. She bristled.

"Well?"

"I'm not an experienced detective, Mother," I said, "but the clues seem to point in that direction," I added, and sauntered off to breakfast. Perhaps I shouldn't have been so gleeful, but I couldn't help it. For once, Mother might be thinking I'm not the worse of her two children, even if that thought lasted only a few hours.

To her credit, my mother wasn't one to wallow in her self-pity all day. She got herself together and decided firmly that she would not be left out of any more decisions concerning the wedding. She got on the phone and called Waverly Taylor, insisting they meet for lunch. Whether it would be true or not, she was determined to give the appearance of having been involved in the wedding arrangements right from the start.

In fact, Mother was soon talking and acting as if nothing contrary had occurred. She was on the phone with her friends, discussing all the details about the wedding as if she had been in on it even before Ellery, much less her mother. This, she claimed, was the way she wanted it to be; this was happening because of her suggestions. Soon the talk, the plans, the excitement all served as a big distraction. No one noticed my comings and goings. More importantly, I was able to add to what

I now considered Del's and my escape money, pilfering periodically from Mother's purse.

So as not to create any more complications, I behaved like a little marionette in school and continued to improve in my studies, even to the extent that Mr. Bloomberg himself made it a point to stop me in the hallway one morning to tell me how happily surprised he was by my healthy new attitude.

"I never had any doubts you could do well, Teal," he said, "if you put your mind to it."

That remark almost shattered the mask of polite smiles I wore. Who did he think he was kidding? He probably had placed a bet on my impending expulsion.

I thanked him as politely and sickeningly sweetly as I could before I continued down the corridor. I was such a perfect young lady that I thought I would puke up my breakfast, lunch, and dinner.

The only one who was really upset with me these days was Carson, who cornered me in the house one night after he had a meeting with Daddy. I never had to try to avoid Carson. Usually he took little interest in me except to give me some warning or short lecture.

We hadn't spoken since the day he came to my bedroom and offered to help me, even giving me the money, which I gave immediately to Del.

"Just a minute, Teal," I heard after he had emerged from Daddy's office. I was halfway up the stairs. I paused and looked down at him. He stood there with his hands on his hips, shaking his head at me.

"You caused quite a mess for me, not keeping our secret," he began.

"Our secret?" I said, stepping down the stairs. "Our secret, Carson? You told Daddy long before you told me, didn't you? And you had already asked Ellery to marry you long before that, right?"

"I trusted you with the news," he countered.

"What news?" I shrugged. "Mother knows the Taylors knew before she did. She's putting on a good act now for her friends, but you and I know she was devastated, Carson, and for once it was you and not me who did the devastating."

"You're such a little bitch, Teal."

"Why, because I tell it like it is, because I'm honest?"

He choked back a laugh.

"You? Honest?" He stopped smiling. "Where's my hundred dollars?"

"I used it to buy bubble gum," I said, turned, and walked back up the stairs.

"You won't have any friends, Teal," he called after me. "When people can't trust you, they won't want you for a friend."

I didn't reply. I went into my room and shut the door. Maybe he was right. Maybe I would never have a real friend. Despite the brave front I put up and my toughness at times, I did fear that I had grown like a weed in a neglected garden. Even though I could claim it wasn't my fault, perhaps, I was still not a nice person, not someone anyone would want for a friend. When I was younger, I imagined my dolls weren't happy being with me. I didn't take especially good care of them, maybe because they were tossed my way like so much pablum designed to keep me quiet in my cage.

I would show all of them finally, especially Carson, I thought, sulking in my room. Del and I would do it. We would run off and leave them standing with their mouths wide open. I counted the additional money I had stolen. It was nearly fifteen hundred dollars. I knew it wasn't nearly enough, and that made me feel sick. How long could I keep up this goody-goody girl behavior? What a fool I had been to give Shirley the diamond bracelet, I thought. I had done it to impress Del, but now it would have come in handy. Maybe I could get her to give it back to me.

I went back downstairs and waited for an opportunity to use the phone. As soon as Daddy left the house, I went into his office and closed the door softly. The phone rang and rang, but no one picked up at Shirley's house. Frustrated, I left and found Mother getting herself ready to meet someone at the golf club. I asked her to drop me off at the mall, claiming I had to buy a new pair of running shoes for physical education class. I even got her to give me two hundred dollars.

"Don't spend it all at the mall," she told me. "Keep something for a taxi home and come right home, Teal, as soon as you buy the shoes. I don't need your father chastising me for letting you run loose."

"I'm not running loose, Mother. I'm doing some important errands."

"I know that, but your father keeps talking about waiting for the second shoe to drop, whatever that means. He makes me very nervous. Just keep being good, please. What I don't need now, with all these plans to work out for the wedding, are any complications."

"I thought everything had been decided about the wedding, Mother," I said.

She smiled gleefully.

"Waverly Taylor is really not equipped to handle such an important social event. I've had to make a number of changes already," she said proudly. "She simply doesn't understand what goes with what, what is the proper etiquette, and what people of quality expect at such an event. She has money but no class," Mother added.

"She's lucky to have you, then," I said.

She looked at me, deciding whether to believe me or not. I tried to appear as innocent and as sincere as I could, and she nodded.

"Yes, she is lucky," she concluded.

As soon as I arrived at the mall, I rushed to the pizza parlor to see Del. Luckily, he was on a break. His face brightened the moment he saw me.

"I was hoping you'd find a way here today," he said. "I've got some good news."

"What?"

I sat beside him quickly. Had he come up with some money, too? Had he found a way for us to leave sooner? We had spent so much time talking about it since I first introduced the possibility. We would lie side by side in his bed after making love and talk until it was late and I had to get home. Someone else might think we were romanticizing, but he or she wouldn't know how serious we were and how desperate we were. Desperate people do desperate things, Del told me, and I could see he had come to believe in us. It had given him new hope, and when he had hope, I had hope.

"My mother got a good job," he said, and I felt my body sink as if all my bones had turned to soft clay. That was what made him so happy?

"What do you mean? What job?"

"Hairdresser, and in a very good and busy salon, too. She's going to make some decent money. She's been clean for nearly a week now, no drugs, no booze. She's even given up smoking, realizing it's damaging her complexion."

"Oh," I said, not hiding my disappointment that well.

"And it all hasn't come a moment too soon, either. We had another visit from the social services department. When she was able to show she had gainful employment, they backed off. Maybe they'll leave us be now. Isn't that great?"

"Yes," I said, but not with as much enthusiasm as he would have liked, I know. "But hasn't she done this before, Del?"

"She has, but not with as much enthusiasm. Something woke her up. Maybe she saw something, someone go bad or something. I don't know. LaShay hasn't been around either, so that's a good sign. My constant nagging finally paid off. The kids are happier, too."

I nodded. In my closed fist, I had the money Mother had given me. Del looked at it.

"What's that?"

"What? Oh. Something more to add to our fund," I told him, and unfolded my hand to show him the four fifty-dollar bills. He stared at it.

"You have to quit doing this, Teal. It's going to become very serious and you'll get into big trouble. I can't take any more of your money," he said. "Absolutely cannot."

"Why not? I thought we had decided that—"

"Don't you see?" he cried, his face in a vivid grimace. "Now more than ever, I have to be very careful for my family, Teal. I have to continue to set an example for my mother to follow. I know it should be the other way around, but it's not, and that's just the way it is."

I closed my fist around the money and pulled my arm back.

"What about our plans?" I asked.

He shook his head and sipped his soda.

"I'm just trying to get by each day for now. Thinking about the future is a luxury."

"Not to me," I said sharply, and stood up. "I'm not going to hang around here forever. With or without you, I'm going to do something."

"Don't do anything stupid," he warned. "You've kept out of trouble this long. Don't mess up, Teal."

"Thanks," I said, and walked away. I heard him call after me, but I didn't turn around.

He's the one who's doing something stupid, I told myself. He'll see. He'll be sorry. I was his best chance and the best chance for his little brother and sister. He'll regret not taking the money, I muttered under my breath, but before I left the mall, my anger turned to sadness and depression. I felt my eyes well up with tears. Even though it was a bright day with the sky a deep, rich blue and the few clouds looking soft and cotton white, I felt a heavy dreariness.

Instead of going to a taxi stand, I just walked and walked. Every once in a while, I felt another tear trickling down my cheek and flicked it off. I wasn't even thinking about direction, so it surprised me to find myself on a street corner near a gas station, at least a good mile or so from the mall.

A young mechanic, his dark brown hair looking as greasy as his hands, bounced a tire on the garage floor and then rolled it over to the side. When he looked up, he saw me standing nearby. He smiled, wiped his hands on a rag, and brushed back the strands of hair that lay over his forehead. I should have just turned and walked away, but I was in a reckless mood. I smiled back, and he strutted out.

"What, ya lost?" he asked, looking around and seeing I hadn't driven up and wasn't with anyone.

"Maybe," I said, and he widened his smile.

In the bright sunlight, the skin on his cheeks looked like gauze because of tiny pock marks. He was dressed in faded gray overalls and was about six feet tall. He wasn't handsome by any means. His nose was too thick and his mouth too wide, but he had nice brown eyes that were fixed with interest on me. I smiled at how easy it was to capture and hold his attention.

"This your garage?" I asked him.

"Might as well be. It belongs to Benny Dodge, but he's away more than he's here. Where are you going?"

"Nowhere," I said.

"Well, you're there," he replied, and laughed. "Wanna soda?"

"Sure," I said, and followed him back into the garage. He took a can of Coke out of an ice chest, pulled the tab, and handed it to me.

I took a sip. With his mouth slightly open, he stood there watching me as if I was doing something very special.

"It's warmer than I thought," I said, and undid the top button on my blouse. His eyes traced every move I made.

"How old are you?" he asked.

"Why?"

He shrugged.

"I don't want nobody sayin' I corrupted a minor."

"By giving me a Coke? Some corruption. Is that all you have to offer?" I challenged, and he laughed harder.

"Wow." He shook his head. "What else did you have in mind?"

"I don't know," I said, and picked up the air hose. I pressed it and blew some dust around the floor. "What are you working on?"

"Rotating tires. Why? You wanna learn how to be a mechanic?" he teased.

I stared at him and drank some more of my Coke. His eyes went from side to side and he fidgeted nervously.

"Who are you?" he asked.

"Nobody," I replied.

"Nobody going nowhere?"

I dropped the air hose and walked closer to him.

"Thanks for the Coke," I said, and kissed him quickly on the lips.

His eyes nearly exploded.

"Since I'm nobody and this is nowhere, that didn't happen," I said. I smiled and started out, but he reached for my arm and seized me at the elbow.

"What are you, crazy?" he asked. He pulled me closer. "You're a tease."

"Let go," I said, but he held on and then he kissed me hard and moved his hands over my shoulders and down over my breasts. I squirmed until I broke loose.

He looked like he was going to come after me again, but a car pulled up to the pumps and he hesitated.

"Stick around," he pleaded. "I'd like to talk to you."

"Sure," I said. "I bet you'd like to just talk."

I left quickly, my heart pounding. What's wrong with you, Teal? I asked myself. That was like playing with matches. You want to start another fire, one that can't be put out with a sprinkler system?

I hated myself for being so self-destructive, so angry

that I would take it out on myself. Maybe I needed to go back to the therapist. Maybe I should be on some kind of medication. Before I knew it, I was crying. I felt the tears streaming down my cheeks as I thought about why lay ahead for me. At home it was all about Carson's wedding. My mother had some purpose. And Del was filling himself with hope and treating our plans and dreams like children's fantasies.

Why was it that I couldn't hold on to anything, care about anything?

My father is right about me, I thought. He's right to ignore me, to try to forget I exist. Maybe I could forget I exist.

I walked on and on. Cars whizzed by me, but I didn't care. At one point a driver leaned on his horn because I had stepped too far into the road, but I didn't move and he screamed something nasty at me as he went by. Finally, I reached a familiar shopping area and called myself a taxicab. It was getting very late in the afternoon, and I was sure Mother would be home by now and upset that I wasn't. She was probably on pins and needles, hoping I would get there before my father.

The moment the taxicab turned into the driveway, I wished I hadn't.

I wished I hadn't come home at all.

There was a police car parked in front of the house, and without knowing why, I knew that it had something to do with me. I got out of the cab slowly and paid him. For a long moment, I just stood there, dreading going into the house. I even contemplated turning around and running off.

But to where?

Del wouldn't want me, and as Carson said, I had no friends.

What difference did it make anyway? I thought. Even if I escaped from bad news here, it was sure to be waiting for me out there.

It was just part of who and what I was. Why that should be, I really didn't know. All I knew was, it was true. Curses float around us and attach themselves to someone, I thought. It could be as simple as that. Born lucky, born rich, born poor, born sickly, whatever, it was just the way it was and would always be. Fighting it was futile.

Surrender, Teal, I told myself.

Give up.

Be who you are.

8

A Disaster Heading for Disaster

Carson, Daddy, and two policemen turned to look my way the moment I opened the door and entered the house.

"There she is," Carson said, and shook his head.

Daddy stepped forward, the two policemen now on either side of him. One carried a clipboard. They all looked like they were poised to charge at me.

"What?" I cried, my hands out.

"Your mother," Daddy began, "actually fainted when she heard about all this. She's upstairs in the bedroom. I have called Doctor Stein, who wants me to bring her into the office to check her blood pressure." He paused, glanced at Carson, and then added in a louder voice, "She could have a stroke, Teal. That's how people get strokes."

"What did I do?" I wailed.

"Tell her," Daddy ordered the two policemen. The

taller and darker-haired man on his left stepped forward. He lifted the clipboard higher and peeled away the top page.

"Do you know a Shirley Number?" he asked.

"Of course she does," Daddy answered for me.

"Dad," Carson said softly. "Maybe you shouldn't have her say anything until you call Gerald Gladstone."

"I'm not wasting good money on any attorney," my father practically screamed.

Carson pulled his lips in and stepped back.

"I would like you to answer the questions," the policeman said. "Not your father. Well, do you know her?"

"Yes, I know Shirley. So what?" I snapped back at the policeman.

Daddy's face reddened until he resembled an overly ripe tomato. I thought he was the one who would get the stroke, not Mommy.

He pointed his right forefinger at me.

"I'd advise you to be contrite, Teal. Your only hope here is that people who don't know you will take pity on you," he said.

I looked away so the policemen wouldn't see the tears in my eyes. There was more love between Del and his estranged father who deserted the family than there was between me and my father, I thought. How many nights had he lain awake wishing my mother had gotten an abortion?

"Shirley Number had a diamond bracelet in her possession. What do you know about it?" the policeman asked. I could see from the look on his face that he already knew the answer.

So that was it. I felt the blood drain from my face. Shirley had given me up. Why couldn't she come up with a story? Say she had found it, anything? Some friend she was. She had obviously led the police to me. She didn't even qualify as a mere acquaintance.

When I glanced at Daddy, I saw that by the expression on my face and my silence, I was confirming whatever he had been told. He nodded as if he had expected no less.

"She knows everything about it, don't you, Teal?" he asked me.

I looked away again. Should I lie? Should I pretend I don't know anything? I could switch things around, maybe. I could put all the blame on Shirley. I could deny, deny, deny. Why should I do anything to protect her? I thought.

"Shirley Number's father contacted the police department and we questioned her. She claims you gave her the bracelet," the policeman continued. "She said you were all playing some sort of a shoplifting game, a contest to see who could steal the most expensive thing at the mall. Is that true?"

What didn't she leave out? What a coward, I thought.

"For God's sake, Teal, at least tell the truth when you have no other option," Daddy said, grimacing.

"Yes," I admitted. "It's true. It was just a game," I added to make it seem innocuous.

"Then you admit that you took the bracelet from Mazel's jewelry store?" the policeman continued, now sounding like a prosecutor.

I didn't respond. I had told him enough. Let him do some work, I thought. The policeman turned to Daddy.

"Once we heard the story, we went to see Mr. Mazel. He checked the bracelet case in question and discovered it wasn't the right bracelet that was in it. He recalled your daughter coming in to shop for a present. He said the bracelet she switched was less than half the value."

"You switched a bracelet? What bracelet was that, Teal?" Daddy asked me.

I folded my arms and stared at the floor.

"Well?" he shouted.

"The one Mommy bought me for my fifteenth birthday," I blurted.

Daddy's head was bobbing like the heads of those toy dogs people put in the rear of their cars.

"I knew it. Buy her expensive gifts. See what it gets you," he recited as if Mother was standing right there.

"Then you admit you switched bracelets?" the policeman asked me.

"Dad," Carson said, caution filling his voice.

"No, we're not protecting her, Carson. Let her pay the price," he told my brother.

I could see it in his face. My brother wasn't worrying about me so much as he was about the family name, especially now that he was engaged to the daughter of a well-respected and influential father. Newspaper headlines flashed across his eyes, filling them with shame.

"Yes," I screamed at the policeman. "I exchanged the bracelets! Are you all happy now?"

"We'll have to take her downtown," the policeman told my father. "This is a pretty serious crime. It might be considered a felony," he said, fixing his cold blue eyes on me.

He's just trying to scare me, I thought, but Carson looked like he was turning paler and paler every passing moment. Most of the time he tried to ignore that he even had me as his sister. Now, he might try to deny it. Maybe he would tell his friends I was really adopted.

"A felony?" he said under his breath.

"The bracelet sells for ten thousand dollars," the policeman told him. "It's a serious theft."

Daddy kept nodding as if he was enjoying the policeman's evaluation. The more he nodded, the tighter the knot became in my stomach. I felt the ache spreading up my chest. He looked so self-satisfied, as if he could predict my whole life and had predicted this scene in detail.

"Take her and do what you have to do," he told the police. He turned away as though he could no longer look at me.

I turned to Carson. He really looked sad for me now, the sadness overcoming any disgust.

"Come along," the policeman ordered.

The two of them stepped between me and my father and brother.

"I want to see Mommy first," I cried.

"She doesn't want to see you," Daddy muttered.

"No. I won't go until I see her," I insisted. She would make him help me.

"You're not seeing her, Teal. She's taken one of her tranquilizers and she is resting quietly," Daddy said. "I won't permit you to risk her health another moment."

"I thought you said you were going to take her to the doctor."

"Later. Right now, no one feels like stepping a foot out of this house," he added. "The disgrace is so thick we can feel it in the air."

He nodded at the policemen, and the one with the clipboard seized my elbow and physically turned me toward the door.

"Mommy!" I screamed at the stairway.

"Dad," Carson cried.

"Leave it be!" my father insisted.

I don't know why I was so surprised, so shocked at my father's attitude. After all, he was the one who had me picked up for stealing our car.

I was led out of the house and quickly down to the patrol car, where I was placed in the rear behind the cage, a place growing more and more familiar to me. The door slammed on me again, and moments later we were moving away from the house. I sank back in the seat, first cursing Shirley and then cursing myself for being so stupid as to trust someone like her.

When we arrived at the police station, the desk sergeant looked at me as though I was a career criminal.

"What happened, you missed your holding cell and just had to get back to it?" he asked through the right corner of his mouth. Then he grinned at the other policemen.

Once again I was put through the booking process and led back to the Spartan cell where there was now a woolen blanket on the bench. A man who looked like a homeless man was sleeping on the floor of a cell across the way. After I was locked in, I realized there was no point in asking for my one phone call this time. Who would I call who could help me? My father wouldn't let me speak with my mother.

I crawled over the bench, put my head on the folded blanket, and closed my eyes. Maybe, if I'm lucky, I thought, I'll fall into a permanent sleep like Rip Van Winkle or Sleeping Beauty and I won't wake up until Del decided I had been right and had come to kiss me and take me away just like the fairy-tale prince. And of course, we would live happily ever after.

I spent all night and half the following day there

before Carson came to get me. Daddy had sent him like some gofer to do some unpleasant chore.

"What's going to happen to me, Carson?" I asked. I was stiff from being so uncomfortable, and very tired.

"Lucky for you, Daddy calmed down enough to realize nothing would be gained for the family to have you convicted of a crime and sent to prison," he told me as we left the station. "He went over to see Mr. Mazel and got him to drop the charges."

"He did?"

"Yeah," Carson said, pausing at the car. "Do you know how he did?"

I shook my head.

"By buying the necklace. That's right, Teal, it cost him ten thousand dollars to fix the mess you created this time, ten thousand dollars! And Mother doesn't want to wear it. She says it will only remind her of the terrible thing you did."

"You going to add this to the profit-and-loss sheet you and Daddy are keeping on me?"

"Go on, be a smart aleck and see how much more it will get you now," he said, getting into the car.

For a moment I actually considered just turning and running off, even without a cent to my name. I'd be better off living in the streets, I thought.

"Get in, Teal. We have a lot to do yet," Carson ordered.

I got in and folded my arms around myself defiantly.

"He didn't pay the ten thousand for me," I said. "He did it for himself and for you, to keep things quiet."

"Same thing," Carson said, driving away from the police station. "We're a family."

"We're supposed to be a family. We're not a family, Carson, not by a long shot."

"Oh, boy. What are we going to hear now, the poor neglected me song?"

"No. You won't hear another word," I said, and pressed my lips shut.

He rattled on and on about the sacrifices our parents had made for both of us, especially me, describing the great efforts they had made and were making to find a way to get me to behave, be mature and responsible, and have a decent future. As I sat there and his words went in one ear and out the other, I thought how much like each other my mother, father, and brother sounded whenever any of them spoke to me. Never before did I feel it was me on one side and them on the other as much as I did this particular morning.

"Dad said you should remain in your room until he gets home today," Carson told me when we reached the house.

"What happened with Mommy?" I asked him.

"She went to the doctor and he put her on a new tranquilizer, but she had a meeting with Waverly Taylor and a wedding planner this morning and hasn't taken any of her medication yet."

"What a trooper," I muttered.

"You know what, Teal," Carson said, his eyes narrowed and dark, "I really don't think anything Dad does will make a difference with you. You're a disaster heading for disaster. It's just a matter of time, a matter of what you will do next to destroy yourself, and frankly, I'm not going to get myself sick over it."

"Like you ever did," I said, and got out, slamming the car door closed behind me.

He drove off before I reached the front door.

I watched his car disappear down the driveway. I've always felt like an only child, I thought. This just confirmed it. I wanted to be glad. I wanted to be defiant and hateful and not care, but the tears still came into my eyes. Why were Carson and I so different from each other? Was it just because I was born so much later? It was truly as though we had two different sets of parents. Why was he the lucky one? Why was he born first, born when they wanted a child more, when they had more time to give and to love?

It's so easy for Carson to look down at me from his mountaintop. He had been brought through all the valleys and over all the difficult terrain comfortably, with loving care, and gently placed in a seat of substantial success. I was still struggling to get a foothold, to hold on to anything that gave me even the semblance of meaning and self-worth. Was it really all my fault?

I went inside and up to my room. The experience of being arrested and held without the prospect of hope had been far more exhausting mentally and emotionally than I had imagined it would be this time. The moment I lay down, I was asleep. Hours later, I felt the bed shake and opened my eyes. Daddy was standing there staring down at me.

"Did you enjoy your second night in jail, Teal?"

I didn't answer. Instead, I turned away and stared out the window at the gray sky.

"Okay," he said, "this is how it will be until further notice. I've hired a driver who will take you to school in the morning and bring you home at the end of the day. He will take you nowhere else, so do not ask him to do so. You will come home, do your homework, have your dinner, and go directly to your room. You will speak to no one outside of this house, accept no invitations, even to go shopping, which to you means stealing anyway. You will be permitted to go with your mother to shop for the things you will need for Carson's wedding. Other than that, you will spend your weekends confined to this house and these grounds. You will invite no one here and accept no invitations."

"I would have been better off in jail," I moaned.

"Maybe I should have let you be tried and convicted and go to jail, Teal. Perhaps that would have been the only way you would know for sure that you would *not* be better off there. However, there are other people to consider here, other people who would be hurt more than you, in fact, and you can be thankful for that. Otherwise, believe me, I would not have hesitated to leave you there. Nothing else I've done or tried to do has had any success with you.

"Let me assure you," he continued, "that if you get into any more trouble at school, if your grades take a dive, this confinement will continue. Your therapist calls this tough love. As hard as it is for you to believe, it is tougher on your mother and me than it is on you. I try not to worry about her and about you at work, but it's not easy to do."

"Maybe I'll die and you'll be happy," I said.

"Self-pity won't work with me, Teal. Don't waste your time on tears and threats and moans. You'll behave yourself. One way or another, I'll make that happen."

He started for the door and then paused and turned back to me.

"The only thing going for you is the fact that you committed this disgusting deed before you were repairing yourself at school. I'm hoping that you did turn a corner and you will do a lot of soul-searching and continue on that track. If you do, we'll ease up on the restrictions. How you live and how you enjoy your life from this moment on is therefore solely up to you."

"It's always been up to me," I muttered under my breath. If he heard me, he didn't care to react. He stared a few moments more and then left, closing the door behind him.

To me it sounded like the door of the police cell, clanking and rattling.

When Mother came home, she looked at me as if I was someone suffering from a terminal illness. Her face was full of pity, her eyes gray with sorrow.

"Teal," she said, pronouncing my name like she would if she were standing over my grave, "Teal. I feel so sorry for you, so helpless. Forget about your father, your brother, and me for a moment. When you do bad things to people, do you ever think about the pain you cause them? Can you imagine how poor Mr. Mazel must have been suffering when he discovered his loss? His is a small, family-owned store. Do you ever think of such things?"

I didn't answer, but I knew the short answer was no. Whatever I did, I did on the spur of the moment. Consequences for myself and for the people involved never played on my thinking or my actions. I was truly like some hysterical person, flailing about, casting myself every which way, looking for some relief from my own unhappiness. The therapists at least got me to see and believe this.

But I didn't even know how to begin to explain that to my mother, so I continued to avoid her eyes. She sighed as deeply as ever and then added, "I guess I have to turn you over completely to your father, Teal. I can't interfere anymore. I can't plead for you anymore. I've failed you," she said, and then I looked up at her.

Oh, Mother, I thought, you don't know the half of it. You have no idea how long you have been failing me:

all my life. Maybe she saw that in my eyes, for she turned briskly and walked away, returning to her favorite topics, Carson's wedding and other social events.

Daddy wasn't kidding about the driver. Apparently, he hired a former gangster hit man, I thought, because the man, a stout, dark-haired man with beady eyes and a neck that looked like it belonged on a young bull, gazed at me with a no-nonsense expression that shouted, "Don't give me any grief." He didn't introduce himself or even say good morning. He just grunted at me and started the car. Daddy had at least told me his name was Tomkins, but I didn't know if that was his first or last name.

At the end of the day he was there standing by the car, looking like a secret service agent. I saw the curiosity on the faces of the other students. To be sure, there were some others who had cars and drivers taking them back and forth to the private school, but most, like me, had been forced to ride the bus.

As I approached the car that first day, Tomkins looked at his watch.

"You're ten minutes late," he chided.

"One of my teachers kept me to explain something. Sometimes, I have to stay after an hour or so for remedial work," I told him.

"This is the time I know to pick you up," he said firmly, tapping his watch. He looked like he could lunge at me and tear off my head. "If there are any changes to be made, it has to come from your father. Otherwise, I'm instructed to go in there and get you. One way or another, I will do that," he added, leaving little to my imagination. He opened the rear door and growled, "Get in."

I didn't know who I was more angry with at the moment: myself for getting into this situation, Del for backing away from our dream plan, or my father, who was like a prison warden. The ride home was dreary— no music, no conversation. When we arrived, Tomkins remained for a while to be sure I went into the house. I expected he would be out there, parked on the street, waiting to see if I would break my father's rule and try to leave the grounds.

I got my second shock after I changed my clothes and went downstairs to call Del at the pizza parlor to see how things were going for him. The phone on the kitchen wall was gone, and the phone in the sitting room was gone. Daddy's office-den door was locked. There wasn't a phone for me to use downstairs. I spun around in the hallway as if I had just gotten off a merry-go-round. I am truly in prison, I thought. It's even worse. It's solitary confinement.

Angry and even in something of a panic, I hurried down the corridor to the stairway and ran up. There were two phones in my parents' bedroom, but to my disappointment, I found that door locked as well. I rattled it angrily.

"You can't do this to me!" I screamed.

One of the maids downstairs called back to see if there was something wrong. I didn't answer her. I went into my bedroom and slammed the door. Daddy's strategy was to put the phones back when he returned at the end of the day. Mother was strictly forbidden to permit me to use their phones. I felt like I was being choked.

I will run away, I thought. I will.

The next day, I managed to talk Lisa Hardwick into letting me use her cell phone during lunch. Del had just arrived at work in the pizza parlor. I hurriedly told him all that had happened to me so that he wouldn't think I was avoiding him or had decided not to see or speak with him ever again.

"I had a feeling something like that might happen, Teal. You went too far when you took that bracelet, and it was stupid to give it to someone like Shirley."

"I know. I was just trying to impress you," I confessed.

That softened him.

"Yeah, well, just be yourself, Teal, the way you are with my little brother and sister. That's enough to impress me."

"I'm glad, Del. I miss them. I miss you. How are things?"

"My mother is still holding on to her job and doing well. I'm holding my breath, of course, but it looks good."

"I'm happy for you, Del."

"Don't do anything to get yourself in any more trouble," he said. "Maybe your father will ease up."

"I doubt it, Del, and I hate my driver. He's like a prison guard! You still want to see me, don't you?"

"Sure," he said.

I wanted to say so much more, but Lisa was standing over me, eager to get back her phone.

"I'll call you again. I'll figure something out."

"Whatever," he said. "Be careful," he added, and told me he had to get back to work.

I closed the phone and handed it to Lisa.

"Thanks," I said. "Could I use it again tomorrow?"

"It's expensive," she replied, grimacing through her braces.

"I'll give you ten dollars for five minutes, okay?"

She shrugged.

"Maybe," she said, enjoying her power over me and my desperation. "I'll see."

How I hated these snob birds and wished I could somehow pull out their feathers and keep them from flitting about, so contemptuous of everyone below them.

My day will come, I told myself. It will come.

9

Ten Thousand Dollars

I managed to steal twenty dollars from Mommy's purse that night. The next day at lunch, Lisa lorded it over me, practically making me beg her for her phone in front of the other girls. I swallowed my pride and did so. Finally, just before the bell was going to ring and make it impossible for me to use the phone, she relented and I gave her the ten dollars.

"Frozen custard for us after school today," she announced, waving my ten dollars like a flag, "on Teal Sommers."

The girls laughed.

I turned and called Del, but was disappointed to learn he wasn't at work.

"He's coming in at four today," the other counterman said, and hung up.

"That was an easy ten dollars," Ainsley Winslow

cried when Lisa took the phone back. The girls laughed again, all smiling gleefully.

I hurried away, never feeling more helpless. I won't let this go on, I vowed. I won't.

With my driver herding me into the car and watching my every move, and with the house locked up like a penal institution, I boiled over with frustration. I couldn't call Del and I couldn't leave school and go to see him. After I was brought home at the end of the school day, I thought about breaking the lock on Daddy's den-office door so I could get to his telephone and actually went down to the kitchen and got a butter knife out of the silverware drawer. What more could Daddy do to me anyway? I decided.

Just as I was at the door, however, I heard the front door open and Daddy and Carson speaking as they entered. Why were they here this early? Was Daddy coming to check on me?

Panicking, I retreated to the powder room across the way. I heard them laughing, and then I peeked out and saw Daddy unlock his door.

"What a pain in the rear this is," he told Carson, "locking and unlocking my own office in my house, but for a while, I have to be sure she doesn't disobey me. And there's no doubt in my mind that she would if she could."

"I know, Dad. I'm sorry," Carson said as if he bore some responsibility for my behavior.

They entered his office, leaving the door open. Maybe they would forget and leave it that way, I hoped, and waited, watching them and listening.

"It was easy for Broderick to pay us the retainer in cash," Daddy told Carson. "We're saving him a ton of money and he knows it."

I saw Daddy put a stack of bills on the desk, open his top desk drawer, take out a key, and then go to his wall safe and take out a metal cash box. Neatly, he put the money into the box.

"Ten thousand tax-free dollars!" Daddy declared. Carson laughed. "I hope you're learning how to handle some of these clients of mine," Daddy continued. "Someday, you'll be in charge of the company, son."

"You're not retiring for a long, long time, Dad," Carson told him, and Daddy smiled at him with such love and pride, I felt my heart ache. Paranoia or no paranoia, I thought, I never felt him look at me like that.

Daddy put the cash box back into his wall safe and put the key to the safe in his top drawer. Then they sat and began to talk about another project.

Boring, I thought, and slipped out and up the stairs. I'd wait to see if Daddy would leave and forget to lock the door. Hours later, Carson left, but Daddy didn't. I heard him come up and go to his bedroom. When I went down to check the office, the door was locked again. Disappointed, but too frightened to attempt anything with the butter knife now, I retreated to my bedroom.

Later, dinner was conducted in the usual fashion it was conducted these days: a cross-examination of my activities, my school work, and my behavior. Mother sat looking as if she was the one being questioned and prodded. She kept her eyes down, held her breath, and nibbled on her food like a squirrel.

"Remember," Daddy ended as he did every night since I had been arrested for the bracelet theft, "I hear that you so much as look at one of your teachers cross-eyed, and I'll tighten the walls around you even more."

What else could you do, lock me in a closet? I

wanted to fire back at him, but I didn't say a word.

Instead, I waited like some predator for an opportunity, which came when he went upstairs to change into more relaxing clothes. This time he had left the office door unlocked. I snuck away from Mommy, who was on the phone, and I slipped into the office, but I didn't call Del. I was too terrified Daddy might come down and find me in his office. Instead, I went to his window and undid the lock so it could be opened from the outside. Then I retreated to my room for the night, working on my homework, more to occupy myself and pass away the time than any interest I had in the material.

Close to eleven, Daddy came up to bed. I heard him go to his bedroom. Mommy was already there, after having given herself a foot treatment. I heard their muffled voices behind the closed door and as quietly as I could, tiptoed down the stairs and out the French doors in the sitting room.

It was a cool, overcast night, with just the ground lighting and some illumination from the house helping me to find my way around to Daddy's office. I worried that he had found the window unlocked and had locked it, but when I went to it and tried, it opened and I was able to climb into the room. I dared not put on the lights. Carefully, I picked up the phone and punched out the number of the pizza parlor. If Del had come in at four in the afternoon today, he would still be there to close up, I thought. It rang and rang until finally someone picked up and I asked for Del.

"Who?"

I was afraid to raise my voice too loudly, but I took a chance.

"Del Grant," I said.

"Del Grant?" I heard a voice I didn't recognize ask.

"Yes."

What other Del would be there? I wanted to snap at him.

"He couldn't come in today. He had problems," the man said.

"What kind of problems?"

"Family problems."

"What do you mean? Anything happen to his little brother or sister?"

"What do I look like, the Albany newspaper?" he griped, and hung up.

Couldn't come in? Family problems? What could have happened? How was I supposed to go back up to my room and sleep? The very thought of having to beg Lisa for use of her phone again tomorrow sickened me. I've had enough of this, I thought. I don't care what happens to me now.

I went back into the house and found the SUV keys where they always were. Daddy didn't hide them. He couldn't even imagine my taking that car again, I thought. He was so confident I was too afraid. Well, I was, but this was more important to me. I wasn't going to let my fear stop me.

Our house was so big and my parents' bedroom was at the far end in the rear, so there was little chance of their hearing the SUV being started. Nevertheless, I drove out very slowly and kept the headlights off until I was out of our driveway and had turned onto the road. Then I gunned the engine and drove as quickly as I could to Del's house.

All the lights were out when I arrived. It was late now, close to midnight, so I shouldn't have been surprised, but after hearing what the man at the pizza parlor had said, darkness frightened me. I wasn't sure what

I should do. What if it wasn't as serious a situation as
the man had made it sound? Wouldn't I cause more
trouble by appearing at Del's front door now? His
mother might become very angry, and I might be
responsible for bringing unpleasantness just when
things were going well for Del and his little brother and
sister.

I sat there, trying to decide, and finally concluded
that since I had come this far and taken this great a
chance, I had to do something. I couldn't just drive off
and forget about it. As quietly as I could, I got out and
approached the front door. Hopefully, Del will wake
first and come to the door, I thought, and tapped lightly.
No lights went on, and I didn't hear any sounds from
within. I knocked harder and waited. Still, no light went
on and no one came.

"Del!" I called. "It's me."

A dog began barking next door. I heard someone
scream, "Be quiet!"

Disappointed, I turned away and started back to the
car, but just before I reached it, a taxicab pulled up
behind it and Del stepped out of the rear, holding Patty
Girl in his arms. Shawn got out after him and immediately took hold of his jacket.

"What are you doing here?" he asked, the moment
he saw me.

"I called the pizza parlor and some man told me you
had family problems."

"You could say that," he remarked, and paid the taxi
driver.

"Hi, Shawn," I said. "Can I take your hand?"

He looked at Del, and then he offered his hand to
me.

"What's happening? What's wrong?" I asked.

"I'll tell you all about it after we get them to bed," Del told me.

They were both so exhausted, it didn't take long. The expressions on their little faces told me the exhaustion wasn't only physical. They were overwhelmed with fear and emotional trauma as well. As soon as we closed the door on their room, Del lowered his head.

"She overdosed," he muttered.

"What?"

"She's in the hospital, still in a coma. I stayed as long as I could with the kids." He shook his head. "I'm disgusted with her. I don't even feel sorry for her. She went off with that LaShay after work and she mixed a few things, including a lot of cocaine. I got the call just before I was supposed to leave for work myself and she was supposed to be home to watch the kids."

"Oh, Del, I'm so sorry."

"Yeah. It's just a matter of time now before the social service worker will be back at that door, this time to tell me they're going to foster homes," he said sadly, and flopped onto the chair at the kitchen table.

"You want me to make you something to eat?"

"No. I had a cheese sandwich at the hospital, and my stomach regrets even that," he replied. He stared so coldly at the wall, I felt my heart ache for him. "I don't know why I let myself believe her."

"Because you wanted it to be true so much, Del. Don't blame yourself for trying to be hopeful."

He nodded.

"You're right. I guess when you're desperate, you're most vulnerable to fairy tales," he said, and then widened his eyes with curiosity. "How did you get out to come here? What's happening with you now?"

"It's terrible," I said, flopping in the seat across from

him. "I bet people in prison have more freedom than I have."

"But you're here," he noted.

"I snuck out, stole the keys, and came when I heard you were having troubles."

"Oh, no, not that again. The police will be at my door and that will bring the social workers here faster," he complained. "You had better get back."

"I don't want to go home again, Del."

"What are you talking about? Where are you going to go? What would you do?"

"What we decided. This is the best time to do it," I told him, my excitement returning.

"Oh. And how are we supposed to do that, Teal? You and I haven't enough money to travel and settle in somewhere else with two young children."

I stared at him and then smiled.

"What?" he said, his lips softening.

"I can get us thousands of dollars," I said. "And tonight, right now."

"Thousands? How?"

"I just know where there is a lot of money, and the beauty of it is, no one wants anyone else to know about it."

He shook his head.

"You're not making any sense, Teal."

"Never mind. If I return with ten thousand dollars, will you leave with me now? Will you, Del?"

The reality of what I was saying sank slowly but firmly into his consciousness. I could see his eyes changing, hope replacing defeat and sadness, as what we thought of as dreams and illusion suddenly began to slide into possibility.

"But where would we go?"

"There's that cousin of yours you mentioned in California, the one you've spoken with about your going out there."

"Yeah, but that was to be by myself, not with two little kids."

"It won't matter. He'll help you, help us. You'll get work right away and I'll look after Shawn and Patty Girl until we get them into a school."

"You just don't enroll kids in a school, Teal. There are legal papers, guardianships, all that."

"We'll figure all that out when we get there, Del. The main thing is, we don't want to stay here. For you it means losing them anyway, and for me it means walking about in shackles soon."

He smiled, and then he shook his head.

"It sounds great, but I don't know."

"Money will make the difference, Del. It always does," I said firmly. "The only thing is, we have to decide immediately. I have to do all this now, before they realize I've taken it and the car and I'm gone. We need the head start," I urged.

"I don't know," he said, but I could see his resistance weakening.

"It's a fresh start for both of us, for all of us, Del. We can make it work. Together, we can."

He looked at me.

"I don't understand about the money. Why do you say no one wants anyone to know about it?" he asked, and I told him what I had heard Carson and Daddy discuss.

"So they won't be so quick to report it missing," I emphasized.

He was thoughtful again.

"We're not incapable of doing this, Del. We'll get to California. We'll do it," I urged.

He lifted his eyes to me. I could see it was on the tip of his tongue. He was going to do it. My heart was pounding so hard, I thought that was what was making the noise, until we both realized, someone was at his front door. The pounding grew louder. For a moment neither of us could move, and then he rose and looked through the front windows.

"It's the police!" he said.

"Oh, no. My father."

"Oh, great," Del said. "I knew it. I just knew it, Teal. You weren't thinking."

"I'm sorry, Del," I moaned.

"Right, you're sorry," he said angrily, and went to the door.

A patrolman stood there gazing in at us. The thought of my being arrested again sickened me. I felt like I would actually faint.

"Del Grant?"

"Yes?"

"The hospital has been trying to reach you. No phone?"

"No, we lost service and I haven't restored it yet. What is it?"

"Your mother," he said, and shook his head. "I'm sorry."

It felt like a bullet had passed through Del into me. Cold and then numbed, I moved up beside him. He was just standing there, nodding.

"You'll have to contact the hospital as soon as possible," the policeman said.

Del continued to nod.

"Is there anything we can do for you, get in touch with anyone else?"

"No," Del said. "Thank you."

"I'm sorry," the policeman muttered. It was easy to see he hated the assignment and wanted to get it over with as quickly as he could. He turned and walked back to the patrol car. Del stood there looking out at the street, unmoving.

Despite how angry he is at his mother almost all the time, she is still his mother, I thought, and she's gone. Surely, he was also thinking about the impact it would all have on Shawn and Patty Girl. I felt so bad for all of them. Any thoughts about my own misery were forgotten.

"Del," I said gently, touching his arm.

When he turned to me, I was expecting to see tears, but instead I saw a face so stone cold, it chilled my heart.

"Go get the money," he said.

"Del?"

"Go on. We'll leave tonight. I'll start packing what I want to take."

He turned away. I stood there for a moment and then hurried out to the SUV.

All the way back to the house, I thought about Del's reaction to hearing his mother had died. How would I have reacted to such news? What did running away like this mean anyway, if not a total break with my family? What did I expect them to do once they had discovered what I had done? Forgive me? Wish me luck? Tell me they understood? Once I left the house with Daddy's money, it would be the same as hearing they had died. I'm sure it will be similar for them in relation to me, I thought.

I had been dreaming and fantasizing about this for so long that now that the reality of our actually going ahead and doing it was here, it still seemed like an illusion. It wasn't until I pulled into our driveway and confronted our big home that I began to feel afraid. Could I pull this off? Could I really do this? Was I a terrible person for giving Del such assurances, such hope?

I sat for a moment in the SUV with the engine off and the lights off, my body trembling. I almost wished I would be discovered, but no lights went on in the house and no one came to the front door.

Back in his house, Del was packing, getting ready to start a new life with me. His grief was being smothered with the fresh new prospects I had given him. I had to succeed now. I had to do what I had promised. I got out quietly and scurried around the house to the window of Daddy's den. There, I took a deep breath and then climbed back through it into his office. For a long moment I stood listening, half expecting to hear the sound of footsteps on the stairs, but I heard nothing. The maids were in their rooms. It was eerily quiet.

I went to Daddy's desk drawer and felt for the safe key. When I had it, I paused again to listen. There was just the sound of something creaking in the walls, a pipe or maybe just the house itself settling into a cozy rest for the evening. My heart started to thump so hard, I could actually feel the blood being rushed through my body when I opened the safe and felt inside for the cash box.

If there was any chance of Daddy forgiving me for my past actions, it was soon to end, I thought, but I had long gone past that moment. I had to harden myself against him, Mommy, and Carson in order to continue. I thought about the way Daddy looked at me now. I thought about Carson's washing his hands of me, and I thought about Mommy telling me I was too far gone for her to interfere. As far as they're concerned, I rationalized, I'm no longer part of the family anyway. What am I risking?

I opened the cash box, took out the money, and stuffed it into a manila envelope on Daddy's desk. Then I closed the box and put it back in the safe. I locked the safe and replaced the key in the top drawer. Once again, I paused to listen and heard nothing.

Good-bye Daddy, I thought as I stepped up to the window. Good-bye to seeing all the disappointment in your face, to hearing your voice harden with threats and the imposition of new punishments. In the end you will be happy I'm doing this. Think of all the relief I will bring you.

And good-bye to you, Mommy. I'm sure you'll be upset for a while, but some new social event will come up, and then you will have all the pressure of Carson's wedding. That will take your mind off me, won't it? It seems to do it for you now, to the extent that I'd just as well not be here.

And Carson, my reluctant brother, how happy you will be. Just think, you no longer will have to make up any excuses for me or try to avoid me. You can go on and believe you were an only child after all. Your sister was a fiction. What sister? Never heard of her.

You're all going to be happier, and there is no question in my mind that I will be, so good-bye, good-bye, good-bye, I thought, and went out through the window. I closed it behind me and walked slowly around the house and back to the SUV. For a moment I stood by it, looking up at the darkened windows and thinking about Mommy dreaming her happy dreams and Daddy feeling safe and contented beside her. I wondered just how long it would take them to realize I was gone.

I even imagined the scene at breakfast.

"Henderson," Mommy would say after sitting awhile and discovering I hadn't come down to breakfast. I hadn't even made a sound: no shower going, nothing.

Daddy would lower his *Wall Street Journal*.

"What?"

"Teal hasn't come to breakfast, and she has to get to school."

Daddy would sigh in annoyance and call to the maid to tell her to knock on my bedroom door. She would, and then she would return to tell them there was no response. Now, infuriated, Daddy would get up and pound up the stairs to my bedroom. He would thrust open the door and stare with confusion at my still-made bed.

"Teal?"

He would look into the bathroom and see I wasn't there. Confused, but more angry than worried, surely, he would come flying down the stairs and announce I wasn't in my bedroom. The bed, in fact, looked unused.

"What?" Mommy would say. "That's impossible. She didn't leave the house, and she certainly wouldn't make her bed."

Daddy would stand there a moment thinking, and then he would turn and march out to look for the SUV. When he saw it was gone, he would come stomping in, screaming about me. He would go to the phone, vowing to have me arrested again and this time, put into jail for years if he could.

Mommy would try to calm him, but soon she would feel she was getting too stressed over it and retreat. After all, she had to be ready for some luncheon or another and she couldn't very well go looking like a ragtag woman.

Daddy would call Carson and they would console

each other and repeat to each other how terrible I was, how utterly hopeless I was.

"Don't get sick over her," Carson would advise.

"I won't do that," Daddy would vow, and he would gather his wits, call the police, and then go to work.

I played this whole scenario in my mind as I drove back to Del's house. In a way it made me feel good about what I was doing, and in a way, it made me feel even sadder.

Whatever, I told myself. It doesn't matter now. It doesn't matter anymore.

It's too late to turn back, and it's too late for regrets.

When I arrived at Del's house, I saw the lights were on and at the door, I saw two old suitcases. It wasn't until then that I realized I had nothing but what I was wearing and the money in the manila envelope.

He stepped out and looked at me.

"Get what you need?" he asked.

"I just got the money," I said.

"Wasn't there something important to you, something you had to have?" he asked. "Pictures, dolls, anything you wanted to take with you?"

I thought for a moment and shook my head.

"No," I said.

And finally, I had a reason to cry.

10

Following the Sun

Fortunately, Shawn and Patty Girl were so exhausted and groggy, they didn't realize we were putting them into the rear of the SUV along with some of their things. We set up pillows and blankets for them and finally started out. Once we left the city streets and got onto highway I-90 toward Buffalo, I remarked how asleep the world looked this late at night. My excitement had kept the adrenaline flowing, but now that we were gassed up, packed, and on our way, my body began to soften.

Del said very little besides dictating the directions. The route west was something he had long ago committed to memory. I remember someone in history class in my public school asking our teacher why it was that people always seemed to head west to start new lives, explore, and make discoveries. He thought for a moment, nodding and smiling at the question, which was apparently a good question to him, something that gave him a chance to leave the prescribed curriculum for a moment, to be philosophical and original.

"I don't know exactly," he replied, "but if you think about it, the sun rises in the east and sets in the west. Maybe we all just follow the sun. Maybe we all believe it knows where it's going," he added with an impish smile. It was one of those rare moments when something was said or done in a classroom that stuck with me.

Do we really know where we're going? I wondered.

As we drove into the night, the darkness, interrupted now with only oncoming or passing vehicles, grew thicker. I know it was just my imagination, but it seemed as if the SUV was battling harder to move forward. I felt like we were inside a balloon, pressing harder and harder against the unexpectedly thick walls, stretching them and waiting to finally pop out and be free.

"How are you doing?" Del asked.

"Okay," I said in a voice smaller than I wanted it to sound.

I wanted him to be assured of my confidence and my determination. I wanted to fill him with courage and resolve, to believe that we could overcome whatever obstacles awaited us and solve any problem simply because we were young and free and bold. We could shut the door on our pasts firmly and finally. We could forget everything and live only in the present.

I remembered another thing from a classroom discussion, this one in science class. My teacher was telling us that one thing that distinguished man from the lower forms of life was his ability to draw upon memory and to foresee. And I remember thinking, but what if your memories were full of pain and what if you saw only danger and trouble in the future? What was the benefit of that? I almost asked him, but I anticipated some scientific, textbook answer that wouldn't really address my thoughts, so I didn't. I simply left class thinking the stupid ant or worm was better off. At least, better off than I was.

"We can't drive all night, although it's probably better. Less chance of being tracked and spotted," Del said. "I'll take over when you feel you're too tired, okay?"

"Yes, fine. I can drive a little more," I assured him.

He turned the radio on but kept it very low so as not to disturb Shawn and Patty Girl. In the rearview mirror, I saw how they were sleeping in a sweet embrace, safely surrounded by their childhood dreams. I envied them.

Del didn't look tired, but he was quiet.

"We're doing the best thing," I said. "You're probably right in thinking the social services people would be at the house in the morning."

"I know," he said.

"Count the money," I told him to help build his confidence. I pushed the manila envelope over, and he opened it and took out the bills.

"They're all hundreds," he commented. "There's so many, they don't look real."

"They're real, believe me," I told him.

He started to count.

"I thought you said something about ten thousand dollars," he said. I saw he wasn't finished yet.

"That's what I overheard. Why?" I asked, afraid I hadn't taken enough.

"I've already reached ten thousand and there's more, a lot more, maybe another ten."

"That's good for us!" I cried.

"I don't know," he said, wavering. The sight of so much money frightened him. "Your father might not want to write off this much."

"Don't worry about it, Del."

"Maybe your parents won't be as happy to see you gone as you think, Teal."

"Trust me, they will."

He continued to count.

"Twenty-two thousand," he reported, took a deep breath, and put it all back into the envelope.

"That should get us where we want to go and help us get started, don't you think?"

"Yeah," he said.

"I'm tired now," I told him. "You can drive."

If he was at the wheel, he would think less about it all, I thought. I slowed down and pulled to the side of the road. Cars whizzed by. More people than I thought traveled late at night. Maybe they were all running from something, too.

Del got out, went around the SUV, and got behind the wheel. I slid over to the passenger's seat. He adjusted the driver's seat, and we were off again. When we drew closer to Buffalo, Del decided we should pull into a motel.

"It will be daylight soon, and I'll feel better if we're off the highway, resting."

"Sure," I said. "Whatever you want to do."

Del wasn't happy with the first two motels we found off the exit. He thought they were too busy and too close to the highway. He drove on until we found a motel that looked out of business. Its sign had some blown letters, and there were only two other cars parked in front of units. The office was small and very dimly lit.

"I'll check us in," he said, taking out one of the hundred-dollar bills from the envelope. "Watch the kids."

He got out and went into the office. I saw he was standing at the desk for quite a while before a short, bald-headed man in a white undershirt came out of a back room. He scratched his head and looked past Del at the SUV. For a moment I thought there would be a problem, but then Del showed him the money, and he nodded and turned around to fetch a key.

"That's Norman Bates's older brother," Del muttered, getting back in. Norman Bates was the name of the psychotic killer in the movie *Psycho*. I laughed nervously.

We pulled in front of unit twelve, and Del handed me the unit key.

"Open the door first, and then we'll bring in the kids," he said.

Calling Shawn and Patty Girl the kids really made me feel that we were a family now. I hurried to do it and prepare one of the double beds for them. He carried the two of them in his arms, neither really waking up. I took Patty Girl and gently placed her in the bed. He put Shawn in, and we tucked the blanket in around them.

"I wish I could sleep like that," Del said.

"Me, too."

"We'll bring in what we need for them tomorrow," he said, and went into the bathroom. I fixed the bed for us and took off my sneakers, jeans, and blouse.

"I'm exhausted," he said, coming out. "I hope they sleep late."

I went to the bathroom and washed up. When I came out, Del was already asleep. I crawled in beside him, bringing myself as close to his warm body as I could without waking him. Then I closed my eyes and wished that Shawn's and Patty Girl's dreams would make their way over to me, even for a few minutes. I underestimated my own fatigue. Moments after I closed my eyes and snuggled up to Del, I was asleep.

The drapes were heavy enough to keep the morning light from jolting us awake. Shawn and Patty Girl were exhausted enough from the emotional trauma and all to sleep late into the morning, too, but when I awoke, I found Del was up. I turned and saw him sitting there, all dressed, staring at me.

"What's wrong?" I asked, grinding the sleep out of my eyes with my small balled fists. He didn't respond, so I opened them and sat up. "What is it, Del?"

"We can't do this," he said. "I don't know what got into me. I was so angry, so frustrated, I didn't give it all real thought."

"Why not? We have so much money. You said so yourself last night."

"It's going to take more than money, Teal, a lot more."

"Why?"

"Why?" He shook his head. "Look at them," he said, nodding at Shawn and Patty Girl. "We've taken on full responsibility for two infants. They have all sorts of needs, Teal, health needs, schooling, everything."

"But the money . . ."

"It's not going to last us forever, and we have to have some legal means, some proof of guardianship. Eventually, the law will catch up with us even if your father and mother are not coming after us. Then what do we do?"

"We can make it work. Somehow, we can, Del," I pleaded.

He lowered his head.

"I haven't even attended to her funeral," he said. "I know I should hate her like crazy, but she's lying back there in some cold hospital morgue, and there's no one going to come around to see about her. They'll dump her in some pauper's grave, and I won't even know where it is. Who knows what they'll do? They might just cremate her and scatter her ashes in a junkyard."

I stared at him.

"Del," I said, shaking my head, struggling to come up with more reasons, more hope.

"I'm sorry, Teal. I was too impulsive. I know I got you into more trouble and you have enough of your own. You don't need to take on ours as well. I'm sorry."

"You didn't get me into anything I didn't want to get into myself," I said petulantly.

Just then Shawn sat up and looked around, confused.

"Hey," Del said, standing and going over to him.

"Where are we? Where's Mama?"

"We took a little car ride for fun," Del told him. "We'll have breakfast in a restaurant soon, too."

Shawn looked at me.

"Hi," I said, and he smiled.

He looked down at Patty Girl and then at Del. Del glanced at me. Shawn wasn't as young and trusting as I thought, and Del knew it, too.

"Where's Mama?" he asked.

"We'll go home," Del said as an answer, and looked at me with an expression that shouted, *"See! See what I mean and why it's going to be so hard!"*

I fell back against my pillow and stared up at the ceiling. Del went out and got Shawn's and Patty Girl's clothing. By the time he returned, she was up and I was helping to get them together. Before we had pulled into the motel, we saw a roadside restaurant that looked like an old-fashioned diner. Shawn and Patty Girl were excited about being there and having pancakes.

I was so nervous about them, about how they were going to take the news of their mother's death, that I didn't think about my own situation until we were a good half hour on the road back home. We bought Shawn and Patty Girl some coloring books and small toys to amuse them for the trip. Del kept apologizing and blaming himself. I was terribly disappointed but kept my tears behind my lids. They fell inside me.

We didn't stop for anything but gas. Del got the kids some candy, and we were driving back into Albany proper by two-thirty.

"Where do you want to go first?" I asked him.

"We'll go home and I'll get their things back into the house. Then I'll contact the hospital and see what I have to do."

"I'll stay with you as long as I can," I said.

"Thanks, Teal."

The look of relief on his face made me sadder still. I was hoping to see that look grow stronger and brighter as we drove farther and farther away from here, not as we drove back here. Was I being too selfish? Was it true that I've always been?

As it turned out, neither Del nor I had much time to ponder these questions. We drove up to his home and got the children out first, but before we reached the front door, car doors slammed around us and we turned to see four men in suits marching toward us, followed by a woman Del recognized.

He groaned.

"Child welfare department," he muttered. "They must have been staked out and waiting for us."

"Just hold it right there, son," one of the men ordered. Del put up his hand.

"Wait," he said. They all paused, the woman stepping a little farther forward. Del looked at Shawn and Patty Girl, who were now terrified and holding on to him. "They don't know anything yet, Mrs. Fromm," he told the woman.

"Something has to be done for them now," she insisted.

Del nodded.

"Okay. Just give me a few minutes, please."

She firmed up her mouth, glanced at me, and then said, "We've been here quite a while. Where did you take them? I know you weren't at the hospital."

Patty Girl, thinking she had something important to offer, piped up with, "We had pancakes."

None of them smiled.

"Ten minutes," Mrs. Fromm told Del, and he turned and took the kids into the house. I started after them.

"Are you Teal Sommers?" I heard, and looked at the man closest to me.

"Yes."

"Do you know that there is an all points bulletin out on you?"

"There always has been," I replied, and walked into the house.

I'm not very old, of course, and I have been well protected all my life, but just when I thought I had seen the saddest things I could see, there's always something sadder, something that wrings your heart more and tears at your very being. The sight of Del sitting Shawn and Patty Girl quietly on the sofa and then kneeling down before them to tell them their mother was dead and gone was something I will never forget.

I suppose when we're young, as young as the two of them were, we have built-in walls of skepticism to keep us from believing in such a thing as death. The finality of it is not easily understood and accepted when you're still young enough to believe in fairy tales and magic. Sick people always get better; they always come home out of the hospital.

"Mommy's not coming home anymore," Del began. "She was too sick to get better."

"Why?" Shawn asked quickly.

"Her body became too weak," he said. "The people out there, Mrs. Fromm, who you know, are worried you and Patty Girl won't be safe here anymore. I can't be with you all the time and work. They want to be sure you're all right, so you will have to go with them to live where people can take care of you for a while. Someday," he said, "I'll come for you and we'll be back together."

I suppose it did Del no good that I was standing there in the doorway with tears streaming down my face. Oh, why did he get cold feet? I cried. Why didn't we just go on and on? We would have made it. Anything would have been better than this, wouldn't it?

Del shook his head as if he could hear my thoughts.

"I don't want you two to cry about it," Del told them. "It will just make it harder for everyone, including yourselves. Be a big boy and a big girl. I'll see you soon. I promise," he said.

"Will we go to a restaurant again?" Patty Girl asked.

"Absolutely, yes," he told her.

He took her hand and then he took Shawn's and they stood up.

"Del."

"There's nothing I can do," he said, close to tears himself.

I lowered my head and stood back so he could walk them out. I was a coward. I didn't go out with him. I remained in the house and waited. Finally, curious as to why it was taking so long, I opened the door just as Del was waving good-bye to the kids. My body felt like it had turned to stone. He lowered his head and then, instead of returning to the house, he started down the street.

"Del!" I cried after him. He did not turn back. He kept walking.

I started after him, but when I reached the sidewalk, a police car pulled up and two patrolmen and Tomkins stepped out. Tomkins, without so much as glancing at me, went directly to the SUV and got in.

"Teal Sommers?" the policeman who had been driving asked.

Tomkins started the SUV and drove off.

"I said, Teal Sommers?" the policeman repeated with annoyance.

Here we go again, I thought.

"What if I say no?" I asked. "Will you leave me alone?"

"Believe me, young lady, we have a great deal more important things to do than chase after a spoiled brat. Get in the car," he ordered.

I looked down the street.

Del turned the corner and was gone.

I didn't know it then, but as far as I was concerned, he was gone forever.

11

The Court
of Last Resort

To my surprise, the police did not take me to the police station this time. They took me directly home. Now I understood what the driver meant when he said they had more important things to do than chase after a spoiled brat. Daddy had used his political influence to arrange all this.

I saw the SUV parked in front, but no sign of Tomkins. It was only then that I remembered the manila envelope containing all the money had been between the driver's and passenger's front seats. I wondered if it was still there. If it was, I might be able to get it back in his safe and have my father believe I had done nothing wrong, but only taken the car without his permission again.

Carson opened the front door for us as we stepped up to it.

"My father wanted me to thank you for him," he told

the policemen without looking at me. It was almost as if I wasn't there.

"No problem," the driver said. He glanced at me, and then the two of them returned to their car.

"Just go to Dad's office," Carson ordered. He stood back for me to enter.

"Where's Mommy?" I asked.

"Just go to Dad's office," he repeated.

"Thanks, Carson," I muttered, and walked down the corridor.

I noticed that the maids weren't working. I heard no vacuum cleaner going, no dishes being washed, no sounds of anyone in any of the rooms. Daddy's den door was opened slightly. I hesitated, took a deep breath, set my mind on how I would act and plead, and then entered.

He was sitting with his back to the door, gazing out the window.

"Daddy?" I said.

At first I thought he wasn't going to turn around at all, but finally, he did, very slowly. He looked at me for the longest time without speaking. His face was oddly complacent, calm. His eyes did not have their usual red rage shining on me.

"When you were little and you misbehaved, we told ourselves it was normal growing pains, adjustments. My and your mother's only real experience with children had been with Carson. He has an entirely different personality, different nature, some of that because he is a male, I suppose.

"Other people, friends, used to tell me all the time that little girls were harder to bring up than little boys. In stories, movies, little boys are always made out to be the ruffians, miscreants, handfuls of trouble. Girls were supposed to be dainty, fragile; but in reality, everyone assured me, that was simply not so.

"And so, we accepted you as you were and tried to teach you, contain you every which way we knew, and even people who were supposed experts knew.

"When you were older, a preteen and then a teen, and you got into trouble, it clearly became more serious. Your mother, mainly, decided we should turn to child psychologists and even a psychiatrist. We sent you to the people we were told were the best, but there wasn't the dramatic turnaround we were expecting, hoping, to see.

"I took a more forceful position, especially after the more recent episodes. I thought okay, you're self-centered. Eventually you'll realize you can't do well for yourself and enjoy yourself if you continue to get in trouble and do poorly in school and you'll change solely to make yourself happier, but that didn't happen, either.

"Your mother—once again, more than me—hoped that if you were placed in a more controlled, richer, more advantageous environment where you would get more individualized attention, you would come around, but you didn't.

"In my heart I hoped you would care about this family, care about us at least enough not to really do us harm. That would be sort of the bottom of the barrel, the last straw, so to speak, wouldn't it?

"Then, you did this," he said, and held up the manila envelope. "You knew what this was, didn't you, Teal? You must have, because you knew where it was. You must have spied on me or something, right?"

I didn't care to answer. The truth was, I was having trouble forming words. My throat was closing up tightly. I looked away.

"Actually, I'm glad you're not speaking. All I'd get from you right now are lies, fabrications, excuses. Don't say anything."

He sat back.

"I'm going to do one more thing for you. You will realize that it's the last thing I'll do, I'm sure. I have, through some influential friends, been introduced to what we can call the court of last resort when it comes to you and kids your age who are like you."

I looked up. What was he talking about now?

"I'm sending you to another school. This one is away from home, Teal, so you won't have to answer to me for a while."

"What school?"

"The name doesn't matter. What it can do for you is all that matters. If you fail there . . . well, you fail. At least I will know that we did the best we could for you."

"I don't want to go to any new school," I said.

"What you want and what you don't want have no bearing on the matter anymore. It never should have had any bearing. That might have been one of my mistakes—caring about what you wanted."

"I want to talk to Mommy," I said.

"She's not here."

"Where is she?"

"She's gone to her sister's, your aunt Clare, for some very much needed R and R."

"I want to talk to her," I whined. "Call her on the telephone."

"She won't speak to you. She didn't want to be here when you were returned this time, Teal. She couldn't stand the idea of it."

"No."

"Yes," he said. "It's true."

He leaned forward on his elbows, folded his hands together, and glanced at his watch.

"There's a car outside, a limousine, waiting for you."

"What are you talking about, Daddy? Now?"

"Now is almost too late for you, Teal. Yes, right now."

"But my things."

"Everything you need is already in the automobile."

I shook my head.

"I'm not going anywhere, Daddy."

"I pulled some strings and, believe me, paid a lot of money, twice as much as your private school costs, to get you a spot right now, Teal. Someday, I hope, you will appreciate it. I realize you won't for a while, but that's a bitter pill I'll swallow."

I kept shaking my head.

"Where is this school?" I asked, seeing how determined he was.

"It's wherever your last chance resides," he said.

Instinctively, I backed up and suddenly hit what felt like a stone wall. I turned to see Tomkins smiling down at me.

"Tomkins will handle your transportation," Daddy said.

Panic swirled around me.

"Where's Carson?"

"He's gone home."

"I've got to go up to my room and see if there is anything I need that you didn't put in the car, Daddy," I said, playing for time.

"You didn't think about any of that when you ran off with your mother's car and my money earlier, Teal, did you? Why would anything matter to you now?"

"Please, let me call Mommy?"

"I don't understand all this interest in us suddenly, Teal. You didn't speak to your mother before you ran off, did you? You didn't speak to me or Carson. I'm giving you some of what you want—an escape from us," he said.

That wasn't what I wanted from my family, I was about to tell him. I wanted love and concern. I wanted attention and I wanted to feel wanted, but I said nothing. We were like oil and water, Daddy and me. For the moment, I was too angry and stubborn to do any more pleading. Send me to another school, I thought. See if it matters.

"Good-bye, Daddy," I said.

"Good luck to you, Teal. I really mean that," he said.

I turned and marched out of the office. Tomkins was right behind me. As we went by the stairway, I glanced up at it. Tomkins thought I might make a mad dash up to my room, I guess. He sped up so that he clearly blocked any such move on my part. He opened the front door.

There it was, as Daddy had described, a long stretch limousine.

At least I'm going in style to wherever I'm going, I thought.

What surprised me was that there was another driver. What was Tomkins here for, then? This driver was in a chauffeur's uniform. He got out as soon as we appeared and opened the rear door for me. To my further surprise, Tomkins followed me into the limousine and sat across from me.

"Are you going to a new school, too?" I asked him.

He stared coldly at me. What was Daddy doing, making sure I didn't have the driver stop and jump out somewhere? This is getting ridiculous, I thought.

The chauffeur got in, and we started away. It was funny how I didn't look back at the house with any sort of sadness the last time I had left it, but for some reason, perhaps because of Daddy's tone of voice and his strangely calm, almost defeated demeanor, I did now.

When I glanced at Tomkins, I saw a smirk on his face.

"That's a lot to throw away," he muttered.

"You don't know anything," I spit back at him.

"Of course not. No one but you knows anything," he replied.

We drove on, and I quickly realized we were heading for the airport. Daddy hadn't been kidding when he said far away. The limousine was permitted to go through a special gate and directly to a small plane.

"What is this?" I asked.

"This is an airport and this is a plane," Tomkins said.

"Very funny. Why am I going on a private plane?"

"You're so special," he replied with that same small cold smile on his lips.

The plane's engines were started as we approached. The door was opened as we pulled alongside. Tomkins got out quickly and held the limousine door open. The chauffeur sat staring ahead. I hesitated, my body feeling like it had sunk into the car seat.

"Let's go. I have other things to do today," Tomkins snapped. When I still hesitated, he leaned in. "Do you want me to embarrass you and pull you out of the limousine?"

"Where am I going?"

"Hey, my job was to bring you here. The guy in the pilot's seat knows where you're going. Move," he ordered.

I had no doubt he would pull me out, so I stepped out

of the limousine. The wind whipped around us.
Tomkins took my left arm, pinching it at the elbow with
his thick fingers and directing me up the small stairway.
I lowered my head and got into the plane. There was no
one else there.

The door was slammed shut.

"Buckle yourself in," I heard. I felt the plane begin to
move.

I looked out the window. Tomkins was getting back
into the limousine. It sped off as the plane turned and
the engines were revved up.

What about my things? I realized. I hadn't seen anything taken from the limousine and put onto the plane.

"Wait!" I shouted at the door between me and the
cockpit.

The roar of the engines drowned out my voice.

"Where am I going?"

The plane began to roll faster and faster and soon
lifted into the air.

I looked out the window.

"Mommy," I whispered.

The sun went in behind a cloud as we rose higher.

Across the way, I saw my face reflected in the opposite seat's window.

I was crying.

"Poor little rich girl," I heard myself say.

PART THREE

PHOEBE

1

Mama's Gone

"Well, she's gone," Daddy announced at my bedroom door. "Your mother has really gone."

I turned slightly in bed and grunted, thinking, *why did he have to wake me so early just to tell me that?* Then, I peered at him through the slits of my barely opened eyes. He stood in my bedroom doorway, his head bowed and his hands on his hips. He was already dressed for work, wearing his gray suit and tie, looking as perfectly put together as a storefront manikin, as Mama would say.

"Right, Daddy, she's gone," I said, and pulled the cover over my head.

"No," he said, raising his voice. "I mean it. This time she's really gone, Phoebe."

I lowered the blanket again.

"What are you talking about, Daddy? She's really gone? Like this is the first morning you woke up and realized she didn't come home all night?"

In the beginning they would have loud arguments about that, Mama crying that he didn't consider how hard she worked and how she needed time to unwind. After a while Daddy gave up complaining and just ignored it, which was usually how he handled every crisis between them.

My mother worked as a waitress in a small jazz joint. Most of the time she spent what she made right there, or at least, that was what she claimed. Either that or she needed this and that for work: better shoes, nicer clothes, beautifying to make better tips. Whatever excuse she came up with, Daddy accepted.

With Daddy on the road selling tools to garages all around the Atlanta, Georgia, area, I was often home alone most of the night. Lately, he had to go even farther to bring in as much income as he had before. Because of that, he often had to sleep in a motel and I'd be alone all night, not realizing until morning that Mama hadn't come home.

"She didn't leave a good-bye letter for either you or me, but she's gone! She packed most of her things and took off."

I stared at him a moment and then sat up in bed. I was wearing one of his pajama tops, which was something I had done since I was four and was still doing at sixteen.

"What things? Her clothes?"

"That's what I said."

That was something she hadn't ever done, I thought. I ran my fingers through my hair before getting up and marching past him to his and Mama's bedroom.

Her closet door was wide open, and there were dozens of empty hangers dangling. Some of her less cherished garments had been tossed to the floor. There was only one pair of old shoes in the shoe rack. Now that the closet was almost empty, the gobs of dust were more visible. I stared at it and shook my head.

"She took all that and left," I said in amazement, mostly to myself. Daddy was standing right beside me.

Mama was really on a fling this time. I was sure it was something she had just decided to do on the spur of the moment. She hadn't given me any hints. I think I felt more betrayed than Daddy, not that Mama and I were all that close these days. She didn't like being reminded she had a sixteen-year-old daughter. Instead, she preferred pretending she wasn't much older than that herself, especially in front of men. I was absolutely forbidden to go to the club to see her when she was working, and she warned me that if I ever did, she would act like she didn't know who I was.

"All her cosmetics, too," Daddy said, nodding at their bathroom. The counter had nothing on it, no jars of her creams, no shampoos, nothing.

"Wow," I said. "I guess she did take off for a while."

"What time did you get home last night that you didn't even know it, Phoebe, and didn't even hear her do all this?" he asked. "I'm sure she wasn't alone," he added in a lower voice.

Anger didn't darken his ebony eyes as much as it turned them into cold black marble.

"I was home early, but she was still at work and I was so tired I went right to sleep," I lied.

Once again I had violated my curfew and come home very late, but I just assumed she was still at the club. I didn't go to her room to look for her, and if I had and had woken her, she would have ripped into me good. The gin I had drunk at Toby Powell's house practically put me into a coma anyway. I didn't even hear my dreams.

"She was threatening me with leaving all the time, but I thought like you," Daddy said, staring at the empty closet. "She's always threatening. But this time, it's obviously more than just a threat, Phoebe. I should have known. I should have expected something like this. I heard rumors about her and that no-account Sammy Bitters."

"What kind of rumors?" I had heard them, too, stories about her being with him, but I made like I knew nothing.

"Not the kind I'd care to discuss," Daddy said. "Anyhow, I gotta go off until late tonight. I don't have any time to worry about this or care. I just wanted to be sure you knew to be home after school and all, Phoebe. No hanging out on any street corners or staying late at some friend's house, you hear? You gotta stay good. Remember what that judge told you," he warned.

Along with two of my friends, I had been arrested for shoplifting at a department store. Sylvia Abramson had one of those tools the cashiers use to take off the thing that sets off an alarm, and we used it to steal clothes a few times before we got caught this time. A saleswoman saw me go into the changing room with a blouse, and afterward she went in and realized I was wearing the blouse under my own. They let me walk out of the store before they stopped me. Meanwhile, Sylvia and Beneatha Lewis got caught stuffing panty hose into their jeans.

This was the second time I was caught shoplifting and brought before a judge within one year. If it wasn't for Daddy, I guess the judge would have done something more than just sentence me to probation and impose a curfew. Daddy kept thanking him. To me it looked like he was begging for mercy, apologizing, taking the blame onto himself, and promising to try to do better as a parent. Before the session was over, the judge did bawl him out more than he chastised me, but he did tag on the threat of having me removed from our home and placed in foster care the next time I got into any sort of trouble.

"It's easy to have children, but it's a real responsibility to raise them," he lectured from his high desk. Daddy just kept nodding. "Too many people have thrown and are throwing their obligations onto the state or society. The court isn't here to take the place of a parent."

"I know, Your Honor. I am sorry to have my troubles in public."

"Um," the judge said. He had asked where Mama was, and Daddy had told him she was at work and couldn't get free. The truth was, she was home sleeping off a hangover. The judge peered at him when he explained that, and Daddy shifted his eyes quickly. It was like he had a glass skull and you could see any attempted lies tangle up and crumble. He kept rubbing his hands together nervously.

I felt more embarrassed for him than I did for myself, even though Daddy always looks respectable and is always nicely dressed. He says it's part of his work as a tool salesman. He sells very expensive equipment and says he has to look like someone who would. He's always telling me a good presentation, a good image, is half the battle in this world. He does his best to get me to dress more conservatively. I tell him he's just too old-fashioned, but he says it doesn't have anything to do with fashion. It has to do with being decent.

I told him being decent is no fun.

"It's like eating sugar-free candy," I said. He didn't laugh. He was laughing less and less these days, and now I wondered if he would ever laugh again.

Anyway, without Daddy around and with Mama out and about, working and such, I often violated the curfew, and the evening before was just such an occasion. Daddy told me I was skidding on thin ice. I almost fell through the day Daddy told me Mama was gone. Now that I knew he wasn't going to be home for dinner, I went off with Sylvia and stayed too long at her house partying with her, Packy Morris, and Newton James, two boys whom the principal herself had encouraged to drop out of school. We made a little too much noise, and Mrs. Gilroy, who lives in the apartment below, went and called the police. They took our names, and I thought they would know I was violating curfew, or they would come arrest me the day after, but no one came.

Daddy found out about it and looked very glum when I came home from school the next day. Mama still hadn't come home, and the reality of her never coming home was beginning to settle in me like a glob of fresh cement. He was sitting at the kitchen table, nursing a cup of coffee between his hands and coming up out of an ocean of thought like someone who had been deep-sea diving for ideas all day.

"I realize I can't do this, Phoebe. I can't look after you, and this can't continue. You're just going to go from bad to worse," he said. He shook his head and drummed his fingertips on the tablecloth, looking like he had spent his last dollar.

His conclusion was that since there was no doubt now that Mama had left us for good, he had decided to deposit me with my aunt Mae Louise, Mama's older sister. He told me he had already had a preliminary conversation with her and my uncle Buster about it.

"What are you talking about, Daddy? I ain't gonna live with no Aunt Mae Louise," I said after he told me. I wagged my head and put my hand on my hip. Usually, I could get him to ease up on any of his restrictions and punishments, but he looked very determined this time.

"This is no life for you here, Phoebe. Not the way things are now. It won't be forever, but it's a way to save you. Maybe the only way."

"I don't need to be saved."

"People who need to be saved usually don't know it," he replied. "Put on something nice. We're going to talk to Aunt Mae Louise and Uncle Buster tonight."

"No," I said.

"You do what I tell you, Phoebe," he said firmly. "If you don't, the law is going to come around and take you off one of these days anyway. They'll go and put you in some foster home with strangers, like the judge said, and I know you wouldn't like that."

"Uncle Buster and Aunt Mae Louise are no better than strangers," I whined.

"Stop it," he snapped, and pounded the table with uncharacteristically intense anger. I actually jumped back. "Now go get dressed, and don't put on any of those blouses so short your belly button peeps out. Go!" he ordered, his finger stiffly pointing toward my room.

I sauntered off reluctantly and changed into something that I knew would make him happy, but I wasn't smiling. All the way out to Aunt Mae Louise's house, I sat sulking in the car. Daddy went on and on about how this was my biggest and best opportunity to escape trouble and grow into a decent young woman, maybe even go off to a college and become something. He said he couldn't be expected to make a living and raise a teenage girl who had already been in enough trouble to bring a grown man to tears. He said bringing a girl like me up in the heart of Atlanta's toughest neighborhood was like planting a rose in a pigsty.

"Not that I'm saying you're any rose, Phoebe, not by a long shot," Daddy added. "I'm not one to be blind to my child's problems and my own. People who do that end up wishing they was born a few minutes earlier or later."

"Maybe Mama will come back," I offered as a last resort when we drew closer to Stone Mountain. "At least we should wait a week or so to see."

Daddy looked at me with those coldly realistic eyes of his, the sort of eyes that would clear fantasies off your own like windshield wipers cleared off rain.

"I don't fool myself about your mama, Phoebe. She was never satisfied with our life, and you know it. She's into bad stuff now. And anyway, I don't want her coming back," he added with more rage in his voice toward her than I had ever heard. "Not after what she's done this time."

I used to think nothing could make him really mad. He seemed to take every insult Mama threw his way. She complained he didn't put up enough of a fuss when his boss made him work harder and cover more territory.

"You sure you got a spine in there, Horace?" she would taunt him.

The most he would do is shake his head and saunter off, but I could see there was no way I was going to talk him out of this. My only hope was that after all was said and done, my aunt and uncle wouldn't want me. If I were them, I wouldn't want me, I thought. I don't even want me now, and probably Daddy didn't, either, and was just using everything as an excuse to pawn me off. Part of me was sick over it, and part of me was understanding.

Aunt Mae Louise and Uncle Buster Howard, who was a civil engineer, whatever that meant, had recently bought a nice home in Stone Mountain, a suburb community of Atlanta. It had two stories, a front yard and a backyard, an attached garage, and enough land between it and the houses beside it so that you couldn't reach out the window and steal bread off someone else's dinner table like you could in the rundown tenement we occupied in downtown Atlanta.

In other words, they had a home that would nourish a rose, even a weed. It was in a safe neighborhood. There were no gangs, and drugs if they came had to come subtly, through back doors, and not be sold in kiosks in the street outside your front door like they did where we lived. I could attend a better school, and, most importantly, Daddy emphasized, help my aunt and uncle with their two children, Jake, age five, and Barbara Ann, age eight.

Daddy, who had been a salesman of some sort or another most of his adult life, put all his skill and logic into his selling of me. There was just no other way to view it. He was there to convince my aunt and my uncle they should take me in, just like they would take in a new vacuum cleaner.

I really hated the idea of living in Stone Mountain, away from my friends and stuck with my snobby relatives, especially my mother's older sister, who was fond of lecturing her about how an African-American woman and man today could make themselves successful if they just had a mind to and had real ambition. Everything they had was real; everything we had was just a temporary fix.

"You know that most of the time my work takes me on the road, Mae," Daddy continued, directing his plea mainly at her. "These days I have to expand my territory to make expenses. She'd be left alone for longer and longer periods of time. It won't be long before the authorities come and take her off."

We were all in the living room of their Stone Mountain home. It was in a housing development that was at least eighty-five percent black. After they had bought the home, Mama told Aunt Mae she just traded one ghetto for another, but even I had to admit that was just envy talking. This was no ghetto. Close your eyes and then open them when no one was in the street in front of his or her house and you would think you were in the finest suburbs, built for middle- and upper-class white people.

"That's why Charlene went bad," Aunt Mae Louise piped up, those black green eyes of hers narrow, dark, and angry. To me she always looked like an alley cat poised to pounce. "She needed looking after, Horace. Charlene was never one to be on her own. My folks only had to leave her in the house by herself an hour for her to do something to add gray hairs to their heads. You should have known that from the day you met her," she told him. "I don't know why you went ahead and married her. Men sure don't think with their heads when they see a pretty thing. I won't deny she was always pretty, but I'll never claim she was anything but selfish and spoiled."

Aunt Mae Louise wasn't ever going to take her sister's side just because she was her sister, I thought. She probably never had, even when they were growing up.

She glared my way.

"You take after your mama too much in that regard, Phoebe. It's sad to have to say it, but she was a very bad influence on you. Lucky for the rest of us that she had only one child."

I knew Mama had almost had another but miscarried in the sixth month, probably because of the alcohol and cigarettes and her wild ways.

Even so, and even though I knew she had run off with a small-time con man named Sammy Bitters, I didn't like Aunt Mae dissin' her. I knew it was the same as criticizing me because, as she just said, in Aunt Mae Louise's eyes Mama and I were cut from the same cloth. She never hid the fact that she had doubts my father was my father, too. I knew it was like someone sticking a pin in his chest whenever she implied or even came out and as much as said it. Daddy was just too easygoing to ever show anger or pain, especially in front of her. Maybe he was just a pincushion after all. Mama got so she thought so. No wonder he didn't want her coming home now. Nothing would confirm that as much as placing me with my aunt and uncle. There was a finality to it, just like a period at the end of a long sentence. This is it; this is the way it will be, and that's that.

Everyone was quiet in the room because the heaviness of the conclusion hung in the air like stale cigarette smoke. They all wished I had never been born, and now there wasn't much choice about what to do.

"Of course," Daddy said softly, "I'd give you money every week for her room and board and whatnot."

He gave me a quick glance of deepest despair.

"We don't need you to pay for her food, Horace, but she will need decent clothes, shoes, and a little spending money," she said.

My uncle didn't look happy about it, but it was clear they were going to take me in. I felt my heart sink. I wanted to do something to stop it, but I was afraid Daddy might just give up on me and call some child protection agency or the court and say he gave up. Mama had left him. His work was getting harder and I was in too much trouble lately, trouble that deepened the lines in his face. He was tottering on the heels of his shoes.

"But first, I want some understandings set down right now, while your father is sitting here, Phoebe," Aunt Mae Louise began.

She stood up to continue, suddenly very full of herself. She was only about five feet two and weighed maybe one hundred and five. It gave her self-confidence to stand when she wanted to be firm and authoritative, I'm sure. Sitting, she looked like a little girl with those thin arms and tiny shoulders.

Unlike Mama, Aunt Mae Louise kept her hair straight and wore almost no makeup except some lipstick occasionally. Mama was five feet five, with a full figure. I had heard men say she radiated sex like a hunk of uranium or something. She could have a man eating out of her hand by just turning her shoulders, swinging her hips, and batting her eyelashes. Even though she drank too much and smoked too much and did drugs occasionally, she was obsessive about her teeth.

"Your smile is your billboard when it comes to men," she would tell me. "Make sure you take good care of your teeth, Phoebe."

As long as I could remember, Mama was giving me advice about men. She always made it sound like a war, like we had to prepare to do battle to defend our treasure. That was literally what she called our sexuality, our treasure.

"We don't need no dragon guardin' the door, but don't let 'em in unless there's more in it for you than some cheap thrill, girl. Otherwise, you'll end up bein' some sorry tramp like what hangs out at the club. I don't have no money to give you, just good advice, so you'd better take it and stuff it in your heart," Mama told me. It was usually after she had drunk too much and was feeling sorry for herself that she gave me these lectures. To me it seemed as if her sexuality had become more of a burden than an advantage.

Although she wasn't exactly a prude, Aunt Mae Louise was a great deal more self-conscious of her sexuality. Uncle Buster was a good-looking man, firmly built at six feet one. He had played football in college, but was never a hell-raiser. His father was a Baptist minister, and whenever Uncle Buster was around Mama, he always looked at her and treated her as if she was a saleslady for Satan. Mama told me that was because Uncle Buster wanted her so much he had to make her seem terrible. I knew she loved to tease him, which was something that made Aunt Mae Louise irate at every family gathering, not that we had all that many besides an occasional Christmas dinner, something we hadn't done for two years.

It was no surprise to anyone, least of all to me, that for me family was as fictional a concept as Oz. The lines between us, the linkage was so thin and fragile, I never felt anything special about it. My relationships with my cousins, my aunt, and my uncle weren't any warmer or tighter than the relationships I had with ordinary friends.

"First," Aunt Mae Louise said, "I want you coming

straight home from school every day. You go right to the guest room, where you'll be, and you finish your homework," she said, turning and twisting like a traffic cop so she could point at each area of the house she made reference to. "Then, you come out and help me set the table for dinner. On weekends, we shake down the house. We vacuum every rug, polish furniture, and do the windows. On Sundays after church, we'll do all the ironing needs to be done.

"Uncle Buster and I play Bingo every Wednesday night at the church. We usually have a neighbor, Dorothy Wilson, baby-sit, but now that you're living here, you'll do it. That doesn't mean you can invite anyone to the house when we're gone. We'll tell you exactly how we want you and the children to behave, and you'll be responsible for them getting to bed on time, after they clean up and put away any of their toys, of course.

"Don't you think of accepting any invitations from anyone you meet until either Uncle Buster or I find out everything we need to know about the person. We see how young people today slip through the cracks because parents don't take enough interest in who their friends are and what they do," she said.

You're not my parents, I wanted to say, but kept my lips firmly glued shut.

Uncle Buster, still looking quite glum, nodded after every point she made as if he was in church listening to his father deliver a sermon. Any minute I expected him to let out with a "Hallelujah."

"Of course, it goes without saying that we won't tolerate any smoking or drinking, and if you do any drug, we'll turn you in to the police ourselves, won't we, Buster?"

"Without batting an eyelash," he confirmed, his eyes

fixed on me like two laser beams that could burn through my face.

"Now, neither Jake nor Barbara Ann ever use any profanity, and I don't want to hear them start suddenly after you move in, Phoebe."

I sat there staring ahead.

"Well?" she asked.

I looked at her with a "Well, what?" expression.

"You understand and agree to everything I've said?"

I glanced at Daddy. He looked like he was ready to break into tears any moment, but I could see the fear in his face, too, fear I would say something nasty and end it all. His eyes were full of pleading.

"I understand," I said.

"Good." She turned to Daddy. "All right, Horace. We'll give it a try, but if she gives us any problem and doesn't listen . . ."

"Oh, she won't give you any problems," Daddy said quickly. "She's a good girl. She's just in with too many bad kids, and she doesn't have me around enough. I appreciate this, Mae. I know she'll do well in a home where there is love, responsibility, and supervision."

Aunt Mae Louise grunted skeptically and looked very self-important. I hated to see Daddy grovel like that, but I was afraid to raise my voice. I just continued to stare at nothing, like someone who could meditate herself right out of hell.

"When you bringing her things?" Buster asked. I saw that he kept his eyes on me instead of Daddy whenever he spoke about me.

"I thought tomorrow, Buster, if that's all right with you."

"It doesn't matter when she starts, Horace. It's how she behaves afterward," Uncle Buster said.

"Oh, right. Of course," Daddy said. "She knows that."

"The room's all ready. I always keep it clean and prepared for guests," Aunt Mae Louise said. "I'll just move some of my things out of the closet tonight so she has all the room she needs."

"What about the school?" Daddy asked.

"I'll get her registered and all," Aunt Mae Louise said. "I've already spoken to the principal, Mr. Wallop, about her, and he explained what has to be done. You sign a paper saying you give us temporary guardianship. We go to all the parent-teacher meetings so they know us well at the school. There was even talk about Buster being on the board," she said proudly.

"Maybe someday," he said, "but I'm a little too busy at the moment to give it the time it requires."

"There's a good lesson for you," Aunt Mae Louise told me. "Never take on any responsibility you can't give one hundred percent to."

I looked at her as if she was totally crazy. What did she think I was going to do, run for student government president?

"Then it's settled," Uncle Buster said. "How is your business going?" he asked Daddy, anxious to get off the topic of me.

They started to talk about the economy. Aunt Mae Louise brought me to the guest room and explained how she wanted things kept.

"You make sure you make the bed before you leave for school every morning, Phoebe. Fix it just like this, with the pillows fluffed and the comforter neatly folded. I don't want people coming to my home and seeing an unmade bed. And no clothes lying about on the floor or over chairs. Everything gets hung up properly. Nothing looks messier than discarded garments. I used to fight with your mother all the time about that. She was just too lazy and didn't care what people did or didn't see."

"I can keep the door closed," I said, "can't I?"

"It doesn't matter if a door is closed and everything behind it is a mess. It's still a mess. Now you be sure you don't drop any makeup or such on this rug. It's practically new," she pointed out.

"You'll be sharing a bathroom with Jake and Barbara Ann, of course. They know how to clean up after themselves. They even wash out the tub after they bathe. Jake does the best he can, and I come in after him and finish, but he's gotten into the good habits."

"I'm not a dirty person, Aunt Mae," I said.

"I never said you were. I'm just telling you how things are here in our home and how I want them to remain. I feel sorry for your daddy. I felt sorry for him two minutes after he said 'I do' to my sister. If you care about him, you'll be a good girl now. In a way," she said, "it might be the best thing that happened to the both of you, your mother running off like that. The Lord works in mysterious ways, and sometimes, something that seems bad really is good. You go to church with your daddy much?" she asked.

"Never," I said dryly.

She pulled up her shoulders.

"Well, we'll see about changing that."

I was going to protest, but Daddy came out and stood in the hallway with Uncle Buster, so I took a deep breath and looked away.

"Now, we'll talk to Jake and Barbara Ann," Aunt Mae Louise declared. "I asked them both to wait in

Barbara Ann's room," she said, and led me two doors down the hallway.

Jake was sitting at a desk working on a puzzle. Dressed in a white shirt and a pair of black pants with his hair neatly trimmed and brushed, he looked older than five. Of course, he knew me well enough, but I also knew that both he and his sister had been warned about me often.

Barbara Ann was sitting and reading a book. They both looked up quickly when we entered.

"Children," Aunt Mae Louise said, "your cousin Phoebe is going to stay with us for a while."

Jake's eyebrows lifted.

"Where's she going to sleep?" Barbara Ann asked, probably afraid she would have to share her own room.

"She'll be in the guest room," Aunt Mae Louise told her, and she looked relieved. "Everyone is to behave and help everyone else. Everyone is to respect everyone else's property," she continued as if we were in a camp and not a home. "The same rules apply when it comes to watching television and to cleaning up after ourselves."

"Is she going to our school, too?" Barbara Ann asked. She was tall for her age and, unfortunately for her, looked more like her father than her mother. Her features weren't as dainty as her mother's, and she had big shoulders and plump cheeks. She looked a good twenty or so pounds overweight.

"Of course she is."

That seemed to interest her more.

"You can sit with me on the school bus," she said as if she was granting me a wonderful opportunity. "I'll save you a seat if I'm on first after school, and you can save it for me if you're first."

Great, a school bus, I thought, with a load of screaming children. That was just what I needed every morning.

"When is she coming to live here?" Jake asked.

It felt funny standing there and hearing everyone talk about me as if I wasn't there.

"Tomorrow. And that's that," Aunt Mae Louise said. "Get ready for bed, Jake. Barbara Ann, I want to see what you did for homework tonight."

We walked out and joined Daddy and Uncle Buster in the kitchen.

"You want something, tea or coffee, Horace?" Aunt Mae Louise offered.

"No, thank you, Mae. We'd better get back and start organizing."

"Good idea," she said. She turned to me. "You help your father now," she ordered. "This is not easy for him, and he's a good man just trying to do the best he can with his terrible burdens."

I flinched at being called a burden, but then I thought, what else am I really?

Daddy and I walked to the front door. Uncle Buster shook his hand, and we started out. As we walked down the sidewalk to the driveway, I gazed back and saw both Jake and Barbara Ann peering out the bedroom window, looking like two children kept prisoners in some high tower. That's how I'll feel for sure, I thought.

The night sky was so overcast I felt like I was moving through a tunnel, even with the streetlights in front of the other homes.

"This will be only for a little while," Daddy said after we got into the car.

I looked at him with eyes as coldly realistic as those eyes of his, and he turned away quickly.

Daddy wasn't good at lying to anyone, even to me. To my way of thinking, that was a weakness. I used to wonder how he could be a good salesman. Everyone lies to everyone about everything, I believed. If the story of Pinocchio were true, everyone in the whole world would have a long nose.

"I'm sorry I can't do more for you, Phoebe," he continued. "I don't like putting my responsibilities on someone else, but I've spent many a restless night worrying about you. At least I'll know you're safe. You understand all that now, right, Phoebe? You've got to be happy about that."

I didn't answer him. I stared out the window. This sleepy residential world looked like another planet. There were no bright lights, no music pouring out in the streets, and no one standing on any of the street corners. Everyone was locked safely behind his or her doors or gathered around television sets like cave people gathered around fires.

Then I thought that somewhere in the night, Mama was laughing. I was sure. She was listening to music and having a good old high time of it. Did she even pause once to think about me? Did she ever wonder about me? Or did she force herself to forget me? I had no doubt that she would probably say I was better off with her sister than I was with her. Mama never tried to pretend she was good.

"I'm born to raise hell," she would tell me, and she would laugh.

Am I born to raise hell, too? I would wonder.

"I hope you'll behave yourself, Phoebe," Daddy suddenly said as if he could read my thoughts.

He said it like a prayer.

And what are prayers, I thought, if not just little lies between yourself and God?

2

At Aunt Mae Louise and Uncle Buster's

I never really believed I was saying good-bye to anyone or saying good-bye to my home in the city. In my heart I truly believed I would be coming back sooner rather than later. Back at the apartment that night, Daddy hovered about like a nervous soon-to-be father, pacing in front of my door while I packed with little or no enthusiasm.

"Don't take any of those wild clothes of yours, Phoebe. You'll just steam up your aunt and uncle. Leave them here," he pleaded. "None of those rings in your nose and your belly button, and no cigarettes. For God's sake, no cigarettes. She becomes a banshee when she sees people smoking, a truly wild spirit warning people of impending death."

It irked me how afraid of Aunt Mae Louise he was.

"I don't have any cigarettes and I don't have any

wild clothes, Daddy. I'm not wearing no old lady's clothes just to please her."

"You've got to make this work," he said. "Take it slowly, a day at a time. I'll come by as much as I can, and I promise I'll take you places on weekends."

"Where you going to take me, Daddy? Some kiddy fun park?" I threw back at him.

"I'm just trying to make it work," he protested. "We'll go to a movie or I'll take you to a nice restaurant, whatever, but I'm not bringing you back here to mingle with those juvenile delinquents, so don't ask."

"Right," I said, looked at a miniskirt I knew would set off Aunt Mae Louise, and then tossed it on the closet floor.

"Maybe I'm better off with some strange foster family," I muttered.

After I packed, I called Sylvia and told her what was happening.

"You're movin'?"

"It's temporary," I said. "Believe me."

"Right. You ain't that far away anyhow," she said. "You come in on weekends and stay with me."

That cheered me up until I considered that Aunt Mae Louise would probably not allow it, and Daddy had made it clear he wouldn't. I wasn't going to put up with it, I vowed. I don't know why I'm packing so much, I told myself. I'll be coming back so fast, it'll make Daddy's head spin. Either that or I'll just run off like Mama.

"Maybe you and Beneatha could come out there, too," I suggested to Sylvia.

"What's to do out there?" she asked.

"I don't know. When I find out, I'll tell you."

"Good luck with that," she said.

I was so depressed I couldn't sleep, so I went back out and saw Daddy was sitting in the living room staring at the television set. I could tell he didn't care what he watched. His eyes were glassy, and he didn't even realize I was standing beside him.

He can't be too happy about how his life was turning out, either, I thought, but I didn't feel sorry for him as much as I felt he should do something about it, prove he had that spine Mama said he didn't have. Why was he so defeated? Plenty of my friends lived with a single parent and got by.

"Why don't you just get a job here in the city, Daddy?" I asked him. "That way you wouldn't be away from home and no one could come take me off. Maybe we could move to a better apartment or something, too."

"Whaaa?" he said. He looked up at me.

"I asked you, why don't you get a different job?"

He shook his head and smiled like I was asking him to go to the moon.

"I've been doing this too long to change now, Phoebe. Soon I'll get better routes with better clients. Someone's retiring. Soon we'll have a better plan."

"Right. Better this, better that, soon," I said, disgusted, and went to bed hoping to bury my frustration and anger deep into the pillow.

Damn you, Mama, I thought. If you were running off, you could have at least taken me along. I fell asleep dreaming of it.

The next morning Daddy was up ahead of me and had my suitcase at the door.

"Can't wait to get rid of me, can you?" I told him bitterly.

"You know that's not so, Phoebe. You know what's

going on as well as I do. Don't make this harder than it is for me. Or for yourself, for that matter," he said.

Sullenly, I drank some juice, smeared some jam on a piece of toast, and drank a cup of coffee. He sat there turning the spoon around and around in his cup, his eyes down. This might very well turn out to be the last breakfast we have together, I thought, and despite myself, I started to feel sorry for him, imagining him all alone in this dump. What would he do for fun? What would he look forward to in his life now?

"You gonna go out with someone new?" I asked, and he looked up sharply.

"What?"

"Someone new? Mama's gone for good, so why wouldn't you?" I pursued.

When I was very young, I saw him and Mama behave more like a husband and wife, kiss each other, hold hands, laugh, and even dance. I had no idea what had changed it all. It seemed almost to have happened overnight.

"I wouldn't go out with another woman while I was still married to your mother, Phoebe. That's adultery."

"Well, she's doing it."

"I'm not her," he said.

"But you're getting a divorce, aren't you?"

He nodded slowly, making it look hard to do, like someone who didn't want to face his troubles.

"So," I said, shrugging. "It's just a matter of paperwork before you can have some fun. Unless you're just going to join a monastery," I quipped. His eyes heated.

"That's enough of that," he said. "Contrary to what your mother might have drilled into your head, sex isn't the end-all of all things, Phoebe. It's a horse that pulls you along, maybe, but you gotta keep it from going wild. All you'll do is end up like she will someday, crying over a glass of cheap gin in some dump bar, deserted by men who found younger women and dumped her like yesterday's newspaper. Just keep that picture in your mind whenever you stop to think about her."

There was no doubt that was what he envisioned, or hoped.

"You really hate her now, don't you?" I asked.

"No," he said. "I really feel sorry for her, but the way I feel sorry for someone with a contagious disease. I don't want to get too close."

"You two weren't always like that, Daddy. What happened to change it?" I asked.

He raised his eyes in surprise again. I thought he was just going to tell me not to think about it or say something to pretend it wasn't so, but he nodded slowly instead.

"I guess you're old enough to know. This is hardly the first time she betrayed me with another man. I caught her with someone once before, someone I trusted, too, and in our own home!"

"Why didn't you throw her out?"

"It's not that easy, Phoebe. I was hoping it would be different," he said. "She seemed remorseful, and I thought if I forgave her, we'd get back to the way we were. That didn't happen, but there's no sense talking about all that now. Let's just think about the future."

"Right," I said, "the future. Like I have one waiting for me out there."

"It doesn't wait for you. You have to make it for yourself," he said.

It was on the tip of my tongue to say, "Like you did?" But I didn't feel that mean. Instead, I gazed around at our small apartment. I didn't have any real affection for where we were living. My room was a two-by-four and we had trouble with roaches all the time, but even a rat gets used to its hole, I thought, and for a moment or two when it was time to leave, I paused at the doorway as if I was saying good-bye to a real friend.

"You won't regret this," Daddy said, seeing my small hesitation.

I said nothing. I just followed him out and into the car. This time it felt like we were in a funeral procession all the way to Stone Mountain. When we arrived, Uncle Buster was at work, and Jake and Barbara Ann were at school. Aunt Mae Louise greeted us without a smile. I supposed that up until the last moment she was praying it wasn't going to happen.

Daddy brought in my suitcase, looking like some exhausted road salesman making his last stop. Afterward, he stood in the doorway with a face so sorrowful it made me sick to my stomach.

"Good-bye, Daddy," I said. He kissed me on the forehead and hurried back to his car, now looking as relieved as a mouse that had outrun a cat.

"Let's get to it," Aunt Mae Louise told me then, and followed me to my room so she could hover over me as I unpacked my things.

"Don't think they'll let you wear that to school," she said, pointing at my abbreviated blouse with spaghetti straps. "I don't know why you bothered packing such a thing and bringing it here. I won't let you go out of this house in such rags. You got to remember that everything you do now reflects on your uncle Buster and me. Every time you have to decide on something, no matter how large or small, you think of that."

I didn't say anything. When I was finished, she said we were going to the school so I could be registered. I was surprised at how much she had done in preparation for my coming. She had given the school guidance counselor information about me, and he had contacted my school in Atlanta. The new school already had my records. We met with the guidance counselor, Mr. VanVleet, a tall, red-headed man who smiled as if he had been waiting anxiously for me to finally arrive, as anxiously as he awaited some exchange student from another country.

"We want you to succeed here, Phoebe," he began. He tapped the folder on the desk. "I see you have had some difficulties at your previous school."

Aunt Mae Louise grunted and said, " 'Difficulties' is too nice a word." She squirmed in her seat, but Mr. VanVleet kept his smile.

Maybe it's a mask, I thought. Anyone would need a mask to keep smiling in Aunt Mae Louise's presence.

"What we'd like you to do is get you at the proper reading level as quickly as possible. We have a class designed to do just that, and for a while, that's where we want you to begin. Once you're at the proper reading level, we'll be able to schedule you into classes you should be in, but we don't want to do that until we're sure you'll succeed. You understand that, don't you?"

I shrugged. None of it mattered to me. I wasn't going to be here long.

"Whatever," I said.

"Well, look at it this way," he continued, "you wouldn't want a third-grade student put in an eleventh-grade class, now would you? How would he or she do? Not too well, right?"

"You saying I'm like a third grader?" I asked, not hiding my indignation.

His eyes shifted to Aunt Mae Louise for a second and then back to me.

"I'm afraid that's about your reading level, but don't you worry. We'll fix that fast if you give it some effort."

"You're going to put me with third graders?"

I'd be sitting in a classroom with Barbara Ann!

"No," he said, laughing. "But with other students who have some temporary reading difficulties. There are some who are older than you, in fact."

I felt a little relieved about that, but still suspicious.

"She'll do what she has to do to succeed," Aunt Mae Louise promised him. "She knows how important it is now," she added, stabbing me with her penetrating glare.

"That's good," he said. "Let me take Phoebe down the corridor to meet Mr. Cody, the remedial reading teacher. You'll find him to be a very good teacher, Phoebe. He has had lots of success."

"Go on," Aunt Mae Louise ordered, and I stood up and followed Mr. VanVleet out.

"I know how hard it is to start somewhere new," he said as we walked. "You don't hesitate to come to me with any problems first, okay?"

Here's my problem, I wanted to stop and say. My mother has run off with a cheap con man. My father is too weak to deal with anything and pawned me off on my ogre aunt and uncle. I feel like Cinderella without any hope of any prince and never a glass slipper. Do you have a pill or something that will make all that go away?

Instead, I was silent and walked along listening to him describe the school, some of its important rules and regulations, and why I could still turn my life around and be successful at something.

Teachers, I decided, live in a world of fantasy, a fantasy of their own making. If they blinked too hard, they would see their students for who and what they were and they would get so discouraged, they would run out the door. At least that was how I had seen the teachers in my school. Most of them looked defeated and taught to the one or two students who showed any promise at all. The rest were just a nagging reminder of how ineffective they were, and who wants to be reminded of failure?

But that was exactly what was happening to me at the moment. Failure was being rubbed in my face.

Mr. VanVleet opened the door, and I looked in at a dozen remedial reading students. There was an expression I had heard at my old school whenever teachers referred to students like this, I thought. They called them mentally challenged. We called them retards.

"This is a new student, Phoebe Elder," Mr. VanVleet announced to the group. Some looked as disinterested as they had been the moment before we came. Some brightened slightly with curiosity, and one girl with a caramel complexion and long, reddish brown hair broke into a wide, happy smile.

I looked at them all and felt as if I had been forced to look into a mirror that hid no blemishes. Was this really where I belonged?

Mr. VanVleet saw the expression on my face.

"You'll make fast progress here, I'm sure," he said, "and get back on track quickly."

The only thing that kept me from turning and running was the realization that I had no place to go. Mama hadn't left a forwarding address.

"Welcome, Phoebe," Mr. Cody said. He was a short, stout man with balding curly black hair, a thick nose, and soft, almost feminine lips. His chin cut in so sharply, it was practically nonexistent. "Sit right here," he said, pulling the chair out a bit at the desk near the girl with the wide smile. She was still smiling at me that way. Is her face stuck? I wondered.

Mr. VanVleet pulled Mr. Cody aside, spoke to him softly, and then handed him my file.

"Okay," Mr. Cody said. "While the rest of us work on these exercises, Phoebe, I'd like you to take this little test I've designed. It will help me understand how I can best help you, okay?"

Everyone is so eager to help me, I thought disdainfully. The truth was, they probably wished I never had come.

He handed me the test, and I reluctantly began to do it.

"You can't fail," Smiley whispered to me.

"What?"

"No one ever fails Mr. Cody's tests."

"I'll try to be the first one," I told her. Her smile finally faded.

"What?"

"Quiet, Lana," Mr. Cody told her. "Don't disturb Phoebe. Just work on your reading exercises."

She pulled back into her chair and squinted, looking like she was going to cry.

Because I had arrived late and all, there wasn't much time for me to do any more than take the test. I heard bells ring at the end of periods and heard students pass through the hallways, talking loudly, laughing, but none of the remedial reading students got up to go anywhere else. It was clear that all we left this room to do was go to the bathroom and to lunch. I hadn't understood.

"Don't I go to a science class or a history class?" I asked Mr. Cody after the first change of classes was over.

"For a while you'll have all that here," he said. "I divide the day into the subjects and work on the reading that applies to each subject. Everything involves reading, Phoebe."

"This is like grade school," I complained. "I guess they just dumped me somewhere."

"Oh, no, no," he assured me. "We give you and the others here very individualized treatment. You're very special."

"I don't want to be special," I muttered.

The others listened to my complaints with some interest. I was sure most of them felt like saying what I was saying.

"For now, it's the best way," Mr. Cody insisted.

How was I supposed to meet anyone or get to know anyone, locked up in here like this? I thought. And when I did get out, they would all know I was one of the mentally challenged. I remembered how those students were treated at my old school. They might as well have had leprosy.

All of this just added to my sense of entrapment. Daddy had thought I'd be like a mole coming up into a world of bright light and hope, but all I did was go deeper into the darkness. At least, that was how I saw it.

It took me hours to finish the evaluation test. Mr. Cody let me go to the bathroom once, and I left hoping to meet someone maybe smoking in a stall and borrow a cigarette, but there was no one else there and besides, I saw they had a teacher monitoring the hallways, checking passes, and making note of the time a student left a room and returned to a room. To my further surprise, the teacher already knew my name. What, was the whole school warned about me? I wondered.

When the bell rang at the end of the day, the teachers were out there herding the students into the buses to keep them from loitering in the hallways. Mr. Cody promised to have my test results first thing in the morning and then design a program for me.

"Every student gets his or her own program to fit his or her special needs," he explained after the others had left. "That way we can be sure we'll strengthen your weaknesses. Sound good?" he asked.

"Sounds like you think I'm sick," I retorted.

His lips held the friendly smile, but his eyes turned a little dark and cold. He was obviously someone who expected to be appreciated.

"Well, in a way that's what's happened. We take your mental temperature and treat your problems and make you a better student," he said, obviously proud of his answer.

I didn't say anything else. I left the room and followed directions to the exit where my bus was waiting. Barbara Ann was standing by the bus, looking for me.

"You gotta hurry so you don't miss the bus or don't get a good seat," she chastised.

That was just what I needed to finish my day—an eight-year-old bawling me out. She stomped onto the bus ahead of me, expecting I would sit beside her. Instead, I slipped in next to a white boy with curly light brown hair who was glaring out the window like he was fixing to smash it with his fist. He didn't even notice I had sat beside him until we were under way. Barbara Ann was sulking in the rear with her friends. I supposed she had bragged how she was going to boss around a high school girl.

Finally, the white boy turned and looked at me. His eyebrows rose and then dipped in at each other.

"Who are you?" he asked.

"The Queen of England," I replied. He stared a moment and then laughed.

"I wish I was in England," he said. "I wish I was anywhere but here."

"That makes two of us."

"You just come to school here?"

"That's right, and not because I wanted to, either."

"Well, where you really from?"

"Atlanta. I'm living with my aunt and uncle for a while."

He nodded as if that was something very common.

"I know why I hate being here. What's your problem?" I asked him.

He looked out the window again and then turned back to reply.

"I just got thrown off the basketball team. My father's going to bust an artery."

"Why'd you get thrown off?"

"Got caught with these," he said, and pulled a pack of cigarettes out of his jacket pocket. "In the locker room. Didn't think the coach was anywhere nearby so I went into a shower stall and lit up. No second chances with Coach McDermott. I was on the starting five, too," he added.

"What's your name?"

"Ashley Porter," he said. "Or it used to be. Now it's Mud."

"Can I have one of those?" I asked.

"Huh?"

"A cigarette. Can I have one?"

"You can't light up on the bus. You'll get me suspended on top of everything else."

"It's for later," I said. "I couldn't bring any from Atlanta. My aunt put me through a metal detector and a body search when I came to her house."

"Did not," he said, smiling.

"Close to it."

"What's your name?"

"Phoebe Elder."

"What class are you in?"

"How to be a millionaire."

"What?" He laughed. "C'mon."

"They put me in some remedial reading class for the time being because I read like someone who just came from another country. I'm not staying here long, so I don't care."

"Where you going?"

"Back to my apartment in Atlanta, one way or another," I told him.

"Sure," he said. He turned away, and then he turned back and gave me a cigarette.

"Thanks."

"I should give you the whole pack. I wish you had asked me this morning and I had," he moaned.

"Maybe your daddy will get him to take you back on the team."

"My mother will try to get him to do that, but my father's a hard guy. He'll tell me I deserved worse and even call the coach and thank him for throwing me off the team. He was a marine."

"Your daddy was?"

"Yeah, and he never lets me forget it, so don't complain about your aunt."

"Who says she wasn't a marine, too?" I told him, and he laughed again.

I liked his smile. When he relaxed his lips, his eyes brightened like two candles of crystal blue light. He had a very small dimple in his left cheek, too. It flashed when he smiled.

"I get off here," he said as the bus came to its first stop. "Wish me luck."

"Good luck," I said as I stood to let him out. He brushed very close to me, pausing to look into my eyes, and then smiled again.

"How do I get into remedial reading class?" he teased.

"Flunk everything," I told him, and he laughed.

"See you tomorrow if I'm still alive."

"Same for me," I called after him. He waved as he went down the bus steps.

Then I flopped back into my seat. When I turned to look at Barbara Ann, I saw she was glaring at me, looking more like her mother now, her eyes full of suspicion and criticism, as if it came natural.

"How come you were talking to that boy?" she asked when we reached our stop and got off.

"Don't they let black girls talk to white boys here?"

"I don't mean that. He's on the basketball team. I saw him at the game. Shouldn't he be at practice?"

"You're awful nosy for an eight-year-old girl," I told her. "Watch you don't get it caught in a door."

"Huh?"

I hurried along until we reached the house. Aunt Mae Louise looked like she had been waiting at the doorway for quite a while to greet me.

"How was your first day at school?" she asked as

soon as I entered behind Barbara Ann. Jake was still attending a preschool at a different location.

"Peachy," I said. "It's run like a prison."

"I'm not surprised to hear you say that. I'm sure you're not accustomed to a well-run school," she replied. "Never mind. Put your things away, change into something you can work in, and come to the kitchen. I'm rearranging the pantry and I want to clean it out first. Then we'll work on dinner, and you can set the table before you wash up and dress for dinner."

"Dress for dinner?"

"We always dress for dinner," she said. "The dinner table is a special place for a family and should be treated with respect."

I looked at her as if she had gone crazy, and she pulled those tiny shoulders back as she usually did when she didn't like something I said or did.

"Hurry up and do what I say," she snapped.

I wanted to say, "Aye, aye, sir," and salute, but I knew it would only make her more angry.

She had me take everything off the pantry shelves and dust and polish. Then, I had to put it all back in an organized manner, alphabetizing soups, pasta, rice, and vegetables and fruit in cans. Every once in a while, she would look in and tell me I had a *d* or a *g* in the wrong place and I had to take it all off and rearrange it.

"Concentrate on what you're doing," she said. "You know your alphabet at least, don't you?"

"What difference does it make if a soup starting with *c* comes after one starting with *t?*" I asked, referring to the chicken noodle and the tomato I had confused.

"I can tell instantly what I need. That's what. Being organized saves us money and time. I can just imagine what your mother's cabinets were like."

I shrugged.

"Most of the time, empty," I said, but she didn't think that was funny.

Finally, I finished it to her satisfaction, and she sent me off to clean up and dress for dinner. I had no idea what she considered proper, but I showered and put on a black dress Mama gave me last year when she remembered she had forgotten my birthday. It was one of hers when she was younger and much slimmer. I hadn't worn it since then, and when I put it on, I realized it was tight, especially around my breasts. It had a V-necked collar and because of the way it lifted and tucked, my cleavage deepened. I was going to change into something else when Barbara Ann opened my door to say, "Mama says it's time to come to dinner. Right now," she added. "Daddy's already sitting at the table and Mama says you got to help serve," she whined.

"Maybe I'll help her eat it, too," I said.

"What did you say?"

"Get your ears fixed," I muttered as I charged past her.

Uncle Buster looked up as soon as I entered the dining room. Jake was already seated and sitting like a proper marionette with his back straight and his hands folded in his lap. Aunt Mae Louise came out of the kitchen and stopped dead in her tracks, her mouth opening and closing.

"What's that you're wearing to my dinner?" she cried.

"You said to get dressed up, and this is the best I have," I told her.

Uncle Buster was just staring, a little wide-eyed.

"That's disgusting. You might as well have come in

here naked," she spit back at me. "Where did you get such a dress? Does Horace know you have it?"

"Mama gave it to me for my birthday last year. It was one of hers."

"Well, that figures."

"You want me to go change or what?"

"No," she said. "We're not eating a cold supper because you don't dress properly. Get in here and bring out the string beans and then the mashed potatoes. Barbara Ann, you bring out the pitcher of cold water, and don't spill any of it."

She placed a roast chicken in front of Uncle Buster. He was still staring at me, now shaking his head slightly.

"Buster, you want to start carving the chicken?" Aunt Mae Louise asked him sharply.

"What? Oh, yeah," he said, and began.

After everything was brought out, we sat and Uncle Buster recited a prayer. Aunt Mae Louise kept her head bowed, but I could see her eyes were lifted enough to watch me.

"You use the smaller fork for your salad," she instructed.

"Why do we need two?" I asked, just curious.

"That's the way a proper table is set. I'm not surprised you haven't ever sat at one except the times you were here and obviously forgot."

"It's been a long time since we had dinner here," I remarked. I had to admit to myself that her cooking was good. She had done something to make the potatoes delicious, too.

"You were always invited for the holidays, but your mother had something better to do, like hang out at some sleazy gin palace, I suppose. Even though she was impossible, I did my best to help that girl, but when the devil gets a good grip on you and you don't care . . ."

"Amen to that," Uncle Buster said, chewing vigorously on his chicken leg.

"How come Mama fell to the devil and you didn't?" I asked. I was really curious about their upbringing, but she took it like a slap on the face.

"What's that supposed to mean? You think our mama and daddy were bad people? They did their best to show that girl the right ways. She was just born to be bad. Nothing they did worked, and they tried. We all tried, even after your daddy made a fool of himself and married her. Just look at you. Look at what she wrought."

Tears felt like little drops of burning acid under my lids, but I didn't let them out. I looked down and ate in silence. I am in hell, I thought. She didn't have to threaten me with it.

"Don't you take another tablespoon of those potatoes, Barbara Ann. You got weight to lose," Aunt Mae Louise snapped, and Barbara Ann's hand recoiled like a snake. She went into a pout. Aunt Mae Louise turned back to me.

"What's this I hear about you and some white boy on the bus?" she demanded.

"What?" I looked up at her and then at Barbara Ann, whose pout changed quickly to a smug smile on her lips.

"Not there five minutes and you make a scene?"

"I didn't make any scene. There was an empty seat beside him so I sat there. What did she tell you?"

"Never mind that. You be sure you don't bring any disgrace to our front door," she warned.

The mashed potatoes choked in my throat. I glanced at Uncle Buster, who still had a little of that look of surprise in his face from when I had come in wearing the dress. He ate and was silent like someone who was himself an invited guest at the table and had no right to speak.

"We'll clear the dishes and bring in the cups for your uncle Buster's and my cup of coffee."

"I don't get any?"

"Children don't need coffee," she remarked.

"I'm not a child."

"Girl," she said, standing and leaning toward me, "until you learn to behave like a proper young lady and not some urban alley cat, you're a child. You don't become an adult because you turn a certain age. That's the trouble with young people today, right, Buster?"

"Amen to that," he said, nodding and wiping his mouth.

"Last Sunday, the minister said we should issue licenses for adulthood and not let anyone drive a car, marry, or have children until they pass a test. We coddle and spoil our youngsters so much, we stop them from learning how to be responsible citizens."

"As ye sow, so shall ye reap," Uncle Buster recited.

"Amen," Aunt Mae Louise said.

"I guess the next thing we'll do is pass the plate for donations," I quipped, much louder than I intended.

Aunt Mae Louise looked like she was going to pop her eyes out onto the table. Uncle Buster dropped his jaw. Little Jake looked like he was going to laugh, and Barbara Ann bit down on her lower lip.

"You go right to your room," Aunt Mae Louise ordered. "No apple pie and ice cream for you tonight. Go on," she cried, her arm out and finger pointing.

No apple pie and ice cream? I guess I'll go and cry my eyes out, I thought, but said nothing. I turned and left them gaping after me. When I got to the room, I closed the door and sat on the bed, pouting. Maybe I should just run off tonight, I thought. I could go to Sylvia's for a day or so. Not having any real money made it all very hard, though. I barely had enough to pay for a bus ticket into the city.

Even though the door was closed, I could hear Barbara Ann moaning about her piece of pie being too small. Uncle Buster took her side, but Aunt Mae Louise was overpowering, and they all grew quiet again. Was this any more of a home than the apartment I had been forced to leave?

At this moment I really did feel like a trapped animal. It tore at my insides, making my nerve endings sing. I rose and went into the bathroom, locking the door. Then I took out the cigarette Ashley Porter had given me and lit up. Doing something as forbidden to me in this house as smoking made me feel a little free at least. I opened the window so the smoke would not be easily detected.

Just after I took one puff, Barbara Ann was at the door.

"I gotta go," she wailed.

"Just a minute," I said.

"I gotta go!" she cried louder.

"Damn it." I took another long puff, blew the smoke out the window, tossed the cigarette into the toilet and flushed. Then I waved the towel about.

"I gotta go now!"

"What's going on here?" I heard Aunt Mae Louise cry in the hallway.

I unlocked the door.

"I was just going to the bathroom. That's allowed, isn't it?" I asked.

"Go, but don't dawdle in there," she said.

Barbara Ann stood looking at me.

"I thought you had to go so bad," I told her.

She glanced at her mother and then rushed in and closed the door.

"Go back to your room. I'll tell you when to come out to wash the dishes," Aunt Mae Louise said.

I started away when the bathroom door opened.

"Come look at what's in the toilet, Mama," Barbara Ann said.

"What?" Aunt Mae Louise looked at me and then went in.

My heart began to pound. I started for the bedroom.

"Stop!" Aunt Mae Louise shouted. "Just stay right there," she ordered, her finger pointing to the floor. "Buster!"

Uncle Buster came around the corner.

"What?"

"You go into her room and tear everything apart. She brought in something she shouldn't and who knows what else?"

"I didn't bring in anything. I—"

"Go on, Buster," Aunt Mae Louise commanded.

"What she bring in?"

"A cigarette. A cigarette!"

He looked at me and marched past and into my room.

"God help you if he finds anything else," Aunt Mae Louise warned, her eyes on fire, "because He'll be the only one who can."

3

A Ravishing
Sexual Hunger

I was sure a correction officer looking for drugs in the most severe penitentiary didn't rip apart a prison cell as completely as Uncle Buster took apart my room. All the while I was made to stand in the hallway and wait outside while he went through my things. So miserable and unhappy, I was like an island with the sea eddying around me.

"If he finds any more or anything else, I swear I'll call the social services people and have them come and take you to be placed in a foster home this very minute," Aunt Mae Louise threatened.

I fought back the urge to turn and curse her, to shout that I didn't care and just run.

"You two get to your rooms now!" she snapped at Barbara Ann and Jake.

They hurried away.

"Smoking, and in my house, in my house! Don't you

know how bad it is not only for you but for the people who smell your smoke, especially younger people like Barbara Ann and Jake? Don't you know that?"

"It was just two puffs of one cigarette with the window wide open," I said sullenly.

"Don't tell me that it was just this or just that. Just like you can't be a little pregnant, you can't be a little bad, girl. It's like a cancer. You don't cut it out right away, it will consume and destroy you. That's what the minister said last Sunday."

"That must have been a very long sermon last Sunday," I muttered.

Finally, Uncle Buster emerged and shook his head.

"Nothing else there," he said.

"You sure, Buster? You look good?"

"Go see for yourself, Mae Louise," he told her, and she stepped up to the bedroom door. Then she turned back to me.

"Get that room looking like it was and then you come out and do the dishes and don't dare drop anything. We'll talk about what this cigarette in the bathroom means tomorrow. Your daddy is going to be very disappointed if I tell him. Not here a day and you already break one of the rules. I'm not surprised."

She stepped back, and I looked in the room. The bed had been turned over, the mattress on the floor. The two pillowcases, the bed sheet, and the comforter had been stripped away and tossed about. All the drawers were emptied, my panties, bras, stockings thrown to the floor. Every garment I had brought was dangling over a chair or over the edge of the bed, especially my bras and my panties.

I shook my head.

"This is sick," I said. "What did he do, get excited over my clothes?"

"Don't you be disrespectful. Clean it up," Aunt Mae Louise ordered again.

I went in and began to put things back. Ten minutes later, she returned and handed me a pamphlet.

"What's this?"

"This is from the church. It tells young people why smoking is bad for them and why the devil himself wants you to light up. You read it and memorize it. Starting tomorrow night at dinner, I want to hear the first page."

"What?" I squinted. "That's—"

"You do what I tell you, Phoebe. I'm taking on my sister's responsibility and I intend to do it right. You read and memorize that. That's how you'll earn your right to eat," she declared, and left.

I looked at the pamphlet. Memorize? Right to eat? I'd rather starve, I thought, and tossed it to the floor.

Almost an hour later, she came by again and told me to look after the dishes.

"I'll be checking them so be sure there are no spots and smudges after you wipe them clean and put them back. There's polish and a rag on the counter. Do the dining room table after that, and I want the floor vacuumed."

"What are you going to do?" I asked.

She smiled at my quick comeback.

"Why, I'm going to pray for you, Phoebe, pray for you every night, and so will your Uncle Buster and your cousins."

"I don't know how to thank you all," I said.

She stood silent a moment and then in a cold, hard voice said, "I won't mention any of this to your father if you do everything I've told you to do. We expected a crisis or two with you. We just didn't expect it so soon, but I'm not about to give up on you. That is what you should be thankful for," she concluded, turned, and left again.

I wondered if Ashley Porter had it any worse when he got home today.

I did all she wanted me to do. While I was vacuuming, the phone rang and she came into the dining room to tell me my daddy was on the phone.

"I kept my promise," she said. "I didn't tell him what you did. He's waiting to talk to you. Go in the kitchen and pick up the phone."

I set aside the vacuum cleaner and did as she asked.

"Hey," Daddy said after I said hello. "How's it going?"

My throat closed up.

"Phoebe?"

"Fine," I managed. What was the point in complaining? He would only moan and groan about how helpless he was until things changed.

"It's a good school, isn't it?"

"Terrific," I said dryly.

"All well with Aunt Mae Louise? She seemed okay."

"Daddy," I said. "Don't call me or come here until you can get me home."

"What?"

"You heard me, Daddy. I am never going to be happy here. There's no sense pretending on the telephone."

"Now don't go and do anything stupid, Phoebe. You have a court record. Your mother's nothing more than a tramp, and I don't have the means to do what has to be done for you at the moment. You listening to me?"

"No," I said, tears finally rushing into my eyes, tears

I had no time to trap beneath my lids. I flicked them off my cheeks as fast as they came.

"I'm working at this, Phoebe. I'll find a way. That's a promise," he said. "Be a good girl. Please," he begged.

"I gotta go, Daddy. I've got to finish my chores or I'll be locked in the basement."

"Phoebe?"

"Thanks for calling," I said, and hung up.

Aunt Mae Louise was standing right behind me in the doorway to the dining room. I knew she had been listening in.

"Didn't think you'd make it easy for him," she said. "Just go do whatever schoolwork you have. I'll finish up."

I walked out without saying a word. As I passed Barbara Ann's room, I looked in and saw her stuffing a chocolate bar in her mouth.

"I wonder what your mother would say if I told her about that," I said.

She stopped and looked terrified.

"That's the difference between us, Barbara Ann. I don't rat. I bet you don't have any friends, do you?"

"I do too."

"They would have to be fellow rats." I shook my head and went on to my room.

It wasn't too hard to fall asleep. The moment I crawled into bed, I realized how tired I was. I didn't want to think about my situation anymore so instead I looked forward to drifting off. The next thing I knew Barbara Ann was in my face to tell me Aunt Mae Louise wanted me up and about to help with breakfast, clear the table afterward, and take out the garbage.

"And Mama says you'd better have this room looking like it was before you go to school," she added, wagging her head.

"Get outta here before I turn your fat ears around," I warned her through clenched teeth.

Her eyes brightened with terror and she ran from my room. For a moment I just lay there wondering if I should simply refuse to do everything and get thrown out. Reluctantly, I rose, washed, and dressed in a pair of jeans and a blouse over which I put on a sweater I had lifted from the same department store I had been caught stealing from last month.

"Squeeze those oranges," Aunt Mae Louise ordered as soon as I appeared. "Your uncle Buster likes fresh juice every morning, and make sure you get out every drop. That's expensive."

Still half asleep, I did it, but she had to show me I had left some juice in every single orange.

"A penny wasted is a penny lost," she recited.

After I served Uncle Buster his juice, I got a lecture on how poorly I ate and why breakfast was the most important meal of the day. Aunt Mae Louise came to my room to inspect it after I had made my bed and went about criticizing everything: how I hung up my clothes, how loosely I had left the cover sheet, how I didn't fluff out the pillow correctly, on and on until I pointed out that I would miss the school bus.

"Don't forget to take out the garbage on the way out," she called after me.

I returned to the kitchen, got the bag, and dumped it in the can.

Barbara Ann was standing on the corner, embracing her books and talking to two other kids who looked about her age. They all turned as I approached, their eyes obviously brightened by the stories Barbara Ann had told them about me.

"Boo!" I said, and they jumped.

When I stepped up on the bus, I noticed immediately that Ashley Porter was sitting alone. He smiled and I slid in beside him.

"You survived, I see," he said.

"Barely. What about you?"

"My father took away my driving privileges, not that I had that much. Both he and my mother work and use their cars all day, six days a week. They let me use my mother's car Saturday nights and Sundays, but that's gone. I'm supposed to come right home after school, blah, blah," he said. "And you?"

"I gotta break a pile a rocks in the backyard with a sledgehammer."

He laughed and then asked me more about myself, about my school in the city and my friends. We talked so much, neither of us realized we were at the school until the driver opened the door.

"Maybe I'll see you at lunch," he said as we walked off the bus.

"I don't even know when that is. I came in after lunch yesterday and they keep us in that room."

He paused at the front door.

"Tell you what," he said. "Get sick about eleven-thirty. The nurse's name is Mrs. Fassbinder, and she's easy. You tell her you have cramps or something like girls have all the time and she'll let you lie down. I'll be there, too."

"What good's that?" I asked him.

"You'll see," he said with a twinkle in his eye, and left for his homeroom.

Armed with the results of my reading test from yesterday, Mr. Cody greeted me eagerly.

"I feel certain that you suffer from a learning disorder we call dyslexia, Phoebe."

I grimaced.

"What's that mean?"

"Well, the short explanation is that you confuse letters or words and write and read words or sentences in the wrong order. This doesn't have anything to do with your intelligence, which I believe is above average," he said.

Was that just to make me feel good? I wondered.

"It still sounds sick," I said.

"More people than you know suffer from dyslexia, Phoebe. Why, Tom Cruise was diagnosed with it, and he hasn't done so badly for himself, has he?"

I looked suspicious.

"Go read about him. You'll see. I don't want to get too technical with you. It's not necessary. You have a problem that affects your reading ability, and that has a big impact on your ability to learn, which would explain why you don't do well in subjects that require a lot of reading. No one wants to do something they keep failing at, so they avoid it, get discouraged. It explains a lot," he said in a voice a little above a whisper as if he and I were now sharing a very important secret.

"So?" I said.

"I'm surprised the teachers, evaluators in your previous school didn't concentrate on this problem for you."

"I'm not," I said.

If I told him how many days of school I had missed, especially when I was in grade school and Mama was either too tired or hungover to take me, he might understand, I thought. Later, in high school, my teachers were happy if I just didn't give them any trouble. They left me alone and I left them alone, when I was in class.

"Well, we're going to attack the problem and help you here," he vowed. "I know I can make progress with you very quickly," he said.

"You mean I'll get outta here, out of this class-room?"

"Sooner than you think, if you work hard at what I give you," he promised.

He put me on some reading machine that included a screen on which words were printed, a pair of ear-phones, and a microphone for me to read into. It also checked my understanding of what I read periodically. I noticed that the other students, including smiling Lana, seemed envious. When Lana asked Mr. Cody why she couldn't work on the machine too, he told her it wasn't for her. It was for someone with a different reading problem.

Instead of being happy about it, she looked disap-pointed. Mr. Cody winked at me, and I couldn't help believing he was telling me the truth. I was different from the other students. I really didn't belong in any class for the mentally challenged.

"That's better already," he said, looking over some of the work I had done the first hour.

Time passed faster than I thought it would, and I sud-denly realized it was nearly eleven-thirty. Remembering the plan Ashley had suggested, I stopped working and doubled over with pretended cramps. It was something that always worked in classes where I had male teach-ers. Most of the time, they looked terrified and didn't hesitate to give me permission to leave the room quickly. Mr. Cody was no different. He told me where the nurse's office was, and I left the room.

Mrs. Fassbinder looked like she was close to eighty. Later, I found out she was a retired nurse who needed to supplement her income. The school had trouble finding anyone to fill the position. Her office was much larger than the nurse's office in my last school. She had a desk and a work area with scales and blood pressure cups, closets full of bandages, disinfectants, and pairs of crutches, but off that office were three rooms with cushioned cots, blankets, and pillows in them.

I told her my problem, and she assigned me a room.

"Just rest awhile," she suggested. "If you need something, it's right here," she told me, and showed me where she kept tampons and sanitary napkins.

Now that I was in the room and lying on the cot, I wondered what had happened to Ashley. I was beginning to feel silly about it when my door opened slightly and he peered in, holding a cold wet cloth over his forehead.

"Hey," he said, and I sat up.

He looked back toward Mrs. Fassbinder, and then he stepped into my room and closed the door.

"Easy, wasn't it?"

"Yes."

"After a while she'll forget you're even in here," he said. "It's almost time for her to go to lunch. I'll be back as soon as she leaves," he promised, and slipped out again.

A little more than five minutes later, he returned.

"She's gone," he said, sitting on the cot, "and when she leaves, she locks the door and puts a sign up telling the students she's at lunch and to go to the office for emergencies."

"I thought it would be harder to do something like this here," I said. "You do it a lot?"

"Once in a while. When I have some good reason," he added with a smile.

"What's your good reason now?" I asked him.

"You," he said, and leaned forward slowly to kiss me. I let him and then leaned back on my pillow.

"How'd you know I'd let you do that?" I asked.

"I was hoping you would."

"You going to try to take advantage of me?" I asked him.

"No," he said, and smiled. "I'm hoping you'll take advantage of me."

We both laughed.

"I want you to know right now," he continued, dropping his smile, "that I'm not easy."

"Listen to you!" I said with some outrage. He shrugged.

"You're a very pretty girl, Phoebe. I don't know how long I can hold out."

"What?"

He leaned down and kissed me again, this time slipping his hands under my sweater and blouse. I held his arms for a moment and then he lifted his lips from mine, looked in my eyes, smiled again, and kissed me harder. It had been so long since I felt this good, I couldn't help but let my resistance slip away, especially when his fingers reached my breasts and his thumbs reached my nipples. I couldn't help moaning softly.

"I really like you," he whispered. "You're an exciting girl."

He lifted my sweater and I let him take it off, and then he unbuttoned my blouse and pressed his lips to my breasts, sliding them over to each nipple so slowly and gently, I tingled in anticipation.

"Man, you really are nice," he said. He surprised me

by bringing his mouth down to my belly and then undoing my jeans to kiss me lower and lower.

Every few seconds I told myself, we're doing this in school, right in the nurse's office. It made it all seem more exciting—so exciting that my heart hammered at my chest and shortened my breath.

If I don't stop him soon, I'm actually going to give up my treasure, I told myself. He had his hands inside my jeans, moving around to cup my buttocks and lift me so he could kiss me lower, his lips now caressing the insides of my thighs.

"I've got what we need," he whispered. "Don't worry."

He backed away to prepare himself and in those seconds, I argued with myself, warning myself that this was my last chance to stop before it was too late. I knew what it was to reach a peak of excitement and then fall over like someone who had lost her footing on a cliff. I would be helpless, caught up in my own ravishing sexual hunger.

You're not here two days, Phoebe Elder, I lectured myself. How can you do this with the first boy you've met? You'll get a bad reputation so quickly it will be impossible to walk the halls. Stop him; stop him before it's too late.

It's all right, another side of me argued. He really likes you and you like him. When that happens, you don't need much time. It's magical. Go with it. Enjoy something in this miserable situation.

He stepped out of his pants and underwear and was between my legs. We were kissing harder now. I held on to his shoulders and waited, but before he could do anything, the door opened.

There was a moment of such deep silence, it was as

if a nuclear bomb had gone off and it was just a split second before the explosion would sound. The silence made the situation seem more like a dream, like Ashley Porter and I were floating and would just fall to earth like two feathers.

Then we heard Mrs. Fassbinder's scream, and Ashley leaped back, scurrying for his clothing. I pulled up my jeans and turned away from the door.

"Get out! Get out!" she shouted at Ashley.

"I'm going. I'm going. Take it easy," he cried.

I got my blouse back on and buttoned it clumsily. Then I sat up and pulled my sweater over myself as Ashley rushed out the door. Mrs. Fassbinder stepped back with her hands still up and shaking.

"Oh, my God," she said, looking in at me. "Oh my, my."

She looked so confused and flustered, I half-expected her to suffer heart failure. Her pallid face was beet red, her lips twisting. Then, finally gathering her wits, she told me to stay where I was and rushed off. I finished fixing my clothes and walked out of the room. Ashley was nowhere to be seen, and neither was Mrs. Fassbinder. After I splashed some water on my face, I wiped it with a towel and returned to the remedial reading room.

"How are you?" Mr. Cody asked when I entered. "You look a little flustered yet."

"I'm all right," I said, and then noticed no one else was in the room. "What's going on?"

"It's your lunch hour, Phoebe." He pointed to the clock. "Be back at one-ten. You know where the cafeteria is and all, right?"

"I'm not hungry," I said.

"Well, you still have a long day ahead of you,

Phoebe. You should get something in your stomach, unless the nurse has said otherwise, of course."

"That's right. She said otherwise," I told him.

"Well, I'm just off to lunch myself. You can sit here or go outside as long as you don't leave the school grounds, okay?"

I nodded, and he left. The truth was I was still shaking, the trembles rattling my very bones. I flopped into my seat and lowered my head to my folded arms. I think I fell asleep for a few minutes because when the door was opened and I heard my name, it was almost one o'clock.

A tall, dark-haired man wearing a tie and a shirt with no jacket stood in the doorway, holding the door open. His shirtsleeves were rolled up to his elbows. He had a firm mouth, a cleft chin, and two brown eyes under thick, dark brown eyebrows.

"Phoebe Elder?" he said again.

"Yes."

"Come with me," he said.

"Who are you?"

"Dean Cassidy," he said. "Let's go."

"Where am I going?"

"To my office, young lady. Move it. I don't intend to have a conversation with you in this doorway," he said sternly.

I rose and walked out.

"Keep going," he said, remaining a foot or so behind me. "Just past the guidance department," he added, and I turned into an office doorway.

The secretary turned from the filing cabinet and looked at us. She had short, auburn hair and was dumpy with a round face. Her eyes narrowed as she shook her head.

"Send for Ashley Porter," Dean Cassidy ordered, and she moved quickly to the phone on her desk.

"In here," he told me, holding a door open.

I entered his office, which wasn't much bigger than the outer office. On the paneled walls were all sorts of commendations, plaques, and awards from a variety of community organizations, congratulating Dean Cassidy for his work with the youth of the community, as well as his college degrees in gilded frames. I saw pictures of a pretty woman and two little girls on his desk.

"Sit," he commanded, pointing to a chair in front of his desk. He didn't go to his chair. Instead, he went to the window and looked out. He stood there without speaking so long, I assumed he was waiting for someone else, but finally he turned and glared down at me.

"I've been here for almost ten years now," he began. "I've dealt with many things, insubordination in class, truancy, theft, fighting, smoking, vandalism, but this is the first incident of something as sordid and disgusting as this.

"And then, on top of that, to have such a thing involve a student that hasn't been in my school two full days!"

I turned away from him and stared at the wall.

"I don't know whether to have you sent to a church, a mental institution, or a prison," he hollered so loudly it made my ears ring and shook my insides, but I didn't cry and I didn't cower.

Slowly, I turned my head back to him and looked up at him. He was frozen with his back bent, his face glaring, his arms out.

"Well, when you decide," I said softly, "let me know."

If a human being could explode and reform himself,

he would have at that moment. His face got so red with blood, I thought the top of his head would blow off and stick to the ceiling. His throat undulated like the body of a snake, his Adam's apple bulging, and then he stammered and pointed at me.

"You . . . you show me some respect, young lady. Your life here is hanging on by a thread."

I turned away again, and there was a knock on the door.

"Come in!" he screamed.

The door opened, and his secretary told him Ashley was outside.

"Send him in here," he commanded.

I heard Ashley enter, but I didn't look back at him.

"Not only is the coach very, very disappointed in you, Ashley, I am absolutely disgusted with your behavior. What was going on in your head?"

I smiled to myself.

It wasn't exactly what was going on in his head that mattered, I thought.

"Wipe that grin off your lips, young lady, or I'll wipe it off for you," Dean Cassidy threatened.

"And how you going to do that?" I shot back up at him.

His eyes widened in surprise. I looked at Ashley, who was just as astounded. He shook his head gently as a warning.

Dean Cassidy got hold of himself and straightened up.

"I wanted the two of you in here together so I wouldn't get one story from one of you and another story from the other. You don't know how serious this is, Ashley. You could be in a lot more hot water than I cook up," Dean Cassidy told him, and nodded at me.

What was he implying? That I would accuse Ashley of trying to rape me?

Ashley looked sufficiently terrified now.

"I'm not going into detail about what Mrs. Fassbinder reported. You know what she saw. Do either of you want to deny it?" the dean asked.

"No, sir," Ashley said quickly.

"And you, young lady?"

"My name's Phoebe," I said.

"And you, Phoebe?"

I looked at Ashley.

"I guess what she told you is what it was, but I don't know what she told you, now do I?"

"Well, I'm not going to get into detail about it," Dean Cassidy said.

He finally sat behind his desk.

"Okay, Phoebe, you wait outside. I want to speak with Ashley first."

I got up and walked out, closing the door hard behind me. I knew what he was going to say in there. I could have written his dialogue for him. He was going to tell Ashley Porter I was a very bad girl with a bad record from my other school and he had gotten himself into trouble because of me. He was going to tell him how devastated his parents were going to be when they heard about it all. He was going to tell him how he was a boy with a good future that he was tossing into the ash can. And then finally, he was going to try to get him to put as much blame on me as he could. By the time he was finished, it would be as Ashley had pretended: I had seduced him.

Ashley will probably do and say what the man wanted, I thought. What did I matter anyway? His parents lived here, and the dean would emphasize that he should be concerned about them.

"She doesn't care how her aunt Mae Louise and uncle Buster look in the community, or she wouldn't have gotten herself into so much trouble here so quickly. You have no reason to be loyal to a girl like that," he would say.

Maybe Ashley didn't need all that much convincing. The truth was, I hardly knew him. For all I knew, *loyalty* was a foreign word to him. He was certainly not very loyal to his teammates on the basketball squad, I thought.

Why didn't you think about all that before, stupid? I asked myself as I sat across from the secretary, who looked at me as though I were a serial killer. She avoided my eyes and worked on files.

After what seemed like thirty minutes, but was probably only ten, the dean's office door opened and Ashley, his head bowed, came out with the dean right behind him. He glanced at me and then quickly shifted his eyes guiltily away.

"Write him a pass back to class," the dean said with his hand on Ashley's shoulder.

"Phoebe," the dean said, and nodded at his opened door.

I stood up, looked at it, and shook my head.

"No, thanks," I said. "I been there, done that."

"What?"

Ashley spun around in surprise as I walked past him out of the office and started down the hallway.

"If you know what's good for you, young lady, you'll march right back in here!" Dean Cassidy called after me from the office doorway.

I know what's good for me, I thought.

That's why I'm not marching right back.

4

Daddy's Gone

I didn't know where I was going, of course. I just left the building and continued to walk down the street. I went about four blocks before a police car pulled up alongside me and sounded its siren. The policeman got out when I stopped and turned.

"Where do you think you're going?" he asked.

"Anywhere but here," I said.

"You can't do that, miss. The school is responsible for your well-being. Now get into the car," he ordered.

He wasn't that tall, but he looked like he could rip a tree out by its roots. His shoulders were wide, and he had a neck so thick, I thought it would look perfect on a bull. He stepped toward me threateningly.

I walked to the car and got in.

"Where do you live?" he asked, and I gave him Aunt Mae Louise and Uncle Buster's address.

"You're taking me home, then?"

"That's where the school wants you brought. Your mother's been called."

"She's not my mother," I said.

"Who is she?"

"My aunt."

"Whoever she is to you, she's been called. What did you do wrong, anyway?" he asked.

"Be born," I said, and stared out the window.

"Kids today," he mumbled. We drove without speaking the remainder of the trip.

I felt certain Aunt Mae Louise would get rid of me now. With all she was telling Daddy and me about how important she and Uncle Buster were in the school community, she would surely be too embarrassed to keep me around. In a way I felt relieved. Daddy would have to take me back, and we would have to find a way to make it work.

When we pulled into the driveway, the front door opened and she stood there with her hands on her hips, shaking her head. The policeman got out and approached her with me trailing behind.

"You her aunt?" he asked.

"Unfortunately, yes," she replied.

He asked her to sign some paper on his clipboard, which made me feel like a package being delivered.

"Good luck," he sang as he returned to his car.

"We'll need it," she called after him, and looked at me.

"Not here two days and you do something like this?" she asked.

"I want to go home," I said.

"Believe me, that's what I want, too. Get in and stay in your room until Buster calls. He's trying to locate your daddy right now."

"Good," I said, marching past her.

I went into my room and shut the door. All the while I hadn't noticed how gray the sky had become. The room grew darker and darker until I heard raindrops tapping on the window with a sound that made me think of tapping witch's fingers, long and bony with sharp, hard fingernails. It was something I heard and saw in recurrent nightmares all my life, only now the witch's face I imagined was Aunt Mae Louise's face.

More often than not, when I was younger and I had a bad dream, there was no one there to comfort me. I would put on my lights and catch my breath, but I distrusted every shadow, no matter how small. Nightmares hid themselves in shadows. They waited and watched until they were confident I was asleep, and then they crossed through the light and came into my head through my ears or my nose or my open mouth. That was what I used to believe and, although I never told a soul, still believed. Even when I was little, I sensed that if I told Mama, she would either ignore me, yell at me for being stupid, or maybe even laugh and tell one of her friends what I had said and embarrass me. She had done something like that often enough.

Now I sat here, unable to stop the trembling inside myself, despite the angry brave front I had put on in front of the dean, the policeman, and Aunt Mae Louise. It was one thing to be alone in a world where there were other girls like myself who were as alone or almost as alone as I was, but to feel like I felt here was harder.

This is all Mama's fault, I thought. If she hadn't been so selfish, she would have considered me and what would happen to me after she had run off. I hated Aunt Mae Louise, but she wasn't all wrong when it came to my mama, I admitted to myself. And she wasn't wrong about Daddy either, about him ignoring all the warnings and about him being too weak.

But he was all I had and I was all he had now. Lucky people had lots of choices for themselves. I had none. Wherever I was in my life, I thought, there would always be bars on the windows. There would always be shadows waiting to pounce on me. Lie back and take it, Phoebe, I told myself. Stop trying to go against the wind.

I closed my eyes and listened to the rain and fell asleep. The sounds that woke me were the sounds of Barbara Ann and Jake returning home. I heard Aunt Mae Louise chastise them for making too much noise, and I heard her warn them to stay away from me. The tone in her voice made me sound like I could contaminate them.

The drizzle turned into a heavy downpour. It went on and off for what seemed like hours and hours. I left the room only to go to the bathroom, and when I walked through the hall, I was struck by how quiet it was in the house. Both Jake's and Barbara Ann's doors were shut tight, and Aunt Mae Louise wasn't nearby. All I could do was wait. Finally, she came to my room.

"Your uncle Buster has not been able to locate your daddy yet. His company is trying to contact him for us, but he hasn't gotten to his scheduled stops, I guess. Anyway, you might as well come out and help me get the dinner ready. Uncle Buster is on his way home."

"Are you sure you want me touching things?" I asked sullenly.

She paused and furled her brow.

"No, I don't want you touching things, but I don't want you doing nothing either. Idle hands get into mischief."

I followed her out and set the table. The truth was, I was getting cabin fever in that tiny room anyway. Even her grouchy face and bitter comments brought some variety. When Barbara Ann came out of her room, she looked at me with different eyes, eyes not so full of herself as they were fearful of me. What did Aunt Mae Louise tell her, I wondered, or what had she heard from the other students on the bus?

As if she could read my thoughts, Aunt Mae Louise decided to tell me immediately why Barbara Ann was looking at me askance.

"The other kids made fun of her on the bus, I'll have you know. Seems the news about you and that boy spread like a bad rash through the school. All of our friends are going to hear about it now. Fine thing to do to us."

I didn't say anything. My tongue stayed glued to the roof of my mouth even though the words were scratching away at the base of my throat. I finished what I had to do and then, when Uncle Buster came in, I sat with my head down.

"Your daddy's going to be very disappointed to hear about this when I contact him," he said. Surprisingly, that was all he said. Aunt Mae Louise said grace, and then we ate in relative silence. Every once in a while, I looked up and saw Jake staring at me wide-eyed.

Finally, I couldn't take it any longer and I slapped my fork down on the table and stood up.

"I didn't kill anyone, you know," I screamed, and marched out of the dining room.

"Phoebe Elder!" Aunt Mae Louise called after me. "You don't get up from the table until you are excused. Do you hear what I said?"

"Let her go," Uncle Buster said.

I slammed the door behind me. What little I had eaten seemed to be caught in my throat. My stomach churned, and I went into the bathroom and threw up. They heard me, but no one came to see how I was. Now I was thinking that I wouldn't wait for them to contact Daddy. I would pack my things and just leave. I could hitchhike a ride back into Atlanta proper, and I knew where we kept our key outside the apartment. There was no sense in staying here a moment longer.

It was still raining very hard, however, so I thought I would at least wait for it to let up. In the meantime, I packed everything and then I sat on the bed with my arms folded, facing the door. To my surprise, it opened slowly and little Jake poked his head in.

"What do you want?" I asked him.

"Are you really going to hell?" he replied.

"Your mother tell you that?"

He nodded.

"No. I am not going to hell. I am in hell and so are you," I snapped back at him.

"No, I'm not. Only bad people go to hell," he said. Even at his young age, he had Aunt Mae Louise's scowl.

"Not just bad people," I said, "also unlucky people."

My answer put some confusion in his eyes. He shook his head and said, "No, they don't."

"You better not come too close to me," I warned, "or I'll take you with me. I'll wrap my arms around you so tightly you won't be able to get loose and we'll go down, down, down."

He started to shake his head and then I went, "Boo!" He backed out quickly and closed the door. I started to laugh, but stopped and suddenly felt more like I should cry.

Maybe Aunt Mae Louise was right to tell her children that. Maybe I am going to hell, I thought. I'm my mother's daughter, aren't I? What chance do I have to avoid it? The only thing I've accomplished in my short life is get myself deeper and deeper into trouble. It was a dark, descending road I traveled, and perhaps hell was at the end after all. I had no idea how or what would stop my fall. It seemed hopeless and useless to think of a way. I guess Mama had the right idea after all, I thought. Have a good time and don't worry about tomorrow.

The rain began to let up. I didn't hear it on the windowpane any longer, and when I looked out toward the street light, I saw the downpour had thinned to a slight drizzle. I decided I would wait until they were all asleep and then I would quietly slip out of the house and be out of their hair forever. Aunt Mae Louise would not have to worry about me corrupting her children, and she and Uncle Buster could make up any story they wanted and tell it to their friends in the community. Everyone but Daddy would be happier, including me.

It grew quieter and quieter in the house. I could hear only the muffled sounds of the television set, some water running in the kitchen, and then Aunt Mae Louise getting Barbara Ann and Jake to bed. Not much longer to wait, I thought. I felt like a racehorse champing at the bit. What lay ahead was not exactly a hike in the country. I had to carry my suitcase and get myself onto the more traveled highway before I could get any sort of ride. I didn't have enough money anymore to take a bus.

A little more than a half hour or so later, I heard the telephone ring. I was anticipating that they had finally contacted Daddy. I had made up my mind I wasn't going to talk to him on the phone. I had nothing to say now. This was his fault, too. He shouldn't have brought me here, and I shouldn't have come.

Why did I come? Did I hope this would work? Did I believe Daddy when he told me my life would change and I could have a future? I'm too poor and too cursed to afford a fairy tale, I thought. I should have known that only the rich and lucky become Cinderellas. Now, I would do what I had to do, and that was that.

Suddenly, I heard Aunt Mae Louise scream, "Lord, have mercy."

Uncle Buster called to her, and there was the sound of his heavy feet pounding the floor as he ran into the kitchen. I opened my door and listened. I heard him ask, "When?" and then, "How? Oh, Christ!"

Slowly, I made my way down the hall and stopped in the kitchen doorway. Uncle Buster had his back to me. He was still on the phone. Aunt Mae Louise was collapsed in a chair, both her hands over her face.

"Yes," Uncle Buster said into the phone, "we understand. We'll take care of it. Give me that address again." He waved his hand toward Aunt Mae Louise, but she didn't see. She still had her hands over her face.

"What is it?" I demanded, and she lowered her hands and saw Uncle Buster's hand.

"Give me a pen and something to write on," he ordered. She jumped up and opened a drawer, found what he wanted, and gave it to him before turning to me.

"Terrible, terrible news," she said. Uncle Buster kept writing.

"What?"

"Your daddy, an accident. He's gone," she said.

I looked at her suspiciously, my head tilted.

"What do you mean, gone? Gone where?"

"To the lap of the Lord," she replied.

Uncle Buster thanked whomever he was speaking to and hung up the phone. With a long face, a face weighed down by gloom, he turned and looked at me. He shook his head, his huge eyes staring woefully back at me.

"What is she saying?" I asked him.

"Horace ran off the road sometime this afternoon. Luckily, some man sticking catfish in a stream came upon the car. It had gone down an embankment, through some woods before smashing into a tree and turning over and landing top down in the water."

"He always wears his seatbelt," I said, shaking my head.

"That didn't matter this time. Matter of fact, it may be why he didn't get out."

"Didn't get out? You mean Daddy drowned?"

"It's ugly," he replied.

What little food had remained in my stomach had long ago turned into a small pool of acid. It came rushing back up my throat. I stuffed my fist into my mouth.

"He was trying to cover too much territory in one day, I'm sure," Uncle Buster continued. "You get careless, go too fast around a turn, lose control."

"The Lord meant for it to be," Aunt Mae Louise muttered.

"What kind of Lord is that?" I shouted down at her.

"Don't blaspheme now, child. Your daddy needs to be with the angels and you will want to join him someday."

"No," I said. "This is all a lie. You're just trying to find another way to get rid of me."

"Boy, I wish that were true," Uncle Buster said.

"It is true. You're lying!"

"I got to make arrangements. We got to try to find your mother, Phoebe. No matter what she's done, she should know about this. You have any idea, any idea at all where she might have gone?"

I kept shaking my head.

"Well, I guess we'll have to get the police to help us," he told Aunt Mae Louise. She nodded.

"You're lying," I whispered.

"Now, you have to be a big girl, Phoebe. You have to be a good girl. This is a very hard time for all of us, and you don't know how hard it is going to be yet," Uncle Buster said. "I've got a lot to do here, and I can't be distracted by any unnecessary trouble, hear?"

I stared at him. My heart wasn't pounding. It felt more like it had stopped or melted. There was a deep, cold emptiness under my breast. I embraced myself.

"You see how hard life can be," he continued. "You see how important it is to be good, to be responsible and not be wasteful. Whatever blessings we have, we've got to cherish and appreciate."

He was going on and on like his father, the minister. I started to back away.

"It's all a lie," I muttered. "Another dirty lie. This is a house built on lies."

"That's it!" he screamed back at me. His voice bounced off the walls and I shuddered. "Stop that nasty talk now."

I couldn't stop trembling and I couldn't swallow. All I could do was shake my head.

"All right now, Phoebe," he said in a softer tone, "you go back to your room and get some sleep. We've got a lot to take care of tomorrow." He relaxed his shoulders. "You sure you can't help us find your mama?"

I shook my head harder.

"What's that man's name, the man she ran off with?" Aunt Mae Louise asked. "I didn't pay any attention to what your daddy told me. You know?"

"Speak up, Phoebe. This is not the time for any silly tantrums. Your aunt asked you something."

"Sammy Bitters," I said. It didn't sound like me talking. My voice was so deep.

"Name fits the situation," she told Uncle Buster. "Bitter."

He nodded.

"Go on, Phoebe. Get some rest," he said. "We'll take care of things. We'll take care of you and what has to be done."

Aunt Mae Louise looked up at him sharply. I could almost feel the new realization sinking into them both like a rock in soft mud: with my mother tramping about and not caring about me and my daddy dead and gone to the lap of God, they were all I had now. Like it or not, fate had more than just delivered me to their doorstep. It had put me smack into the middle of their lives. They couldn't send me back.

Aunt Mae Louise nodded.

"The Lord tests us," she said, more to herself than to Uncle Buster and me. "He gives us burdens to make us stronger and stronger."

First, I was a distraction, an annoyance, a responsibility my mama didn't want and finally denied, and now I had graduated to being a burden, but not just an ordinary burden, oh no. I was a blessed burden, a gift from God. The way she made it sound, I should be grateful. Think of all the young women my age who weren't a burden, who had a family that loved and cared for them, who were good students and behaved and said their prayers without being reminded to do so. Of what use were they for the struggle to reach the pearly gates Aunt Mae Louise saw parting for her celestial entrance? If there were no poor, there would be no charity, and how would my aunt get herself blessed?

I turned and walked back to my bedroom. When I got there, I closed the door and then I pressed my back to the wall and slid down slowly to the floor, where I sat next to my suitcase. I wanted to cry for Daddy, but I couldn't. None of this seemed real to me. Surely, Uncle Buster and Aunt Mae Louise would be coming to my door any moment to tell me that was all just meant to put the fear of God into me and make me behave.

"Now go to sleep and count your lucky stars that it isn't so," she would say.

Right? The little voice inside me, a voice I hadn't heard since I was no more than Jake's age, was asking.

Whether they felt sorry for me or what, I don't know, but a while later, there was a gentle knock on my door. I didn't open it or call out, but Uncle Buster opened it and peered in, confused at first when he didn't see me.

"What?" I asked him, looking up.

"What are you doing on the floor? Why is your suitcase out?" he asked quickly.

"I was going to leave," I said.

"No, no, no. You can't leave now, Phoebe. You're just confused and in shock," he told me. He didn't understand that I meant I was going to leave before the phone call. "Everything will be fine. You just get some sleep. I came by to see if you needed anything."

I stared up at him, and he looked uncomfortable.

"You should go to bed, Phoebe. It's going to be hard for the next few days. Go on. Get some sleep," he advised, and backed out, closing the door.

I lowered my head again and soon, I was feeling so tired I had to get up and go to bed. I was afraid of sleep, afraid of those shadows. They were closing in around me, encouraged by the news of Daddy's accident. Now there was definitely no one to come to help me chase them off. They would sink into my brain and make a home for themselves, swimming to the top of my thoughts whenever they pleased. Shout and scream, run and hide, I could do whatever I wanted and it would make no difference, not to them.

I kept my eyes slightly open as sleep crawled over me, slithering around my legs, my waist, and my breasts until it could tighten like a vise and close me in darkness. The shadows kept coming. I could almost hear them swishing over the walls and over the floor.

"Daddy!" I moaned, and then I closed my eyes completely and saw him again, rushing away, leaving me behind forever. It did no good to run after him. My nightmare diminished into a blob of darkness, and I woke with a start. For endless hours, I drifted fitfully on the rim of sleep, never finding the peaceful oblivion I desperately sought.

A cloud of silence came over my aunt and uncle the next morning. They kept Jake and Barbara Ann from making much noise and got them both off to their respective schools. When they spoke to each other in front of me, they practically whispered. Uncle Buster said he had to drive to where they had taken Daddy and make an identification. He never asked if I wanted to go along.

"I spoke with the police last night, and they are trying to locate your mama," he said. "Your aunt Mae Louise and I are making arrangements for your daddy's final resting place. We'll have a nice service for him here. My father will conduct it for us."

I listened to everything he said, but I didn't say anything.

"You better eat something," Aunt Mae Louise told me. "This isn't the time to get sick yourself."

I looked up at her. She almost sounded like she cared, but on second thought, I imagined her concern was that I might add some unnecessary complication. While Uncle Buster went to see about Daddy, Aunt Mae Louise left to talk to her father-in-law and make the arrangements for the funeral. She didn't ask me to go along, either.

Not more than an hour after she left, the phone rang. I wasn't going to answer it, but it rang so long, I finally decided it might be Uncle Buster.

"Is this Mrs. Howard?" a man asked.

"No, it's her niece," I said.

"Well, is she home or is Mr. Howard home?"

"No."

"Well, this is Detective Morgan. I was able to track down Mrs. Elder," he said.

I held my breath.

"Where is she?"

"She's in the detox unit of a hospital outside of Macon," he said. "She was admitted two days ago after causing a disturbance in a nightclub and being taken to the emergency room. You can have the telephone number and address," he continued, and I jotted them down. "Have either of them call me if they would like," he concluded.

I didn't thank him. I hung up the phone and stared at the notepaper.

Then I crumpled it in my fist, but I didn't throw it away. I put it in my room.

But I never told either Uncle Buster or Aunt Mae Louise about the call.

Uncle Buster returned before Aunt Mae Louise. I saw from the look on his face that I would have had a hard time. It really wasn't until he walked into the house and stopped to look at me sitting there in their living room that the full impact and reality of Daddy's death hit me. For a while I was able to put it out of mind, pretend it never had occurred, that it was all one of those nasty dreams the shadows brought into my sleep. Most of the time Daddy was away from me, out there doing his selling. It wasn't hard imagining that he was doing that now, and that some day he would return or call, even though I had told him not to bother unless he was going to take me home. Now, he would never take me home; he would never call.

"Was it really my daddy?" I asked Uncle Buster, and his droopy eyes widened and even brightened.

"For a few seconds after they showed him to me, I had doubts," he replied. "Seems he didn't have his seat belt on after all, Phoebe. It must've slipped his mind. He was carrying a lot of worry. He hit the windshield pretty hard," he added, and immediately shut his lips, regretting that those words had somehow gotten out.

"Are you blaming it on me?" I asked in a voice much shriller than I had expected it to be.

"I'm not blaming nobody," he said. "That's the Lord's work. If you have a guilty conscience, you bring it with you to the church. Your mama should do likewise," he added, and then he thought a moment. "Where is that woman?"

He mumbled something I didn't understand and then went into the kitchen to use the phone. In the meantime I heard Aunt Mae Louise come in. She looked at me, shook her head, and sighed deeply.

"It's all arranged," she said. "Day after tomorrow, whether we find your mother or not."

"We found her," Uncle Buster announced, and returned from the kitchen. "Why didn't you tell me, Phoebe? Why didn't you tell me the police had called?"

"You knew and didn't tell?" Aunt Mae Louise exclaimed. "Why not?"

"What difference does it make? She's no good to anybody," I said, and left the room with both of them staring after me.

I should be feeling more pain, I kept telling myself. I shouldn't feel numb. I should feel sad. I should be crying hysterically, beating the walls, something. My daddy was killed. He's gone for good. My mama is in some nuthouse babbling helplessly. I had seen people lose their loved ones. A girlfriend of mine lost her five-year-old brother last year when he got caught in between two gang members shooting at each other. I never had seen so many tears, heard so many wails of agony. The pain in their hearts was so thick I could feel it in the air.

And then there was Rodney Marks's father, who had a heart attack playing basketball with Rodney and his friends. A tall, healthy-looking man who had something called an aneurysm and died right there on the court. I was watching them play and saw the look of disbelief on Rodney's face. I used to be jealous of his relationship with his father. They were together lots of times. He wasn't just losing a parent; he was losing a friend.

Maybe that was what was wrong with me and my parents. I never thought of them as friends, just as keepers of the cage. There was never much holding us together, but whatever there had been was now gone.

That's why I feel so numb and light all over, I told

myself. I'm like a feather, floating. I have no interest in
staying where I am and I have no idea where I should
go. I'm in the hands of the wind.

That's how I felt over the next few days, like someone
being carried along. Uncle Buster's father being the minister and all made it easier to arrange the funeral and bur-
ial. None of my friends back in the city came, and I was
sure by now word had spread. Bad news had a way of
working its way through walls. Maybe people were just
happy to talk about terrible things happening to someone
else and not to them. Maybe it made them feel safer.

Daddy's boss showed up with one of the other sales-
men in the company. Some of Uncle Buster's and Aunt
Mae Louise's church friends attended out of respect for
them, or maybe out of pity for them being weighed
down now with the responsibility of me. I could feel it
in their eyes when they looked my way, and I saw it in
the almost imperceptible shaking of their heads. They
probably didn't realize themselves how clearly they
were showing their thoughts and feelings. I didn't
blame them. Like Uncle Buster had told me, there's no
one we can blame. That's not our job.

I never looked upon Daddy in death. Because of how
badly injured he had been in the accident, the coffin
was kept closed and I didn't want any private visit. It
was easier for me to keep pretending he wasn't dead,
but just gone. I heard his name mentioned in the sermon, but I reacted with surprise every time.

Afterward, after Daddy's boss and fellow salesman
and all of Aunt Mae Louise's and Uncle Buster's
friends had left the house, she came to my room.

"Uncle Buster and I have been thinking about you,"
she said.

I kept my eyes down. I had found a comfortable,

warm, and dark place inside myself, and for the time being, I didn't want to leave it.

"We decided we would give you another chance here, Phoebe. I had a long talk with Dean Cassidy and the school authorities. Your teacher thinks he can help you, too, and really make progress with your reading. It's going to be up to you entirely. If you behave, if you listen to people and you do your work, you can still save yourself.

"I don't hold up much hope of your mother ever straightening herself out, but who knows the will of the Lord? Maybe someday, she, too, will wake up and realize she can be a decent person, and the two of you can help each other."

I raised my eyes toward her. What enabled her to live in such a world of fantasy? I wondered. Her faith? Or was it just her ignorance of how hard it could be?

"All I ask of you is that you try, Phoebe, you really try. You going to do that for yourself? Well?"

I looked down again.

"I hope so, Phoebe. I really pray for it. You should go back to school tomorrow. It's not healthy for you to hang around here doing nothing but stare at four walls."

"What about my father's home?" I asked.

"All that's being handled by Uncle Buster. He's trying to get all he can to keep in trust for you so you'll have something out of all this misery, but I got to tell you, right now it doesn't look like there's much. That old furniture in that rented apartment isn't worth trucking out, and from what we can see so far, your daddy didn't keep up his payments on his term life insurance. I'm sure he needed every cent he could earn just to keep up ordinary expenses. And your mother, your mother is in the hands of welfare."

So I have nothing but Aunt Mae Louise's and Uncle Buster's charity, I thought, nothing but the few rags that hang in this closet.

"I'm sorry, child," she said. "But this is why you have to try harder to be good."

With that she left me.

Try harder to be good? She might as well have said try harder to fly like a bird.

What did being good mean? Doing everything they wanted me to do and never doing anything I wanted to do. That was the way I saw it. That was the way I always saw it.

And that was the way I always will, I thought.

Maybe I would go on the roof, wave my arms hard, and jump.

5

An Invitation to a Party

During the funeral and after, I saw that my cousins Barbara Ann and Jake looked at me with fear and expectation in their eyes. I felt they were waiting for me to go crazy, scream, and be wild, or maybe just explode as if a bomb of misery and sorrow had finally been ignited inside me. I understood they were expecting me to be as destroyed and distraught as they would be should something as horrible happen to Uncle Buster. I was at least smart enough to realize that for children their age, parents were their whole world, even if it had never been true for me. Parents brought sunshine and happiness, laid out their daily lives, and moved them about with godlike power. Nothing made you see that you could get sick or have an accident, whatever, and die too as much as the death of your daddy or mama. You look down into your own inevitable grave when you look down into theirs, and that puts the ice into your veins.

I suppose my lack of a real relationship with my daddy and with Mama helped me face a world without them. Maybe that was a good thing after all. I wasn't thinking all that much about them after I had been brought here, except in anger. In other words, we didn't miss each other the way parents and children should miss each other. They were almost completely gone when we lived together. This numb feeling that kept me from crying at the cemetery wasn't something I could explain or wanted to explain to Barbara Ann and Jake. They would eventually understand it themselves by just watching me go on, plodding through my day instead of crawling under my bed.

Barbara Ann didn't talk to me at all in the morning. Jake avoided my eyes. When it came time to go on the school bus, Barbara Ann hurried away to sit with her friends. Since my trouble at school and the death of my daddy and his funeral, it was easier for her to pretend she didn't know me. I didn't blame her for that. Actually, I thought, if I was her I would probably have acted the same.

Ashley was sitting with another boy when I got on behind Barbara Ann. He looked at me quickly, and then he and the other boy whispered something and laughed. I was disappointed, but not all that surprised. By now I was sure he'd had enough time to characterize me any way he wanted to and make himself look like some sort of victim. His parents were surely happier about that, and, from the way his friends gathered around him on the bus and in the halls, I could see he was something of a hero.

That's funny when you think about it, or just plain unfair. When a boy gets into trouble with a girl, his friends pat him on the back and he struts through the school corridors like some heroic war veteran. When a girl gets into trouble because of being with a boy, she's supposed to keep her eyes down in disgrace and be ashamed. Well, I wasn't going to keep my eyes down. I'd eyeball anyone who dared to look at me with disgust, not that I looked forward to it.

In fact, I didn't think I would be happy about being stuck in one classroom all day, but for now I was grateful. I didn't have to face the students here as much and see those crooked smiles on their faces and watch them whispering about me. The others in my class seemed unaware that anything had happened at all. Mr. Cody certainly treated me the same as he had when I first entered his classroom. He didn't mention anything except to tell me how sorry he was to have heard about my father's tragic death.

"You're lucky to have an aunt and uncle like the Howards," he added to make me feel better, I'm sure.

I didn't say thank you or anything. Suddenly silence had become a good and close friend. The quick comeback, smart remarks, sticking it to people I didn't like, none of that mattered. I was still moving in a very narrow, dark hallway of my own, and I had no interest in stepping back into the light of day. I buried myself in the work Mr. Cody gave me. I ate my lunch alone. I continued my work, and then I sat in the rear of the bus going home, my eyes looking blankly on the world outside, my ears shut to the gossip and laughter around me. I knew in my heart that, like a time bomb, sooner or later I would explode.

At least for a while at home, Aunt Mae Louise eased up on what she had described as my chores. She didn't call me out to set the table for dinner or help with any of the food preparations. I wanted to believe it was out of some kindness, some compassion, but it occurred to me that she wasn't all that eager to have more to do with me than necessary. At least for now, it was more comfortable for her to keep some distance and not have me at her side in the kitchen.

Death had brushed its hand over my face and left its dark shadow under my eyes. My mama was spinning about in her own lunacy, and I was an immigrant from that mad world. Like some unwanted foreigner who had to be tolerated, I was pushed off, driven by indifference into my own place. My room had become another ghetto. In fact, Aunt Mae Louise didn't even look in to check on how I was keeping it anymore.

I also noticed that at the dinner table, the conversation rarely, if ever, involved or included me. As if I was no longer there, they talked only about themselves. Aunt Mae Louise asked Barbara Ann and Jake about their school work, but never asked me anything. Uncle Buster talked about his job, a trip he planned for the family soon, and they both talked about things they wanted to do for the house.

I began to consider that I might really not be there. Maybe I was the one who had died in the car accident and this was my punishment, my hell, just as I had once told little Jake. Silly and wild imaginings like that kept occurring. Sometimes, they put a wide smile on my face, so wide and bright that Aunt Mae Louise was forced to ask me what I thought was humorous.

Interrupted, I looked at her as if I had just noticed she was there. It spooked her, I know, because she looked away or at Uncle Buster for help.

"Are you all right, Phoebe?" he would ask me softly.

"All right? Sure. I'm fine," I would tell him and return to eating.

I knew Aunt Mae Louise warned both Barbara Ann and Jake to keep their distance from me and be in my company only when it was absolutely necessary. Neither ever came to my room anymore, and when they passed me in the hallway going or coming from the bathroom, they kept their eyes down and their lips pulled tightly shut. Barbara Ann's puckered mouth was drawn up like a drawstring purse. She continued to ignore me completely on the school bus and walking to and from it. The two of them were keeping themselves in an invisible plastic bubble when it came to having anything to do with me. I didn't really care. It was just something curious because I wasn't quite sure if they had the bubble around them or I had it around me.

I continued to behave the same way in school, only vaguely aware of how many of the students were laughing at me until one afternoon, while I was eating my lunch at an outside table, two girls approached me.

They were both white, the taller one prettier, with hair like spun gold and turquoise eyes as bright as polished stones. She had a runway model's figure and a very confident air about her, telegraphed in her correct posture and the arrogant turn in her shoulders when she walked or spoke.

The other girl wasn't as pretty as she was voluptuous, with a fuller figure, dark brown hair, and hazel eyes. Her features weren't as dainty as the taller girl's, but her lips were thicker, sexier, like someone who had gotten those cosmetic shots to make them so. I had the feeling she was a work in progress and would probably have her nose redone.

"Hi," the taller girl said. "I'm Taylor Madison and this is Rae Landau. We heard about what happened with Ashley Porter," she added, and sat.

"Yeah," Rae said, sitting beside her.

I looked at the two of them and smirked. Pride tightened my throat and lifted my shoulders back.

"Big deal. I guess you'd have to be deaf not to have heard," I said.

"Exactly," Taylor said.

"So what do you want? More details to spread?"

"No. We want to tell you we feel sorry for you," Rae said. "Ashley has been telling all sorts of stories about you, exaggerating and embellishing to make himself look better for sure."

"I don't care what he says," I replied. Then I paused to scan their faces, searching for their real intentions, since they said they weren't here to get more details. "Why would you two care so much, anyway?"

"He did something like this to me," Rae revealed. "And it was just as unpleasant for me afterward. I almost had a nervous breakdown."

I know I looked skeptical. I could see Ashley picking on a new girl, especially one like me who had no friends here, but not a girl who looked like she could buy and sell whatever she wanted, especially friends.

"A nervous breakdown?"

"She's telling the truth," Taylor said. "He tried to get me to go on a date with him after he dumped on Rae, but I wouldn't give him the time of day so he spread rumors about me, disgusting rumors."

"Like what? What do you think is disgusting around here?" I challenged.

"Saying I was more interested in girls and that was why Rae and I were such good friends."

I raised my eyebrows and wondered if there was a seed of truth to any of it.

"Someone like Ashley thinks that's the only reason a

girl wouldn't be with him," Rae said. "He's too egotistical to believe anything else. He can never be wrong or the cause of any trouble."

"Yeah," I said with a deep sigh, "I can't deny I did agree to meet him in the nurse's office. I can't blame anyone else but myself for what happened."

"You certainly can and should blame him," Taylor cried, raising her voice. "You were here hardly forty-eight hours. He didn't care if he got caught. He knew he would get away with it. They didn't even suspend him, and guess what," she continued. "He's back on the basketball squad."

"He is?"

"As of this afternoon. There was a hearing or something and his parents came and pleaded and the school decided he had suffered enough being suspended from the team this long."

"I thought his daddy was a marine and was happy he was punished," I said.

They looked at each other and shook their heads.

"Ashley lies to people so much, he probably doesn't know himself what's true and what isn't anymore," Taylor said. "His father was in the army, not the marines, and he's an influential attorney who always finds a way to cover up his son's mistakes, especially speeding tickets."

"Of course, Ashley promised the school and the coach to be a good boy and never do anything like that again," Rae added.

"Believe that, and you'll believe in the tooth fairy," Taylor said, and they laughed.

"It doesn't matter to me. I couldn't care less who is on and off the basketball team. And I don't care if he gets away with murder around here," I said, and finished my sandwich.

"You should care. He got you into trouble and barely blinked," Rae said, her face scrunched in anger. "And on top of it, just as we told you, he hasn't stopped spreading nasty stories about you."

"Maybe they're true," I said.

"I hope for your sake they're not," Rae fired back without hesitation.

"They're even worse than the stories he spread about me," Taylor added.

I stopped smirking.

"What stories?"

"He said you were a professional, that you made money in the streets of Atlanta, and that your mother was one too and made you work with her," Taylor said. "He said that's why you were brought here, to get away from all that, and that's why he didn't get into as much trouble. He even said the dean took the money from you that you made Ashley give you."

"He said I took money from him to give him sex in the nurse's office?"

"Exactly," Rae replied. "Today he told everyone that your father was killed by your mother's pimp because he sent you to live with your aunt and uncle and took business from him. The kids believe him because they think his father has some in with the district attorney," she continued.

"It's not true, is it?" Taylor asked, her eyes somewhat narrowing with suspicion.

"No, and nobody better say it in front of me," I told her, "or it will be the last thing they say."

They looked at each other and then back at me.

"What?" I asked, seeing the hesitation in their faces.

"That's not the worst of it," Taylor said. "He's getting some of the boys to put money in a pot so they could buy sex from you. Someone's going to offer you money to come to a party, but there will be no doubt as to the reason why."

I bit down hard on my lower lip, trying to keep from showing my emotions. When you had no one in the world you could trust or believe in, you felt helpless, as helpless as an astronaut accidentally cut loose in space. Instead of coming to live in a better, safer community with a superior school, I felt like I had been forced to come to a den of poisonous snakes just waiting to pounce on someone like me.

"Thanks for warning me," I told them.

"What are you going to do about it?" Rae asked.

"About what?"

"She means, what are you going to do when the boys approach you?"

"Tell them where to get off," I said. The two of them just stared. "What else?"

"Taylor and I have a better idea," Rae said.

"What?"

"Agree to go to the party," Taylor said.

"What, are you crazy, girl?"

"Just listen," Rae said, moving closer. "We think the party's going to be at Ashley's house this weekend. His parents are going somewhere. Besides offering you money for sex, they'll have drugs. We know Ashley can get Ecstasy whenever he wants to. He's done it many times before."

"So?"

"Tell her who your father is, Rae," Taylor urged, and nudged her with her elbow. Rae smiled slyly.

"My father is a police detective. We're going to tell him what the boys are up to, and he'll be there with some other policemen and arrest them all."

"But what good is that to me? I'll look like I really am a whore," I said.

"No. Rae's father will know you are working with us and them," Taylor explained. "The police do things like this all the time. They call it a sting operation, right, Rae?"

"Exactly. Everyone will know how you cooperated with them. You'll look a lot smarter than those boys."

"Finally, we'll wipe that smug, arrogant smile off Ashley Porter's face and no one will believe anything he says about any girl anymore," Taylor said.

"You'll be doing us all a big, big favor," Rae continued.

"It'll be easy," Taylor said. "And just think how you'll feel watching them take those boys to the police station and calling all those parents, especially Ashley's, who will have to come home from their weekend holiday."

"Mr. Perfect goes in the toilet," Rae said, and Taylor nodded, both of them turning to me eagerly.

"Well, what do you think?" Taylor asked.

"I don't know," I said.

"You can do it," Rae urged.

"I know I can do it," I snapped back at her. I didn't need encouragement from this lollipop.

"So?" Taylor said. "What do you say? We'll be with you the whole time."

"Revenge is sweet," Rae sang, and beamed.

"There's no better way to put a cork in Ashley Porter's sewer mouth," Taylor emphasized.

"Why should I care if he talks garbage or not? It's not going into my ears," I muttered.

"Don't you have any self-respect?" Rae asked, pulling back.

No, I wanted to say. I don't even have a self anymore to respect. I don't know who I am, much less who I will be. I was living with relatives who really didn't want me. I had a learning disability and a court record. My father was dead and my mother in a madhouse detox unit. Nothing that happened to me or that I did seemed to matter.

"Everyone here, especially every girl, will see you as a heroine," Taylor said. "I bet your relatives will be proud of you, too."

"No one messes with Phoebe Elder," Rae declared as if she was writing a headline on a television news program.

"Will you do it?" Taylor pursued eagerly.

I took a deep breath. If I really didn't care, what difference did it make if I did it or not? I thought. I might as well do it. At least, it was something to do.

"Okay. What's first?"

"Wait to see if any of the boys approach you with the offer. Maybe it's all talk. If it isn't, however, Ashley will expect you to be indignant, angry about it, and chase the boy off. He's probably hoping for that and getting his explanation for that all ready, but you'll surprise him by accepting the offer. Now he'll have to put up or shut up, and he'll put up," Rae explained.

"He won't want to look stupid to his friends," Taylor added.

"Right. So you'll have a date and a place," Rae continued. "I'll tell my father and we'll plan out the trap."

"This is great," Taylor said. "I can't wait."

"One thing," Rae continued. "We don't want to spook them, so Taylor and I won't be friendly with you in school until afterward, okay?"

"They're not stupid," Taylor said. "If they see the

three of us consorting, they'll back out or do something to ruin the sting."

"Just write down when and where and slip a note into my locker. It's number 103. You pass it every morning on the way to your classroom, okay?" Rae said.

"We'll call you the night you get the note into my locker and give you whatever instructions Rae's father wants you to have."

"What if he doesn't want to do it?"

"Are you kidding? My father is a very strict disciplinarian. He thinks kids are way too free today and would jump at a chance to make an arrest like this," Rae replied, "especially if there are any drugs involved, and especially with someone like Ashley, who thinks he's above the law. My father doesn't like his father either. He says he's helped too many criminals escape justice."

They both got up.

"Remember, locker 103."

I nodded and they walked away. At the door, Taylor turned and gave me a small wave good-bye.

Life in the perfect suburbs was turning out to be just as nasty as life in my neighborhood, I thought. One good thing that would come out of this would be my aunt Mae Louise would have to stop riding on her high horse and bragging about how much nicer and safer it was living here. That alone seemed reason enough to go through with it.

Nothing happened that afternoon, and no one approached me during lunch the next day. I was beginning to think it was all just a lot of talk, just as Rae thought it might be, something the boys bantered about to show how brave and sophisticated they were. And then, as I was walking back to class, two boys I had seen with Ashley came up beside me. One was about my height, with curly black hair and a pug nose. He was wide in the shoulders and wore a wrestling team jacket. The other boy was taller, with long straw-colored hair and a sharp, pointed nose over thin lips and a cleft chin.

"Hi," he said. "We heard how you got into trouble."

"Good for you," I said, and kept walking.

"We don't think it's right that all the other girls in the school are such snobs and don't have anything to do with you," the boy on my right said. "They should be welcoming you here, not ostracizing you."

I continued walking, keeping my gaze straight ahead, and they remained right alongside.

"Is that right?" I asked.

"Yes, it is. I'm Gerry Balwin. My friends call me Grog. And this is Skip Lester."

I stopped and turned to him.

"Okay, what do you want?" I demanded.

He smiled and looked at his friend.

"We just thought that maybe you'd like to come to a party we're having."

"What party?"

"A cool party," Skip said. "There'll be some other girls there, but three of us really want you to come. We thought, that is . . ."

"We'll give you three hundred dollars, that's a hundred apiece," Grog offered quickly. "That's what you got before, isn't it?"

A big part of me wanted to lash out and slap the side of his face so hard his head would spin around. My heart was thumping with anger I didn't expect, but I figured Taylor and Rae were right about how to get back at these boys. Just smacking them wouldn't do much and in the end, they would surely deny what they had said and I'd be the one getting in trouble again.

"Where's the party?"

"It's at Ashley's house. I wrote down the address for you," Grog said, "with the time. It's Saturday night." He handed me a slip of paper. "We'll have the money there and promise to give it to you as soon as you come. We'll keep it a secret, too."

"Most of the other girls in the school, the ones who look down on you, will be jealous you got invited and they didn't. We won't tell them why. You'll be invited to other things afterward," Skip assured me.

"What kind of a party is it going to be? I hope there's something else to do," I added.

"Oh, don't worry about that," Grog said, smiling. "Ashley's prepared. He'll have some good stuff."

I looked at the slip of paper and then from one boy to the other.

"Three hundred as soon as I get to the house?"

"Guaranteed."

"I want half tomorrow."

"Huh?"

"We got to trust each other, don't we?" I asked.

They looked at each other.

"Well?" I said, seeing the hesitation in their faces. "You want me there or not?"

"You'll have it lunchtime," Grog assured me.

"Then I'll be there for sure," I said, smiling. "Now you go break open your piggy banks," I told them, and walked away.

I heard them laugh and saw them hurrying excitedly back to the cafeteria. When the police pounced on them, I would have sweet vengeance, but I'd also have one hundred and fifty dollars, and I had no intention of giving it up.

At the end of the day, I passed locker 103, paused, and dropped the slip of paper through the slot. That night, to my aunt's surprise, I had a phone call. She came to my room to tell me there was a girl on the line asking for me.

"She said her name is Rae," Aunt Mae Louise told me, her eyes full of suspicion. "Who is she?"

"Just some girl I met in school. Her father's a policeman," I added.

She relaxed.

"Oh. Well, we want you to have nice friends here, Phoebe. We're just going to always be concerned about your welfare," she explained.

She tried not to make it obvious, but I knew she was following me to the kitchen. She should be working as a spy for the government, I thought.

"What?" I said instead of a hello.

"I'm just calling you to confirm I have your note, and I've spoken to my father. He's very excited about this, and he wanted me to tell you thank you beforehand," she said quickly. "He says just pretend to be going along with everything, and he'll take it from there."

"What's that mean?" I asked, keeping my voice as low as I could. Although she wasn't in the kitchen, I was sure Aunt Mae Louise was just outside the door eavesdropping.

"You know, start like you're going to go through with it so they can't claim it wasn't what we know it is. You'll have to go into the bedroom with the first boy after they pay you. They'll do some Ecstasy first to build up their courage, and my father and his partners will be watching all the time. I know you're probably afraid, but . . ."

"I'm not afraid and I know what to do," I said. I didn't need my courage built up by the likes of them.

"Good. We'll have our own little celebration afterward. I promise," she told me, and hung up.

"Where's the party?" I pretended to ask after she hung up. "I'll have to ask my aunt and uncle. Thanks," I said, and hung up.

As I anticipated, Aunt Mae Louise was right outside the door.

"The girls are having a party this weekend and asked me. Is that all right with you?"

"Where is the party?"

"At Rae's house. Her mother and father will be there," I said. "It's like one of those pajama parties, girls getting to know each other and all."

"That sounds fine. I'll see about Uncle Buster taking you there."

"He doesn't have to," I said quickly. "Rae's going to pick me up."

"Oh. What's her name again?"

"Rae Landau," I said. "Her father's a detective."

She made a mental note of it and told Uncle Buster. I overheard them talking about it. He phoned someone to check on my story. They were being extra careful all right, I thought. However, when he returned and reported I was telling the truth that there was indeed a Detective Landau, I had to admit to myself I felt better about it, too.

Anticipating Saturday night and how sweet my revenge would be put some excitement into my life. I actually looked forward to going to school and seeing how the boys looked at me, Skip and Grog smiling and winking, and how excited both Taylor and Rae looked whenever I confronted them.

On Friday, right after I entered the cafeteria and got my lunch, Grog came up beside me and handed me an envelope.

"Just put it away quickly," he said, looking around nervously. "We can both get into lots of trouble for this."

I dropped it into my purse and later, in the girls' room, I took it out and counted seven twenties and one ten. I smiled with glee. Won't those rich arrogant boys be surprised? Just the thought of it put some pep into my steps and gave me new energy. I worked hard in class, so hard Mr. Cody gave me a compliment.

"You keep going like this, Phoebe, and you'll be on reading level and back where you belong before you know it."

The others looked at me with envy.

That's exactly where I'd like to be, I thought. Back where I belong.

That evening and all the next day, I tried to be Miss Perfect at home. I didn't want anything to happen that would interfere with our plans. I offered to help Aunt Mae Louise with the dishes before she asked. In the morning right after I rose and dressed, I started to vacuum, cleaning my room and then going into the halls and the living room.

Aunt Mae Louise smiled and nodded. Later, Uncle Buster asked if I would like to go with him, Barbara Ann, and Jake for some frozen custard. I thanked him and told him I had to get myself ready for my party. I chose the most conservative thing I had to wear and asked Aunt Mae Louise's opinion, something that took her by complete surprise.

"Yes," she said, "that's appropriate." She thought a moment and said, "Once your father's estate is straightened out, we'll use whatever there is to buy you some new clothes, Phoebe. A girl your age needs a nice wardrobe. Some day you'll go off to college or a business school and need nice things to wear."

I nodded. Me in a college, even a business school? Get real, I thought, and then, for a moment, I tried to imagine it. Every image seemed silly. I was sure I'd end up like Mama, a waitress in some restaurant. It made me angry and even more eager to go to this party and turn those rich boys and their friends upside down.

Rae and Taylor showed up exactly at seven o'clock. Aunt Mae Louise insisted I bring them into the house to meet her. They looked more nervous about it than I was.

"I think it's real nice of you girls to welcome someone new to the community like this," Aunt Mae Louise told them. "It shows a warm heart, a charitable and compassionate heart, and that's how we all walk in the light of the Lord."

They smiled at her and looked to me to get them out quickly. As soon as we left, Rae pounced.

"You didn't mention the sting operation to your uncle and aunt, did you?"

"No. You don't have to worry about that. I know what to say and what to do," I told her sharply.

These spoiled girls with their fancy clothes and cars weren't going to make me feel innocent and incapable of handling myself. They hadn't seen half the things I had. If they had, they'd be the ones hiding in a closet, I thought.

"Rae's father told us we're supposed to act like we don't know anything," Taylor explained. "The boys will be sitting around, drinking. There'll be music and then Ashley will bring out the Ecstasy. You should take it just to keep them from being suspicious. You ever do that before, take drugs?"

I raised my eyebrows.

"Where I come from, it's like candy," I said.

"I bet. After this is over, I want to have a real party at my house so the girls can get to know you. Some of them are so naive and simple, they'll think you're out of a movie or something."

"But not you, huh?" I said.

"Taylor and I are a lot more sophisticated than our friends," Rae explained, "mainly because of things I hear my father talk about, things he doesn't even know I've seen and heard."

"That's nothing. That's like watching it on television," I said.

They were both quiet. We traveled through another neighborhood where the houses looked bigger and more expensive than the ones in my aunt and uncle's development. It had been mostly cloudy all day and had grown darker and darker until the wind picked up and some drops of rain struck the windshield. By the time we drove up a long driveway lined with lanterns and beautiful cypress trees pruned to the exact same height all the way up to the circular driveway, the raindrops had become a steady drizzle.

I was impressed with the size of Ashley Porter's house, but I didn't want to gape and sound like I was. It was a two-story home with a steeply pitched roof and tall, narrow windows. I could see the chimney on the left side. The walls of the house were solid brick. I saw five other cars parked in front.

"Looks like everyone's here," Rae commented.

"Where's your father?" I asked, gazing around.

"They're either here already or right behind us," Rae said. "Don't worry about them. If we can see them, then the boys might be able to see them."

The moment we opened the car doors, I could hear the loud music within the house.

"They're starting early," Taylor said. "Good. They'll be too wasted to be careful."

The front door was slightly open, which explained why the music leaked out so loudly.

"Hey, we're here!" Taylor cried.

We heard a whoop from the room on the left. I tried not to gawk at all the artwork, the statues, expensive-looking rugs, and gilded mirrors. In the living room there were pieces of furniture that looked built for giants. The fireplace was the biggest I had ever seen, not that I had seen that many.

I recognized most of the boys and saw only one other girl. Some of the boys were sitting on the floor and some on the long sofa and oversized chairs. What looked like two bottles of vodka were on the large, oval coffee table with soda water, juice, glasses, and a bucket of ice. Most everyone was smoking, and it didn't smell or look like plain cigarettes.

Ashley, who was in front of a stereo, turned and smiled. There was no doubt in my mind that something slippery and ugly was hidden beneath those laughing eyes.

"Hey, the party's here!" he cried. The boys cheered.

I had seen people my age wasted on drugs and drink. I had been at many a party where sex, booze, and drugs were common, but there was something about this scene, about being among so many rich kids that made me nervous, as well as our secret plan I had to make work. Maybe it was just the size of the house and all the expensive things. I was in unfamiliar territory, and even though I wasn't afraid of any of them, I couldn't help feeling like a fish out of water. Even a shark has trouble there, I thought.

"What would you like to drink?" Ashley asked. "Or do you just want to go right to the party?"

I looked at Rae and Taylor. Rae nodded slightly.

"Why waste time? Ain't time money?" I fired back at him, and the boys all whooped again.

"Well, enjoy an E," he said, and handed me some Ecstasy. "It's a fringe benefit."

"Thanks," I said, and pretended to take it, but kept it in between my fingers.

Grog jumped up.

"We already decided," he said. "I'm first."

"Lucky you," I said, and there was another cheer.

I looked at Rae, and again she nodded. I glanced at the windows. Were the police watching? Were they already in the house? Could they hear everything?

"Right this way," Grog said, taking me by the right elbow.

"Hold on," I said, glancing at Rae. "Where's the rest of your money?"

"Oh, right, sorry," Grog said, and dug into his pocket to produce a fifty-dollar bill. He held it up.

The other boys seemed hypnotized, even Ashley. Soon, he would be choking on his nasty words, I thought.

Taylor and Rae watched me pluck the bill from Grog's fingers and stuff it into my purse. I tried to make the action as big as possible so Rae's father would be satisfied, wherever he was. Then I turned toward the door.

"He won't be long," Skip Lester called after us. There was another whoop of laughter.

We crossed the hallway and entered what looked like a big office.

"Right through here," Grog said, continuing to a door in the rear.

I walked slowly behind him, anticipating Rae's father's arrival any moment. Grog opened the door to what looked like a small bedroom that had been created out of a big closet.

"What is this?" I asked, surprised.

"Ashley's father's little hideaway. Perfect, huh?" he asked.

I shook my head. There wasn't a window. Behind me, the music got louder. Where were Rae's father and the other policemen?

"Well, let's get to it. Just pretend we're in the nurse's office in school," Grog said, unbuttoning his shirt quickly and then undoing his pants.

I looked back. Something was wrong. Something was very wrong. Silent screams stuck in my throat when my heart began to pound warnings.

"What's up?" Grog asked, standing there with his pants half down.

I turned without replying and headed back across the office, but when I reached the door, all the other boys were standing there.

"Where are you going, Phoebe?" Ashley asked. "He wasn't that fast, was he?"

I tried to look past them for Rae and Taylor.

"Where's Rae? Where's Taylor?" I demanded.

"Oh, they had another appointment," Skip said. "They told me to tell you, don't worry. They'll be back."

"What? Be back? What are you talking about? Where are they?" I demanded, and tried to look past them.

"Hey," I heard Grog call from the little room, "I'm ready!"

"He's ready," all the boys chorused.

"What's the matter, Phoebe?" Ashley asked, stepping closer. "Expecting someone else?"

"Let me outta here," I said, feeling I was snared in some spider's web that was partly my own making. I tried to push past them, but they held fast, not making any space for me.

"Don't tell me we didn't pay you enough," Ashley said. "You don't get this much on the street, plus benefits."

They were all looking lustfully at me, their eyes burning with pornographic fantasies. I backed up. This was really a trap, and I had walked right into it, arrogantly, confidently, stupidly. There were no policemen; there was no sting operation. What kind of girls would do this to me? The boys stepped forward, moving in a clump.

"Tell you what," Ashley said. "For another hundred, we'll all be able to watch. What do you say?"

I spun around. Grog was in the doorway behind me, his pants and shirt off.

"Bastards!" I screamed at them, scooped a small statue off the desk, and held it like a club.

"Put that down," Ashley ordered.

Panicked now, I swung it and hit Skip Lester, who was moving up on my right. I caught him on the side of his forehead, the small pedestal of the statue cutting deeply and quickly into his skull. Blood spurted instantly, and all the boys washed back like a wave at the sight of it. Skip staggered and fell toward them. I saw my opportunity and ran past them through the office doorway.

I heard them screaming after me, but I didn't hesitate. I went right to the front door and out, charging down the steps.

"Get her and bring her back here!" Ashley ordered the others from the open doorway.

I ran as fast as I could down the driveway, almost slipping on the slickness from the drizzle, and then I cut across the lawn and into some bushes and trees. I heard the boys' footsteps clacking behind me on the driveway. I continued to charge forward, bushes catching my dress and tearing it, but I didn't stop until I was out on the road. I could still hear them shouting after me. I kept running until I reached a street corner and paused to catch my breath and listen.

They had stopped chasing me. I no longer heard them. After a few minutes, I continued walking quickly until there was nothing behind me but the darkness and a bad memory.

6

The Best of Nothing

I walked for hours because I didn't know where I was going or how to get home. First fear and then rage filled me with energy, my fury carrying me along like some magic carpet on the wind. I couldn't wait to get my hands on that Rae and Taylor. Their meanness in conspiring with those boys was lower than anything I could remember. I had never been so betrayed. How could I have been so trusting, so gullible? I blamed myself for wanting to believe in them, for being desperate to have friends.

Despite the rage boiling inside me, I was a lot calmer because of the distance I had made between me and Ashley's house. Now, as I walked, I felt the ache in my calves and thighs and some sharp pain on my right side where a bush branch had slapped against me. I realized my feet were muddy and wet, too. The slight drizzle had stopped, but my hair was wet, soaked from the rain and my own sweat.

Finally, I stopped at a fast-food store and got some directions. I didn't realize just how far out of my way I had gone until the counter girl explained the directions back to my uncle and aunt's home. Grudgingly, I started out again, worried about every car I saw pass me by, half expecting some of those boys to jump out and attack me.

By the time I turned into my aunt and uncle's housing development, it was close to midnight. I was tired, damp, and dirty, and there was that long rip through my skirt. Aunt Mae Louise was surely going to raise the roof, I thought. How was I going to explain all this?

What caught me by surprise, however, was the sight of a police patrol car in our driveway. I stopped to think. Why would the police be here? Did it have something to do with what happened tonight, or did it have something to do with Mama? A part of me wanted to turn and run again, but my curiosity was strong, too. I had no reason to run, I told myself. I didn't do anything bad. Bad things were done to me.

Before I could decide which way to go, the front door opened and the policemen stepped out, with Uncle Buster beside them. They all saw me standing half in shadow, half in the light at the foot of the driveway.

"Phoebe?" Uncle Buster called. "That you, girl?"

"Yes," I said.

"You come right up here," he said sharply.

I walked up the driveway slowly. He turned and shouted into the house.

"She's home, Mae Louise!"

I heard her running up the hallway to the front door.

"Where have you been, Phoebe?" Uncle Buster asked me.

"I got lost," I said, looking from one policeman to the other.

"Everyone's been looking for you, girl," Uncle Buster said.

Aunt Mae Louise came up behind him.

"Where you been?" she shouted at me.

"She said she was lost," Uncle Buster said.

"Oh, she's lost all right, but unlike the prodigal son, she's not lost and found, no, sir. Not by a long shot. How could you do something like this now? With your daddy not even cold in his grave, how could you be so bad?"

"What did I do?" I moaned. I looked at the scowling policemen and realized they weren't here about Mama. They were here about me. Those boys had told some other lies. I began to babble. "They're the ones who deceived and trapped me. They're the ones who lied."

"What are you talking about? They lied? Talk about lies. You said you were going to that girl's house when you were going to a party with lots of boys instead," Aunt Mae Louise said sharply. "You don't know how to do anything else but lie and you're still doing it now."

"That's not true," I moaned.

"You hurt a boy real bad tonight," Uncle Buster said. "He's in the hospital. You know that?"

"He deserved it. They all deserve to be in the hospital."

"Oh, just listen to her," Aunt Mae declared to the policemen. "She's much too much for us to handle."

"You'll have to come with us to the police station," one of the policemen said. "Serious charges have been lodged against you, miss."

"Charges? What about what was done to me?"

"You'll have your chance to tell your side of it," he said.

"Oh, sure. I'll have lots of chances," I snapped back at him.

"Come along," he said, moving to take my arm.

"Uncle Buster, it's not what they say. I was fooled into believing something else was going to happen tonight. They were all out to get me."

"You better just go with them for now, Phoebe. I'll be along," he said in a tired, skeptical voice.

"But—"

"This is very, very serious. Just do what the police want you to do, Phoebe."

"Right. Just do what they want," I mimicked. A lot of good it was going to do me appealing to him for any help, I thought.

"Let's go," the policeman said, moving me more forcefully toward the police car. The other patrolman opened the door, and they practically pushed me into the car. Aunt Mae Louise stood on the stoop shaking her head at me and mumbling some prayer under her breath.

"It's not my fault! I'm not lying!" I screamed back at her.

The policemen got in, and we started out of the driveway. I looked back and saw Uncle Buster arguing with Aunt Mae Louise, and then we made a turn and headed out of the development. Fuming, I sat back and glared straight ahead. Daddy sure made my life more miserable bringing me here, I thought. I would have been better off living in the streets of Atlanta.

When we arrived at the police station, they put me in a room by myself. It was brightly lit, with bare walls and a mirror. They sat me at a long table, but no one came for so long, I fell asleep with my head down on the table. Then I felt someone nudge me, and I raised my head slowly and looked at a policewoman. She had short, dark hair, beady eyes, and a small mouth. There was a small bump in the bridge of her nose. I had seen policewomen before, but she looked too small and fragile to be one.

"All right," she said. "Let's hear your side of this."

I stared down at the table, my arms folded under my breasts.

I didn't want to talk to anyone. What good would it do? What good did it ever do?

"You had better start talking. That boy, Skip Lester, he has a concussion and fifty stitches. He'll have a scar. His parents are pretty angry," she said calmly. "They want us to charge you with more than just assault and battery. They think you tried to kill him."

"If I was trying to kill him, he'd be dead," I said.

"An inch or so to the right, and you would have hit him in the temple and done just that," she shot back at me. "I don't think you should be such a smartass, girl."

I pouted, still fuming too much to speak.

"Now, if you don't tell us your side of it, all we'll have is their side, and that doesn't look too good for you. There's an assistant district attorney coming here soon to decide how to charge you and what to do with you now. You don't have to be charged as a minor if it's a serious felony. You could go to adult court, Phoebe. That's your name, right, Phoebe?"

"Yeah, that's my name."

"Well?"

I took a deep breath and sat forward, wondering just where I should begin. Perhaps I should start with the day Mama left me alone when I was only four and I accidentally pulled a pot of boiling water off the stove, scalding my hand and wrist and screaming so loud, I brought neighbors to the door. Mama yelled at me and shook me so hard, I thought my teeth would fall out. From then on it always seemed to me it was me against the world. This was just another in a series of attacks, attacks that would never end until I did.

"I got into some trouble in school," I began, and told her the story from start to finish, right to the moment I walked up to my aunt and uncle's driveway. She listened, which was more than my uncle and aunt were willing to do. After I was finished, and actually as I was speaking, I had the sense other people were watching and listening. The mirror on the wall was probably a one-way window, I thought.

"Okay," she said when I stopped speaking. "You want something to drink?"

"Some water."

She got up and a few moments later, brought me a bottled water.

"Just relax awhile," she said.

"Am I going to jail?"

"We'll see what's what soon," she told me, and left again.

Nearly another hour went by before she returned.

"Okay. For now you've been released back to your uncle and aunt's supervision," she announced.

I looked up, surprised.

"I am?"

"Yes. It's not like you're on bail, but your uncle has vouched for you and promised he would make sure you came to the court when you have to come. He could get into trouble if you don't listen or try to run away. He's going to take you home now," she said.

"What about the charges against me and such?" I asked.

"They'll decide about all this in court later," she explained. "For now, go home, listen to your uncle and aunt, and keep your nose clean."

When I walked out, Uncle Buster was sitting with his head down in the lobby. He looked up at me and then rose.

"This wasn't all my fault," I told him in a hoarse voice.

"Let's just get home and get some sleep, Phoebe. It's been a long, long night," he said, looking almost as exhausted as I felt. "Your aunt's sick over worrying about you."

"I'll bet she's worrying about me," I said.

I followed him out to the car.

"You can't go anywhere but to school and back," he told me when we got in. "Otherwise, you could end up right back here and things will go very bad for you when we do go to court, Phoebe. It might be a lot different here than where you lived. They don't see as much of this sort of thing, and they might be a lot sterner."

"I don't know why I'm the one who has to go to court. They're the ones who tried to rape me!"

"Let's not talk about it anymore," he said.

"Let's not."

I fell asleep again with my head against the side of the car and woke up when we pulled into the driveway and then into the garage. Wrapping her bathrobe around herself, Aunt Mae Louise came out of her bedroom when we entered the house.

"Don't say anything more now, Mae," Uncle Buster begged her before she could begin. "Let's all just get some rest. You want to be up early for church and make those corn muffins for Dad."

"Seems we all oughta be up early for church," she muttered, her eyes fixed stone-coldly on me.

I didn't reply. I went into my room and without even taking off my clothes, went to sleep. Collapsed was more like it, because I didn't even take off my muddied shoes.

I heard my door opening in the morning, but I kept my eyes closed.

"She doesn't even have sense enough to get undressed for bed," Aunt Mae Louise said.

"Just let her rest, Mae," I heard Uncle Buster tell her. "She'd only fall asleep in church and embarrass us both and you'd be more upset."

"Ain't that the truth," she replied, and the door was closed.

I lay there listening to them move about the house, Aunt Mae Louise snapping orders at Barbara Ann and Jake and even Uncle Buster until they were ready to leave. When the door closed and the house grew silent and I was absolutely sure they were gone, I rose.

I took off my clothes and had a hot shower. Then I dressed in a pair of jeans, a blouse, and a light leather jacket. I slipped on some running shoes, ran a brush through my hair, and then packed my suitcase, taking only the things I absolutely wanted. I dug out the hundred and fifty dollars I had taken from Grog in school. I had buried it in a drawer under my panties. I scooped up my purse and put the money in it along with the fifty I had kept from the night before.

On the way out, I drank a glass of orange juice. I wasn't very hungry, but I thought I had better take a piece of bread anyway. I paused in the doorway.

"Good riddance to you all," I told the house. "I'm

not hanging around here to see whether or not I get put in jail or something."

I closed the door and walked out of the housing development. First, I thought I would just go back to our apartment in Atlanta, hoping it was still ours and the landlord hadn't moved Daddy's things out yet. But as I rode the bus toward the city, another thought entered my mind. When we reached the bus station, I stood considering for a while before deciding to take the next bus to Macon.

I decided I was going to see Mama. Maybe if I went to see her, she would be encouraged and want to start her life anew. Maybe we could be together after all, just up and go somewhere we had never been and be a mother and a daughter for once and for all. She can't want to stay in a detox ward, and she might be disgusted enough with her choices to see the light and want to be with me.

For all I knew, she didn't know about Daddy, too. Perhaps that would affect her. She would realize I had no one now and she would care, especially when I complained about her sister, my aunt Mae Louise. Mama never liked her own sister. She'd understand why I was so determined to get away.

Sure she would. She would have to, I thought. The more I thought about it all, the more excited I became, so excited, I wished the bus would go faster. When we pulled into the station in Macon, I practically knocked people out of my way to get off. Then I found a taxi stand and had the driver take me to the place I knew Mama was being kept.

After I spoke with the receptionist, she made me wait in a small lobby, but I didn't wait long before a tall, thin African-American woman in a lab coat came out to see me. Her hair was a thin reddish brown, and she had freckles on her caramel cheeks, a long but nicely shaped nose, and lips that were almost orange.

"I'm Doctor Young," she said, extending her long arm and thin fingers at me.

I took her hand and stood.

"I want to see my mother," I replied.

"You're Charlene Elder's daughter?" she asked as if she didn't believe Mama had a daughter.

"Yes."

"We've been trying to locate her husband. Where is your father?"

"He's dead," I said. "He was killed in a car accident recently."

"Oh. I'm sorry to hear that. We actually tried contacting . . ." She paused to look at her clipboard. "Contacting a Mrs. Mae Louise Howard, but she hasn't returned any calls. That is your mother's sister, isn't it?"

"She's probably trying to forget she's related," I said dryly.

"Well, who do you live with?"

"Nobody," I said, not hiding my impatience. "I just want to see my mother. Can I see her?"

"Yes, yes. I think it might do some good. Come along," she said eagerly. "What do you know about your mother's condition?" she asked.

"Nothing," I said. What was I going to do, tell her my life story?

"Your mother has been suffering from serious substance abuse and is still in a period of withdrawal."

"How did she get here?" I asked as we continued down the corridor.

"As far as I know, she was dropped off at the emergency room, but whoever did that didn't hang around.

It's quite common," she added quickly as if she thought I would get hysterical over it.

"Is she going to be all right?"

"These things take a lot of time," she replied. "They require a great deal of therapy and a willingness on the part of the patient."

She stopped and touched my arm.

"I don't know how much you know about what happened here."

"I don't know much. She left my daddy and me and ran off with someone."

"I see."

She hesitated and then, from the look I saw in her eyes, decided she had to be truthful, even to someone as young as I was.

"Your mother tried to commit suicide," she told me.

"Suicide? We didn't know that."

"I did leave a message for your aunt."

I shook my head.

"She never told me," I said more to myself than Doctor Young.

"It's not uncommon to see patients with problems like this get this depressed and try to take their own lives."

"What did she do?"

"She cut her wrists with a ballpoint pen, but fortunately, an attendant was nearby and we were able to prevent serious consequences. At the moment she's quite withdrawn. It's not uncommon, given the drugs, the alcohol."

"Nothing seems to be uncommon," I commented.

She stared at me a moment and then nodded.

"I'm just trying to prepare you. You don't look that old," she said as we continued. "With whom do you live now?"

"I was living with my aunt."

"Your aunt? But I thought . . . I mean, as I said, we've tried to get her to call us. Does she know you've come here?"

"I'm making other living arrangements," I said quickly, hoping she would stop asking so many questions.

She widened her eyes.

"I see. Okay. We have your mother under twenty-four-hour observation in here," she said, taking me through another door. We paused in the hallway. "She's in this room. Don't be alarmed about how stark it is. With cases like this, we have to limit the patient's ability to find ways to harm him- or herself."

A tall black man in an attendant's uniform peered out of a doorway, holding a cup of coffee.

"How is Mrs. Elder doing?" Doctor Young asked.

"No different. No problem," he said.

She reached into her pocket and produced a key chain. Then she unlocked the door of Mama's room and opened it. Mama, in a patient's light blue gown, was sitting on a bare bed looking at a bare wall. There was no other furniture, not even a chair.

"Charlene?" Doctor Young said. "I have a visitor for you. Someone's come to see you."

Mama didn't turn. She didn't look as if she had heard.

Doctor Young nodded to me, and I stepped forward.

"Hello, Mama," I said.

Mama's eyes fluttered, and then she turned and looked at me, but her expression didn't change. I saw the bandages on her wrists, but shifted my eyes away quickly. Just the sight of that made my heart thump hard and fast.

"Your daughter has come to see you, Charlene. Isn't that nice?"

Mama looked at Doctor Young.

"I want a cigarette," she said as if I came to see her every day and it was nothing unusual.

"Now you know you can't have cigarettes yet, Charlene. Why don't you just visit with your daughter now. Have a nice visit, and we'll be talking again this afternoon."

Mama pursed her lips the way I knew her to do when she had an angry or unpleasant thought. Then she grunted and turned back to the wall. I looked at Doctor Young, who nodded some encouragement.

"I'll be right outside," she said, and left the room, but leaving the door slightly open.

"Hi, Mama," I said.

"What are you doin' here?" she snapped back at me. "This ain't no place for you, girl."

"I came to see you. I had to see you, Mama. I was hoping you'd be better and—"

"You got any cigarettes?"

"No, Mama."

"They keep me from having cigarettes. I'm dying for a drink. It's like prison. I get outta here, I'm gonna get even with Sammy for dumpin' me like that."

"What happened?"

"I don't know," she said, and then looked at me sharply. "Your daddy send you here hopin' I'd come back?"

"Didn't anyone tell you about Daddy, Mama?"

"They don't tell me nothin' 'bout nobody. All they tell me is what I can eat and drink, when I should sleep, and how I should try to care more about myself. That doctor drives me crazy with all her talk. Makes my head spin. If you got a cigarette and you're not givin' it to me, Phoebe . . ."

"I don't have any cigarettes, Mama. Aunt Mae Louise won't let a cigarette ten feet near her."

"Mae Louise?" She blew some air between her lips. "She only let that man of hers near her twice, to have those brats, and that was that. I can see it in his face when he looks at me. Man's starving for some lovin'," she said, smiling. "Mae hates it when I'm around."

She looked at me again, angrily.

"Why didn't your daddy come here himself? Man has no spine, sending a girl to do his work."

"Daddy can't come here even if he wants to, Mama. Daddy's dead," I said.

She tilted her head a bit and narrowed her eyes.

"I don't know why no one has told you that. Maybe they have and you forgot," I added, more for my own thinking than hers.

"Dead? How's he dead?"

"He was killed in a car accident, Mama. I've been living with Aunt Mae Louise and Uncle Buster since you ran away with Sammy Bitters. Daddy thought it was better than my being alone in the city, only it's been worse," I continued, since she looked like she was really listening to what I had to say now. "It's a snobby place and—"

"You say Horace is gone?"

"Yes, Mama. Daddy's gone."

She nodded and then rocked herself.

"He was like dead anyway," she told herself. Then she stopped rocking and looked at me.

"So who you living with now?"

"I just told you, Mama. I'm living with Aunt Mae Louise and Uncle Buster, but I can't stand it there so I ran away."

"Ran away?" She smiled and then chuckled. "I wasn't much older than you when I first ran away. Runnin' is in the blood, I guess."

"Mama, I want you to get better and come out of here. We could go off together, start a new life somewhere, far away from people like Aunt Mae Louise."

"You can't ever get away from people like your aunt Mae Louise. They're everywhere, like locusts," she said angrily, and started rocking herself again.

"We can, Mama. Just you and me."

She looked at me with a smirk.

"You and me? Girl, you don't even have a cigarette," she said. "You come here and you don't even have a cigarette for me."

"Mama, you can get all the cigarettes you want when you come out of here and we're together. We'll get jobs together, maybe even in the same restaurant or something, and we'll have a nice apartment and take care of each other."

"Who told you to say all that? Your daddy tell you? He'd try anything to get me to come back."

"No, Mama." I squinted at her. "Daddy's gone. I told you. He was killed in a car accident. Don't you understand? We don't have anyone but ourselves now."

She stared at me, looking like the things I was saying were finally taking hold.

"We can't go off, Phoebe. I gotta wait here for Sammy. We're goin' to California. His cousin owns a beauty parlor in Encino and there'll be a job for me. I always used to talk about goin' to California," she said, smiling. Then she stopped. "He shouldn't have left me here so long." She leaned toward me. "Those people, that doctor, they ain't nice at all. They want to keep you here because they get more money that way from the state." She smiled and nodded. "They don't think I know about such things, but I do."

"You can get out of here, Mama. You can get out of here and be with me. We'll go to California. I promise," I said. "I'll just get some part-time work and raise the money for our trip. I can do that."

"Can you go out and come back here?" she asked.

"Yes, certainly. I'll find some place to stay and I'll find some work."

"Well, go on and buy some cigarettes and come back," she said, and waved her hand as if I was dismissed.

"Mama, why are you talking about cigarettes? I'm talking about starting a life together, a whole new life."

"I started a new life," she said. She rocked herself again. "I don't know where my clothes are or anything." She stopped and looked at me. "You know what I've been thinking, Phoebe? I've been thinking your daddy did this. Somehow, he did this, got me in here. Well, you go home and you tell him it's not going to work. I'm not going back there, you hear me, girl? That's my message and make sure he understands it's firm and final."

I stood there staring at her, watching her rock herself, start to say something, stop, and then rock on.

"Mama," I said softly. I reached out and touched her shoulder. She didn't turn to me. She kept staring ahead.

Whatever it was that you had to reach back into to find yourself was still quite buried under confusion in her, I thought. I had been too optimistic, even arrogant, to think that I merely had to appear and all sorts of good thoughts and dreams would be revived, the mother in her would come rising to the surface like some corpse dead and under water for too long. The sunshine would resurrect it. The new hope would renew all that naturally binds a mother to her child and a child to her mother. Memories of the umbilical cord would be vivid and startle her and she and I would walk out of here like mother and daughter should.

When do you stop believing in fairy tales? I wondered. Or is it that you never stop? Even on the day you die, you think about doorways to paradise, to places without pain and sorrow where the only shadows that hover alongside you are the ones that want to dance with you.

Well, you don't dance, Phoebe, I told myself. You walk out of here alone.

I lowered my head.

Doctor Young appeared in the doorway and opened it a bit more. I shook my head at her, and she beckoned me to come out.

"I'm going now, Mama."

She didn't turn to me. I drew closer and I kissed her on the cheek. She felt my tears, tears that moved to her skin, and she brought her hand to it.

"Am I crying?" she asked me.

"No, Mama, I am," I said.

She nodded.

"Doesn't surprise me," she said.

"Me neither, Mama. It never does anymore. Goodbye," I said, and walked out.

"You shouldn't be discouraged," Doctor Young said. "We've only just begun to work with her. Give it time."

I smiled at her. Another one who believes in fairy tales, I thought.

"Where are you going now, Phoebe?" she asked.

"I'm not sure," I admitted.

"Come to my office and rest awhile. We'll talk some

more about your mother's condition and maybe I can help you understand," she suggested. "Are you hungry?"

I hadn't realized it, but I was now that she mentioned it.

"Yes, I am."

"Good, let's get you something to eat first."

She took me to a cafeteria and told the cashier to charge everything to her. She told me how to get to her office and left me. I had a small salad, some macaroni and cheese, and a piece of chocolate cake, much more than I thought I would eat.

Afterward, I walked to her office. She said she had to attend to a patient, but she would be right back and told me to make myself comfortable. There was a very soft leather sofa, and I sat on it and glanced at some magazines. My eyelids grew heavier and heavier. I wasn't aware of how tired I was from the strain of traveling here and the emotional tension I had just experienced with Mama.

I'll close my eyes for a little while, I thought, and leaned back and to the side on the sofa. I guess I fell asleep quickly. I woke up when I sensed someone looking down at me. My eyelids fluttered like the wings of a newly hatched baby bird, and I focused on a pair of gray pants. My eyes traveled up until I confronted a state policeman.

Doctor Young stood right beside him. I sat up quickly.

"You weren't supposed to leave your aunt and uncle's home," the state policeman said gruffly.

I looked at Doctor Young.

"They say you ran away, Phoebe. Is that true?" she asked softly.

"I wanted to see my mother."

"But you didn't tell your uncle and aunt you were coming here," she said. "Everyone was worried about you."

"Sure they were. Just sick with worry," I said. Then I narrowed my eyes. "I thought you couldn't reach her. I thought she wasn't interested."

"Your uncle spoke to me when I told him you were here. They have the police looking for you. You don't want to be on the road alone, Phoebe. You'll only get yourself into more trouble."

"Thanks a lot," I said.

"We have to do what's best for you, Phoebe. You won't help your mother's situation by getting yourself into trouble. I'll keep your uncle and aunt informed about your mother's condition," she promised.

"Don't waste your time," I said.

"Let's go," the state policeman told me, and shook his head at Doctor Young, who stepped back.

"I wish you the best," she called after us.

"Best of what?" I muttered.

I already had the best of nothing.

What else was there for someone like me?

7

Waiting for the Music

I was surprised when the state policeman did not bring me straight back to Uncle Buster and Aunt Mae Louise's home. I wasn't even sure we were going in the right direction. Most of the roadside looked unfamiliar to me. The late afternoon sun played peekaboo through trees and around houses, putting me in a daze. I dozed on and off. After about two hours on a main highway, the policeman pulled off and into the parking lot of a roadside diner. It was one of those silvery-sided ones shaped like a railroad car that looked like it had been built fifty years ago. It wasn't very busy. There were only four cars in the dimly lit parking lot.

"I'm not hungry," I said immediately.

"I'm not bringing you here to eat," he replied. "Get out."

Confused, I got out of the vehicle.

"Take your suitcase, too," he ordered.

"My suitcase?"

"Your uncle is waiting for you in there," he said, nodding at the diner.

I looked at the other cars and realized one of them was my uncle Buster's. I could see he was sitting in a booth by a window and looking out at us. I gazed back at the state policeman, who was standing by his car door, and I shrugged. Then I reached in, took my suitcase, and shut the door.

Thanks for nothing, I thought, and strolled up to the diner's entrance. As I opened the door, the state policeman drove off. I entered the diner. The sound of some country-western female singer with a very heavy twang in her voice came through the small speakers on the wall behind the counter. Two elderly ladies sitting at the farthest booth on my left turned to look at me and then went back to their conversation like two swimmers who had raised their heads for a breath.

I walked down to Uncle Buster's booth and stood there. Where is Aunt Mae Louise? I wondered. Why would she miss an opportunity to tear into me as soon as it was possible for her to do so?

"What's going on, Uncle Buster?" I asked. "Why did that policeman bring me here?"

"Sit down, Phoebe," he ordered gruffly through his clenched teeth. His eyes burned up at me like two small candles flickering in a hot breeze. Rage tightened his lips at the corners. Here we go again, I thought.

"Before you start," I said after I put down my suitcase and sat, "I wanted to see my mother. I should be able to see my mother if I want."

"You don't pack a suitcase to go visit someone, Phoebe. Don't you ever stop lying? Even when you're caught with your hand in the cookie jar, you claim you didn't do it."

"I took my suitcase because I thought . . ."

"Thought what, Phoebe? Huh?"

"I was hoping Mama would want me to live with her again," I said quickly.

He lifted his eyes toward the ceiling and pressed his lower lip up into his upper, scrunching his chin.

"You thought she would want to live with you again? Come on, Phoebe. The woman ran out on you and your daddy. If she was so worried about you and wanted you with her, she wouldn't have done that, now would she?"

"People change. I was hoping—"

He slapped his palm on the table.

"None of this is the point," he said sharply. "You were released from police custody into our care, and in order for that to happen, I guaranteed the district attorney and the judge that you would not run off and you would be there to answer the charges. How did you get down to Macon?"

"Bus."

"Where did you get the money?"

"I had some money."

He straightened his back and peered at me.

"I kept some of the money those boys gave me."

"What boys?"

"You wouldn't listen to my side of the story," I said, "so you don't know."

"Listen to me, Phoebe. It's one thing to slap someone, to kick someone, even to punch him, but when you hit someone with a statue and so hard you hurt him seriously and put him in the hospital, you are always going to come out looking like the bad one, so whatever your story is, you better first face up to that."

"If I hadn't done it, they would have jumped me, Uncle Buster. That's what they got me over there to do that night. That's what I've been trying to tell you."

The waitress came to the table.

"Just some more coffee," Uncle Buster said. "You want something, Phoebe?"

"Coffee's fine," I said.

"What were you doing over at the house with all those boys anyway, Phoebe?"

"We were there to . . ."

"To what?"

"Get revenge. But they lied to me."

"Who lied to you?"

"Those girls, Rae and Taylor. They said her father was going to arrest the boys for having drugs and for paying for sex."

"Paying for sex? Is that why you went there?"

"Not to really do it. Just to pretend and get them in trouble."

"And that's the money you have?"

"Yes."

He shook his head. The waitress brought the coffee.

"Anything else?" she asked sullenly.

"No, thanks."

She ripped off the check and dropped it on the table like a policeman giving someone a parking ticket.

"Trouble just seems to know your name, Phoebe. All the times you were in trouble in Atlanta, being arrested, going to court, we worried for you and for your daddy. I knew your mother wasn't going to be much help in that area, being she was in trouble a lot herself most of the time. Mae Louise doesn't know it, but your daddy called me first, called me at work and pleaded with me to get your aunt to agree to taking you into our home."

I kept my eyes down and stirred my coffee.

"He was desperate, Phoebe. At one point he sounded like he was crying."

Hearing that brought tears to my eyes, but I held them back for fear that if I didn't, I would cry forever.

"He said he had no doubt in his heart and mind that you were headed for big trouble, that you were mixing with the worst sort of people. He said we'd be saving your life by letting you live with us."

I looked up, but not at Uncle Buster. Instead, I gazed out the window and watched a white ambulance pull up and park. No one got out. All that was written on the ambulance were the words Emergency Transport.

"Mae Louise was very worried about Barbara Ann and Jake, but I turned her around so she would at least consider taking you in with us. We even spoke to my father, who helped convince her it would be the charitable thing to do."

"I'm no one's charity," I muttered, still without looking at him.

"We're all someone's charity, one way or another," he said. "Anyway, you can imagine how she feels now. First, you smoke in the house. Then you get into serious trouble in school after less than two days there and then get arrested and charged with a felony crime. On top of that, you violate the agreement I made with the authorities, and we look very bad in the community."

"I get the idea, Uncle Buster. I'll just get up and walk out of here and you won't hear from me again," I said defiantly.

"I can't let you do that, Phoebe. Aunt Mae Louise wouldn't take you in without your father assigning full guardianship to us, remember? She didn't want any arguments down the road as to whether we had the right to do this or that. You know your daddy agreed to do that," he said.

The tears were burning under my eyelids now. For some silly reason, a memory returned, the memory of Daddy and me going to a fun park together. I couldn't remember exactly how old I was, but I wasn't more than seven or eight at the most. He won a doll for me at the baseball game by knocking over milk containers and I carried that doll everywhere, clutching it as if it was a real baby sister. We rode a modified roller coaster and screamed and held on to each other. I thought we'd never let go of each other.

Now I was in that car alone, and I was going down very fast.

"Your mother deserted you, and she's not capable of taking care of herself, much less a teenage girl like you."

I looked at him sharply.

"Like me? I guess I'm just a curse on everyone I meet, right?"

He sighed deeply and looked down at his cup of coffee.

"You're not a curse, Phoebe, but it's not much of an exaggeration to say you're a handful. Mae Louise is right about that, and she's right that we just don't have the time and the ability to change you."

"So?"

"So," he said, "we don't want to see you go to women's prison, either. Young girls your age don't come out of there any better. Most come out worse."

"I'm not going to any prison," I said.

"Keeping you out of places like that means hiring expensive lawyers, Phoebe. That's not something we can do. Mae Louise is right. It's just a matter of when, not if, you'll be put in with hardened criminals and become more like them. We both feel we'd be letting your poor daddy down something terrible if we let it happen."

"Daddy's dead," I said sharply.

"When someone dies, you don't lose or forget your obligations to him or her. If anything, what you promised becomes more important because it's really all up to you. That's a lesson I guess you were never taught, but then there are many lessons you were never taught and should have been. That's why we're sitting here like this right now."

I squinted at him.

"Why are we sitting here, Uncle Buster?"

I didn't think he was going to answer because it took him so long. Finally, he looked up at me.

"When we came home from church and realized you had run off, I had to call the police, Phoebe. Your aunt Mae Louise was hysterical about it, too. The police sent that policewoman over to speak with us. She was concerned, and she told us about a school that might be able to help you."

"What school?"

"A school for girls who get themselves into too much trouble, much more trouble than most parents or guardians can handle themselves. We know you've got a history with the devil. This time you almost killed someone. Next time, you might do that or something almost as serious. Then what, Phoebe? We would be to blame, too."

"I don't see how another school makes any difference, especially any school around here. The girls and the boys here are just too stuck-up and fancy."

"This school's not around here, Phoebe. You won't be living with us anymore."

I raised my eyebrows. That should have sounded good to me, but something in his voice made me hold back my glee.

"Where is it then?" I asked.

"That boy you hurt, his father has a lot of influence in the community, Phoebe," he replied instead of answering my question. "This situation isn't going to disappear, especially now that they know you broke the agreement and ran off. They'll expect you to do it again. I can't chain you to the bed in your room, can I? And your aunt doesn't want to stand guard outside your door, and I can't be called away from my work to go looking for you or to solve some new crisis."

"I get the point, Uncle Buster. I never wanted to live with you and Aunt Mae Louise. You know that."

"Right. Right," he said. He sounded too relieved.

"But I don't understand about this school."

"It's a school that's run by people who know how to help you, to save you from yourself."

"What is it, some Bible-thumping, hymn-singing camp? Because if it is . . ."

"Now you listen to me," he said, pointing his thick right forefinger at me. "This is precisely your last chance. After this, no one's going to take your side or be bothered with you, Phoebe. You'd be left out there with the sharks and you wouldn't last long, no, ma'am."

He nodded after his own thoughts.

"You be grateful you have this opportunity, and you don't fail at it, understand?"

"Whatever you say, Uncle Buster," I told him.

He lowered his hand.

"Your aunt's right about you, girl. You do need this."

"Yeah, everybody has always been right about me, except me." I pushed the coffee cup away, spilling some coffee on the table.

He took out his wallet and put down some money.

"We're going now, Phoebe," he said. "You want to

use the bathroom? You have a trip ahead of you."

"What do you mean, a trip? Aren't we going back to the house first?" I asked, a small sense of panic balling into a lump in my throat.

"No. Your aunt would rather she didn't see you right now. You need the bathroom?"

I slid out of the booth and headed for the ladies' room without answering him. After I went, I stood by the sink and looked at myself in the mirror. I was tired, very tired. I could see it in my eyes, eyes that had seen too much sadness and too much disappointment. They wanted to just close and remain closed forever and ever. For a moment I understood why Mama had tried to cut her wrists. Sometimes, it all gets to be too much, even for someone as young as I was.

I ran the cold water and splashed it on my face. Then I ran a brush through my hair. I stood there staring at myself and didn't realize how long I was there until I heard a voice behind me and turned to see a tall woman with very short hair. She wore a blue jacket and a pair of dark blue slacks.

"Your uncle sent me in here to see what was keeping you," she said.

Now he was asking strangers to help. I grimaced and picked up my purse.

"Nothing's keeping me. That's the point," I told her, and walked past her and out the door.

I returned to the booth, but Uncle Buster wasn't there. And neither was my suitcase!

I looked around the diner. The woman from the bathroom came up beside me.

"Just keep going out the door," she said.

"Who are you?" I asked, pulling myself back.

"Your escort," she replied.

"My escort?" I didn't know whether to laugh at her or tell her to get lost. "Where's my uncle?" I cried, and headed for the diner entrance.

She followed right behind me, spooking me with how closely she kept to me. I stepped out and looked over the parking lot. I didn't see him or his car anywhere.

"We're here to escort you to your new school," the woman said, stepping up beside me.

"You're taking me to a school?" I pulled my head back. "Where's my uncle? What happened to my suitcase?"

"He took it and he's gone," she said. "You just come with us now."

"Why would he take my suitcase? My uncle didn't say anything about any escort."

"Trust me," she said. "That's who we are."

The lack of any emotion and the firmness with which she stood facing me actually frightened me. That surprised me because I had seen things and been confronted by people who looked a great deal more threatening than she did, but there was something so cold about her calmness.

"I'm going back in there and call my aunt," I said.

"That would be a waste of time. Just get into the vehicle and we'll get started," she said, blocking my path back to the front entrance of the diner.

"What vehicle?" I looked in the direction she nodded. "I only see an ambulance there."

"That ambulance is for you," the woman said.

"What?"

She nodded again at the white ambulance I had seen pull up. A man sat behind the wheel staring at us.

"This is really stupid. Where's my uncle?" I asked again. I could feel my chest tightening.

"I told you. He's gone," the woman said. "You don't see his car anymore, do you?"

She was right about that, which only increased my anxiety. A state policeman had brought me here to meet him, and now Uncle Buster had just disappeared without saying good-bye? And he had taken my suitcase! This didn't make any sense at all.

"Why would he just leave me? What is this?"

"Your last chance," she said through tight lips. "Go on," she urged, her hand now on my shoulder. She pushed me a few steps toward the ambulance.

I turned out of her grasp sharply and then heard the ambulance door open and close. The driver came walking toward us. He was wearing what looked like a pair of construction man's overalls with deep pockets and a T-shirt that his firm and thick muscularity was stretching to the limits of its seams. He had a shock of black hair and sleepy brown eyes.

"Trouble?" he asked.

"No, not yet," the woman said. "She's just a bit tired. You're tired, aren't you, Phoebe?"

"I'm not tired. I want to see my uncle," I said, sounding a lot more frightened than I had wanted to sound. It was just hard to put up a brave front under such weird circumstances.

"We don't have time for this," the man said to the woman.

"I know what time it is and what we have and have not time for," she told him irritably.

He lifted his hands as if he was going to have nothing to do with any of it anymore and stepped back.

I turned in a circle. Where was Uncle Buster? How could he just leave me? Why would I be going anywhere in an ambulance? And how could they call that an escort service?

"I gotta get out of here," I moaned.

"Now you just relax," the woman said, and before I

could take another step, she put her arm around my
shoulders. I tried to pull away, but she was amazingly
strong and had my arms pinned against my sides.

"Let go!" I screamed. An elderly couple who had just
pulled up and parked looked at us, but the sight of the
woman holding me just made them walk away faster.

"Okay," she told the driver. "You'd better give her
the first-class ticket."

"Glad to be of service," he said, smiling. He stepped
up and pulled a syringe out of his deep pocket. I felt the
needle go into my arm, and again I tried to pull free,
even kick her. Then he stepped back and walked
quickly to the rear of the ambulance. She held on to me
as I continued to squirm and cry out.

Suddenly, though, I felt so numb. I wasn't even sure I
was making any sound even though my mouth was opening and closing. The whole parking lot went into a spin.

"Hurry up, will you!" I heard her shout at the driver.

"I'm coming, I'm coming. Man, you're getting to be
a slave driver."

A stretcher was wheeled toward me, and I felt
myself being lowered to it. First, I sat and then, despite
willing myself to put up resistance, I was easily made to
lie back. Straps were pulled over my legs and across my
chest under my breasts. A pillow was shoved down
beneath my head.

I heard someone ask what happened and the woman
say, "Epileptic fit."

"Oh, poor thing."

"She'll be all right," the woman said.

I vaguely felt myself being lifted. I had no pain. It
was actually a pleasant sort of feeling that came over
me. I wasn't exactly asleep either, but I wasn't fully
awake. I was caught somewhere in between and I was

drifting. I heard the door shut after I was moved farther into the ambulance.

Then another door opened and shut. The woman was beside me. I sensed her, but I didn't see her. My eyes were closing.

"I never like it like this," the driver said.

"Shut up and drive," the woman told him.

I was sinking farther down now. I thought I was falling through the stretcher. It was like my whole body was melting, too, and seeping into it. Was this death?

I began to hear music. The driver started to sing along with a song.

And then I heard other music, a tune coming from a black marble pedestal upon which two ballerinas twirled. I remembered it well. It was at my bedside, a birthday present. I was hypnotized with it, with their graceful movements as the male dancer twirled and swung the female.

How wonderful it must be to dance like that, I thought, to be airy and unafraid of your body failing you. How I wished I could be a dancer.

"It's pretty," I heard myself say.

"The moment I saw it, I knew I had to get it for you, Phoebe," Daddy said.

There he was, standing at my bedside, smiling down at me. Then he lost his smile and put his hand on my forehead.

"Still got some fever," he muttered, and straightened up quickly, concern on his face. "She still has some fever, Charlene," he called behind him.

"It's nothing," Mama shouted back. "Kids get fevers all the time."

"Maybe we should take her to the doctor. She's been sniveling and coughing for days."

"She'll be all right. Everything scares you, Horace. I swear you were brought up a mama's boy, frightened by the sound of your own footsteps. You going with me or not?"

"Going? We can't leave her, Charlene. The girl's sick. What, you crazy?"

"Suit yourself," she said. "You know where I'll be."

Daddy wound up the music box again and I watched the dancers.

"I'll get you some hot tea and honey to drink, Phoebe. You feeling all right?"

I nodded, unable to take my eyes off the dancers.

Daddy left, but he didn't come back. The dancers stopped and the music ended.

I wanted it all to start again.

"Daddy," I called. "Daddy."

He didn't reply. I struggled so hard to get to that music box, but I couldn't reach it.

The dancers waited. This was all they were created to do, dance, but it was enough to give them purpose and beauty. Silence and neglect were the two sides of the same cruel sword cutting their lifeline. And they weren't just waiting for any music. They needed the music that belonged to them, the music they were born with, the music that had become a part of them. They looked so helpless, waiting there, so full of disappointment, too.

They started to disappear.

I felt myself drifting pleasantly again, but I kept thinking about the dancers.

And then it came to me.

I'm just like them, I thought.

Waiting for the music that belonged to me.

POCKET BOOKS
PROUDLY PRESENTS

MIDNIGHT FLIGHT

V.C. ANDREWS®

Coming soon in paperback
from
Pocket Books

Turn the page for an introduction to
the three heroines of *Midnight Flight*. . . .

Prologue

Just like someone rising to the surface of a pool filled with ink, I slowly awoke from what felt like a month-long coma. My eyelids flickered, but they were two tiny lead curtains slamming closed repeatedly until I managed with determined effort to keep them open. Shadows swirled and wavered and then gradually came into focus. However, the shapes they began to form made no immediate sense to me.

Something was roaring in my ears. For a moment I thought I was right beside a waterfall and then as my eyes focused I read the instructions on the back of the seat in front of me: KEEP YOUR SEAT BELT BUCKLED WHEN IN FLIGHT.

In flight?

I lifted my head and looked about. I was in a small airplane that had room for what looked like twenty or so people, and I wasn't just buckled in the seat. There was a thick, black leather strap around my upper body, tightened just below my elbows, keeping my arms so close to my sides. I could barely move my hands.

There wasn't anyone else in the plane!

I had been in an airplane only once before in my life when Daddy and Mama took me to see Daddy's father in an old age home in Richmond just before he died. I was only five at the time, but I never forgot being on a plane. Mama wouldn't let me sit by the window. She wanted me between her and Daddy so I wouldn't really think about being up in an airplane. Daddy thought she should let me sit by the window, but she wouldn't have it.

"I don't want no kid screamin' and cryin' 'bout being afraid. It's enough I agreed to go on this depressing trip," she declared.

Mama never cared about raising her voice in public, and the only way Daddy could stop it was by looking away and stopping the argument.

I wasn't afraid of being on a plane. Actually, I was fascinated with everything, especially the feeling of being lifted into the sky. When my heart started to pound, I closed my eyes and smiled to myself. It was better than the time Daddy had taken me on the Ferris wheel. However, when it came to my getting up to go to the bathroom, I was very nervous. Daddy wanted Mama to take me and she was annoyed.

"She can go to the bathroom herself at home. She can go in a plane," she told him.

I went myself and when I came back to my seat, I curled up and fell asleep. The next thing I knew we were getting off the plane in Richmond. Because I behaved well, Mama let me sit by the window on the way back. I couldn't stop looking at the clouds and the earth below where houses looked like toys. I thought to myself that this was the way God saw the world every day. He rode inside a cloud or on the back of the wind.

But this plane ride was different, so different. I felt as if I was being transported from one dream to another. Was this real? Or would I wake up any moment and realize it had all been a terrible nightmare?

I was so busy looking around that I didn't realize immediately how I was dressed. Gone were my clothes. Instead, I wore what looked like a thick, faded white nightgown created from an old potato sack. It was that coarse. Whatever was on beneath it didn't feel like my panties either. Where were my jeans and blouse? And my watch? Even the ruby ring Daddy had brought back for me from one of his sales trips was gone.

I squirmed in the seat and glanced down at my feet. I was wearing white stockings, the sort of stockings I saw nurses wear, and instead of my pink-and-white sneakers, I wore a pair of the ugliest looking black shoes with thick heels I think I had ever seen.

What was going on?

"Hello!" I screamed.

The only response was the continually monotonous roar of the engines. Whoever was in the cockpit might not be able to hear me, I thought.

I looked around the plane again. How had I gotten here? Who had strapped me into this seat?

I struggled through the maze of blurred memories, desperately trying to understand, to remember, and then, as if a dam in my brain had broken, it all came rushing back over me and as soon as it had, I wished it hadn't.

After Mama had left Daddy and me, and I had been in trouble too often in Atlanta, Daddy had convinced

Mama's sister and brother-in-law, my aunt Mae Louise and Uncle Buster Howard, to take me into their suburban home in Stone Mountain and enroll me into a better school. Daddy was on the road too much to keep an eye on me. Unfortunately, there I got into trouble quickly with a boy named Ashley Porter who came from a wealthy white family, and then after Daddy had been killed in a car accident, I had decided to run off.

I had learned that Mama had been left in a clinic where she was being treated for substance abuse addiction, and I was headed there. I was hoping she would be well enough to get out and go somewhere where she and I could start a new life. I was hoping she would be as excited about that as I was, but when I arrived at the clinic and went to see her, she was so confused. She just couldn't or wouldn't understand what I was telling her about Daddy being killed in a car accident and me being forced to live with her sister, Mae Louise.

Unbeknownst to me while I was visiting Mama, the doctor at the clinic had called my uncle and aunt, and my aunt called the police. The state police were sent to bring me back. I wasn't supposed to leave Stone Mountain for any trips since I was to go to court for hitting a boy named Skip Lester with a small desktop statue when he, Ashley, and the other boys all ganged up on me. Girls from my new school tricked me into being involved in what they called a sting operation to permit the police to arrest Ashley who had been spreading stories about me and them. He was going to be arrested for selling and using drugs. Of course, the girls were in cahoots with Ashley and his friends to trap me and have fun with me. I still couldn't explain why I was so stupid and gullible enough to believe them. That's how you get when you're so desperate to have friends. You can have only one friend, I concluded, yourself.

The state policeman who picked me up at Mama's clinic dropped me off at a roadside diner to meet my uncle Buster. I thought my uncle was just going to bawl me out without my aunt being present and then he was going to take me home. Instead, he left me there to be taken to what he called some special school for troubled teenagers, like me, girls whose parents and guardians could no longer contend with them and their problems.

No one wanted to listen to my side of things, especially my aunt and my uncle. My uncle didn't even have the courage to tell me what he had secretly arranged to take place at the diner. He tricked and betrayed me. I went to the bathroom and when I came out he was gone, and so was my suitcase.

The man and the woman who had come for me came in an ambulance, and when I resisted, they stuck a needle in my arm and gave me something that made me dizzy and confused. I passed out as I was being loaded into the ambulance. That was the last thing I remembered.

And that was what my aunt and uncle had done to me, and I was supposed to be the bad one in the family?

Now, here I was alone in this strange plane. Had I died? Had they given me something to kill me? Was this how people were really transported to the other world?

"Hey! Anyone! Please!" I screamed. "Someone, help me!"

I twisted and pulled and tried to kick the seat. Frustrated and frightened, I went numb inside and the tears in my brain flooded and washed my screams onto my face.

Still, no one responded. I gazed out the window at the wing and the engine. It was twilight, that time when the earth became a giant sponge and absorbed all the light around it. The dark sky laying in wait came rushing in behind like a black velvet ocean. I saw some stars appear. Their growing brightness comforted me until we flew into a wall of puffy, gray clouds that whirled about like so much smoke.

Every nerve in my body grew tighter and tighter, threatening to snap. My throat was so dry and my shoulders ached, the fingers of pain stretching down from the base of my neck. I continued to struggle against the strap, but it was too thick and too securely fastened. All I was doing by struggling was irritating my skin. Helpless, I relaxed and closed my eyes, trying to keep a lid on my boiling rage. Whoever had done this to me was going to be sorry, I vowed. As soon as they unfastened this belt, they'd see. How dare they take my clothing and put me in this rag and these ugly stockings and shoes!

As best as I could, I wiggled my fingers and explored what I was wearing beneath. It felt like . . . like a diaper, firm as plastic on the outside like one of those special undergarments women who have bladder trouble wear.

What was going on? Who dared to undress me? Was someone playing some sick joke on me? How long have I been on this plane? Where was I being taken? I thought I was going to some school. Why wasn't there anyone else with me? What if something terrible had happened to me? What if I was being kidnapped to become someone's slave? Who would know? Would that satisfy my uncle and my aunt? All they cared about was getting rid of me. Whatever happened to me wasn't important.

As I thought of these things, the rage began to boil over again. I tried to turn and press my body against the strap in hope of breaking loose, but nothing helped. It felt woven out of steel thread. Beads of sweat popped out on the back of my neck and my forehead because of my efforts. It was another futile attempt. I was just wasting my energy—energy I might need the moment I was finally released.

Inside, my stomach was churning, grinding rocks of frustration into sand: I closed my eyes and, taking deep breaths, again tried desperately to calm myself.

"Get hold of yourself, Phoebe Elder," I muttered. "Easy. You'll get out of this soon. You've been in worse places."

No, I haven't, I thought.

I opened my eyes and looked at the closed cockpit door. Why wasn't anyone at least interested enough to see if I had regained consciousness?

"Damn you!" I screamed. I could feel the veins in my neck becoming embossed in my skin. I shouted and then just released a long, animal cry of pain.

As if my scream effected the plane, it bounced and then dropped. I balled my fingers into fists and pressed them against my sides, gasping. What was happening now? Were we crashing? The plane bounced again and again and then rattled. Looking out the window, I saw how we dropped lower and lower until we were out of the clouds. Way off in the distance, I could see the lights of some small city, but other than that, the land-scape was dark, just like that pool of ink out of which I had imagined myself rising.

The plane continued to descend. Finally, I heard wheels being lowered and locked into place and then the plane touched down with a small bounce. It slowed and taxied until it turned. Wherever we were wasn't much of an airport. Maybe because of the angle I was at, I couldn't see any lights or people or cars. I heard the engines being shut down and the propellers slowing. When it all stopped, I waited in anticipation to see who would come out of the cockpit. The door did not open for so long, I began to think no one was flying the plane.

Then, the two pilots emerged. They looked so young to me, too young to be in charge of an airplane, but they had wings on their white shirts and gold threaded bars on their shoulders.

"Where am I? Who did this to me? Why am I tied down?" I fired my questions at them in machine gun fashion.

They looked at me, but neither spoke, making me feel like I wasn't really there. Instead, one of them undid the door and lowered the steps. I heard a woman outside ask if everything was all right.

"Just peachy keen," one of the pilots said and the two left the plane. No one else had emerged from the cockpit. Who was in charge here?

"What about me? What is going on?" I shouted after them. I watched the doorway and then tried to kick at the seat in front of me. "What's going on, damnit!"

Finally, a young woman with very short dark-brown hair appeared. She was as tall as I was, about five foot ten or so, and she was wearing a dark-blue uniform jacket with brass buttons and a pair of blue slacks. I thought she wasn't much more than nineteen or twenty years old. She was wide in the hips and small on top with narrow shoulders, making it look like two different bodies had been slapped together when God was busy attending to other matters.

"Who are you? What's going on?" I demanded.

"Keep your voice down," she said sharply, and approached me. When she drew closer, I saw she had a pudgy face with thick lips and wide nostrils. There was a streak of freckles bursting down the bridge of her nose on both sides and over the crests of her puffy cheeks. She wore no makeup, not even lipstick and there was a small, thin scar on the left side of her chin.

"Where am I?" I asked as softly and as calmly as I could. *First, I had to have some answers. Then I could take some action,* I told myself.

"You'll see," she replied and began to unfasten the strap.

"Who are you? Am I at some school? Where is this school that I had to be flown here?"

"You're wasting your breath asking me questions," she said stepping back. "Get up and get out."

"What happened to my clothes? Why am I wearing this rag dress?"

Her untrimmed eyebrows lifted and I thought she smiled, although it was hard to tell because her lips were so stiff.

She seized my right arm and tugged to get me to stand. When I did, I wavered for a moment and she had to grab my shoulders to keep me from falling.

"I'm so dizzy," I said. "They put me to sleep. Maybe they gave me something poisonous."

"Oh, you poor little thing," she said with exaggerated sympathy and sweetness. Then she snapped, "Walk!" She poked me at the base of my spine with her thick, right forefinger which felt like the barrel of a gun.

I scowled back at her and made my way down the small aisle to the door. For a moment I was dizzy and nauseous again. Then I caught my breath and navigated the half-dozen metal steps. The outside area was well lit, but all I saw was what looked like a building made of concrete. It had bland gray walls and a metal door with no windows in it. There were no windows in the front of the building either.

The first thing I noticed when I started down the steps was how hot it was. It was dark, but it felt like the middle of a summer day in Atlanta, especially in the poorer part of the city where we had lived. It wasn't true that people of African descent didn't notice the oppressive heat and humidity as much as white people.

"Where is this? It's so hot."

"Hell," I heard her say behind me. "Keep walking toward the building before I have you carried there," she threatened and I continued slowly. Where had the two young pilots gone? Why wasn't there anyone else around? I stopped to look and she gave me another shove to move me toward the building.

"Where are we going?"

"Just walk to the building and keep your mouth shut," she ordered.

Every time I turned my head to look around, she pushed me.

"Keep your hands off me," I warned.

"We've got a long night ahead of us. Move it," she commanded.

When we reached the door, she stepped ahead and opened it. The hinges squeaked like it hadn't been opened for a hundred years. It was like opening a tomb. How could this be a school? Why was I being brought here?

"Go in," she said.

I hesitated and she reached out, seized my wrist, and pulled me forward, driving me into the building with such force, I nearly stumbled and fell.

The inside was poorly lit by some weak overhead neon lights, but I could see it was just a dusty, empty warehouse or something. At first I didn't realize there was anyone else there. They were both so quiet and so still. Then I saw a petite rust-color haired girl sitting on a stool in front of a desk on my right. Her hands were folded, the fingers gripping like the fingers of someone in pain. Her knuckles looked as if little white buttons had been sewn onto them. She was dressed in the same sort of one-piece rag I was wearing and I could also see she had the same style shoes.

Sitting off on my left was another girl with styled pecan brown hair. Even though she, too, was dressed like me and the other girl, she held her head with a more arrogant air, her posture firm, but her arms folded under her breasts. I thought I could even make out a small smirk of impatience on her lips. Who were they? Was this concrete building supposed to serve as a classroom? Why was it so poorly lit then? A hailstorm of questions peppered my brain.

"Sit," my escort ordered and pushed me toward the empty stool and desk at the center.

"What is going on? Why am I in here? This isn't any school. I'm supposed to be taken to a school. I want to know where I am," I demanded more loudly, my hands on my hips. My voice echoed in the tomb-like building.

"Just sit and shut up," she blared. "The longer you act stupid, the longer this is going to take."

I looked at the other two who glared back at me with an expression of annoyance that suggested I was making things harder for them as well. Reluctantly, I did what she said.

"Now what?" I snapped back at her.

She finally did smile.

"Now, it begins," she said, and turned and walked out of the building, closing the door behind her.

I was right about that door. It sounded like a lid being shut on a coffin.

Visit

V.C.ANDREWS®

At the Simon & Schuster Web site:
www.SimonSays.com/vcandrews

*Read excerpts, find a listing of all titles,
and learn more about the author!*

Pocket Books